Dear Reader,

Welcome to a

Award-winning author Kristin Gabriel is back with
Bachelor By Design, book 2 in the delightful CAFÉ
ROMEO trilogy, about a coffee shop that doubles as a
dating service. *What better place to find both lattes and
love!* And popular Superromance author Kay David
joins the Duets lineup with the sizzling *Too Hot for
Comfort.* Something is definitely cookin' in Comfort,
Texas, between Sally and Jake—and it isn't steak!

Duets #28

Talented Jill Shalvis delivers her version of
MAKEOVER MADNESS. *New and...Improved?*
questions whether life is any better for the heroine
when she goes from geek to goddess—and has to fight
off men day and night! New author Jennifer LaBrecque
serves up a delicious hero in *Andrew in Excess.*
Andrew Winthrop is gorgeous, filthy rich—and in
need of a temporary wife. Kat Devereaux knows just
the woman—herself! But can these two make it down
the aisle?

Be sure to pick up both Duets volumes this month!

Birgit Davis-Todd
Senior Editor, Harlequin Duets

Harlequin Books
225 Duncan Mill Rd.
Don Mills, Ontario
M3B 3K9 Canada

New and...Improved?

"Are you going to look this way every day?"

Kent swiped a hand over his face and frowned. "This isn't real. You do not suddenly look this...hot."

Becca's smile widened and he pointed. "Stop that, stop that right now."

"I'm just looking at you."

"Yeah, like you want to eat me for breakfast. Now, knock it off, Becca," he said. "Be good. Speaking of which, I suppose you're planning yet another adventure?"

She laughed. "Of course."

"You're not going to a club, right? Because men are slime, trust me on this."

"All men?"

"Most definitely all men."

She actually seemed intrigued by that, but before they could discuss it, Dennis poked his head in and grinned at her. "Pick you up at eight. Wear your dancing shoes."

The door closed and Kent repeated, "Slime. Complete slime."

For more, turn to page 9

"Which side do you prefer?" Andrew asked.

Kat shrugged, lifting the hem of her lime-green, oversize T-shirt to just above her knees. "It's your bed. You choose."

Andrew wondered if she always wore the hideous shirt to bed, or if, fearing he'd lose his head after seeing her naked earlier, she'd done it deliberately. "Go ahead and take the side closest to the bathroom."

While Kat got Toto settled, Andrew stripped down to his briefs. Doubtless, Kat would have expected pajamas.

By the time she'd finished with the dog, he'd settled between the sheets. Her eyes widened when she turned and noticed his bare chest. She didn't know whether he was naked below the sheet or not. He grinned. Let her wonder.

Kat didn't stay disconcerted for long. "I checked my ovulation prediction kit and it seems now's a good time," she said briskly.

Andrew's jaw dropped.

"So I guess we might as well just get the sex thing over with..."

For more, turn to page 197

HARLEQUIN DUETS

ISBN 0-373-44094-4

NEW AND...IMPROVED?
Copyright © 2000 by Jill Shalvis

ANDREW IN EXCESS
Copyright © 2000 by Jennifer LaBrecque

JILL SHALVIS

New and... Improved?

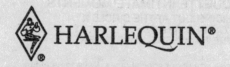

HARLEQUIN®

TORONTO • NEW YORK • LONDON
AMSTERDAM • PARIS • SYDNEY • HAMBURG
STOCKHOLM • ATHENS • TOKYO • MILAN • MADRID
PRAGUE • WARSAW • BUDAPEST • AUCKLAND

Dear Reader,

It has always been my fantasy to...no, not that! To get totally made over. You know, be turned into Cinderella. But permanently, since I can't seem to tell time and would never make it home by midnight.

Anyway, my chemist heroine gets this chance when she wins a makeover. Only problem, she's never had such a fantasy. In fact, she's a bit of a tomboy, so when all her workmates are now staring at her dazed by lust, it's a bit baffling. But then, her boss is doing it, too, and he *is* her fantasy, so suddenly looking like a sex kitten has its appeal.

But is it just lust? Of course not, but don't tell them yet—let's let them figure it out by themselves. After all, they are brilliant chemists—but love isn't a science, is it?

I hope you get a kick out of Becca and Kent's wild ride into head-over-heels love. Happy reading!

Jill Shalvis

Books by Jill Shalvis

HARLEQUIN TEMPTATION
742—WHO'S THE BOSS?
771—THE BACHELOR'S BED

SILHOUETTE INTIMATE MOMENTS
887—HIDING OUT AT THE CIRCLE K
905—LONG-LOST MOM
941—THE RANCHER'S SURRENDER

Don't miss any of our special offers. Write to us at the following address for information on our newest releases.

Harlequin Reader Service
U.S.: 3010 Walden Ave., P.O. Box 1325, Buffalo, NY 14269
Canadian: P.O. Box 609, Fort Erie, Ont. L2A 5X3

1

IT WAS JUST ANOTHER DAY in the life of Rebecca Anne Lewis. Work, work, work.

As a chemist for Sierra Scientific Laboratory, Becca did little else. It was in her blood. All her life she'd been a fine, responsible, steady human being. A rock.

And wasn't that just the problem? Rocks were solid, but boring.

Last month she'd turned the big three-oh. *Thirty.* And while her life was fine, her condo was fine, her job was fine, she wanted to scream from all the humdrum fineness.

As it had more and more, her secret fantasy came to her, the one where she threw all caution out the window. Where she became mysteriously beautiful and bold, different and exciting.

She definitely wouldn't have to struggle to remember if she'd had sex in the last decade.

The lab door opened, and steady, confident footsteps headed down the hall toward her. For a moment, Becca closed her eyes and pretended those footsteps belonged to a tall, dark, gorgeous man who was about to make her every fantasy come true. He'd take one look at her and reach out with a powerful swipe of his long, strong arm, sweeping the counter clear. He'd lift her up, then slide his hands down her hips to her thighs, which he'd open and slip between, still watching her with those smoldering eyes. His tennis shoes squeaked and—

Wait a minute.

Her dream man didn't wear squeaky tennis shoes. Becca sighed as reality intruded on the only sex life she had at the moment—the one in her thoughts.

The footsteps still came. Not her mystery man, but her boss Kent Wright. "A change," she muttered, fanning herself. "I definitely need a serious change."

"What? You're going through the change?" Kent stood in the doorway, looking tall, dark and annoyingly amused.

"Not exactly."

"You sure? I mean, you *are* officially old now." He came toward her, shoulders straight, stride long-legged and confident. Not cocky or full of ego, just incredibly comfortable in his own skin.

Laughter twinkled in his dark eyes. "Practically over the hill," he added.

"Funny." Jeez, a girl turned thirty and everyone felt free to remind her of it daily. Just yesterday the staff secretary had brought her black roses. "And not that it's any of your business, but I meant change as in *adventure*. Not the change of life."

"Adventure." He glanced at her speculatively, and she could hardly blame him. She was the epitome of nerdness. In school she'd been voted mostly likely to have her picture used in the dictionary to describe the word dork. College hadn't been much better, but at least then, with all her various science classes, she'd been surrounded by people more like herself.

"What kind of adventure?" he wondered. "As in blowing up your work station?"

He spoke mildly, with good humor in his deep voice, but Becca blushed all the same at the reminder of how she'd lost her last chemist position. She had an incredible amount of book smarts, always had. But what she more than made up for in IQ, she seemed to lack in good, old common sense. It had gotten her into trouble more times than she liked to admit.

And had lost her more jobs than she cared to think about.

Thankfully she'd had a really good interview with Kent, and he appeared to believe in her. But she didn't want to press her luck. Outlining her new plan for an exciting personal life might scare him off. Actually, it would scare off anyone that knew her. "And that particular incident with the explosion didn't count," she said defensively. "I didn't mean *that* kind of adventure."

"Ah." He nodded sagely. "So this time you're going to do it on purpose."

"Yes. No!" But she laughed at herself because what else could she do? "This has nothing to do with work. I'm talking about my personal life."

"What's wrong with it?"

"It's…fine." She rolled her eyes. "But it's so boring I can't think of a thing to say about it. That's going to change."

"Should I be worried?"

"Of course not. I'm not your responsibility."

Thankfully, he let that go. "Saw your report on the TD virus," he said. "Fine job."

Fine. There was that word again, and though she tried to not take it personally, she wasn't entirely successful. "Could you think of another adverb?"

"But fine is the one that fits."

"I hate that word."

"Because...?"

"Because it's as boring as the rest of my life is!"

He blinked slowly. "Which brings us back to this change thing, right?"

"Yes." She glared at him. "So if you don't mind, please don't tell me my work is fine."

Another man might have looked at her perplexed, or laughed, but Kent merely absorbed her request. Then in a deceptively serious voice said, "I'll put out a memo. *All employees take note, use the words 'fine' and 'Becca' in the same sentence at your own risk.*"

Oh, as if *he* could understand. He had dark hair, even darker eyes and a lethal smile when he used it. He was tall, lanky but muscled, and stunningly gorgeous in a dangerous sort of way that, according to his staff who were all too happy to talk about him when he wasn't within hearing range, never failed to garner him female companionship when he chose.

And yet, despite looking like a Greek god, he didn't choose often. She might have only been at Sierra a short time, but one thing she'd already learned through the watercooler gossip train was that he liked being alone, liked not having anyone to account to, and most of all, liked keeping his feelings and thoughts to himself. It gave him an edge that made him all the more appealing to the opposite sex.

But it wasn't his appeal that bothered Becca. It was her own *lack* of appeal.

With one finger, Kent reached out and stroked the spot between her eyes that always wrinkled when she concentrated or frowned. She was frowning now. "Didn't your mother ever tell you your face could freeze in that position?"

They'd never touched before.

It was only a finger, and yet the strangest thing happened. A bolt of awareness shot through her. It was so strong as to be almost painful. Her glasses fogged. Even her tongue got into the action, tying itself into knots.

And Becca rendered herself completely stupid.

"That was some strong static electricity," Kent said, staring, perplexed, at his finger.

"Was *that* what that was?"

"Definitely." But now he frowned too, and stepped back, slipping his hands in the pockets of his white lab coat. "Couldn't be anything more."

"Absolutely not." After all, Kent had an aversion to "more," to anything that tethered his precious freedom.

What she didn't know was why, but she had other things to think about. Such as her decision to make a major change in her life-style. Really, it was overdue.

She'd spent her entire childhood as a mousy, chunky, sharply intelligent child, playing in the shadow of a vibrant, gorgeous, fun-loving sister.

She'd spent her teens pretending she loved to study more than getting noticed by boys.

Little had changed there, she was afraid.

As an adult, she spent most of her time wearing a white chemist coat, thick glasses, her hair stuffed into a backward baseball cap, peering into a microscope trying to find a cure for the common cold. When she wasn't at work, she was at school learning more, still pretending it was more fun to work than have a social life.

That's who she was. Plain-Jane, total fashion nightmare, nose-in-a-technical-book, Becca.

And yet...she had the secret heart of a rebel, she just knew it. So she turned away from Kent, buttoned up her lab coat, sat at her stool and thought, *someday I'm going to figure out how to knock a man's socks off.*

"I'm sorry." Innocently, he looked at her with those deep, unfathomable eyes, which should have been her first hint—he'd probably never been innocent. "Did you say something?"

"No."

"Yes, you did. Something about my socks, which is very unusual, since I've noticed on Monday mornings you're all work and no play. So there must be something..." His fingers swept aside his white lab coat, and he pulled at the soft, faded denim encasing his powerful, long legs. Two white athletic socks were revealed, tucked into white running shoes with frayed laces. "Hmm. They look fine to me." He studied them seriously and rotated his ankles. "They actually match today, which is new."

"They have a pink tinge to them," she said, as if she didn't care that even his calves were perfect. "You ought to try bleach."

"Yeah, that's what happens when they get washed with red lace panties."

Her eyes went wide as she jerked her gaze back to his. "You're kidding."

"Maybe." He let out another of those killer smiles. "Maybe not."

"Humph." She crossed her arms and turned away, unreasonably annoyed with him.

"You could be happy for me."

"Might be happier," she muttered, reaching for her notes. "If I was getting some too."

"To get some, Becca, you actually have to *date*." With wry amusement, he leaned back against the counter as she fussed at her station, the picture of rough and ready trouble.

"How do you know I'm not?"

"Well, you told Cookie, who told Tami, who told—"

"Ah." She ground her teeth. "The gossip mill."

He smiled, which only magnified the mischief dancing in his eyes. But there was something about discussing her nonexistent sex life that really got her going, and it was only slightly mollifying to know he actually thought she was *rejecting* date requests, instead of not receiving any.

"Of course you'd have to break away from work long enough to have a good time," he added conversationally, reaching around her to flip on a second light over her work station.

He smelled good, she noted reluctantly. Not like cologne, but more an outdoorsy, male sort of smell that made her yearn. And that annoyed her all to heck, too.

"I'd ask you what you did this weekend but I could probably guess." He smiled. "You worked on school stuff, and for some extra excitement, you came in here to put in a little time on your latest project.''

Was that really what everyone thought? That she was all work? No play?

That it was true didn't help. "How do you know?''

He waggled a daring brow, every single hard-muscled inch of him oozing sin. "Because you have that not-relaxed, still-tired-even-though-I-just-had-a-weekend look.''

A quick glance in the small mirror over one of three sinks confirmed the painful truth. It was there for the entire world to see. Pale skin, paler green eyes rimmed with fatigue, the hair beneath her baseball cap a dull, nondescript brown.

Who had time to worry about hair? The glasses she wore hid most of her face, which was fine since she didn't wear an ounce of makeup. Not that she didn't like makeup, she thought defensively, it was just that when she applied it she had the tendency to resemble Frankenstein's bride.

Her body was blah, not curvy, not lean. Just average. And totally hidden under baggy jeans, T-shirt, sweatshirt and lab coat.

But that was because she didn't like to worry about what to wear in the mornings. Thankfully

S.S.L. provided the oh-so-bulky lab coats, so really, it hardly mattered how she dressed.

Bottom line though—she wasn't great date material. Not even *average* date material.

"Another frown." He sounded surprised and wary, too, as if he knew he was the cause, but didn't quite know what to do about it. "Maybe you should work," he said with genuine concern. "That always seems to cheer you up."

"Oh yeah, there's the answer, more work."

He blinked at her reaction and she felt a spear of guilt. "I'm sorry. I guess I've got the Monday blues."

"No, that's not it," he said slowly, cautiously. "You're different today."

Yes, she was different. At least, she wanted to be. "Well, to tell you the truth…"

"Uh-oh. You want a raise already."

"This isn't about work!"

"Okay." He leaned back and crossed his ankles, looking totally at ease, while her hopes and dreams gnawed at her. "Shoot."

But the phone rang, and while Kent studied her thoughtfully, she answered it. "Sierra Labs."

"Becca!"

Summer, her sister, had a carefree, happy, infectious voice that instantly made people smile. Becca resisted.

"Hey, you there?" Summer asked. "What's the matter?"

Becca broke eye contact with Kent and shoved her glasses higher on the bridge of her nose. "I haven't said a word. How do you know something's the matter?"

"I just know. Work or school?"

"Life," Becca said without thinking, then wished the words back.

"Well you work too hard. You never give yourself a break, much less a good look in the mirror. But that's why I'm calling, I have just the thing to fix that."

"You always have 'just the thing'," Becca said. "And the last time I fell for that, I ended up with green hair."

Kent raised his eyebrows.

"I was just learning to use color effectively," Summer said into the phone with great dignity. "I've come a long way since then."

From the corner of her eye, Becca watched Kent bend over his own work, his wide shoulders flexed with intense focus, his hands steady and sure.

He'd already forgotten about her.

Made sense. He was only her boss. They barely

knew each other. So why couldn't she look away? His muscles were clearly outlined down the length of his taut, lean back. His long fingers stretched and worked, and suddenly, with a shocking heat, she wanted those fingers on her.

It was the craziest thing.

Kent reached for his coffee and took a sip, his strong throat muscles working as he swallowed. Such a great swallow, she thought, entranced. But since she apparently couldn't look at him and still have a functioning brain, she readjusted her baseball cap and turned away.

Still, the strange and unwelcome lust pulsed through her.

Oh boy, this was bad. Getting hot over her boss. Very, very bad. She definitely, really, *really*, needed an adventure, and fast.

"Becca?"

"Yeah." She cleared her husky voice and tried to get control of her hormones. "I'm here. Listen, Summer…" She lowered her voice. "Remember how we always talked about having a wild adventure together? Like flying to Italy on a whim without a travel plan? Or learning to deep-sea dive? Or going to a strip joint?"

Behind her, Kent choked on his coffee.

In her ear, Summer laughed. "You mean when we were young and stupid?"

Had it been that long since she'd dreamed? Carefully she avoided Kent's curious gaze and said, "Let's do it now."

"Oh Becca, you're so funny. As if either of us could just take off now that we're so busy. And speaking of that, let me get to it. I just wanted to congratulate you."

Becca sighed. "For what?"

"You won our first monthly salon makeover. Here at the salon. Isn't that cool?"

"But I didn't enter any—"

"Now I know you won't take this the wrong way," Summer interrupted smoothly. "But no one is more deserving of *Summer's Place First Giveaway Makeover* than you."

"Gee, thanks. I think. And when did you decide to run a contest for a makeover?"

"I've been dying to get my hands on you for years now, you know that."

A makeover. Good Lord. "Look, I'm going to be really busy having an adventure—"

"No one's ever too busy for salon treatment."

"I will be," she promised, but then she glanced down at her plain white tennis shoes, then turned her head and looked at Kent, who'd again immersed himself in work. He had files open, slides prepared and his light on. Even his face was tight with concentration as he scrupulously studied…a lingerie catalogue?

He caught her watching him and sent her a lazy smile that illuminated his face and made her catch her breath. His eyes were heavy-lidded, sensual, and for a moment, Becca allowed the fantasy to root. To put that look in his eyes, to be responsible for all that maleness…

But a makeover?

The whole thing was vain, narcissistic…and embarrassingly appealing.

"Think of all the publicity it will generate for my shop," Summer coaxed.

"Yes, but…"

"I'll need before and after pics because no one is going to believe the change in you, going from…well, absolutely *no* style, to—"

"Hey!"

"—to the height of fashion! I know you've never let me help before—"

"Because I do fine by myself." Right. Uh-huh. Which was exactly why she'd just turned thirty and hadn't had a date in so long her date-only lipstick had dried out. Again she looked at Kent, who'd gone back to studying his magazine, and her tummy tingled.

"Oh, Becca." Summer's voice lowered to plea level. "You *are* going to do it, aren't you?"

Becca didn't have a lot of family, Summer was basically it. For as long as she could remember, her sister had been after her to do something with herself. *For* herself. "I just don't think—"

"That's perfect," Summer said quickly. "Don't think."

"A new hairdo is hardly going to change my life."

"No, but it's a start. It's the works, Bec. Hair, makeup, clothes, *everything*."

"Why do I get the feeling you're making this up as you go along?"

Her sister laughed lightly. *Quickly.* "Don't be silly."

But it *was* silly. And yet... "I don't wear makeup."

"I'll teach you."

"My clothes are fine."

"Yeah, if you're into Blue Light Specials."

"Well at least my hair is..."

"Mousy. Baby, I'm sorry, you need a change. I can do it for you, let me."

She sounded so sure, so excited. But then again,

Summer—as her name implied—was everything Becca was not. Tall, thin, beautiful.

Pride was an ugly thing. "Let me think about it." Setting the receiver back in place, Becca stood there for a long moment. She hated to disappoint Summer, it was like kicking a puppy. Her sister was just so happy and excited and bubbling and...perfect. All the time.

It wasn't as if she was jealous, she loved Summer with all her heart. They were all each other had, but sometimes being with her was strangely deflating.

Kent tossed his catalog aside. "A strip joint?"

"Is that the only part of the conversation you heard?"

"It's the part that grabbed me," he admitted. "Are you going to do it?"

Truthfully, the idea of a makeover actually scared her. Gave her a weightless feeling deep in her stomach. Made her wonder, just for a weak little second, how things could be if...

Kent's gaze filled with shock. "You're thinking about it."

Was it so unreasonable? So ridiculous? "So?"

"Well...I guess I can't believe you'd go to a strip club."

She gaped at him. "I'm talking about the make-over."

"Oh." The bad-boy grin he shot her had probably melted hundreds of hearts. Thousands. "And here I thought you were all work and no play," he said softly, challengingly.

Okay, that did it. Sealed the deal.

Yanking up the phone, she pounded out the number to Summer's Place and waited impatiently, foot tapping. "I wanted adventure," she muttered. "I wanted a change. And darn it, that's exactly what I'm going to get, if it kills me. This makeover is just the beginning. When I'm done there, watch out."

"Watch out what?" Kent wanted to know, sounding unsure.

Good. "I just might go find a strip club for real!"

The look on his face might have been priceless if she wasn't so worked up. "To watch or participate?" he asked carefully.

"Both."

All amusement had drained from his face. "Okay, wait a minute."

"I'm tired of being good. *Why isn't Summer answering?*"

"Hold on a sec," Kent said. "Back the train up."

"No more boring and predictable."

He watched her pace as far as the phone cord would allow. "What did you put in your Wheaties this morning?"

"I need action." She whirled and paced some more, waiting impatiently for Summer to pick up. "I need red lace panties."

"What?"

"Never mind," she whirled away, but Kent turned her back to face him. "Becca—"

Shrugging him off, she clutched the phone tighter to her ear, relieved when Summer finally answered.

"I'll do it. All of it," Becca snapped, then before Summer could gloat, she hung up. "There. That should get the ball rolling."

2

HOURS LATER, Kent watched Becca fidget on her stool as she bent over her microscope.

She wasn't a fidgeter.

Her wriggling was what had originally gotten his attention, but what held it was *how* she wriggled.

His gaze fixed on her hips as she scooted herself first one way then another.

It was difficult to tell her exact shape beneath all those layers she wore, just as he had no idea what she looked like without glasses on her face. He'd never seen her with her hair down, either, and because of the way she twisted it up out of her way, he had no idea how long it was.

Which was fine. He liked her—everyone liked Becca—she was generous, open, warm. And because he liked her, he was careful not to be attracted to her. It was a law with him, written in stone. *Don't ever like the women you date.* Lust after them, yes. Sleep with them, whenever safe and possible. But absolutely do not like them. It was a well-known fact that friends and sex should never mix because then there were expectations.

He hated expectations.

So when his mouth opened and said, "I think we should talk about this adventure thing," he both surprised himself *and* broke his personal law number two, which was *don't pry, because once you do, you're involved.*

Becca ignored him.

Good. He should let it go. That was the smart thing to do, and he was nothing if not smart. But Becca seemed to be itching for trouble, and while he understood the need for trouble all too well, the thought of *her* going after it, and maybe even finding it, disturbed him more than he cared to admit.

It wasn't that he didn't think she could take care of herself. He actually didn't know her well enough to make that decision. But she seemed sweet and kind and yes, dammit, naive. "Becca."

She shot him a smile filled with nerves, and it was such a dazzling one his heart actually skipped.

Not a good thing.

Not when, earlier, he'd touched her in concern and felt that heady shock of awareness. And now a mere smile tipped his inner organs out of whack.

Food, he decided. He must be hungry.

"I need to run," Becca said suddenly. "I don't want to be late."

Everyone else had quickly scattered at exactly five o'clock. Normally Kent would have scattered with the best of them, but something had held him back tonight. "Late?"

Her pencil broke. "Darn it." Her lips tightened as she patted herself down, searching for another one.

Pointedly, he looked at the one she had behind her ear, but she was grumbling, not paying any attention. "I can never find—"

Reaching close enough to see the few freckles scattered on her nose, he slid it out and held it up. "This what you're looking for?"

"Thanks," she muttered, making a grab for it, but he held firm.

"Late for what, Becca?"

"I'd rather not discuss it." She gave up on the tug-of-war and pushed at her glasses. Then once again glanced at the clock.

"It's still six o'clock."

"Yeah. I'd better go."

She didn't seem too eager, which upped his worry factor. "What's with you today?"

"Nothing. Look, don't you have something to

do? Like maybe, oh I don't know, read your catalog?''

He let out a grin. "You know very well it's not *my* lingerie catalog. It came for you, but you tossed it. I couldn't just stand by and let you waste paper that way.''

Her gaze shot heavenward. Then at the clock yet again. "I've got to go.''

"So you've said.''

Her voice held a bit of something he couldn't put his finger on. Panic? He really hated this. She was going off to find some sort of excitement.

Who would look after her?

He knew the answer to that, but he didn't have to like it. "Okay, dammit, I'll come with you.''

She looked confused. "What?''

"To keep you out of trouble. Nothing more.''

She cocked her head. "To keep me out of trouble?''

"That's what I said, didn't I?''

"You know, if this were anyone else in the lab, say *Sherry*—'' She dragged out the name of his secretary. "If *she* were going out, you'd want details. Lurid details.''

"Hey, I've caught you listening to the stories, too.''

"My point is, I find it interesting that you never worry about anyone else in the lab."

She had him there. "Sherry can take care of herself," he said finally, knowing by her instant flash of temper he'd said the wrong thing.

"I'm eight years older than she is!"

How could he explain that she seemed like an innocent? He decided not to explain at all, not to do anything to drag himself in any further.

"I think I'll just head out," she said stiffly, sliding off her stool. She walked to the door, lifted her purse and coat off the wooden hanger there. Then she hesitated, her back to him. "I'm wondering why you treat me as if I were your baby sister. Is it because we work together? Or because I look...the way I do?"

Uh-oh. He sensed this was one of those girl traps. "This has nothing to do with your looks."

She crossed her arms, cocked her head and gave him one of those long-suffering, mock-patient expressions every woman has perfected. "What *does* it have to do with?"

"Well..." With longing, he glanced at his own coat, and the door.

"Oh, never mind," she said, disgusted. "Men." The door shut not so quietly behind her.

BECCA DROVE ALONG the narrow, curvy, two-lane highway of Incline Village, thinking things were going to change from this day on.

The sun disappeared behind the horizon, and in its wake a glorious array of colors bounced off Lake Tahoe where it glimmered on her right. Its waters were a shimmering, brilliant blue that spoke of its amazing depth. The Sierra mountains towered on her left, magnificent and still peaked with snow, though it was already May. And as she drove through Incline, a place she spent both her days and nights, she thought it sad it was a place she'd never played.

Never really lived.

Well that was going to change too.

She turned into the parking lot and looked at the old wooden building that served as the lake's equivalent of a mini-mall. The structure was two stories tall and built to resemble a cabin. It dated from the early part of the twentieth century, when Lake Tahoe had been an exclusive resort for the rich and famous from the San Francisco Bay area. Nearly a hundred years later, little had changed. Not the look of the place, or the wealthy tourists.

The area, especially this building, exuded charm and nostalgia, just as the various entrepreneurs inside the building wanted.

Summer's Place was at the end of the mall, newly converted from a small but exclusive dress shop. The rent in this district was unspeakably high, as it was throughout Incline Village.

Income Village the locals had dubbed it.

And though Summer was wonderful, resourceful and very talented, even she couldn't have possibly afforded the rent by herself. The story in town was that her sweet, kind, rich ex-boyfriend had given her a rent-free ten-year lease.

That was true, but only half of the real story.

She'd actually won it from him in a game of poker. Strip poker. Becca had expected Summer to hide that little tidbit, but she was actually proud of it.

And Becca was proud of her. But a makeover?

Faltering on the steps, she looked out to the lake. A small company that took tourists parasailing was set up on shore, bringing in the latest paying customer, who was hooting and hollering with delight.

Becca turned and stared up at the bright, cheerful sign that read: Summer's Place, Full Service Salon.

Her stomach tap danced. Her nerves skittered.

She wanted this, she reminded herself. It was

just step number one to a more exciting, satisfying life.

When she almost believed it, she went inside.

TWO HOURS LATER she sat beneath a hair dryer, a cup of steaming tea on her right, a glamour magazine—which might as well have been printed in Latin—on her lap. She wore nothing but a robe and some scented lotion that smelled heavenly.

There was something decadent about being so completely naked beneath the robe in a room filled with people. Summer sat at her right, happily chatting away to two other customers as she held Becca's hand.

Becca assumed it was to hold her still, to keep her from running screaming out of the salon. But she no longer felt like screaming at all.

The salon was incredibly homey and relaxing, not at all intimidating, as some salons could be. The colors were bright and cheerful, much like Summer herself. There were all sorts of snacks available—nothing made clients happy faster than something yummy to munch on. Soft rock blared discreetly from hidden speakers overhead. The reception area had been designed to look like an expensive but approachable clothing boutique, and since one of Summer's closest friends, Monique, designed and sold clothes right here, it actually was.

An entire wardrobe had been picked out for Becca, and it hadn't been simple. She'd wanted easy-to-wear clothes that she could both work and play in.

Summer had insisted on two *different* looks, one for Becca's work and one for the nightlife she was hoping Becca would have.

They'd settled somewhere in between, but it was the lingerie she'd purchased that still had her blushing. The silks and lace seemed decadent, especially since she didn't get all that many opportunities to show off her underwear, but there was something almost thrillingly naughty about wearing such exotic things beneath her clothes.

She'd had a delicious massage by Pierre, who'd somehow managed to convince Becca she would love to have his hands all over her body.

He'd been right. For about one-millionth of a second, she'd agonized over lying face down and naked except for one little scrap of towel barely covering her essentials. She'd asked for a bigger towel and Pierre had laughed.

She was certain every square inch of her had furiously blushed, especially the not-so-toned inches.

But Pierre had a voice made for comforting and a touch that was out of this world. If her massage, which had been very professional and proper, had gone on for two more minutes, she was convinced she would have mortified herself and had an orgasm right there on the table. She could have said the same about her pedicure and manicure.

But some of her euphoria died when Summer led her back to her work station. Her sister insisted on styling her hair, without letting Becca face the mirror.

"I'm nervous," Summer admitted as she finished.

"Oh God, really?" Becca braced herself for the worst. "Did you turn my hair green again?"

Summer bit her lip. "How do you feel about magenta?"

"Summer!"

"Just kidding. But gee, thanks for the confidence."

"Just tell me," Becca said urgently. "How bad is it?"

"It's fab, stop it. All I meant was, it's exciting for me to do something for you for a change." Summer squeezed her shoulders affectionately. "Especially since you've done so much for me."

Becca didn't want to take any credit for their

past. Their parents had been killed when she'd been only eighteen, and Summer just sixteen. Becca had taken care of her sister, but anyone would have done the same.

"You're always right there," Summer said quietly. "I've wanted to give you something back, anything. For so long, I've wanted that." She smiled. "Thanks for letting me do this."

Slowly she turned Becca to face the mirror.

Ooohs and aaahs filled her ears as everyone around them gave their opinion. Becca hardly heard. Her gaze was locked on the mirror, her heart suddenly thundering. Her head spun. Her eyes glowed, and thanks to the magic of makeup, seemed huge and green. And her hair...it wasn't green or magenta. Instead, it was shiny, loose to her shoulders and the most glorious color of honey she'd ever seen.

"Well?" Summer demanded, looking at no one but Becca. "Say something. *Anything.*"

It was a miracle, was all she could think. "I had no idea I had such good genes."

Summer laughed and hugged her. "You ought to take that trip to Italy after all. Reward yourself."

She couldn't stop staring at herself in the mirror.

"Oh, I intend to reward myself," she said slowly. "And you, too. But not with Italy."

"I see the wheels turning," Summer said cautiously. "But I don't think—"

"*Exactly.* Don't think," Becca said, echoing her sister's earlier words right back at her. Right out the window she could still see the parasailers. She smiled and turned back to Summer, who looked out the window and gasped when she saw someone hanging from a parachute one hundred and fifty feet above the lake's water. "Oh no."

"Oh yes," Becca said, smiling.

"Okay, look." Summer drew a deep breath. "I understand you're going through some sort of mid-life crisis. You're only thirty, but you hear your clock ticking, or something equally stupid. Becca, stop laughing, I'm serious! Going out and dangling from a tiny little string a million feet in the air isn't going to—"

"Chicken."

Summer closed her mouth and glared at Becca. "I'm not a chicken. You take that back."

"Double dare," Becca said and waited, knowing full well Summer had never, in all her life, been able to refuse a dare.

"You'll ruin your hair and nails," Summer said

with an insulted sniff, as if this was her only concern.

"*Triple* dare," Becca whispered.

Summer dropped the sophisticated air and swore the air blue. Then she grabbed her purse. "Okay, you're on. But last one there goes first."

3

THERE WERE A DOZEN THINGS Kent should have been doing, but instead, long after everyone had gone home for the day, he stood in his office, staring blindly out the window.

Normally he could stand right in this spot, with his picture-perfect view of Lake Tahoe, dotted with sailboats and whitecaps, and be so satisfied with his life he couldn't stand it.

He loved this place, it was his heart and soul. It was also a symbol of all he'd accomplished in his life, of how far he'd come from the young, homeless street rat he'd once been. It had taken every ounce of courage and grit he'd had to manage college, then to procure an internship. Even more to start up his own company, but he'd done it.

Though he was no longer a nobody, some of the stigma had stuck to him, and it wasn't often he let people inside. For so much of his childhood and young adulthood he'd had no control over his life, and now as a direct result, he valued his independence above all else.

Even his friendships were treated with kid gloves and some distance.

Until Becca.

There was just something about that woman. That he couldn't put his finger on exactly what it was was more than a little disturbing. It wasn't attraction, he assured himself. Not sexual attraction, anyway.

Yeah, right.

But sleeping with her would be a very bad idea. Sex, great as it would be, would ruin everything because afterward he'd be looking for a way to escape and she'd be planning their two-point-five kids and a white picket fence.

Today, though, when she'd been talking about making a change, talking about adventure and strip clubs, he couldn't help but take notice. She was running hot and itchy, and she intended to get that itch scratched.

Something akin to panic filled him at that thought. *Platonic* panic, he assured himself, but panic nonetheless. After all, anyone could see she was a baby when it came to affairs of the heart.

And she was going out looking for action.

It was simple really. He had to do something. She'd made it clear that tonight was the night.

Like a caged lion he paced his office, knowing what kind of man she'd attract at a strip club. A bad one. An unkind one. One who would take advantage of her.

Dammit!

Someone was going to have to look after her, help her, protect her.

Someone was going to have to find out what the hell she thought she was doing, and he hoped it would be someone who cared about her. Someone who understood she just wanted an adventure. Someone who wouldn't hurt her.

Someone like him. God. *Him.*

He swore again and grabbed his keys, hoping he wasn't too late. Luckily the town was small, there were only a limited number of places she could have gone.

If she even stayed in town that is. She could have gone to South Shore, where there were any number of places she could go find her trouble.

Summer. She'd know what Becca was up to.

He hoped.

BECCA DID GO FIRST. Not by choice, but when she and Summer walked up to the man in charge of the parasailing, he took one look at Becca and said, "You first."

"Me?" she squeaked in tune to Summer's nervous giggle. "Why me?"

"Because, and no offense here, lady, you look as if you might back out after your friend here goes."

"She's my sister."

"Ah," he said, nodding. "All the more reason for you to go first."

Well it had been her idea, she told herself as she was strapped into a complicated—and hopefully very safe—contraption. Only fair that she go first.

Right?

Sounded good in theory. But she screamed when the first rush of wind lifted her from the launch pad, and she gripped the strap in front of her so tightly her fingers promptly went numb.

She screamed when Summer waved to her from the shore. Summer, who was one little tiny dot on the sand. *Oh my God,* Becca thought, slamming her eyes closed, screaming again.

Adventure, a very teeny voice reminded her.

So she opened her eyes. And continued to scream when she looked down from her height of over one hundred and fifty feet and could see the entire Tahoe Basin spread out beneath her.

Oh my God!

When they started to lower her, and her stomach switched places with her now scrambled brain, and she kept on screaming. The rush was amazing, huge, and worth every penny of the exorbitant fee she'd paid to be scared witless.

At fifty feet she started breathing again. At twenty-five feet she waved triumphantly down to Summer, who was standing next to a tall, dark, handsome looking man... Twenty feet...

Kent.

He was standing there next to Summer, head tipped back as he studied her descent with an inscrutable look on his face.

Still okay, Becca told herself at fifteen feet. *You're okay.* Exhilaration raced through her, both because she'd had her first and second adventures already, and now Kent was looking at her in a way that made her think her third adventure might be far more interesting than she could have imagined.

Their gazes met, his dark and strangely fierce. A tingle started in her stomach, which was now thankfully back in it's rightful place behind her belly button.

Ten feet.

And she remembered, she was looking pretty hot. Her hair, her makeup...had he noticed?

Oh yeah, she could tell by the way he was staring at her that he most certainly had noticed.

Yep, everything was going pretty darn good, and it remained that way...right up until the time she missed the launch pad on her descent and hit the icy, cold water of Lake Tahoe.

SHE DREAMED ABOUT IT, the mascara running down her face in oh-so-attractive rivulets, her clothing plastered to her body like a second skin as they'd hauled her out of the water, dripping like the catch of the day.

And was rudely awakened by the alarm.

Groaning, Becca buried her head because it wasn't just a dream—it had really happened.

She wasn't sorry she'd tried parasailing, she wasn't even sorry she'd hit the water. That Kent had witnessed the whole thing was the sorry part. It was one thing to willingly make a fool of herself, but it was quite another to have an audience while doing it.

He hadn't laughed when they'd unceremoniously dumped her back on the launch pad at Summer's feet, he hadn't dared, but she thought maybe he'd wanted to.

And what had he been doing there anyway?

After making sure she was okay and as warm as possible behind the heater in her car, Kent had vanished as quickly as he'd arrived.

Had Becca only imagined that flash between them? The sun had been setting, she remembered as she picked out one of her new outfits. It could have easily been a trick of light, that look in his eyes. Yeah, that was it.

A few minutes later she stepped into her new panties. The red lace thong immediately gave her a wedgy, but Summer had insisted she try them.

Doubtfully, she pulled on one of her new dresses and wondered if she would be able to go all day without yanking at her underwear.

She also wondered what Kent would say to her today. Would he mention the new look?

Probably not.

She supposed her next adventure would have to be something other than jumping her hard-to-read boss. But what?

Well it would have to come to her. Thoughtful, she drove to work and walked in the front door of Sierra Scientific Laboratory.

Cookie, the receptionist, was on the phone, her feet up on her desk as she simultaneously chomped on a piece of gum, polished her nails metallic green and took a message.

Becca shut the door behind herself.

Automatically straightening, Cookie set her feet down, a professional smile and a finger raised to indicate she'd be off the phone any second.

Then her jaw dropped.

Smiling weakly, a little startled by this reaction, Becca waved at the stunned woman and headed toward the back.

Then she stepped into her favorite place in the world. The lab. Her home away from home. It was here that she felt accomplished, as if she was making a difference. And she was, she reminded herself. At S.S.L. she *was* making a difference. Viruses were their specialty, and after intense study, they were coming closer to understanding them better. Her goal was to be able to treat them.

Without blowing anything up.

The lab wasn't large. There were six work stations, all of which were filled at the moment with various projects. Through the lab and down another hall were a set of offices, including Kent's.

Dennis, a junior chemist, sat at the first work station. He was superbly intelligent, funny, cocky, and a born troublemaker. He had at least one date a weekend, the details of which he enjoyed sharing with everyone on Monday mornings. Though he joked around with Becca as much as he did everyone else, she knew he thought her sweet, kind and...well, a bit stuffy.

Wait until he heard about the parasailing incident.

At the next work station sat Jed. He was the second most reserved one in their midst, after Becca herself. In his late twenties, Jed was quiet and generous. He would give a complete stranger the shirt off his back, and had. Which maybe explained why he also had dates every weekend. He just rarely shared the details as Dennis did.

They were both wonderful, but tended to treat her as if she didn't have a female bone in her body.

She was about to test that theory.

Her new and very high heels clicked noisily on the floor. Since she'd never worn anything but tennis shoes in the lab, it sounded startlingly loud. Both Jed and Dennis glanced up.

And took a comical second take. Then a third.

"Wow," Jed whispered.

Dennis let out a low, soft whistle. "Rebecca Anne Lewis, where have you been hiding all my life?"

She couldn't help it, she grinned at his meaningless but sweet flirtation. "Right in front of your nose."

Slowly he rose from his stool, his eyes on her body as he shook his head. "Oh baby."

It embarrassed her. She knew how she looked, hadn't she just spent every red light on the drive here staring at herself in the rearview mirror? The pastel yellow shirtdress flattered both her coloring and her body style, showing off her limbs, which were usually covered. She knew this, she'd wanted this, but it was going to take some getting used to.

Dennis couldn't get over her. "If I'd known what you've been hiding all this time, I'd—"

"Um...Dennis?"

"Hang on a sec, Jed," he said, still smiling at Becca. "Anyway, I'd—"

"Dennis—"

Dennis shot his closest friend a disgusted look. "Man, this is why you don't get women—"

"I get plenty of women, and your slide is on fire."

Jed and Becca both laughed as Dennis whipped back to the burner, swearing as he rescued his work.

"You look great," Jed whispered while Dennis jumped around and swore some more.

"Thanks." Becca headed past them, turning to

smile at them as she backed into the third station, feeling all warm and fuzzy and happy. She dropped her purse and reached behind her to steady herself as she prepared to sit on her stool. "I can't tell you how much your support—"

Not an empty seat, she thought vaguely as she sat. Beneath her thighs she felt two, hard, muscular ones. Beneath her bottom she felt the unmistakable lap that matched the male thighs.

Two strong, warm arms came up to steady her as she squealed in surprise and twisted to meet the dark, intense gaze of the man she'd convinced herself she wasn't attracted to.

"Well, if it isn't the resident parasailer," he said. "I see you warmed up nicely."

4

BECCA LEAPT UP, but not before Kent's body heat seeped into her skin, seeming to warm her from the inside out.

She stared at him, unable to think. Her mind had gone mushy, but it was okay because he stared right back at her.

"Those legs were made for dancing," Dennis called out. "Let's try that new swing club tonight, you and me."

Locked into Kent's gaze, she couldn't move. He didn't either.

"What do you say, Becca?" Dennis asked.

"She's busy."

Surprised at Kent's words, Becca responded. "I didn't say that."

"No, I believe *I* did."

So much heat in his gaze. Heat was good, she told herself, her heart in her throat.

"Don't you like to dance?" Dennis asked her.

How to admit she'd never done it? That no one

had ever wanted to take her before? "Yes," she said, determined. Anything to get her mind off her gorgeous, unsuitable boss.

"Another adventure?" Kent asked for her ears only. "You know you could have been hurt last night."

Was that rough, urgent tone all for her? Couldn't be, much as she was starting to secretly wish otherwise. But she knew he wasn't a one-woman man, not to mention she wasn't his type. "But I wasn't hurt."

His jaw tightened. "Could I see you alone in my office?"

"You're the boss," she said flippantly while her poor, drumming, overexcited heart threatened to burst out of her chest. She passed Jed, who sent her a sympathetic smile. Dennis winked.

Kent's office door shut behind him, the sound abnormally loud in the silent room. She stood facing his window, not quite daring to look at him. He stood directly behind her, she could *feel* him. Could feel his gaze on her hair, on her body, everywhere.

She knew this because everywhere he looked, she got hot. It was unladylike, and definitely not romantic, but she was going to start to perspire if he didn't say something. "Nice view," she said inanely, nodding her head toward the beautiful lake.

"What's going on, Becca?"

"You tell me. Why were you at the lake last night?"

"I thought I was rescuing you from—" He shook his head. "Never mind." A muscle in his jaw worked, and his eyes were so dark they looked black.

"You thought you were rescuing me from..." The lightbulb clicked on in her brain and she let out a disbelieving laugh. "You really thought I was going to a strip club, didn't you?"

"Well you did mention it."

"I mentioned Italy, too."

"I knew you weren't going to Italy on your salary." He couldn't seem to take his eyes off her. "You had the makeover. You look...amazing."

"Same as last night."

"Hardly. Not when you were a hundred feet in the air, waving your feet and screaming like a banshee, and certainly not afterward when you missed your landing and came out of the drink looking like a drowned rat."

"Oh, yeah." Curiously deflated, she straightened. "Well...I need to get to work."

Kent followed her, then held the door shut when

she would have opened it. "You never answered my question, Bec. What's going on here?"

She put her arms out and twirled around, modeling herself. "I was looking for a change, you know that. Is there something wrong with it?"

His quick intake of breath gave him away. "No." Betrayed by the thickness of his voice, he cleared his throat. "That dress..."

She had turned away from him, facing the door again, but now she peeked at him over her shoulder to find him staring at her behind.

"Are you...wearing anything under that?" He sounded hoarse.

And looked so irresistible. Why couldn't they explore this attraction? What would it hurt? The need made her bold. "Thong panties," she whispered, feeling the blush creep up her face, and deciding she very much liked the way the heat in his eyes sparked to a full flame.

"Thong—" He closed his eyes, groaned, a sound so serrated and sexy and thrillingly dangerous she shivered. "Where did *yesterday's* Becca go? The one that liked her quiet life and baggy jeans?"

"She's on vacation. Permanently."

He lifted his confused gaze to meet hers. "I

don't think I get it. You were fine the way you were.''

"I told you," she said gently, because clearly she had completely baffled the poor man. "Fine is no longer enough for me. Now if you'll excuse me..." Again she turned to the door, reached for it. "I have work."

At her back, his fingers settled against her arm, and that same bolt of attraction, the one she'd felt yesterday, staggered her. "There are safer ways to flex your wings," he said very quietly, his hard chest against her spine and shoulders.

"Just some friendly concern?"

He went absolutely still, then dropped his hand and stepped back. "I'm sorry," he murmured. "I shouldn't have—" He shoved up his sleeves, revealing those arms she loved. They were lean, tightly muscled, allowing all sorts of wicked images to float across her mind.

When he caught her staring, he swore and backed up farther, bumping an elbow into a microscope on the credenza, which he had to be quick to catch as it went flying. With another oath, he set the expensive equipment down and crossed his arms over his chest, tucking his hands away as if he didn't trust them.

He looked edgy, dangerous. And so cute she wanted to hug him. "Kent—"

"You've got work."

He was trying to resist her, with all his might, and it gave her a wonderful, delirious sense of feminine power that she'd never felt before. He was attracted, and for whatever reason, he didn't want to face it. But he didn't want to hurt her, either. "You're sweet, Kent."

"Sweet?" A bark of hard laughter escaped him. "If you could read my thoughts when I look at you in that dress, you'd rethink that word."

Smiling would definitely ruin the moment. "Would it be so bad if I knew what you were thinking?"

"Yes!"

"Why?"

"Because...dammit, just because!"

"There's a good reason."

"This is not going to happen."

"What isn't going to happen?" she asked innocently and he rubbed his temples and groaned.

"I mean it," he told her. "Not happening."

Her smile escaped then. "Okay, but—"

"No! No buts! God—" he swiped a hand over his face. "Are you going to look this way every day?

"Yep."

He looked miserable. "This isn't real. You do not suddenly look this...hot."

Her smile widened and he pointed. "Stop that, stop that right now."

"I'm just looking at you."

"Yeah, you're just looking at me. Like you want to eat me for breakfast. Now knock it off." When she laughed, he glared at her. "I mean it. Be good."

She shook her head and walked to him. "So what you're saying is that you don't feel anything when you look at me. Other than...friendship."

He flattened himself to the door. "That's right. That's all I feel."

On her tiptoes now, because he was very tall, she touched his rock hard jaw. "If you're sure," she whispered.

He groaned again, and beneath the hand she'd rested on his chest, she felt his every muscle tense. "And friends don't...don't touch," he grated out.

The intercom buzzed, startling them both, and Cookie's voice filled the air from the intercom. "Becca? Was that you that came through here a minute ago?"

Becca backed away from Kent and at the loss

of her incredible body heat, he drew a careful breath.

What was happening?

"It's me," Becca said to the intercom, her eyes still on Kent's.

He meant to look away, but couldn't. He had no will left, it was busy warring between his need to grab and kiss her and run like hell.

Running seemed like a much smarter move.

"Well let me say, you look fab," Cookie said.

"Thanks." Becca blushed.

Kent had just enough blood left in his brain to find her embarrassment amusing. Yes, she was much more beautiful than he'd ever imagined, but that didn't mean anything because they weren't involved. Not at all. Not even one little bit. He cared for her, maybe more than he meant to, but he could control that.

No involvement with someone he cared about. *None.*

But because he did care, he waited until Cookie had clicked off the intercom and said, "Okay, come clean. What's your next adventure?"

"Why?"

"I want you to be careful, that's all."

"Careful is my middle name."

"This isn't funny, Becca. You're not going to

a club, right? Because men are slime, trust me on this."

"All men?"

"Most definitely all men."

She actually looked intrigued by that but before they could discuss it, Dennis poked his head in and grinned at her. "Just wanted to tell you, I'll pick you up at eight. Wear your dancing shoes."

Becca frowned. "Dennis—"

The door shut again, effectively cutting off whatever she'd been about to say.

Slowly, she let out her breath.

"*Slime,*" Kent repeated. "Complete slime."

THE CLUB WAS PACKED. First of all, it was a new place, and secondly, the hors d'oeuvres were on special. There was nothing the locals enjoyed more than a good deal.

Oh, and the band was hot.

That's what the guy at the door told him. Kent reserved judgment, or attempted to as the big band sound from the forties bombarded his eardrums.

He preferred good old-fashioned rock and roll.

He had no business being here, but he'd been unable to think of anything except Becca being taken advantage of. He hoped to God she hurried up and got this adventure thing out of her system soon, because frankly it was exhausting trying to save her.

It took him a moment to adjust to the lighting, and then he wished he hadn't. On the dance floor, in the arms of a friend he suddenly wanted to slug, was Becca. She had on one of those black, shimmery, mouth-watering, body-hugging dresses he had been drooling over just yesterday from her catalogue. Just like in the glossy pages, the spaghetti straps and scooped neck, snug body and short skirt were all systematically designed to drive a man insane with wanting.

Dennis had one hand on the small of her back, nudging her close so that there wasn't a spec of light between their two bodies. His other hand held Becca's as they gyrated to the music.

Becca's face was flushed with her smile of concentration, and she nodded at whatever little secret Dennis was whispering in her ear.

Rejecting a server's offer of a drink, Kent strode directly onto the dance floor. The music changed tempo, from lightning fast to soft and slow. *Great*, he thought with a groan. Make-out music.

Becca was a sitting duck.

Over her head, Dennis saw Kent coming, and winked.

With what Kent felt was a remarkable calm, he pushed his way between them.

"Kent!" Becca blinked at him in surprise. "Hello."

"Move it," Kent suggested to Dennis.

"You're cutting in?" Dennis kept his hold on Becca. "But you hate to dance."

"I. Love. It."

Dennis laughed and shook his head. "No, you don't. Remember last month? We took those blond twins out? Tish crushed your toe beneath her five inch heels, and you said—"

"I remember what I said," he grated. "Now get your hands off Becca's ass and go somewhere. Preferably somewhere far away before I decide I don't want to pay you anymore."

Dennis grinned. "You can't fire me because I'm dancing with Becca."

"How about for sexually harassing her?"

Dennis's jaw dropped for a second, then he laughed before turning to Becca. "Are you being harassed, Becca? Sexually?"

She divided a curious glance between the two men and chewed on her full, lower lip.

A full lower lip that had on the most tasty-looking lip gloss Kent had ever seen.

"I've never been sexually harassed in my life," Becca said quite seriously.

Dennis shot Kent a wide, guileless smile. "See? She's fine. I'm fine. Now why don't you go somewhere and be fine, too?"

Kent knew he should back off and let Becca make her own mistakes. In fact, that's what he was going to do right this minute, and he turned away but not before he saw the flash of uncertainty on Becca's face. Sighing, because he couldn't very well leave now could he, and he held out a hand to her. "Do you *want* to dance with me?"

In a move that was both touching and terrifying, she gave him her hand in return. "Yes," she said without hesitation, then blinked, horrified, as she turned to Dennis. "I— Oh, Dennis, I—"

With typical nonchalance, Dennis smiled and shrugged it off. "Go ahead. Dance with him. But watch out for your pretty toes, he's got two left feet."

"I'm sorry," Becca whispered.

Dennis shook his head. "Don't be, it's just one dance." He looked at Kent and leaned close enough so that with all the music and other conversations going on, Becca couldn't hear him. "You've got it bad."

"You don't know what you're talking about," Kent said.

"Don't I?"

Kent grabbed Becca's hand, moving her farther in on the dance floor. The music had changed again, and the tempo raced as fast as his thoughts.

Over the loud, drumming beat Becca asked, "What was that about?"

It was about rescuing you, dammit. "You looked like maybe you needed a break."

Her eyes, the ones that had lit up at the sight of him only a few moments before, suddenly cooled ten degrees. "I look tired to you?"

No, not quite. She practically vibrated with life. Her hair, the shimmering color of a fawn's coat, shone beneath the sparkling lights. Her skin glowed. There was just something about her, something that drew him, and it bewildered him because he didn't want to feel this way.

Around them, people were dancing, swirling and rocking to the licentious, happy music. Becca stood there, a frown growing on her previously excited face.

Oh perfect, now he'd stolen her fun. "Becca—" He reached for her, but she backed away.

"No, don't," she said in an overly polite voice,

looking like an infuriated goddess. Her dress glimmered, her lipstick beckoned him, and he wanted, quite recklessly, to nibble it right off.

"Let me get this straight," she said over the throbbing beat. "We're friends."

"Yes," he said with relief. One of them had to remember that.

"But earlier, when I touched you, you freaked."

"Well actually, *freaked* is a pretty strong word."

Her eyes glowed with some hidden emotion that made him nervous. "And you hate to dance, but for some reason you're here, on the same day and at the same time I am." Her foot tapped to the beat of her impatience. "Would this be a coincidence?"

"Not exactly."

A man bumped into her from behind. She smiled when he apologized, then became serious again when she turned back to Kent. "Okay, look. I know you think this is silly, this whole new me thing." She glanced down at her dress and shook her head. "And it's really none of your business, but I turned thirty this year."

Thirty had never looked so good. "You know I already know that. What different does that make?"

"*Lots*…I want more for myself. I want—"

"Adventure," he said with her and she gave him a sad smile.

Again the music changed, deepened. Slowed. Helpless against the strange pull of it, and her, he stepped close, but she held up a hand to stop him. "You need to stop doing this," she said quietly. "Stop following me, trying to save me from myself. It's going to give me the wrong idea."

He closed his eyes and let out a slow breath. "But I can't get that 'wrong idea' out of my head." He opened his eyes again to discover he was talking to air.

5

BECCA STRODE DIRECTLY BACK to her table. Dennis was nowhere in sight. Still, she grabbed her purse and whirled, prepared to walk home if necessary.

But she was blocked, by none other than the man who had the singular ability to drive her crazy with the conflicting emotions of need and frustration.

Kent took in the sight of her purse slung over her shoulder and winced, even as he reached for her, putting his big, warm hands on her arms.

Now was not a particularly great time for her to feel that shock of reaction to his touch, a shock that shook her to the core.

He, too, went completely still.

A waitress stopped next to them with a tray of drinks, but when neither of them moved, she sighed with irritation and moved on.

Becca's heart raced unnaturally. Kent was looking at her, *really* looking at her, with a slightly confused yet unmistakably desirous expression.

"More static?" she asked sarcastically.

"Or something," he murmured, watching his hands on her with an intensity that made her want to melt boneless to the floor. "You look incredible."

"It's the lighting, and friends don't touch, remember?"

He lifted his slumberous gaze to hers. "It's not the lighting," he said, ignoring her reminder.

"The dress then."

"Well, it is an incredible dress."

"Thanks." She backed up so that his hands fell away from her. Definitely time to move on. "I'll see you."

"What? Where are you going?"

"Nowhere you need to worry about."

He let out a breath. "You're on your next adventure already, aren't you? What is it?" he asked grimly, clearly bracing himself, which stirred her temper all the more.

"Obviously it bothers you greatly to even think about it, so why don't you just let it go? I'll see you tomorrow."

She walked away from him, said her goodbyes to Dennis and exited into the cool night. And if she felt a strange yearning for what might have been, she firmly squelched it.

Kent Wright was not for her.

But adventure number four was, and she could walk right to it. The night was lit by a blanket of stars that dazzled her mind and boosted her spirits. The air blew chilly around her bare legs, but she welcomed the delicious scent of spring.

The town was alive with both tourists and locals, as people hustled between the eclectic mix of historical and new hotels, shops and galleries.

One block later she stood outside the sushi bar and smiled. It might seem really silly to most, but she'd eaten bland food all her life. Simple, easy dishes she could take right out of her freezer and toss into her microwave.

Never, not once, had she had the nerve to challenge her palate, though she'd thought about it.

"Raw fish? *This* is your grand adventure?"

Sighing, even as a secret thrill raced through her, she turned to face Kent. "You've been following me. What a surprise." Without waiting for an answer, she entered the small restaurant and was immediately seated.

When Kent sat next to her, she said nothing. He didn't order, but she more than made up for it by ordering a large sampler platter.

"Becca—" he started, but she glared at him. He lifted his hands in surrender. "I suppose you don't want to hear that they say ten percent of all sushi can make you sick."

"Who's they?"

"I don't know. *They.*"

"Humph."

"They also say it's bad for you. Rots your insides."

She ignored him as the waitress brought her order.

"And they definitely say you ought to take it easy the first time," he warned as she started eating.

She paused. "They say that about a lot of things?"

Tension and awareness crackled between them. Kent broke eye contact first. *Telling,* Becca thought, popping another bite into her mouth. She chewed slowly, absorbing the new taste.

Different, she decided as she swallowed nonchalantly because Kent was watching her so carefully. Very different. The rice part was good, but as for everything else, she wasn't quite certain. She picked up yet another, then another. "I'm not as naive as you seem to think I am." She licked her lips, then her fingers.

His gaze took in the motion of her tongue and she was grimly satisfied when his eyes darkened with heat. She ate two more pieces.

"Becca, do you have any idea how they get that stuff? They—"

"It's delicious," she said, lying only a little. Oh boy, was she ever full. But she'd ordered this huge platter and couldn't imagine letting it all go to waste. "And I told you, you'd better be careful or I'll get the wrong idea about all your touching concern." Another bite before she looked at him. "Which comes from what again, exactly?"

"It's a bit complicated." He lifted a brow when she took yet another piece, but refrained from commenting.

"I do consider myself fairly intelligent." She chewed carefully now, thinking that last piece might have been a mistake. Her stomach rolled. "Try me."

"You're not going to like it."

Definitely a mistake, that last one had been. She pressed a hand to her grumbling belly. "Why is that?" she managed to ask, thankfully sounding perfectly normal.

His jaw clenched again. "Truth?"

"Preferably."

"Okay then, I—"

Uh-oh. Her stomach roiled again, violently, and despite desperately wanting to hear what Kent said, she had no choice but to leap up and run for the door, her hand over her mouth.

Not here, oh God, not here. Please don't let me be sick all over this nice carpeting, in front of the sexiest man she'd ever not wanted to be with.

"Becca, here." With calm urgency, Kent pulled her out the door.

"Go away," she said miserably, frantically pushing at him. She'd just *had* to have that last bite, she just *couldn't* resist.

The pain in her stomach doubled her over, grayed her vision.

Kent whipped her around the corner of the building to the alley, by the dumpster.

She didn't quite make it that far. But at least she didn't throw up in front of him.

She threw up *on* him.

SHE WAS SITTING on the salon steps the next morning, wallowing in humiliation, when Summer came bouncing up.

At the sight of her sister's troubled face, Summer stopped short, carefully popped the bubble she'd been making with her gum and sucked it in her mouth. "Uh-oh."

"Tell me again why I wanted this makeover?" Becca demanded. "Was it so I could make a fool of myself over and over?"

"I take it you've done just that?" Summer jingled her keys until she found the one she needed. Eyeing her sister up and down as she let them in, she said with disgust, "I thought we tossed out all your jeans and T-shirts."

Becca lifted a shoulder. "Little problem came up. I still had the clothes in my car and last night... Well, let's just say I just dropped them all off at the dry cleaners."

They entered the silent, dark saloon. Summer flipped on the lights and music, and immediately the place took on that warm, comfy air that went a long way toward calming Becca's nerves.

Summer pushed her into one of the chairs. "You can borrow something of mine, soon as I fix that whirlwind hair. What did you do, sleep in a wind tunnel?"

"I didn't sleep." Miserable, she groaned. "I was with Kent last night."

"Cool."

"I ate too much sushi and threw up on him."

"Oh." Summer popped another bubble. "Not exactly romantic."

"This whole makeover/adventure thing, it's not

really working out for me. I'm thinking of forgetting the whole thing.''

''But you can't!''

Becca sighed. ''I know. All that trouble you went to for your contest.''

Guilt flashed over Summer's face so quickly Becca decided she must have imagined it. ''It has nothing to do with the contest,'' she said. ''You just looked so great.''

''It was easier being boring. I didn't get wet or cold or sick. And if I was still that person, I'd know Kent was following me around because he liked me. *Me.* The old me, not the new me.''

''Are you speaking English at all?''

''Maybe it's just about my new looks. Maybe I'm dazzling him, you know? I can't stop wondering about that. If I go back to the old look, I could find out for sure.''

Summer's hands stilled in her hair. ''Okay, say that one more time, I'm starting to follow you, scary as that is to admit.''

Becca sighed, closed her eyes and admitted the truth she hadn't yet faced herself. ''I like him. Too much.''

''Then don't give up.'' Summer squeezed her shoulders gently. ''Remember your new lease on life. Go for it. Just stay away from raw fish for God's sake.''

"You're right. A few roadblocks and I'm ready to give up. What kind of determination is that? I can do better.''

"Absolutely. There's all kinds of things you haven't tried.''

"Are we talking about fun and adventure, or catching a man?''

Summer grinned at her in the mirror. "Both.''

A FEW MINUTES LATER, dressed in borrowed clothes, Becca ran down the stairs of the building, into the glorious, clear day and directly into a hard block wall of a chest.

Kent's chest.

With a low murmur of concern, he grabbed her, and before she could say a word, gently brought her down the last step, past the cement bench, to the trash can there.

Hanging over it, with Kent's strong arm around her waist, his other hand holding her head, she could do nothing but stare into the bottom of the can, which had three oozing, rotting bananas in the bottom.

"Why are you out of bed?" he demanded. "Damn, I knew I should have gone home with you

last night and stayed. You should have let me."
He stroked her forehead, holding back her hair,
and she had to laugh.

"I'm not sick, Kent."

"You were running, of course you're sick.
Don't worry, I've got you."

Man, did he ever. She was held against his
warm, strong body and she could have stayed there
all day if it hadn't been for the stomach turning
stench of the can. "I'm okay."

"You're sure?"

"Unless I have to keep breathing this air down
here."

He pulled back a little, peering into her face
with understandable wariness. "You're not still
nauseous?"

She shook her head. "And I was really hoping
last night was just a bad dream."

"So were my shoes."

Wincing, she said, "I'm so sorry. I've never
done that before."

"If it makes you feel any better, sushi doesn't
agree with me, either."

She smiled and his gaze followed the move-
ments of her lips for one long moment before he
let her go. Then he picked up a brown bag he must
have dropped on the bench.

She recognized the slogan and her mouth watered in response. *"Donuts,"* she whispered reverently.

"Got an extra jelly roll in here." He watched as she opened the bag and dug right in. "So what's the next...?" When he trailed off, she glanced up, mouth full, hands covered in powered sugar. Embarrassed, she licked her lips and Kent's eyes glazed over.

She nearly choked when she realized he was getting turned on by watching her eat. The power of it, the sheer delight in being able to render him speechless was amazing. Feeling a bit wicked now, she licked her lips again.

A strangled sort of sound escaped from deep in his throat.

She bit back her grin as renewed hope surged. "What's the next what?"

He shook his head as if to clear it and looked purposely away from her mouth. "What's the next adventure?"

You, she almost said. "Something warm with no food."

"Good. Something safe."

"Didn't say that." She swallowed her last bite and dusted off the sugar. "I was thinking rock climbing."

"Rock climbing," he repeated. "You ever been?"

"Nope."

He groaned. "How did I know you were going to say that? Look Becca, you really have to know what you're doing for that particular sport."

"Don't worry, I'm a quick learner."

"I thought heights disagreed with you. Remember parasailing?"

"It was the cold water that disagreed with me."

He stared at her, then sighed. "All right, fine. Be stubborn, that's nothing new. Rock climbing. I'll pick you up at six. We'll go to The Wall at Squaw Valley."

"*You* know how to rock climb?"

He looked grumpy. "Just said so, didn't I?"

"Actually, no you didn't."

"Yeah, I know what I'm doing. Good thing too, because someone has to follow you around and make sure you don't kill yourself."

Is that all he was doing? "I'll be fine," she said stiffly. "I don't need a keeper."

"It's not for you, it's for me." He looked mightily unhappy. "I won't be able to sleep unless I know you didn't hurt yourself."

"Well gee, when you put it that way. Oh, please come."

"Six o'clock," he repeated. "Dinner afterward."

Her heart stopped. "Dinner. As in...a date?"

"You wanted adventure." His dark eyes were clear, full of an intriguing mix of annoyance and temper. "Unless you got it all out of your system?"

The way he was looking at her made her legs quiver. "Oh no, not yet."

"No Dennis this time, and definitely I pick the restaurant."

A date with Kent. It was her greatest fantasy. Okay, not quite her greatest—her greatest involved him and her, silk sheets and a moonlit bedroom, but this was close enough.

Suddenly he reached out and cupped her face. The touch startled her, warmed her. Aroused her. His thumb slid over her lower lip, arousing her all the more. "Powdered sugar," he whispered. "You still have a speck...right here."

Long after it must have been gone, his thumb played over the most sensitive part of her mouth. Back and forth until she parted her lips and his eyes darkened even more. "You're touching me. Thought that was a no-no."

"It was. Is." But he still did it.

Before she could stop herself, her tongue darted

out and touched his finger, drawing it into her mouth.

A half growl, half moan came from deep within his throat. Her knees threatened to give at the erotically shattering sound.

"Tonight, then." His voice was deep and sexy.

"Yes." And as he walked away, she had the feeling her next adventure had already begun.

6

WORK WAS BECCA'S SALVATION that day, it kept her mind busy. She sat talking with Dennis, going over some of their latest samples, correlating some of their findings.

Or at least *she* was correlating, Dennis was teasing.

He slid a finger up her arm, bared by another one of her new shirt dresses. "Come on, one more night," he coaxed. "Give me just one more night and I swear, I'll ruin you for all other men."

Because she knew he was just kidding, she shot him a sultry smile. "But then I'll ruin you for all other women, too, and then what would you do?"

He laughed and they bent over their work once again. "I had a great time with you the other night," he said after a moment. "I just wanted you to know that."

His pretty blue eyes were genuine, and for once he wasn't crowding into her space, flirting. "I had fun, too," she said.

"Before or after you danced with Kent?"

She opened her mouth, but had to close it again.

"It was hard to miss those sparks flying between the two of you. Real hard."

She busied her hands. Dennis stilled them by setting his bigger one over hers. "You're looking pretty amazing, Bec. If good old Kent keeps getting hives over the thought of a relationship, let me know. I betcha I could get it right."

He probably could. And maybe a few days ago she might have let him try. But suddenly her heart wasn't in any sort of casual relationship adventure. No, she wanted more.

She wanted it all.

THIS IS STUPID. Kent told himself over and over again as he showered, dressed and drove to pick up Becca. A date. With a woman he not only worked with, but one who was his friend. It was trouble with a capital *T*, no matter how he looked at it. Stupid, stupid, stupid.

But then her door opened and Becca was standing there, smiling at him, such an absolute vision she took his breath. She wore a long floral dress, with a row of tiny, delicate buttons down the front that begged a man to go after them one at a time. The lace bodice scooped low enough to show off rich, warm looking curves and the skirt flared gently over her slim hips.

He thought he might never get used to seeing her, *really* seeing her. But it wasn't the outfit that stunned him, or even her glorious body.

It was her eyes, and the way they sparkled with excitement, fear, nerves…everything he was feeling. Warning signals went off in his head, blaring, honking, tooting. *Beware. Attachment alert!*

You're falling, your parachute has failed and there's no back-up equipment.

Vacate the premises immediately.

No. No, he was fine. All he had to do was remind them both, right this second, that this was just fun. No future. No commitment. Just fun.

Yeah, that's all he had to do. He took the last step, until he stood in the doorway with her, gripping the jamb with either hand, a mere inch separating their bodies.

Say it.

Oh, man. Her eyes were huge and full of mysteries, and he had this strange, burning desire to know each of them.

And just when he needed it the most, the panicking little voice inside his head went silent.

When her breath caught at their closeness, his

blood surged with heat, but it was the tenderness and affection that floored him.

It felt right to run his hands up her arms, over her shoulders, to her throat, until he cupped that now serious face in his palms.

And it felt even more right to smile down at her and gently, lightly, glide his mouth over hers. Again.

Then again.

When he pulled back, her eyelids fluttered open and she drew a deep, unsteady breath. "What was that for?" she whispered.

He hadn't an earthly clue. He couldn't even remember the thought process he'd used to go from reminding her they were just friends to kissing her. His mind was mush, complete mush.

There should be some sort of back-up process for when this happened. After all, he couldn't be the only man on earth to lose all the blood in his brain over one little embrace. "It was our goodnight kiss," he improvised.

"We haven't gone out yet."

"Oh yeah." He cleared his throat. "We'd better hurry then."

"Well," was all she said. She gripped her hands together and smiled shyly, but there was a good amount of mischief in that smile as well. "So you were only planning on giving me *one* goodnight kiss?''

His pulse leaped. ''I didn't want to seem too forward.''

''Not at all,' she whispered, her lips parting as he slid his fingers in her hair to better angle her head for another kiss. ''And if you wanted to give me another one, too...you know, while you're at it, I wouldn't mind.''

They were laughing when their mouths connected again, and Kent had time to think that he'd never felt like laughing and kissing at the same time before, that it was the most lovely, joyful feeling in the world, but then he couldn't think at all because the touch of her, the taste of her, closed off his brain to everything but sensation.

Immediately their sizzling connection spiraled out of control. There were other sensations; the sounds of the street behind him, the wind rippling the pines, the soft music playing from inside her condo, but it all faded away. Everything was gone except for this woman in his arms.

She felt it too, he could hear it in her sigh of shock, surprise, need. It was the last that made him groan and pull her closer, deepening the kiss because he had to have more, just a little more.

She gave it. Wrapping her arms around his neck,

she pressed tight and opened to him. More sensations burst in his head, white-hot passion and an unquenchable desire.

He turned and pressed her against the door, holding her body captive, only it wasn't necessary, she was willing and able and making small, needy little murmurs in her throat as she tried to get even closer to him.

This had never happened, came his vague thought. *Never.* In another two seconds, they were going to be clawing at their clothes, dropping each other to the floor to ravish, and...

"Holy smoke."

At the sound of Summer's voice, Becca jerked and moved back, but it took Kent longer to blink himself into awareness and remove his arms from around her.

She stood behind them, in Becca's condo, her mouth open, her eyes wide. "Wow. Just wow." She was tall, willowy and stunning. Her long blond hair was perfectly groomed, not a one out of place. She wore a snug, short black dress, thigh-high boots and looked so glossy and finished, Kent could easily imagine her walking down any model runway in the world.

By contrast, he was standing there with his shirt untucked and half-unbuttoned—when had that happened? He supposed he should consider himself lucky his pants were fastened over an uncomfortably hard erection.

Her very red lips smiled as if she could read his mind.

"I thought you were gone already," Becca said shakily, running a hand through her hair. Her lips were wet and swollen. Her lipstick was long gone, he'd chewed it off and could still taste the strawberry flavor.

"Nope," Summer said, grinning.

Becca let out a long breath and looked down at herself as if checking to make sure she was all together. "We were just…"

"Yes, I can see that." Summer laughed when Becca blushed. "I was getting hot just watching the two of you go at it." She eyed them both. "You ought to think about taking it inside next time. Like to a bedroom."

"My sister thinks she's amusing," Becca said, throwing Summer a warning look.

Summer ignored it and turned to Kent. "What do you think of Becca's new look?"

Becca shifted uncomfortably. "Summer—"

"I think she looks nice."

"Nice." Summer nodded. "Well, there's a word, huh? Quite the description. Every little thing

about her is completely different. Her hair, her makeup, her clothes, everything.''

''Not *everything* is different,'' he said, turning to look into Becca's carefully made up face, sans lipstick. She seemed a bit wan suddenly. Stressed. ''You still have the same insides, don't you?'' he asked.

She only stared at him.

''You know, guts and blood and stuff,'' he clarified.

Unexpectedly, she laughed. ''Yes, I do.''

''And your heart,'' he added, though he didn't know why, he just wanted her to keep smiling at him like that, like he was the best thing since sliced bread. ''Your heart is the same.''

Summer moved next to Becca. Her eyes were bright, filled with something odd. *Approval?* He had no idea why, and other than not wanting Becca to be uncomfortable, he didn't care what her sister thought of him.

But she hugged Becca. With a soft sigh, she hugged him too. ''You're a very sweet man.'' She drew back and smiled at him. ''Take good care of her,'' she whispered.

Then she was gone.

Uh-oh, Kent thought, the warning signals finally coming back. There was that sweet thing again.

He wasn't sweet. He didn't have a damn sweet bone in his body and he liked it that way.

And *take good care of her?* What did that mean?

How had this happened to him? One minute he'd been vaguely concerned about Becca getting hurt in her adventures and the next he was kissing her as if his life depended on it.

In the silence, Becca clasped her hands, still looking embarrassed. "I'm sorry about all that. She likes to put people on the spot and see how honest they are. It's a thing with her. She didn't mean anything by it."

Okay, that was good. This was still light and easy. Temporary.

And he was the tooth fairy.

Damn. "Let's go rock climbing," he said gruffly.

She sent him a curious glance. "I can go by myself if you've changed your mind."

He had visions of her hanging from the rope thirty feet in the air. A hundred things could go wrong. No, actually, with Becca a *thousand* things could go wrong. "I'm going."

"Because there's probably people there who could show me what to do—"

"Becca, I'm going."

Her smile widened. "Okay, if you insist." She picked up the gym bag that sat next to the door and led him out.

HE'D REMEMBER LATER that he'd insisted. The good news was that Becca loved rock climbing.

The bad news was that he loved watching Becca.

She climbed the thirty-foot wall with ease, laughing and smiling and so thoroughly enjoying herself that he couldn't take his eyes off her.

She climbed the forty-foot wall, too, and then looked up at the fifty-foot wall. "Race you," she called out breathlessly.

He'd been climbing for years. Years. So the only excuse he could possibly offer for losing was that the view from beneath her, and the snug pink shorts she'd changed into, were so incredible, it kept him one pace behind her.

At the top she smiled at him, flushed with success and thrill and excitement, and never in his life had he wanted to kiss someone so much.

Luckily they were hanging from ropes, so kissing would have been not only impossible, but incredibly stupid.

Coming down, Becca bounced away from the wall, still laughing and smiling, and still looking so damn wonderful and appealing it should be illegal.

"Watch what you're doing," he told her. "You're going to hurt yourself."

"I'm watching." She grinned with pleasure from ear to ear as she slowly and correctly lowered herself to the ground. "See? Perfect."

Yep, just about, he decided, still watching her. Which explained how he slipped and fell the last eight feet to the ground with agonizing pain twisting up from his ankle.

"How's your ankle?"

Kent shrugged, and the movement shifted the cold pack. They were in the emergency room, waiting for his X-rays to come back from the lab.

Becca leaned across the hospital bed to adjust the cold pack, but Kent's hand caught hers. "It's fine," he said through his teeth.

"Uh-huh." Becca looked at him with exasperation. "Why do guys do that, hide everything? You're pale and shaking and looking like you might throw up. Why can't you say it hurts like crazy? What would it kill you to admit a true feeling?"

His brow lifted. "I can admit my feelings."

"Oh, really." She crossed her arms. "Then tell

me what this is all about, could you? Because I don't have a clue.''

Wariness filled his pained expression. ''A clue about what?''

''About us.''

''Us?''

''I admit, at first I didn't think about there even being an 'us',''' she said. ''I just wanted something new and exciting, which I planned on doing by myself. But then you kept interfering. And then there's that attraction problem,'' she added lightly.

''Attraction?''

She narrowed her gaze. ''Are you sounding like a parrot on purpose?''

He grimaced. ''Sorry.''

''So...are you going to come clean?''

''Uh, yeah...''

The doctor came in, interrupting the moment. ''No break,'' he said cheerfully. ''You'll need to stay off it, though, while it recovers.''

Becca listened politely to his instructions, but the minute he was gone, she gave Kent a pointed stare. ''Where were we? Oh yeah, you were going to tell me what's really going on. And don't even think about using the worry excuse. I'm not the one who got hurt here.''

Kent sighed. ''Fine. I'll tell you the truth.''

"Good."

But then a nurse came in with forms. While Becca waited, nervousness filled her. *The truth.* Suddenly it hit her—she couldn't handle the truth! She didn't want him to say something he didn't mean, or was it just that she didn't want to confront the fact it was entirely likely he was attracted to an illusion?

A few minutes later, she helped Kent to the car. They walked in silence, their bodies close. And hot.

"I'm sorry you hurt yourself trying to keep me safe," she said, her mind racing, her body throbbing, yearning. "I think you should sit out the next adventure."

"That won't be possible."

She stopped. "Why?"

"Because I intend to *be* your next adventure."

"Oh. Oh my," she whispered, and Kent's dark, heated gaze held hers. She could hardly breathe for the pure joy and terror of it all.

7

THE EVENING WAS CLEAR, crisp and beautiful, as only a night in the high altitude Sierras could be. And pain throbbed like crazy through Kent's system, centering in his ankle, making him delirious.

That had to be it; he couldn't think of any other reason why he'd said what he'd just said.

"You didn't mean it," Becca said lightly enough, but not so casually that he couldn't hear her uncertainty. "You couldn't have meant it. You don't do relationships with women, other than for..."

"For...what?"

"You know. S. E. X.," she whispered, looking everywhere but at him, which must have been difficult since she was supporting at least half his weight and he was draped all over her.

"What are you talking about?"

"I work for S.S.L. don't I? Everyone there knows everything there is to know about everything, just ask any one of them."

over the thought of showing her exactly what it felt like to explode with ecstasy.

"And truthfully, even in the adventurous spirit, I feel a little intimidated by the differences in our experiences."

"Becca." His voice was thick, husky. He couldn't help it. "First of all, I have a fraction of the 'experience' you seem to think I do, and second—"

"Oh Kent...really?"

"Really." Her eyes were wide and on his. Her body, so nicely showed off in those snug punk shorts and a T-shirt, had his fingers itching to touch, to skim over all that creamy skin and explore to his heart's content.

Heart's content.

When had that happened? When in the world had she sneaked beneath his defenses? The moment she'd fallen right out of the sky and into the water at his feet, he realized.

"What?"

She was blinking at him and he groaned. "Did I say that out loud?"

"What happened the moment I fell out of the sky?"

"Fresh air," he decided. "I need fresh air."

"We're standing in it. Doesn't get much fresher."

"Humor me."

"Okay." She helped him into the car. "But I'll have to drive."

"No."

She pointed to his bandaged ankle.

Damn. She wanted to drive his baby, his pride and joy. "I can handle it."

"Don't be silly. Hand over the keys. Come on," she coaxed. "You can do it. Just drop them into my hand."

He clutched them tighter. "You might get a ticket, most people do in a car like this."

"Kent." She wriggled her fingers for the keys.

"But—"

"Kent."

In the end, she had to pry them from him and he sat in the passenger seat, agonizing over the two minute drive. "Be careful."

"Yes, dear," she mocked.

"Watch for cops."

"I'm watching." She went to turn the key and he slammed a hand over hers.

"The clutch," he said through his teeth. "You have to put in the clutch first or—"

"Oh!" She laughed. "Of course." She slipped

in the clutch and sent him a sweet smile. "Got it."

He had a very bad feeling about this. "How about we walk?"

"Don't be ridiculous." Slowly she eased out of the parking spot, Kent grinding his teeth all the way.

"Relax." She revved the engine, going faster. Then faster. Up ahead, the light went from green to yellow.

She didn't slow.

From yellow to red.

No slowing.

"Becca."

"I see it." She hit the brake but not the clutch.

They jerked forward until Kent was kissing the windshield.

"Sorry," she muttered, catching the clutch just before they stalled.

He pried himself off the glass and glared at her. "Careful."

"I am," she said, insulted.

"You're going to get a ticket."

"I am not going to get a ticket." She looked at him. "You know, you're more concerned about your car than—"

"A stop sign," he said quickly, bracing himself against the dash. "Don't get a—"

"I told you, I'm not going to get a ticket!"

"Watch out. Don't go through it—"

She did.

And *that's* when she got a ticket.

"NICE NIGHT," Becca said. They'd stopped at the lake after her ticket because Kent needed more fresh air.

He was considering sitting on the beach until he could drive, even though that conceivably could be days. He didn't mind.

"I still want to take the deal," she said suddenly. "That is, if you're still offering."

"The deal?"

"You know, the adventure. With you."

Small, relentless waves hit the shore noisily, only feet from them, while Kent drew a deep, careful breath. "I think we just had our adventure," he said.

She laughed. "Well, okay, if you consider getting a ticket the best adventure you've got in you."

He narrowed his eyes and looked at her. "Don't you dare twist that ticket around to be my fault."

Again, her laughter floated around him, warming him even though he preferred to hold on to his irritation. If he was irritated, she couldn't turn him on. Right?

Wrong.

"You know, you never talked about yourself," she said, tipping her head back to look up at the incredible sky. "You grew up here."

"At south shore."

"Any brothers or sisters?"

"No."

"Do you get home often?"

"No." He tried not to tense, but it was impossible. He hated talking about his past.

She studied him thoughtfully. "So talkative."

She was beautiful in the moonlight. Soft, sincere. And she wanted to know him. How many people in his life had really wanted to know him?

How many had he *let* know him?

He clasped his arms around his knees, ignored the shaft of pain in his ankle and stared into the most amazing night he'd seen in a while. "I grew up with my mother, she worked at one of the lower-class hotels. Cleaning, cooking, whatever kind of work she could find, when she could find it. I never knew my father, she said she didn't, either."

"It must have been rough," she said quietly.

Rough about summed it up, but he shrugged.

"We lived day to day, sometimes with her friends, sometimes out of her car. I hated it then, and I hate remembering it now."

Her gaze was luminous, filled with the compassion he didn't want, and other things he *did* want. "You've come so far, done so much for yourself. It's a miracle."

"For a street rat, yeah."

"Summer and I grew up here in Incline, and had a house right on the lake. We had a tennis court, an indoor swimming pool, servants, everything we could want."

"Sounds nice."

"Everything except parents." She smiled when he looked at her. "They traveled extensively, they were rarely home. Sometimes I used to have nightmares that they'd forgotten us, that they'd never come home again. We'd worry about what would happen if the servants ran out of money, if they'd take off and just leave us alone to fend for ourselves."

He shook his head, angry for the two helpless, little children they'd been. "What happened?"

"One day my parents really didn't come home. Their plane crashed somewhere in Europe, where they'd been vacationing."

"Becca...God. What a nightmare."

She shrugged. "I'd just turned eighteen. Summer was only sixteen, but they let her stay with me because I'd always been so—" She broke off, let out a self-deprecating smile. "Good. Responsible. We turned out fine," she said softly.

Fine. There was that word she so resented, and he thought now, finally, he could really understand why. "So...we're both fine?"

With a smile, she turned to him. "Yeah." Her humor faded a bit as she held his gaze, replaced with nerves and awe and something else, something he couldn't quite name. "Actually, I feel very fine right now," she whispered. "Right here, with you."

She was pressed to his side, held there by his own arm. He could feel the heat of her skin beneath her clothes. Her hair smelled wonderful and he shifted just a bit closer still, more relaxed and comfortable than he could remember ever being.

He considered kissing her senseless, he knew he could do it. Considered taking that adventure right now. It'd be incredible, with only the sounds of the water and the moonlight for company.

Making his move, he slowly drew her in his arms and looked at her mouth, which trembled open.

He leaned closer, all sorts of hot thoughts tumbling though his head. Hot thoughts and light—

Light?

Bright, glaring light. "What the—" Turning, he shielded Becca.

A cop stood there, wielding his flashlight. He sighed, loudly, at the sight of them. "You guys are too old for this necking at the lake stuff," he said grumpily. "Take it to a hotel, will ya?"

8

"I DON'T WANT TO HAVE TO write you up," the cop said when neither of them moved.

Becca let out a laugh at that. She clamped her hand over her mouth and blinked her huge eyes up at the officer.

"Everything okay?" he asked her, frowning, shining the light in her face for a moment. She nodded, but he didn't relax. "Let me see your identification please," he said to Kent, who inwardly groaned, but reached into his pocket.

"You wouldn't believe the evening we've had," Becca told him.

"Try me."

"Well, first Kent hurt his ankle trying to show me how to rock climb, then I got a ticket in his car—"

"You got a ticket? This evening?"

"Just a little one. And getting another would sort of ruin our plans."

The cop studied Kent's driver's license. "What plans, ma'am?"

"Another adventure." She looked at Kent and smiled. It wasn't a casual, oh-let's-go-eat-sushi smile either. No, it was the mother of all smiles, a cat-in-cream smile.

"An adventure," the officer repeated doubtfully, dividing an annoyed look between the two of them. "And would this include anything illegal?"

"Absolutely not," Becca said sweetly, with contrasting fire in her gaze.

Kent's heart stopped. Desire flooded him.

The policeman sighed in annoyance. "Just make sure you go home first, could you? I don't know what you people see in these woods. It's damn cold out here."

"You've never been in love," Becca decided.

No, Kent thought. Not love. Never love.

Vaguely he heard Becca answer another question before they were left alone, but he couldn't concentrate on any of that now.

He'd only offered an adventure, nothing else, he assured himself. He hadn't led her on.

Not on purpose anyway.

"Whew, that was close," she whispered with a smile, moving close again. Happiness shimmered from her. "This must be what it's like to be a lust-struck teenager. I think I like it."

Her eyes were shiny with excitement. Just excitement, he told himself, but that was a lie, too. There was more in her gaze, much more, and he felt his heart crack.

Dammit!

He'd known this would happen, that his fondness for her as a friend would war with the part of him that lusted after her. They hadn't even done anything more than kiss, and already he was feeling responsible for her, worried that he was going to hurt her.

He wasn't even aware of moving back away from her until she sighed, a wealth of sudden sadness in the sound. "You have that panicked look on your face," she said quietly. "The one that Cookie told me about. She said it's the look you had last summer when your girlfriend brought up the price of diamonds."

"She wasn't my girlfriend."

Wrong answer. Becca's face blanked, all emotion cleanly wiped away. "Oh, would you look at that?" she said, glancing at her watch. "It's late. I'm sorry." She rose gracefully. "I'll walk."

"No, you won't." He managed to hobble after

her and after a brief hesitation, he handed her his keys.

"What if I get another ticket?" she asked coolly.

"You won't." He held the driver's door open when she would have shut it on his face. "Becca...I'm sorry."

She looked straight ahead through the windshield. "Nothing to be sorry for. You've changed your mind. You can't handle it. No biggee." Disturbingly distant, she put the key in the ignition. "Get in, Kent. I'll drive you home and walk from there."

"And then what?"

"Then you leave me alone."

Leave her alone. Was he really supposed to be able to do that?

Hunkering down, ignoring the pain in his ankle, he leaned into the car, putting a fist on either side of her hips, caging her in so that she had no choice but to look at him. "Becca—"

She simply started the car and put it in gear. "Better get in," she said casually, revving the engine. "I know how fond of your toes you are."

AT SIERRA LAB'S weekly staff meeting, everyone currently involved in a project read off their latest progress.

Becca was up.

She had the most erotic voice, Kent thought, lost in it like a stupid lovesick fool.

Around a table laden with donuts, bagels, croissants and various juices sat Dennis, Jed and two of Kent's other lab techs, Sally and Tiki.

Despite himself, Becca continued to hold Kent's attention. Her eyes were intent, her body leaned forward toward the others as she spoke.

She loved her job and it showed.

She was upset with Kent and that showed, too.

She hadn't spoken to him all morning, despite his repeated attempts to get her to talk. He'd asked, as he'd trailed her down the hallway, if she was okay.

Yes.

That was all, just yes.

He asked if she was mad at him.

No.

She wasn't mad. She wasn't anything, but late for their meeting, and could he please remember they were at work and not on their own personal time?

Dammit, I'm the boss, he'd called after her as she'd rushed down the hall, away from him, hips gently swinging, skirt flying, legs flashing.

Frustrated, he'd followed her into the meeting.

Her hair shone under the lights and so did her green eyes. Kent sat there morosely and lost the train of what she was saying. Instead he tapped his pencil against his thigh and wondered yet again how he'd never noticed her eyes before, when they intrigued him so much now, and knew it was because she no longer wore her glasses.

"I liked those glasses," he muttered.

"I'm sorry, Kent...what?"

Startled from his sulk, he looked up to find everyone looking at him. Everyone except Becca. *Great.* "Nothing."

Jed took the floor next and Kent quickly lost track of his project too, as he stared at Becca. The *new* Becca. He liked her all pretty and polished, anyone would. She was beautiful.

But the truth was he liked her natural, too, without the makeup and the hair. Without the fancy clothes.

He missed her jeans.

"What?" several people asked him at the same time.

"What *what*?" Kent said, confused.

"Jeans," Dennis repeated patiently, his eyes full of mischief. "You miss her jeans. Should I bother to ask *whose* jeans you miss?"

Kent didn't dare glance at Becca, but he heard a clunk and couldn't resist.

She had dropped her head to the table. Her ears were red.

"Nothing," Kent mumbled. "I don't know what you're talking about."

Dennis nodded seriously, his mouth quirking with barely repressed laughter. "Uh-huh. Maybe you ought to try to stay with us here today, boss."

"Just continue." He couldn't believe the calm in which they did, especially Becca.

How had she forgotten what had almost happened between them? Had she forgotten their kiss? She couldn't have. He could live to be a hundred years old and never forget that kiss.

Suddenly he registered everyone's collective gasp. With dread, Kent looked around. Becca was beet-red again and he closed his eyes. "Don't tell me, I said that out loud too."

"Yep." Dennis didn't bother to hide his grin now. "Is there maybe something you'd like to share, Kent? Something about..." He glanced at Becca, who studiously avoided everyone's gaze. "About a kiss, perhaps?"

"Yes," Tiki said, laughing. "Tell all."

"Or maybe we should be asking Becca?"

Everyone in the room seemed to be enjoying Kent's and Becca's discomfort immensely. Becca on the other hand, looked as though she wished a huge hole would open up and swallow her alive.

"How about it, Becca?" Dennis lifted one eyebrow. "Anything new?"

"Dennis?" Kent interrupted politely.

Dennis turned to him, still grinning. "Yes?"

"Shut up."

Everyone laughed at that, but there was more than one speculative glance divided between himself and Becca, who had stopped avoiding him to glare at him. He couldn't blame her. "I'm sorry," he mouthed and she rolled her eyes and looked away, doubling the distance between them.

He wasn't helping his cause any. And what cause was that? Hadn't he'd known this was a bad idea from the very start?

He should just let it go.

That would be smart. No more rhapsodizing over her voice, no more mourning like a lovesick dweeb over her eyes. They'd just forget about this attraction. They were grown-ups, they could do it.

Becca passed him a quickly sprawled note. *You're off the hook. I'm going to find another adventure. Go away.*

Good, he thought, waiting for the relief to hit him. She'd made it so easy.

There would be nothing more between them, they were free to go on with their lives. He liked his life, quiet and simple. No permanent ties.

Yep, things were good.

Really good.

But damn if a small part of him wondered what she'd do now. Becca was different, special, she needed someone who would appreciate her, and he had the sinking feeling by turning away, he'd made the biggest mistake of his life.

Around him, the meeting continued. Tiki was speaking and everyone was listening.

Yeah, Becca had made it real easy for him. So why did he feel so miserable?

Across the table, his gaze met hers. "I can't do it, I can't go away," he said to her. The thought of his life stretching out in front of him, long and lonely, didn't seem to hold the same appeal it used to. "I don't want off the hook."

Abruptly, Tiki stopped talking, and everyone stared at him.

Becca rose to her feet in one fluid move. Another few steps and she was at the door. "This is really my fault," she said to him. "Don't feel badly."

"Wait!" he called to her as she turned to leave.

"I thought I knew what I wanted," she said, clearly conscious of their audience as she kept her gaze down. "And it was all great, really great. Especially the makeover, which gave me the in with you. But it's no longer enough, Kent. I'm sorry."

Wait. Makeover? Did she really believe that had made any difference to him? "Becca—"

"No." Her smile came straight from the gut, and it was so sad and wrenching, it nearly broke his heart. "Don't say anything. Goodbye, Kent." She closed the door behind her.

When she was gone, everyone turned to Kent, eyes wide and curious.

"Well, that meeting went well," he said.

LAKE TRAFFIC WAS LIGHT, it took him only a few minutes to get to the salon.

Summer looked up from her client when he limped in. She gave the woman's hair a gentle pat, whispered something, then came toward him with a welcoming smile.

No tight black dress today, but a snug skirt beneath a cropped top and an open denim jacket. Young chic. She was gorgeous, and by the confident way she sauntered over to him, Kent knew that she knew it.

"Dr. Dreamboat," she said, laughing when he grimaced at the nickname. "What can I do for you? A manicure? Pedicure?"

"No," he said, backing up a step, imagining himself tied to a chair and having his ticklish feet worked on. "Nothing for me. I came about Becca."

Summer's smile faded. "Is she okay? Hurt? Sick?"

"No."

But something in his expression must have tipped her off. She took his arm and led him past her client, smiling at the woman and promising to be right back.

Her office was a cool, white, comfortable room made interesting with lush, green plants. She gestured him to a chair, and once he sat, she leaned back against a small, neat desk. "What's the matter with Becca?" she asked.

"Me, mostly. But it's also your makeover."

"Excuse me?"

Kent rolled his shoulders. "It's confusing, but she wanted this new adventurous life-style and she thought the new look could give it to her."

Summer crossed her arms. "Don't be silly. This

makeover has been good for her. She's even gone out on a *date*. She would never have done that before, she'd never have made the time for herself.''

While that was fascinating information Kent filed away for later, he couldn't let this go. ''Yes, she's definitely come out of her shell. She's on a mission for a good time.''

''So give her one.''

That he'd wanted to do exactly that didn't escape him. ''I'm off the hook apparently,'' he said wryly, and at her narrowed brow, he shrugged. ''Her words.''

''You idiot. What happened?'' She sighed when he didn't answer. ''And here I thought you were so smart.''

''Are you going to help me here or not?''

''Why?''

''*Why?* What kind of question is that?''

''A good one,'' she said evenly. ''You care about her.''

''Yeah. So?''

''You also love her.''

As far as shock value went, it was a good one. He could feel his lungs constricting, closing off air. ''I've got to go.'' He was at the door, his throat tight, his heart pounding, when Summer stopped him.

"You know what I think, Dr. Dreamboat? I think you're a big phony." Her voice softened, filled with sympathy. "You're far more involved here than you want to be, aren't you?"

Well there was a news flash. "Look, are you in or not?"

She studied him, then smiled. "You can put away that dark, gorgeous scowl. I'm going to help your sorry hide, even if it means I have to resort to bribery."

9

THE NEXT MORNING Becca literally had to drag herself out of bed. What she really wanted was to bury herself beneath her blankets.

But in the warm bed her problems were only magnified. Some good this makeover had done, she thought crossly as she showered, ignoring the blinking answering machine. She knew who the messages were from, but she wasn't ready to hear what the tall, warm-eyed, far-too-sexy Kent had to say.

Fine. He was probably sorry.

So was she, because now she needed a *new* adventure when what she really wanted was him. Grabbing a bagel, she surveyed her closet. It was…empty?

Great. She'd forgotten to pick up her dry cleaning. Again. Glancing down at the sunshine yellow demi-bra and matching bikini panties she wore, she had to laugh. All the hot lingerie in the world wasn't going to dress her suitably for work.

Tossing on old jeans and a T-shirt, grumbling about the waste of money for the silk and lace, when clearly she was going to go to her grave without ever experiencing an orgasm, she got into her car.

Ten minutes later, she came to a stop in the parking lot of the small dry cleaners and could only stare in shock.

A large hand-lettered sign in the window said "Electrical Problems. Closed Till Noon."

"Everything I own is in there," she muttered. Everything except her underwear, she reminded herself. There was always a silver lining. She still had the best lingerie in town.

With a sigh, she got out her cell phone and called Summer, begging her to meet her at the salon where she could pick out an outfit for the day.

Then she got back into her car and headed for Summer's Place, which was locked. She sat on the steps to wait, but twenty minutes later, she looked at her watch and frowned.

Where was her sister? Without her, Becca was stuck going to work looking like...

"Well, *there's* the Becca I know."

At Kent's husky and oh-so-familiar voice, Becca pulled her baseball cap closer around her ears and stared resolutely at the water.

"I was hoping you hadn't tossed those jeans and that hat."

She heard the smile in his voice and knew if she looked at him, his killer grin would melt her.

So she kept her eyes on the lake.

"Ah, you're still upset with me." Uninvited, he sat next to her. "That's okay, I'd be upset with me, too. Anyway, I figure you'll have to talk to me eventually." His body brushed against hers. "Even if only to tell me what you think of me."

"Oh, I have no problem telling you what I think of you," she said. "You have a big mouth. You're a chicken. And—"

He laughed a little, and her tummy tightened at the sound. "Yeah, I get the picture."

Sighing, she turned and found him looking at her with such affection, her heart squeezed. He'd folded his long, rangy body beside her. It was silly, embarrassing, but she melted a little at just the sight of him and that stirred her temper because he didn't feel the same way. "Why are you here, Kent?"

"I'm actually not certain," he admitted.

Flattering. "Well go be not certain somewhere else, would you?" She tried to move away, but he stopped her, put his big hands on her arms and looked deep into her eyes. "You're making this difficult."

"*I'm* making this difficult?"

"I care about you," he said carefully, making her go absolutely still. "Very much."

Her heart simply stopped.

"And I want you in my life, but—"

With an abrupt thump, her heart started again. "No." She stood up, backed away. Dammit, not again. Her ticker couldn't take this roller-coaster ride. "No buts."

With a grip of gentle steel Kent held her still, made her look at him. "*But,*" he said firmly. "The reason Summer isn't here is because she called me and I told her not to come."

She broke free and stared at him. "You *what?*"

"I thought—"

When he found himself talking to her back, he groaned. Becca didn't care, she kept going, heading directly for her car, but despite his limp, he passed her and blocked the door. She tried to evade him, but it was like trying to go around a pit bull. A six-foot tall, one-hundred-seventy-five pound pit bull with determination and grim regret blazing from his gaze.

"Don't you want to know why?" he demanded.

Because it was useless trying to get past him,

she blew a stray hair out of her face and glared at him. "Okay, I'll play. Why did you come instead of Summer?"

"Leaning on Summer to create an image of yourself isn't necessary." Ruthlessly, he held her gaze even when she felt the blush of embarrassment creep up her face. "You don't need to look perfect to change your life-style."

"Then why don't you want me?" she blurted out, then covered her face. "Forget I said that. I have no idea why I—"

"I want you," he assured her. "But there's more than just wanting involved here."

Thinking was difficult since he'd somehow managed to plaster his body to hers again, all his tough, ready muscles to her softer, more giving body. He felt big. Hard. Sexy. But it was his scent that did it; his familiar, male scent that had her yearning and aching, and far too close to tears. To lose it now, in front of him, would just top off the day. Again, she tried to turn away, but with a heart-breaking wordless murmur, Kent pulled her even closer, slid those incredible hands of his over her back, then cupped her head, so that her face was pressed to his throat.

"Let me go," she whispered shakily. "You don't want to be here."

"I can understand why you'd think that, seeing as I've been an ass, but I really do want to hold you."

Pride demanded she resist, but he paid no attention to that, just continued to hold her tight, one hand softly, gently, rubbing her spine, his other stroking her hair as he gave her a hug that wrenched at her emotions as nothing else could have.

For that moment, she felt so protected. So cherished. But the compassion, the utter empathy pouring from his gaze, humiliated her.

"You're important to me," he said when she struggled free. "I don't want to lose you, Bec."

"But you don't want to keep me, either."

"Define *keep*."

"A commitment."

He tilted his head. "The let's-go-out-to-dinner-every-Friday-night kind of commitment, or the let-me-park-a-toothbrush-in-your-bathroom kind of commitment?"

Hating the sudden neediness that swamped her, she closed her eyes. "Forget it. Okay? Just forget it. It's not your fault, I changed the rules on you in the middle of the game, wanting more than you can give. Not very fair of me, I know, but I can't seem to help myself. But I really need you to just drop it. Right here, right now.''

She turned away then, she had no choice, not when her own emotions were so dangerously close to the surface. Not when, with the slightest encouragement from him, she would have followed him to the ends of the earth.

THE KNOCK came at dinnertime. Becca glared at her front door, certain it was Summer coming to make amends for being a no-show that morning.

But Becca wasn't ready to make amends, even if she did know most of her anger was self-directed. She'd had plenty of time to dwell on that since she hadn't gone to work. ''A mental health day,'' she'd told Cookie when she'd called in.

She'd convinced herself she deserved it because she'd never taken a personal or sick day before.

At first, she'd attempted to distract herself with reading. Then with school work. But nothing could make her forget how she'd left things with Kent. She didn't want to think about the hurt in his dark, lovely eyes, or what would happen now.

To take her mind off her troubles, she'd gone shopping, thinking it was time for yet another adventure.

She'd purchased a mountain bike, and it sat in her living room, shiny and inviting.

Another knock came, far less tentative than the first one.

With all her frustration, Becca yanked open the door, but everything she'd planned to say to her sister died on her tongue.

Kent stood there, one arm braced on the jamb, the other low on his hip. He wore all black: black long-sleeved shirt, black jeans, black boots. His dark hair was ruffled, as if it had been shoved back from his face by agitated fingers. In the dim light of the early evening, even his blue eyes looked black.

He was bad attitude personified.

Automatically, her heart responded, begged her to reach out to him, but her brain intercepted with good sense just in the nick of time.

Silent, he straightened and held out the hand that had been braced against her door. Wildflowers.

He'd brought her wildflowers.

Disarmed by the gesture, Becca took them, automatically lifting them to her nose to inhale their beautiful, exotic scent.

He hadn't smiled, not once, but his gaze was soaking in the sight of her in a way that made her anger turn. Instead she became hot and trembly. Confused.

"Missed you at work," he said.

"I'm sorry."

He waited, but when she just looked at him, he said, "Are you going to invite me in?"

His expression was nothing short of fierce. His body was so tense she could see each and every muscle delineated beneath his shirt and jeans. Not for the first time she wondered, a bit wildly, how a desk-bound chemist managed to look so mouth-wateringly magnificent.

"Yes or no, Becca."

Never had she sensed such a temper in him, and even though he held it perfectly in check, it gave her pause. He hadn't made one move toward her, but she backed up a step just the same. "I don't think coming in would be a good idea—" She began, but squeaked in surprise and nearly swallowed her words when he simply picked her up and set her aside, giving him room to walk past her.

"Well, gee," she said dryly, slamming the door. "Come on in—" The sarcastic words backed up in her throat when he put his big, warm hands on her arms and set her against the closed front door.

"You know you're driving me crazy, right?" he asked roughly.

"Kent—"

That was the last word she managed to get out before his mouth came down on hers.

10

THE KISS WAS as combustive as ever. More so.

Kent's mouth moved over Becca's, relentless, urgent. Anxious. He didn't realize how tense he was, how desperately he needed a sign from her, until he felt her fingers dig into his shoulders, binding him to her. Murmuring his encouragement, he pushed closer still.

In answer, she trembled, a shiver he hoped was anticipation because this, *this* was what he'd needed all day. Hell, it was what he'd needed for the past few weeks. *Her* in his arms, arching her body to his, wrapping her arms tightly around his neck, whimpering her need and desire in arousing little whispers that threatened to undo him right then and there. Needing more, he dragged his mouth over her jaw to gently nip at her ear.

She moaned his name.

"Mmm, love that sound." He nipped at her again just to hear it. "Love my name on your lips, in that voice that says I'm driving you half-wild."

"More than half," she assured him shakily. "Why are you here?"

"I missed you."

"Really?"

"Very much." Her body was warm and round beneath his hands. "You're so lovely, Becca."

"It's the makeover."

He opened his mouth to deny that, but she cupped his face, brought his lips back to hers. Incredible need twisted, knotting him up. When she writhed against him, the knots tightened. "Becca...about earlier. About us—"

"No," she said quickly, breathlessly. "It's okay."

He slid a finger over her cheek. "But I wanted to explain—"

"Kiss me." Her fingers against his mouth stopped anything else he might have said.

Kissing each finger, he brought his hand up to hold hers. "So you're not upset anymore."

"You talk too much, Kent."

He had to smile at her irritation. "But I hurt you. I wanted to tell you how sorry I am."

"I know." She returned the smile, and the mesmerizing heat remained in her eyes, invitingly.

Go for it, a little voice said. *She's hot, you're hot, go for it.*

But they had to talk first, before she got the wrong idea. He wouldn't hurt her again. "Becca—"

"Later." She tugged his head down to hers. Her voice was a breathy whisper. "Whatever it is. Much later." And she took over.

Oh man, Kent thought weakly, how she took over.

Sinking her fingers into his hair, she angled his head for her kiss, arching her body into his so that he could feel every inch of her.

A stab of pure heat tightened his belly, and logic warred with heat—he had to get enough air to his brain, to make sure she understood he wasn't just using her, that he truly felt something for her, something deep and scary and almost flu-like—but then she nibbled at him. First one corner of his mouth, then the other, and lust began to win.

With everything he had, Kent willed his hands to remain at her waist, but they weren't listening. Every part of his body responded to the heavy-lidded sensual gaze in her eyes, some parts more than others.

He had her sandwiched between his hard body

and the even harder wood. But this was Becca! She deserved better, deserved more than what he could give her shoved up against the door. "Becca—"

She went up on tiptoe to breathe in his ear, and the sensation that caused made him smack his head hard on the wood. "Ouch!" Pain and desire exploded in his head and all thoughts vanished.

"Stay with me." She pulled him back to her. "I want to be out of control. I want to be wild. *Hot.*" She clutched him, rubbing her body to his in an eager hug that nearly undid him. "Please, Kent. I want to let loose, I want my feet to leave the earth. I want to see stars. I want to explode, for once in my life! Is that so much to ask?" She blinked at him, frustration swimming in her gaze.

"No," he said softly. "It's not too much to ask."

"Then help me."

Oh yeah, he could help her. As if he could refuse her anything, especially this. "Come here then," he said hoarsely, dragging her close for a slow, wet, deep kiss that left them both breathless, and painfully ready. She gripped him trustingly and a heavy ache settled in his heart. When he scooped her up in his arms, she laid her head against his chest and the ache deepened.

She gave him a sexy, wicked smile and delicately bit his lower lip. Tempted to devour her right there, he kissed her again. *Don't take her against the door*, he reminded himself. *Think*. As if he could. "Your bed," he rasped out.

"Yes." She ran her fingers over his chest, and he stumbled in his haste, nearly killing both of them.

Her breathless laughter goaded him, and he licked his suddenly dry lips. Staring at the motion, she slid her fingers into his hair, looked him in the eye and asked with a heart-stopping mix of anticipation and awe, "Are you going to…" She blushed furiously.

"What?"

"Are you going to…use your tongue? You know, on my body?" Her teeth dragged over her lower lip. "I've always wanted to know what that felt like," she admitted.

They were only in the hallway, but he stopped to press her against the wall, his body poised and dying for her. Need pulsed inside him, biting, sharp need. With his arms planted on either side of her head, he cupped her face and tilted it up. Her lips were still wet from his mouth and he traced her lips lightly with his thumb. "I'm most definitely going to use my tongue," he said. "On every single inch of you."

"Oh my." She sounded a bit pressed for air. "Kent?"

He was walking again, and staring down at the drumming pulse at the base of her throat, at her hardened nipples. "Yeah?" he croaked.

"I want to taste you, too."

He swallowed his groan and struggled not to crash into a wall. By the time he dropped her to the mattress, they were grappling to touch everywhere at once, completely beyond finesse.

She wore some sort of flimsy robe that simply begged to be opened past her long, trim legs. As promised, he kissed every inch of her calves, knees and thighs. By the time he dipped and kissed her inner thigh, she was halfway to that explosion she'd wanted.

He slid his hands beneath her, to her curved bottom, and he pulled her closer, opening her legs to make room for his shoulders. The robe had parted now, and her sunshine yellow silk panties were hardly more than a wisp of material. They were wet, clinging to her flesh, and he stared down at her, so unbearably aroused he could hardly think.

Becca couldn't think, either, she was far beyond that. All she knew was a deep, piercing, relentless ache, centered in the core of her. She managed to gasp his name, though she didn't know if she was pleading or demanding. *Both,* she decided, and he reared up above her, looking down at her with so much heat and need she nearly cried.

"Becca." That was it, just her name. Then he pulled off his shirt and her mouth went dry. *Wow,* was all she could think. And then he unzipped his pants, revealing white cotton and the bulge of the most impressive erection she'd ever seen. Her mind blanked, her body sizzled.

His hands came up to the arms of her robe and he slowly pushed the material aside, looked down at her matching silk bra, at the curves spilling out of it and let out a low sigh. "Becca, you're so beautiful."

She reached for him, eyes closed.

He touched her face and whispered, "Becca, did you hear me?"

"I... No," she admitted, unable to hear anything past the roar of blood in her ears.

His hands settled on her quivering stomach and slowly, so slowly, his fingers slid up until they covered her breasts. "I said you're beautiful," he repeated. "*You,* Becca. Not some glossy image you made up, but the real Becca."

She couldn't stop her surprised, indrawn breath nor the delighted shock that reverberated through her system when his thumbs rasped over her nipples.

"Did you hear me this time?" His hot, intense gaze held hers. "You're the most incredible woman I know. Inside and out." His fingers continued to stroke her. "Tell me you believe that, Becca."

"I... *Kent,*" she breathed, arching into his touch. "More."

In the next shattering moment, her bra came unfastened and he ran his warm hands over her taut curves, over the hard, aching points of her breasts, which were thrust out, dying for attention. The sensations were so incredible, so intense, she cried out.

"Tell me," he demanded.

She could do nothing but toss her head back and let out a shockingly dark, needy sound.

"Open your eyes, Becca."

At his erotically rough voice, she obeyed, and with his gaze he let her see everything he was feeling. He tugged her robe and bra down to her elbows so that her arms lay trapped at her side.

"Do you know you're my every fantasy lying there like that?" he whispered, bending over her, his dark hair falling across his forehead, his eyes full of heat and desire. "Your bedroom eyes, your creamy skin—" A fingertip skimmed over a nipple and she gripped fistfuls of the bedding beneath her, biting her lips to keep from shamelessly crying out. "You want me, don't you?" His fingers continued to touch her. "Not just an orgasm, not just fun and adventure, but *me?*"

"Yes!" she gasped.

"Then tell me," he murmured, dipping his head to drag his tongue over her quivering skin. "Tell me you believe I find every part of you beautiful. Inside and out."

She wanted him now, right now. It took little effort for her to wrap her legs around his hips, to rock the neediest part of her over the neediest part of him.

He went completely still, letting out a low groan at her touch. "Becca." Now *he* made the rocking motion, sliding his huge erection over her wet, throbbing flesh. "Dammit, tell me now or this is no good."

He meant it, she could see the agony in his eyes, swirling there amid the hunger and passion. His muscles were tense and trembling, he was hot and hard and dying with need, but still, he would leave if she didn't acknowledge his words.

He thought she was beautiful.

She so wanted to believe that, but the small doubt couldn't be erased. She'd practically forced him into this.

And yet, for this moment, for right now, she wanted so badly to suspend reality and tell him what he wanted to hear. Struggling free of her shirt, she slid her arms around his neck. ''I believe you,'' she whispered.

Above her he was shaking with the effort to hold back, but at her words, he kissed her.

His fingers slid beneath her panties. He stroked her until she was shuddering before he tugged them down and off. Again he kissed her breasts, each of them, slowly, thoroughly, while his fingers traced their way back up her thighs and between. When he sank a finger inside her, she arched off the bed and whimpered his name before he slid his body down, dragging his mouth over her belly, to her hip. With his fingers playing over her, she could do nothing but toss her head on the pillow as he stroked, pressed and caressed, dragging out her tension until she was poised, trembling, dying… Then he shifted and his mouth was hovering over her, hovering, hovering.

"Oh, please," she whispered. "Kent, please."

He said her name once before running his tongue over her hot center. She exploded instantly. Shattered. Shuddered. And slowly came back to herself, and him.

"You okay?" he asked softly.

She'd never been so okay in her life. "I think...that's a fairly safe assessment."

He reared up on his knees and smiled wickedly. "Let's make sure." He slid off her robe, then watched her with a hot, fierce expression as he retrieved a foil packet from his pocket.

She gasped at the sight of him, silky smooth and throbbing, and he let out a groaning laugh, his fingers fumbling as he protected them both.

"Now," she demanded, pulling him close.

"Yes, now." Dragging her hips to meet his, he thrust into her, letting out a hoarse groan. He felt it, too, she realized dimly, this incredible connection. She could see it in the strain of his beautiful face as he concentrated so intently on her.

Slowly he pulled back, only to thrust again. And again. Then again. She couldn't keep still, she had to help, had to rock her hips, had to sink her fingers into his sleek back. Things went from wild to off-the-scale urgent then, and she couldn't stifle her cry as he sent her over the edge once more. Hands in her hair, he bent, tenderness and heat in his gaze as he took her mouth.

From deep within her, the tremors began yet again, and this time when she convulsed around him, he flung back his head and followed her over the edge, her name on his lips.

"Wow."

Against her neck she felt him smile. "We're still alive, then?" he asked hoarsely.

"I'm still breathing." Barely.

He stretched, groaned, then lifted his head and gave her a smile so sexy, so satisfied and male, it made her toes curl. He kissed her softly, and then again, not so softly. "In that case, I'll move when I can feel my legs."

"Please don't."

"I'm heavy."

He was and she loved it, so much so that when he tried to lift himself off of her, she held him tight. "No." Her muscles clenched around him.

Arousing heat sparked in his misty eyes. "If you do that again—" He groaned when she did. "Yeah, that. I won't be going anywhere."

"Aren't you...tired?" she asked politely, her hands sliding through his silky hair.

He shifted between her thighs, proving just

how "tired" he wasn't. "You feel so good," he murmured.

Her heart caught, quickened, then soared as he moved inside her, in slow, long strokes. "Again?" he whispered, dipping his mouth to hers.

"Please."

And it was even better than before.

BECCA FELT TINGLY, relaxed and so full of joy she couldn't stand it. She could hear Kent in the kitchen, getting himself a glass of water. Nearly dancing, she bent for his shirt, which lay crumpled on the floor. It smelled heavenly, and she inhaled deeply because she couldn't get enough of him.

She felt absurdly happy, and silly too, standing completely naked with his shirt pressed to her nose. She slipped it on over her head. Because she was still hopelessly giddy, she grinned at herself in the mirror over her dresser.

Then frowned.

She was a sight, and not a good one. Her makeup was all over her face, her hair such a wild mess it should be considered a national disaster. Embarrassed, yet unable to tear her gaze away, she went completely still.

She looked like the wicked witch of the east. No, like Bozo the Clown.

She had lipstick smeared across one cheek, eye shadow on her forehead. She had black rims of mascara under her eyes.

And yet Kent had looked into these eyes and called her beautiful. But that had been before he'd finished. Now that he was done, he was in the kitchen.

Come to think of it, he hadn't been able to escape fast enough.

He was already sorry, she figured, already wondering how to leave. In fact, he was probably staring at the front door in panic. Well, what had she expected? She had no one to blame for this heartache but herself.

Feeling numb, she went into the bathroom and turned on the faucet to wash her face. Not waiting for the water to warm, she started scrubbing. As she did, only one thought raced through her mind, and she couldn't get away from it.

They'd just made love; bone-dissolving, earth-shattering love. They'd moved as one, their hearts and souls had beat in rhythm.

Somewhere along the way, no doubt far before

today, she had tumbled hopelessly in love with him. And it was a permanent kind of love.

Unfortunately, she'd let herself forget, Kent didn't do "permanent."

11

GOING BACK INTO Becca's bedroom was the hardest thing Kent had ever done. Especially since he could no longer fool himself. What they'd just shared hadn't been merely fun.

It hadn't even been just great sex.

Whatever he'd experienced, it was going to be difficult to recover. Hell, who was he kidding? Recovery was going to be nearly impossible.

And what would happen now? They certainly couldn't go back to their previous relationship.

For the first time in a long time, indecision and fear gripped him. All his life he'd made a habit of avoiding all ties, of keeping things simple and commitment-free.

Well he'd just had the best, most loving, most joyous moments of his life. Not to mention he'd seen the earth move. Nothing simple or commitment-free about that.

Dammit. Panic swirled in his belly as he filled up yet another glass of water from the kitchen sink, stalling. He looked longingly at the back door. His first instinct was to tear it open, run out and never look back.

Come to think of it, that was his second instinct, too, but there was one little problem.

He was buck naked.

He needed his clothes, his car, his own space, and not necessarily in that order. Resolutely, he walked through the living room—and stopped short at the sight of a brand-spanking-new mountain bike. Oh God, there was an accident waiting to happen, he thought. Becca on a mountain bike.

On the other hand, she'd look great in her little shorts, wind in her hair, the world at her feet as she rode. He could go with her, just to keep her safe—

Oh yeah, he was definitely out of control.

By the time he walked back into Becca's bedroom, she was fully dressed, wearing his shirt and hugging herself.

He was utterly unable to help his body's response to the way his shirt fit over her body. It looked as if she'd attempted to tame her hair, and while she seemed to have delicate rings of exhaustion beneath her eyes, her gaze was flashing with temper, not fatigue.

She turned away and something deep inside him

hurt at that, even though just a second ago he'd wanted to turn away, too. "Regrets already," he murmured.

"You're...naked."

"Yeah. I thought maybe you would be, too."

"Maybe you should go," she said weakly, studiously avoiding his nude body.

Yeah, that's what he'd thought, too. Actually, up until about one second ago, he'd wanted that with every fiber of his being. So why was he still standing there staring at her? Reaching out to touch her?

She stepped back, away from him, tightening his shirt around her body. The modesty of that gesture was both touching and mysterious, considering all they'd just shared. And the look in her eyes, that hurt, bewildered look, did something painful to his chest, when he didn't want to feel anything at all. "Did I hurt you?" he asked quietly.

A blush rose up her cheeks. "No."

"Then why the distance between us when we could be in that bed, wrapped around each other, skin to skin—"

"*Kent.*" She closed her eyes. "You're going to make me melt again."

"Okay with me."

"I don't think that's necessarily the truth."

He raised his brow and looked down at himself, where the "truth" was there for both to see.

She reddened even more. "You know what I mean. Look, you're dying to run. I'd appreciate it if you'd just do it now before I make a bigger fool out of myself here."

"Hey, it was a just a teeny-weeny moment of panic," he said, feeling another one right now at the determined, resigned look in her eyes. "It's gone."

"Well mine isn't. I'm sorry, please excuse me." She left the room and, stunned, he followed. In the living room she strapped on a helmet, mounted her bike and coasted toward the front door.

"Your helmet is on backward."

"Oh." Looking sheepish, she kept going. "I'll fix it outside." Somehow she managed to pick up speed in the small space and his worry about her helmet faded to be replaced by a new one.

"Becca, slow—"

Too late. She let out a squeak at the sight of the looming front door, started to frantically pedal backward, but didn't slow down.

"The brakes are on the handles," he shouted. "Watch—"

She crashed into the door.

"—out," he grunted to himself and rushed over. "You okay?"

"Fine." Her face was red as she straightened away from the door and opened it. "I knew about the brakes, I just forgot." She pulled away from him, still straddling the bike, then promptly got caught between the door and the screen.

Muttering beneath her breath, not looking at him, she finally freed herself and awkwardly maneuvered down the stairs.

"Becca—"

"Goodbye, Kent." She rode off without a backward glance.

"At least let me fix your damn helmet!" he yelled, terrified for her. "Come back here." But before he could blink, she was gone, and he was alone in her condo.

The realization galvanized him into action. He went after her, skidding to a halt at the top step. "Becca! Wait!"

The cool Sierra breeze hit him full on the chest, and in regions south that made him yelp.

Still naked as a jaybird.

A jogger moved past, giving him an alarmed look before she picked up her pace.

Terrific. He raced back to the bedroom to shove his legs into his pants. No shirt, it was still on

Becca, which slowed him down some. She was long gone, and clearly wanted to be alone. She was confused, and the truth was, so was he.

He was a man who liked to fix everything himself, but this time he didn't have the tools.

Or did he?

IT TOOK LITTLE EFFORT for Kent to find what he was looking for in her bathroom.

Less effort to haul the trash can from beneath the sink and start loading it full of everything he considered to be at the root of the problem: lipstick, mascara, hair-styling gel...whatever beauty element he found, he trashed.

Grabbing the can, he stalked outside, grumbling about the danger of mountain bikes, even though he'd ridden one for years. He intended to fill the dumpster, only to be halted on the front step by a bony finger to his chest.

An old woman, imposing for all her barely five-feet, stood glaring at him, her blue-silver hair glittering in the light of the porch, her finger still drilling a hole in his middle.

"*Hold it right there,*" she commanded, her voice a curious mix of squeak and rage. "Mrs. Fritzle, landlord, and I'm making a citizen's arrest!"

"What?"

"I've called the police, young man. You aren't going anywhere until they get here. Now get your hands up. Up where I can see them!" She emphasized this command with another hard poke of her finger.

"You've got to be kidding me." But the digit she had against his now aching chest told him she wasn't.

"What have you stolen from that sweet, little Becca, you...you *hoodlum?*"

Baffled, Kent stared down at this little roadblock. "I haven't stolen anything, I'm a friend of hers."

"Uh-huh." She peered into the trash can that he still held in his hands. "Makeup?" A frown creased her already very creased face. "You're stealing makeup? Oh my God, you're not one of those...what do they call 'em? Those men that want to be women, wearing panties and stockings and high heels and the like?"

Kent blinked, opened his mouth, but before he could answer, a sheriff's jeep whipped around the corner.

"Officer!" the woman screeched, jumping up and down with an agility that defied her age, because she had to be at least eighty. "Here he is!

Here he is! The burglar!'' Settling down, she turned her sharp gaze back to Kent. ''No hurry though, he's not dangerous, he wears women's panties and makeup!''

Kent sighed and promised himself he would not, absolutely would not, hold his inevitable arrest against Becca.

IN A SMALL TOWN where the local population is small, everyone knows everyone.

Everyone talks about everyone.

And everyone embellishes everything.

Incline Village was no different.

It was no surprise then, that the news of Kent's questioning at the police station was the big talk at the lab the next morning.

It was also no surprise that when Becca walked in, the sudden silence was loaded with barely repressed curiosity.

Sighing, she hung up her coat and turned to face the inevitable. ''Where is he?''

Dennis grinned. ''The women's panty-wearer?''

Everyone laughed except Becca, who crossed her arms and glared at Dennis.

He gave in. ''He's holed up in his office pouting.''

''Pouting?''

"Well, sulking at least. He wasn't happy with me for spreading the news."

Becca sighed again. "I'm not even going to ask how you found out."

Dennis lifted his eyebrows suggestively. "Dating the receptionist at the sheriff's station. Comes in handy."

"I don't suppose it occurred to you to keep it to yourself?"

"What, and miss the laughs when I told everyone that our straight-laced boss wears your panties?"

"He does not wear—"

The door to Kent's office on the other side of the lab opened. At the sound, even Dennis had the good sense to scatter with the rest of the gang.

"Traitors," Becca muttered, but managed to hold Kent's even gaze as it landed unerringly on her.

"Nice of you to show up for work today. Glad you're all in one piece," he said politely. He leaned his rangy frame against the counter of a work station and crossed his arms over his broad chest.

A casual pose, not such a casual man.

He wore jeans beneath his lab coat and there was something about the authority that the white jacket implied, combined with the casual sexiness of his jeans and T-shirt. Especially since she now knew exactly what lay beneath those jeans.

The memory of his hard, warm, muscled body, and what it had done to hers, made thinking difficult. And then she got a good look at his rugged, unrelenting...and indeed sulking face.

For some insane reason, she had the urge to wrap her arms around him and melt away that dangerous expression. But she couldn't. Too much had happened. "I was just going to—"

"Come here." His tone was quiet, low. Turning his back on her, he headed into his office, clearly expecting her to follow.

"Yeah, that's just what I was going to say." With yet another heartfelt sigh, Becca walked into his neat, roomy office.

She found him silent and distant, staring out the windows at the bright spring sunshine. "How are you?" she asked.

"Gee, great, thanks. Nice day, isn't it?"

Rolling her eyes, she moved closer. "I suppose that's guy talk for 'I'm mad as hell'." He remained silent and she let out a regretful breath. "Kent...I'm sorry."

His broad shoulders and taut back still faced

her. "Sorry you ditched me, or sorry you forgot to mention you have the neighbor-from-hell?"

"Both."

"At least they didn't arrest me. I might have had a hard time with my cell mates, being known as the panty thief."

She bit her lip. "You certainly would have been popular."

"Everyone in town is assuming I'm a kinky pervert disguised as a chemist."

"I'm so sorry," she whispered.

He didn't move, didn't look at her, didn't do anything but stare blindly out the window. Regret brought her forward, until she stood directly behind him, between his tall body and his desk. She set a hand on his taut back. Beneath her fingers, his muscles tensed, and it became impossible not to slide her fingers over him, wondering if the touch soothed him as much as it did her.

"I was throwing away your makeup," he muttered. "In case you were wondering."

That was a surprise; her makeup had been in its usual place this morning. She had no idea what the exact details had been, other than Mrs. Fritzle had decided he had been trying to steal from her, but had returned whatever it was to Becca's apartment. "Why were you throwing away my—" She remembered what she'd said about the makeover being the only reason he'd noticed her. *"Oh."*

"Yeah. *Oh.*"

"No one really thinks you're a..."

"Panty-loving pervert?" He shook his head. "I was trying to make a point. And I never even touched your panties other than to take them off you before we—"

"Yes," she said quickly, suddenly breathless. "I remember."

"So I have no idea how that whole thing started."

"Mrs. Fritzle gets ideas."

"Mrs. Fritzle is insane."

"Yes, well. I'm sorry I left you that way."

He turned his head and looked at her then. His eyes were deep, dark and full of things that unnerved her. "I'm sorry, too. But you were right. For one second there, right after we made love, I did want to leave. You scare me, Becca. Right to the bone."

Well that made two of them. It was shockingly easy to slide her hands around his waist and hug him, her cheek against his back. He was tall and lanky, but muscled, too, and she loved touching him. Desire fluttered in her stomach. "And anyway, I understand," she murmured. "Really."

He turned then, slid his hands to her hips, trapping her between his hard desk and even harder body. "What do you understand exactly?"

His voice was a rough whisper. He'd used that same thrilling tone with her before, just last night as a matter of fact, as he'd urged, coaxed and helped her to the most explosive orgasm of her life.

"I understand we got carried away during…sex." She bit her lip. "We're really connected that way, but I know you don't want me to get the wrong idea about it being anything more then it is."

Shock took him aback for a moment, then he let out an unsteady laugh. "*Carried away.* Quaint term. Is that what happened last night, Becca? We got *carried away?*"

Though his embrace wasn't exactly tender, she slipped her arms around his neck and kissed his hard jaw, wanting to relax him, wanting to give him something of herself, wanting…wanting so much she couldn't even put words to it.

"You knocked my world off its axis," he whispered hoarsely, his voice thicker than it was before. He stroked his hands over her. "I still haven't recovered."

She felt breathless already. And she could hear his own ragged breathing.

"Dammit, maybe I didn't want this," he said roughly. "But even I can admit the truth. It's more than merely 'carried away'." He lifted her chin. "Say it."

If she did, she would have to admit the rest, she'd have to tell him she'd fallen hopelessly in love. Instead, she dropped kisses over his neck.

He groaned when she darted out her tongue and touched his earlobe, but didn't lose track of the conversation. "Say it!"

Their gazes met, hot and tense and needy. *Mirrored souls.* The thought came from nowhere and shook her into seeing the truth. "It's more," she admitted on a serrated sigh.

His eyes glittered. His hands, hot on her, tightened. Then he let go of her, slammed the lock of his office door into place, and came back to lift her onto his desk. Looking at her from dark, dark eyes, he took the pencil she had behind her ear and tossed it over his shoulder. "Hand over the rest of them," he said, holding out an open palm.

With a little laugh, she took another pencil from her breast pocket.

"Only two?" He tsked while she laughed nervously. "I know better than that." Playfully he patted her down, raising a brow in triumph when he found one in her side pocket. "I don't want to get stabbed anywhere...vital."

"That was it," she promised and he drew her close, seeking her mouth. His lips were warm and firm, his tongue coaxing as he ran it over hers. He nibbled and urged and she felt her pulse go crazy. "Kent."

While he held her gaze safe in his, his filled with a terrifying combination of protectiveness and possessiveness, he slid his hand up her thigh, beneath the hem of her dress. His fingers found her and in a barely there touch, slid over her. Again, but beneath the edge of her panties.

She gasped and her head fell back as she shamelessly, urgently opened her legs wider and arched her back. "Here?"

"Oh, yeah. Here. Right here." He punctuated each word with a hard, sexy kiss to her mouth.

A thrill raced through her. "Now?"

Again, his fingers teased, coaxing a low moan from her lips before she could hold it back. "Now."

TEN MINUTES LATER, she was severely air challenged. There was a file beneath her hip, a stapler stabbing her back and the delicious weight of a sated man slumped in her arms.

Her leg tightened, threatened to cramp, but she wouldn't have shifted him to save her life. As she sacrificed her own limb, Becca listened as the racing of Kent's heart slowed and came back to normal, and she knew the startling truth.

He was right.

"Carried away" didn't begin to describe what was between them. "Fine" didn't cover it, either.

Not even close.

12

SUMMER'S PLACE was still open when Kent drove up, as he knew it would be. It was a Thursday evening, which meant the weekend was looming. Incline Village, for the most part, consisted of a wealthy, eclectic group of people. Properties were expensive, so were the resorts. The women liked to look good.

In light of that, the salon was hopping. There was a new receptionist—a small, petite, twenty-something young woman with green hair, black fingernail polish, at least ten earrings and a pierced eyebrow, who gave him a smile and the serious once-over. "Welcome."

"I'd like to talk to Summer."

Even with her pierced brow, she managed a look of regret. "I'm sorry, she's busy with a client. But we aim to please here. Can I help you?"

Her smile told him she wasn't necessarily referring to any service the salon could provide.

There'd been a time in Kent's life when he

would have jumped all over that promise in her eyes. But things were different now, both the times and himself.

He still enjoyed women, no doubt. But suddenly all he could think about was one woman—Becca. And though the thought still brought an abrupt and terrifying change to his pulse, he couldn't just ignore it.

"I'd really like just a moment with Summer," he said to the young woman. "I can wait."

She frowned slightly, an expression exaggerated by her black lip gloss. "She'll have another client waiting after this one—"

The phone rang, and Kent listened as she reluctantly accepted the cancellation of Summer's next client.

"Well, then," Kent said with a smile, when she'd hung up. "Summer will be free soon."

"Sure." Cool now, she folded her hands and looked at him. "For a client."

He gave her his best I'm-so-charming smile. "I just need a moment."

"Sorry. If you want to talk, you'll need to make an appointment. How about a cut and style? Or a manicure?" Her gaze ran over his body, past the dark polo shirt tucked into even darker jeans. "Massage?"

"You're kidding me."

"Obviously you've never had one. Here—" She bent and took out a deep green robe from a drawer. "You just strip down to the buff and—"

"I don't think so."

"We have a male masseuse, if you'd prefer. You know, for modesty's sake."

Kent couldn't believe it. "You're telling me that in order to talk to Summer, I need to let someone put their hands all over me?"

"Yep." Her smile turned a bit naughty. "Of course, if you're shy, or…whatever, you can always just have your hair done."

Oh what the hell, his reputation was already shot thanks to Mrs. Fritzle. What more could one little beauty salon treatment cost him? "Fine. Haircut."

"And style," she added, penciling him into Summer's schedule. She lifted her triumphant, laughing gaze. "Name?"

"Kent Wright."

Her pencil froze. Slowly she lifted her gaze to stare at him. "*Dr.* Kent Wright?"

"Yes."

She laughed, revealing a pierced tongue. She tucked that tongue into her cheek. "Heard about what happened with the police. And the—'' She leaned close and whispered, *''—panties.''*

Perfect. He hadn't been nearly humiliated enough here. "It was makeup," he corrected wearily. "Not panties."

"Uh-huh."

"Look, why don't I just wait over there for Summer?"

Before he could turn to the reception area, his green-haired torturer asked sweetly. "Are you sure you wouldn't like a beauty treatment as well? Maybe a facial?"

"Just get Summer," he said through his clenched teeth.

"So...EVERYTHING BACKFIRED on you, I heard."

It was difficult for Kent to reply since he lay stretched out, his neck on the edge of a chilly sink, his head in that sink getting "the full treatment."

Above him, Summer shook her head. "At least you didn't get arrested." Squirting some conditioner into her hand, she slowly massaged it into his head. Despite feeling silly and uncomfortable, he couldn't prevent the distinct uncurling of his toes as she kneaded his scalp.

"Good?" she asked, working more magic with her fingers.

He shrugged nonchalantly. "It's okay."

Summer snickered. "Liar. You're positively melting."

"I never melt." Well, not quite. He melted over Becca's smile. Over her kisses, her touch. He melted every time she so much as looked at him.

Which really threw this just-fun theory all to hell.

"Why is it so hard for a guy to admit he likes being pampered?" Summer wondered. "Look, I could have told you breaking and entering Becca's wasn't exactly the smart route to take."

"Well thanks for coming up with something better."

Summer started to rinse him out. With cold water. He sucked in a breath.

"Sorry," she said sweetly, and the water magically warmed.

"And I didn't break and enter," he corrected. "I was already *there*."

Abruptly, the water flipped off. Summer's face appeared above him, creased in a frown. "Already there? Doing what?"

"None of your business."

Their eyes met and Kent waited while Summer assessed, decided. Then smiled. This time, when the water came on, it was deliciously toasty. "You love her," she breathed.

He made a noise that he most definitely meant as a denial.

"You do."

He snorted and pushed out of the chair as soon as she'd finished. "By the way, thanks ever so much for that help you offered."

"Hey, don't blame me, you said you had it all figured out." But she sighed. Bit her lip. "And I did help." She sighed again. "Today. If you're interested."

"I'm interested."

She looked him solemnly in the eyes. "I love what I did for her," she said quietly. "The makeup, the clothes, especially the okay to go for it. It'd been a long time coming. But I'm also the first to admit she took it wrong. She honestly believes it's all that extra stuff that finally caught your attention."

"I couldn't care less about that extra stuff."

Summer gave him a long, thoughtful look. "Does *she* know that?"

He shifted uncomfortably. "I thought she might when I tossed away her stuff."

Summer looked disgusted. "*Words,* Kent. Women need words."

"This was supposed to be just casual," he muttered.

"And is it?"

Yes.

Hell, no.

When he didn't—couldn't—answer, she led him through the busy salon, where he was subjected to more than a few whistles. They made Summer laugh, and made Kent grit his teeth.

Then, finally, they were in her office.

On her desk lay a garment bag, filled with clothes.

"Becca's new clothes," she whispered, even though they were alone. "She hasn't even worn these yet."

"You went breaking and entering too?"

At his surprised and delighted laugh, she lifted her chin. "No. But the dry cleaner owed me a favor. And I figured if you *loved* her enough to do it, I did too."

He cringed as if struck. "Would you stop flinging that word around?"

She blinked innocently. "What word?"

Kent unzipped the garment bag and tried to ignore both her and that funny feeling deep in the pit of his belly, not easy to do when he was deathly afraid she was right.

The *L*-word just might be involved here.

"Not ready to talk about it?" she asked, tsking sympathetically. "Don't worry, Dr. Dreamboat, this will all work out."

"So glad you think so. You're not the one on notice at the police station." He fingered the stack of elegant clothes, the same ones he'd seen on Becca for the past few weeks. "Tell me you left her nothing but—"

The knock on the open door surprised them both.

So did Becca as she walked in. "Well hello there," she said with a genuine smile for both of them. "What's this?"

Kent froze. Out of the corner of his eye he saw Summer do the same.

"Sorry, did I startle you?" Becca asked. She wore a soft blue sweater over a matching skirt that managed to be sophisticated yet sweet and still show off her lush body. Her eyes sparkled, her skin glowed. When she turned to look at him, her hair danced over her shoulders in a way that made his fingers long to touch.

But it wasn't the physical attraction that jolted him now. Her smile twisted at him, warmed him from the inside out. Not for the first time, he was struck hard by his feelings for her, by the very strength and depth of them. He just didn't know what to do with them. If he went with the flow, and things didn't work out, he'd lose her. There'd be no more daily chats, no more laughter and shared jokes. No more easiness, or affection, and he'd miss her with all his heart.

But if he didn't go with these new emotions, if he backed off now, he'd lose her anyway.

Screwed either way.

There was still a smile of greeting on her lips. Her laughing, bewildered eyes took him in, from the black smock he still wore, to his wet hair dripping down his back.

"Becca..." Summer shot Kent a warning glance and smiled at her sister. "Hon, what happened? I thought you had school tonight."

"I had a bit of an attitude." Her gaze met Kent's. They'd made love on his desk only hours before and yet none of the need had faded, it was a tangible thing between them. So was affection and overwhelming tenderness. Helpless against the pull of that last emotion, he found himself moving closer to her.

"Well it's great to see you," Summer said brightly. Too brightly. "But I'm right in the middle of giving Kent a great new 'do'—" She moved toward the door, her arms outstretched, trying to shoo everyone out, especially Becca. With one nervous glance at the stack of clothes on her desk—*Becca's* clothes—she said quickly, "Let's go on out there and you can give me tips while I work."

But Becca ducked beneath Summer's arms. She was still looking at Kent, with a sweet, baffled smile. "I didn't know you were going to get your hair cut. Here."

It was a clear question, and he opened his mouth, but before he could say a word, she turned to Summer's desk.

And saw her clothes.

Kent groaned silently.

Summer groaned, not so silently, and made a move to stop her sister.

Avoiding Summer's hand, Becca evaded and rounded the desk, then touched the open bag. As she flipped through the clothes one at a time, her jaw tightened. Her expression darkened. "What's this?"

Summer's smile faltered. "Uh, hon? Remember yesterday when you didn't press charges against panties-man here?" She bit her lip. "Think you're going to be that generous today too? Jail time really wouldn't suit my schedule."

Kent sighed and pinched the bridge of his nose with his thumb and forefinger.

Becca let out a sound of disbelief. "What's going on?" She glared at Kent. Crossed her arms. Cocked a hip.

Waited.

And basically looked so damn irresistible he had to slip his hands into his pockets to keep them off her. "Yeah, about the clothes..." He peeked at Summer, who had apparently found something fascinating on the ceiling to stare at.

"*You* stole them?" Becca asked him incredulously.

Kent again looked at Summer, expecting her to jump in and explain, but she still studied the ceiling intently, as if counting the squares were of utmost importance.

"How could you?" Becca asked him, hurt.

He'd had no intention of dropping a dime on Summer, really he hadn't. But she was humming nonchalantly, looking amazingly innocent, while he was sinking fast.

And the woman he was hoping to coax back into his arms—soon—was sending him a withering look, and this time, dammit, he'd done nothing wrong!

Carefully he weighed his options, but he had

none. "Summer stole your clothes. And if I were you, I'd sic Mrs. Fritzle on her."

"Snitch," Summer hissed beneath her breath.

"But...why?" Becca asked Summer.

Inhaling a deep breath, Kent reached out and took Becca's hands, then drew her resisting body closer.

"It's the makeover," she said quietly, still angry. "Isn't it? It's how I pushed you into..." Hesitating, she blushed, then looked at Summer.

She covered her ears and turned her back to them. "I'm not listening," she said, sneaking a peek over her shoulder. "Unless it's good."

Becca sighed and returned her attention to Kent. "It's because of how I pushed you into sleeping with me, when you didn't want to."

"Didn't want to?" He laughed incredulously. "Is that what you think?"

"I don't know." She lifted a shoulder, her misery barely masked by her coolness. "Since you rarely tell me what you're really thinking."

Gently he lifted her chin. Kissed her. For a second she remained impassive, but he persisted, giving, urging, desperately trying to reach her.

Only when her fingers curled into his shoulders, when she made that soft, helpless sound of awakened desire, did he lift his head. "Did that feel like something I *had* to do?"

Her eyes were luminous. And sad. "I want the words, Kent."

"Well, duh. I told you that much, Ace," Summer broke in helpfully.

When they both glared at her, she covered her ears again, and also closed her eyes. "I'm not even here," she assured them. "Unless you need me."

"You've done quite enough," Kent muttered.

"I'll take my clothes," Becca said to Summer, backing away from the both of them. "And you might as well tell me the truth. There never was a contest for the makeover, was there? It was just a way of roping me in."

Summer dropped the hands from her ears and made a disparaging sound. "I just wanted to help."

Becca let out a smile that was both warm and sad. "I know. And you did. Actually, both of you did." She scooped up the garment bag, walked to the door. When she had her hand on the handle, she turned back. "I understand what you tried to give me, Summer. And it was wonderful. Exciting." She looked at Kent and her eyes clouded, which broke his heart. "I understand what you tried to give me, too," she whispered to him.

"And it was also wonderful and exciting. But I still want more, Kent."

"I know," he said to the door after she'd shut it. "Dammit. I want more, too."

Summer grinned at him, making him swear colorfully.

"Love, love, love," she sang, then laughed. "Oh don't worry, Dr. Dreamboat. I'm going to make a great sister-in-law."

He nearly passed out at the thought.

13

IT WAS LATE, but Becca didn't feel like going home. She'd been riding for an hour already now and her legs had long ago turned into rubber, but she didn't stop. Instead, she rode to the lab, hoping to be able to be alone and think.

Quivering muscles or not, it was time to face the facts. She'd set out to have a good time and had ended up falling in love, and the man she'd fallen in love with didn't "do" love.

Oh, he cared for her; she had only to look into his expressive eyes to see that. He wanted her, too. Every time he held her in his warm, strong, capable arms, that wanting surged like a live, tangible thing between them.

Thankfully the lab was empty. No one to see the stupid tears on her cheeks, no one to witness the self-pity she so rarely allowed herself.

All she wanted now was to lose herself in work. Unfortunately, some data she needed sat on Kent's desk waiting his approval.

Letting herself in his office, she took a moment to stand there and simply absorb his favorite space. She could feel him here, could imagine him standing tall by the window, his eyes flashing wickedly when he shot her that just-for-her smile.

She got what she needed from his desk, then stared in surprise at the trash can. The lingerie catalogue. This was a prized possession, favorite reading material, fought over by every single male in the lab on a daily basis.

Why had Kent thrown it away?

It didn't matter, she told herself. He could do as he wanted. So could she. Wild, fun, adventure. Her new motto. Yeah. She was a new woman.

But some of the wind left her sails when she realized she was a new woman who still had to ride home. Alone.

FINALLY, KENT THOUGHT as relief washed through him. Finally. When Becca got off her bike, he rose off her top stair where he'd been waiting and worrying.

She stood there in the light of the moon's glow looking soft and vulnerable. Automatically, as if it was the most natural thing in his world, he reached for her, but at the last second, he stopped himself.

She'd been crying.

"You're hurt?" he demanded in a voice gritty with concern as he took her arm to turn her toward him so he could get a better look at her. Years of nasty tumbles had him checking out her knees and elbows first, but she shook her head.

"I'm not that pathetic," she said. "I can ride a bike."

He knew then, without her saying it, that *he'd* given her that sad, haunted look. In light of that, he had no right to haul her close the way he wanted to do. To bury his face in the soft spot of her neck, to wrap his arms around her and hold on tight.

While he was still standing there like an idiot, she crossed the threshold and surprised him by walking directly into his arms.

She felt like heaven. "I'm so glad to see you," he whispered.

She simply pressed closer, put her cold nose to the crook of his neck and held on. "You threw away your lingerie catalog," she said, her voice muffled. "How come?"

The question completely baffled him. "What?"

She pulled away and looked at him. "You've never thrown one of those away. You and the guys save them—I *know* where you hide them."

"Uh, yeah. Well." Embarrassed, he cleared his throat. "I threw this one away, okay?"

"Why?"

He sighed. "Wouldn't you rather know why I'm here?"

She lifted a shoulder. Studied her feet. Blew out a breath. "Okay."

"So enthusiastic."

"Okay, fine. If you must know, I'm a little nervous you're here to say something like, 'you drive me crazy, Becca. You ruined a good pair of my shoes, twisted my ankle and got a ticket in my car. You're too much trouble, so stay out of my life.'" She flashed an uncertain smile that both warmed and broke his heart. "That's what I'm thinking you should be saying to me."

"You can't really think that." But she did, he could see that more clearly than the nose on his face. "Okay, I'm not good at words, but I'll try. For you, I'd try anything."

"You...you would?"

"I let you drive my car, didn't I? Come with me."

"Where?"

"Your bedroom," he said, his voice already husky at the thought of her there.

Her eyes darkened, her lips parted. "You want to show me something?"

"I want to tell you, with those words you want, but it has to be there."

She bit her lip and nodded, and he scooped her up in his arms. There was no wild kissing this time, no forays in the hallway, no pressing each other against the wall in desperate hunger.

But she looped her arms around his neck. "I can walk."

"Maybe I want to hold you. Makes me feel tough," he said, huffing only a little. "Manly."

She laughed, then grew quiet when he pushed open the bedroom door, carried her to the bed and slowly let her slide down his body until her feet hit the floor.

With a hand that was suddenly unsteady, because this was so important, he reached out and touched her face. "I can run a company. Manage a staff. I can do just about anything that needs to be done in my lab, but formulating my thoughts and putting them into words where you're concerned is the hardest thing I've ever done."

She closed her eyes. "I understand—"

He pressed gentle fingers to her soft lips, then leaned close to whisper, "Let me show you." He touched her hair, then took a step closer, eased out the clip that kept everything so neat and sank his fingers into the thick, glorious depths.

She made a sound of wanting. He bent to kiss her. She made another sound, of desire this time, and her eyes fluttered closed again. The pulse at the base of her throat matched his racing heart.

He kissed that throat now. "I love your hair," he murmured. "Love it up, love it down, love it any which way, but I especially love it stuffed into that baseball cap of yours, with all those little strands hanging out."

When his fingers brushed against the curve of her ear, she drew an audible breath. "Nice earrings," he said softly, carefully unscrewing the back of her gold hoop and setting it on his dresser. "Without is even better." And then he put his mouth to the sensitive lobe and sucked.

She clutched at him, but managed to say, "You seem to have plenty of words now."

"You inspire me." He took her face in his hands and tipped it up. The room was fairly dark, all he could see clearly were those eyes of hers, but it was enough. He kissed her, stealing what little breath he'd managed to save up, a deep, slow, soulful kiss. When he finally raised his head, they were both shaky.

He went to work on her elegant sweater next.

"Mmm, you look good in clothes…" The soft material slipped down her arms and hit the floor. His fingers went to the zipper on her skirt. "But I love the way you look without them even more."

Now her skirt lay pooled on the floor, too, leaving Becca standing in nothing but a silky camisole, matching panties and thigh-high stockings. She was breathtaking, so much so that he had to stand there looking at her in awe. "You're so beautiful." Gently he slipped the straps of her camisole down her arms. "And that's without the veneer of all the fancy clothes, or any part of the makeover, which by the way, has absolutely nothing to do with my desire for you." He sank to his knees before her, running a slow hand up the back of her calf.

She let out a trembly smile, but she crossed her arms over her chest, holding the flimsy material of the camisole to her.

He didn't tell her she'd just emphasized her full breasts, their rosy peaks, hard and begging for his attention.

They wouldn't have to beg long. He tipped his head back and smiled at her. "Have I ever told you how much I love those torn jeans you used to wear?"

She shook her head, sucking in a harsh breath when his fingers played over her skin.

"You have the greatest legs, all long and lean. Your jeans really show them off."

Air seemed to get stuck in her throat when his fingers danced along behind her knees, then up the backs of her thighs. His fingers dipped between those thighs and she gasped.

While she was still trying to catch her breath, he tugged on her camisole, gently and slowly, until she let it free. Immediately, she crossed her arms again, covering her bared breasts, but he'd get to them in good time. "Step out of it," he whispered, coaxing her to lift one foot, then the other, slipping off her heels.

He tossed the silk over his shoulder and moved in close, kissing her quivering belly. While his mouth made its way to her hipbone, he rolled her stockings down until she stood before him in nothing but panties.

Sitting back on his heels, he reached up and took her hands in his, holding them at her sides. Her face was flushed, her eyes limpid pools of desire he could happily drown in. "I have some more words," he told her softly. "Lots of them. We've had fun. We've had adventure. Both were nice. Great. But I don't want to go back to the way we were. I'd miss you too much.''

Her hands clutched his.

He held her tight. "You said you wanted more. I want more too. The grandest adventure of all. You and me. Together.''

"You...really think of me that way?''

"I think about you every moment of my waking day,'' he said honestly. "I dream about you all night long. I wake up hard and aching and dying for you. I love your body, every inch of it, but I love what's inside even more. We're magic together, Becca. We're soul mates. Please, if you believe nothing else I've told you, believe that.''

Her hands flexed in his, but he held them tight. Again, he kissed her softly, high on her thigh now, then higher still, in that smooth, sensitive groove between her thigh and hip.

"Kent...'' Her voice wavered, nervous and excited. "Did you just tell me...''

"Yeah. I love you.''

She let out a sigh that stirred his blood, stoked the fire burning with him. Gently he nuzzled at her, and instinctively her hips undulated. When he did it again, a helpless sound escaped from deep in her throat. Then he slipped his tongue between the edge of her panties and slid it over her.

She cried out then, and when he opened his mouth on her, she shuddered violently. "I can't...Kent, my legs...they won't hold me."

Surging to his feet, he lifted her against him and laid her in the center of the bed.

She watched as he undressed, her chest rising and falling shallowly, her eyes on his magnificent body. "You were right...you had plenty to show me." Her voice was low, her eyes dark and direct.

He let out a groaning laugh. "This isn't the half of it."

"No?" Her breath quickened even more, and he thought he just might lose it right there.

Simply because she was getting hot looking at him.

Then her gaze met his and there was far more than just hunger and passion there in those green depths. "Did you mean it?" she whispered.

"Yes." Leaning over her, bracketing her hips with his hands, he looked deep into her eyes. "I love your wit, your smarts, your voice, your eyes, your *everything*."

"Except the way I drive."

"I'll get used to it, I swear."

She lifted her arms. He sank to the bed, slipped into them and covered her. Her mouth sought out his. The scent of her hair, the need in her gaze, the urging of her hands, it all swamped him. She was everything he'd ever wanted, everything he ever *would* want, and since he could no longer remember why he was afraid of this, he poured himself into the kiss.

She moaned his name, pressed closer still, giving him everything she had. With tenderness and lust driving him, he ran his hands over her breasts, her belly, to the throbbing spot between her legs, and when she opened them further and arched up to him, he filled her. She was gloriously wet and hot, and though he was on the edge, though she thrust her hips impatiently, he held them both still. "Look at you," he whispered. "You take my breath away, Becca."

Gazes locked, she lifted slightly, driving him more deeply inside her. He could see her, all of her; her warm spirit, her compassion, her need for him.

It was the last that had his heart overflowing. Hunger and passion and so much more roared through his veins. He was deep inside her, in her body, her heart. She was most certainly in his. It was almost too much, this joining of the body and soul, so much pleasure and sensation, he could hardly take it.

Planting his forearms on either side of her head,

cupping her face, he kissed her, lost himself in her taste, in the feel of her. "I love you," he said again, in a voice so thick and raspy he hardly recognized it. And he moved within her.

With a small cry, she arched back. He thrust again, and again. Claiming. Staking. Promising. In the most intense moments of his life, they moved together, mind and body. When she came, her body rippling with blinding pleasure, it triggered his own earth-shattering release.

14

KENT WAS HUMMING when he walked into the lab the next morning. He was also grinning like an idiot, just because he could see Becca's car in the parking lot.

Yeah, he was gone. *Far* gone.

And it felt damn good.

She'd slept with him all night, not that there'd been much sleeping involved. Which brought a dreamy smile to his lips, and he walked past Cookie with a wave, thinking he'd been a fool to put off combining this friendship with this new, wildly satisfying element.

"Hold it," Cookie said, snapping her gum, narrowing her eyebrows.

He stopped at her desk. "Yes?"

"Are you...singing?"

"Nope. Humming."

"You got lucky last night," she guessed.

"Depends on what you call lucky," he called,

moving down the hallway to the tune of her surprised laughter.

Though he didn't really need the jolt of caffeine—who would, after having made love with the most incredible woman all night—he grabbed a cup.

The only thing that could hurt his mood was if he dwelled on the fact that Becca hadn't told him she loved him. But he refused to agonize over that. Yet.

DRAWING A DEEP BREATH, Becca entered the lab. Memories of last night danced in her head, of Kent telling her with words, with kisses, with his incredible body, just how much she meant to him.

It had been magical, perfect. Well, nearly, because she had made one crucial mistake.

She'd neglected to tell him just how much he meant to her in return. It was something she intended to fix, today, right this minute if possible, despite the butterflies wreaking havoc in her belly.

Then Kent was standing at her work station, staring at her in that heated way he had, the one that told her he was remembering last night, and thinking of many nights yet to come, and those butterflies morphed into stomach-liner-eating dragons.

He watched her approach and a slight frown marred his brow.

She knew why. She'd dressed carefully for this morning. Jeans, backward baseball hat, glasses, the white lab coat with at least six pencils, the works.

The old Becca.

Kent wore a white lab coat, too, but his showed amazing shoulders, the chest that only hours before, she'd covered with kisses.

She stopped a few feet away, vividly aware of everyone's direct interest, as they pretended to work while unabashedly eavesdropping. "Good morning," she said, her voice unintentionally husky.

"Thanks to you, it's a great morning."

Around them, everyone shifted closer, trying to capture each and every word, while still pretending to work.

"Nice jeans," he said. "What's the occasion?"

She shrugged nonchalantly while her heart raced. "Maybe I just wanted to make sure I had your attention."

"Oh, but you most definitely have my attention," he assured her, his own voice warm and thick. "You always have."

Acutely aware of everyone's undivided attention—they'd given up even the pretense of being busy—she lowered her voice to a whisper. "Are you sure?"

"You can doubt it? After what we shared, especially last night?"

Heat flooded her cheeks, but she'd started this, she would finish. "I was just wondering, you know, because before the makeover, you never looked at me in that way that makes...my knees buckle."

"I make your knees weak?"

She nearly smiled, but there were those dragons working at her stomach. "Oh yeah, you make everything weak. But—"

"But it comes down to the makeover," he finished for her. "And why we didn't go out before that. Right?" He sighed and shook his head. "The truth is, I had it in my head I couldn't have both your friendship and your love. And they were both so important because I'd never had both before."

"Of course you can have both."

"Can I?" he asked softly. "I wanted you before, Becca, you can believe it. But the most important part of our relationship had nothing to do with sex."

Someone snickered. Kent dropped his arms to his side and glared at his staff, all of whom immediately ducked their heads and looked busy.

He turned back to Becca, who bit her lip.

"I liked the sex part," she admitted in a whisper.

He let out an agreeing laugh. "Me, too." Purposely, he removed her glasses, put his big warm hands on her arms and shook lightly. "And for someone who wanted the words, you've been awfully miserly with your own."

Within her, courage and hope blossomed painfully. "I just didn't think I had a chance."

"Take one now," he suggested, dropping his hands from her to cross his arms over his chest.

Take a chance. Her biggest adventure of all. Could she?

Biting her lip, she took that last step between them and blinked him into focus, not easy without her glasses. She touched him and could tell by the warmth and affection that filled his eyes that he truly felt all he'd told her.

He loved her, no matter what.

It was empowering. And awe inspiring.

To be loved for herself! Not for her brains, not for her looks, but for herself. To be loved by a man she loved back, with all her heart. It was the thrill of a lifetime. No, it was the adventure of a lifetime, and all she needed. "Okay." She drew in a deep breath. "Here's me, taking a chance."

She swallowed, licked her lips. "*I* know I'm the same woman on the inside, no matter what the outside looks like. I just wanted to know that you love me regardless of that outside."

"Then know it."

"Well, I think I would if..."

He looked at her, for the first time allowing his hope to show through. "If...?"

"If we were married." She smiled, a bit wobbly, but then again, how often did she ask a man to be hers forever? "I was wondering if, considering all that you've said about us being soul mates and all, if you'd like to have me change my name to yours."

He didn't move a muscle. "Are you asking me to be your husband?"

Why wasn't he jumping for joy? Saying yes? Kissing her? "Yes," she whispered.

"Because you know, it really didn't sound quite like a marriage proposal." His voice was solemn, not a trace of his thoughts showed on his face.

"What do you mean?"

"Well for one, I haven't heard you say you love me."

Drawing in a shuddering breath, she lifted her head, tossed back her hair. "Okay, I'm trying too hard," she muttered. "Give me a minute here."

Gently he squeezed her hand, and desperately, she searched his gaze. She found what she was looking for in a small, barely there twinkle. "I'm sorry. I'm not very good at this."

"Together, we're good."

Her eyes stung. "Yes, I think you're right. I love you, Kent. I love you with all my heart." She let out a slow, shaky breath.

He looked shaken, too, but shot her a devastating grin. "There, that wasn't so hard, was it?"

"No." She smiled back. "There's more. You make me happy, you make me laugh. And you love me back."

"No matter what you're wearing," he clarified. "Say that part."

Her eyes filled, her throat swelled. "No matter what I'm wearing. Will you—"

His fingers caressed her lips, holding the words in. His other hand slipped around her waist, drew her close. "Be mine, Becca. My best friend. My lover. My wife. Forever and always."

A smile burst through her happy tears. "Forever and always." She hugged him tight. "No matter what I'm wearing."

"Speaking of which..." His hands slipped down the backs of her thighs and up beneath her coat to squeeze her bottom. "I was wondering about these jeans... Think you can shrink them a couple of sizes?''

She laughed. "I could try."

He kissed her. "Try hard."

Her laughter filled the lab, but it was smothered quickly by another kiss.

At their audience's collective whoop of encouragement, Kent lifted his head. "Don't you people have work?"

Dennis popped up over the divider. So did Jed. Then Cookie. Others followed. They were all grinning.

Kent grinned, too, then bent Becca over his arm and kissed her to the music of catcalls and laughter.

JENNIFER LABRECQUE

Andrew in Excess

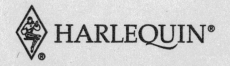

HARLEQUIN®

TORONTO • NEW YORK • LONDON
AMSTERDAM • PARIS • SYDNEY • HAMBURG
STOCKHOLM • ATHENS • TOKYO • MILAN • MADRID
PRAGUE • WARSAW • BUDAPEST • AUCKLAND

Dear Reader,

I have long believed there are two keys to happiness: moderation and organization. Now, if I could at least manage just one!

Have you ever baked a pan of brownies and wondered whether you should either not touch them at all or just go ahead and eat the whole pan to get them out of the house? You know you have. If you answered no, then you, my dear, qualify as a person of moderation.

Kat Devereaux knows she's a woman of excess. And does it ever get her in all kinds of trouble! But Kat's biological clock is in express mode and she wants a baby. Marrying Andrew seems like the answer to her problem. If she can just master moderation...

So hunt down some chocolate, find a comfy spot and indulge in *Andrew in Excess*. And best of all—it's calorie free!

Enjoy,

Jennifer LaBrecque

P.S. I'd love to hear what you think about my first book. Write to me at P.O. Box 801068, Acworth, GA 30101.

To Robert, my husband, who tossed me the ball
and pushed me to play the game.
To Anna Adams and Susan Goggins,
who helped me move the ball downcourt.
And to Brenda Chin, who caught it and slam-dunked it.

Prologue

"I'VE LOST MY MIND." Kat Devereaux slid onto the leather car seat and slammed the door. "Why'd I let you talk me into coming? I hate cocktail parties. No, that's too mild. Loathe. Despise." She reached for the door handle even as her best friend hit the gas.

"Do you or don't you want to have a baby?" Bitsy Winthrop Sommers demanded.

"Yes, of course I do. Desperately. I feel my eggs aging as we speak. In fact, they may be scrambled already. But marrying a total stranger seems a bit excessive. Sort of like last year when you talked me into—"

"Let's not even go there. I didn't know about Rusty's side job as a circus freak. Anyway, *that* was last year." Bitsy jammed her brakes at a traffic light. "*This* is perfect. Daddy insists his heir have a wife if he wants to make partner. And Andrew's wanted that partnership since he started kindergarten and got himself elected class president. What he doesn't want is a wife. You want a baby more than anything, but you know the school board isn't going to go for a teacher being a single pregnant woman. And after that jerk ex-husband of yours skipped out on you, you don't want another husband. So, the two of you set up temporary house, you both get what you want and everyone's happy." Bitsy preened with self-satisfaction. The light turned and she shot the car forward. "I'm brilliant."

Kat recognized herself as a woman of excess. She either ate the entire pan of brownies or she didn't touch them. God knows she tried, but moderation was not her strong suit. Marrying Bitsy's older brother, Andrew, in order to have a baby smacked of potential excess—but she was running pretty darn low on choices.

"Isn't 'Mr. One of Florida's Most Eligible Bachelors' dating someone? Plus, from what I've heard of him over the years, we're not exactly each other's type."

"He is something of a stuffed shirt." Bitsy agreed. "Very conservative. Actually, even though I love him to no end, he's sort of a stick-in-the-mud. But he's rich, successful, doesn't belch in public, so, of course, he's dating someone. Claudia van Dierling. She's horrid, and she wants to marry him. You can see the dollar signs dancing in her eyes every time she looks at him."

"Well, I'm not interested in his money. With my teaching salary and the trust fund my grandparents set up, I live very comfortably. I can certainly support my own child."

"Exactly, my dear independent friend. I'm glad you agree with me."

"Whoa. I didn't agree with you—"

"And the fact that you're opposites—well, therein lies the beauty. You're in no danger of going overboard, are you, 'cause he's not your type—although I swear I don't know how you have a type considering you haven't had a serious relationship since Nick."

"Relationships are tricky for someone with all-or-nothing tendencies. I gave Nick my all. When he left, it almost did me in."

"Yeah, Nick wins the creep-of-the-decade award. But that's just it. With Andrew, you don't need a relationship. A simple agreement will do nicely."

"One of those prenuptial things. He'd have to agree to give up the baby."

Bitsy looked momentarily nonplussed. "I don't know. He's never wanted a wife, so I guess that means he never wanted a kid. Although, he's really great with Juliana. I bet he'd make a great dad.''

It didn't matter how great he was with Bitsy's daughter, joint parenting was a no go. "Uh-uh. I won't have my child caught up in some kind of joint custody. I was nine when my parents divorced. From then on Jackson and I were shuffled back and forth between our parents, and our stepparents clearly wishing we'd just go away.''

"Get Jackson, that legal-eagle brother of yours, to draw up the agreement. Make that one of your terms.''

"It'd be *the* term." Kat checked her appearance in the visor mirror. She'd been fighting the hair battle against her curls for years, but West Palm Beach humidity always won. It claimed victory again today. "Actually, just thinking about the social obligations that would come with being his wife make me queasy.''

"Huh?''

Bitsy pulled into one of the reserved spots flanking the Winthrop, Fullford, and Winthrop, Attorneys-at-Law building, and they stepped out of the car.

"You know what I mean, Bits. We both grew up in families chock-full of lawyers—our fathers and brothers—and I just hate the awful cocktail parties and all the schmoozing you have to do to get ahead. In fact, I can't believe I let you talk me into coming. I've managed to avoid these horrible events for six blessed years. Getting out of them was one of the high points of Nick leaving.''

"It's a great opportunity to check out Andrew without any pressure. Yes, the social stuff is a pain in the butt. Is it enough that you're willing to give up the idea of having a baby? Because, face it honey, you've exhausted every other possibility.''

Kat paused before the double doors of the building and recalled the options she'd considered since deciding to have a baby by herself—almost two years ago. Sperm bank—too many loose ends and she was afraid she'd lose her job. Adoption—waiting lists and one close, emotionally wrenching call. A chance encounter—too risky medically and that pesky school board. Finding Mr. Right—not likely. Did she really want to hit thirty-five in a few years and find herself still in the same boat?

A temporary marriage with a great genetic contribution and no strings attached... Bitsy was right. Two years and counting and no closer to her own little crumb snatcher. Desperation lent her resolve. She could do this. They'd reach a nice civil agreement. A neat and tidy prenuptial—he'd give up rights to the baby and she wouldn't touch his money. She squared her shoulders and opened the door. "I guess this doesn't have to become one of my excessive disasters. I just bought a dozen behavior-modification tapes geared toward people with my all-or-nothing tendencies."

"A dozen?" Bitsy sighed and hustled her into a waiting elevator.

"I obviously need them. I don't consider a dozen excess. It's insurance."

Bitsy read her wavering stance. "Listen, you've only heard about Andrew through me. Go ahead and check him out today. You can present a plan to him later. This is the last week of school and you've got a nice break before summer school. The timing is right, girl! Everything's falling into place. Go with the flow."

The elevator dinged open and they entered the hall.

"Well..."

"This will work out great. Trust me..." Bitsy opened a door to reveal a well-dressed milling crowd.

Kat's glance flitted about the room. "Where's Juliana?"

"Eddie took her for an ice-cream sundae. A little father-daughter time together. They should be here soon."

Kat edged back toward the door. "I'll just wait out here for them."

Bitsy hauled her back. "Nonsense. That's not why

you're here. There's the reason you're here—my brother. Your next husband. The father of your child.''

Kat followed the direction of Bitsy's finger. One look shattered her resolve. ''You want me to marry him? The one right there? I don't think so.'' She shook her head for added emphasis.

''Aw, come on, Kat. He can't help the way he looks. Anyway, looks aren't everything. He's really smart. He's got a great brain.'' Bitsy wheedled.

''I don't suppose it's his fault he's drop-dead gorgeous....'' Lust had her tingling in places that barely remembered how to tingle.

''Hey, you don't want to have an ugly baby, do you?''

''I just want to have a healthy baby.'' Kat forced herself to think logically. Good genes were good genes. Would anyone in their right mind not want to seriously work on baby-making with the black-haired hunk? Steady. She needed to ground herself. ''He does look stuffy and uptight. But I suppose that hair and those chiseled features softened by baby fat would be striking.''

''You bet your sweet patoot it would.''

Kat's attention shifted to the blond woman on his arm. ''Claudine, I presume.''

Bitsy sniffed with a nasty look on her face. ''Close enough. Claudia. The witch.''

Kat eyed the woman—tall, thin, polished, sophisticated. More than enough reasons to dislike her on general principle. But certainly not enough to think about yanking a marriage prospect out from under her. Confused, Kat wished for a sign. Could she really pursue Bitsy's crazy scheme or should she return to waiting for chance to drop Mr. Right into her life.

She watched as a young man sporting a red power tie approached Andrew. With an apologetic look at Claudia, Andrew followed the young man out another door.

Kat grabbed Bitsy's arm. "Come on. I want to meet her."

Bitsy eyed her as they skirted the various groups. "Good idea."

They were just about to make their way around a towering areca palm to the blonde beauty when they saw Juliana run up to Claudia. Juliana's reedy, childish contralto easily carried past the palm that hid them. "Hey, Ms. Vander. My dad and I just got here. Where's my Uncle Andrew?"

"It's van Dierling. Shoo, you pesky brat. He's busy." Through the palm leaves, they could see a smile pasted on Claudia's face that was deceptively pleasant. Her tone was saccharine sweet.

"You're mean and I'm gonna tell."

"If you were a smart little girl, you'd watch your mouth and your manners. I'm going to be your new aunt very soon."

Bitsy made a strangling noise. "I told you she was a witch. Excuse me while I go defend my child."

Juliana held a special place in Kat's heart. The poor darling could kiss any relationship with her uncle goodbye if he married Claudia. And he'd probably never even entertain a clue as to what was going on. Men could be so stupid.

She'd wanted a sign. By golly she had one.

She'd save Juliana and the Winthrop family from the evil Claudine.

She'd marry Andrew Winthrop.

And finally, at long last, she'd have her baby.

1

ANDREW MARTIN WINTHROP III in the buff was a sight to behold. Bitsy had not told all. Of course, she probably hadn't seen his spectacular, splendid bare butt in the past thirty years or so.

Kat lowered the binoculars unsteadily and popped a handful of M&M's into her mouth. Get Andrew Winthrop III out of that starched shirt and those immaculately creased trousers, and there was more to him than she'd supposed.

She washed down the M&M's with the worst coffee imaginable. She sighed. What she wouldn't give for a good cup of joe right now.

Kat squinted through the binoculars again, not that she was trying to be voyeuristic and catch another glimpse of Andrew III's well-formed buns. This was research. She could have hired a P.I. to investigate him, but since he topped her marriage list—okay, he *was* her marriage list—she'd decided to check him out herself. If he happened to move around sans clothes, she'd consider it a bonus. She scanned the bedroom, but Andrew had disappeared.

She settled in behind the oleander at the edge of his property and reached for the one-pound bag of chocolate candies beside her on the ground, scanning the house once more. Still no sign of Mr. "Stiff as His Shirt Collar" Winthrop III. His elegant yet sedate Mercedes sat in front of the cottage. He'd probably be starched and buttoned-down before he ventured out for the Sunday paper.

Bitsy had suggested she introduce herself while he was at his beach house for the weekend. She theorized he'd be more relaxed here than at his in-town home or office. If she only knew!

Kat trained her binoculars on the kitchen. She'd wait until just the right time to introduce herself. Maybe he'd gone in to fix a sandwich. Would he wander around his kitchen in his altogether? Hmm, interesting to find out...

Suddenly, a masculine arm wrapped around Kat's midsection and hauled her to her feet, making her spill bad coffee and her M&M's, and momentarily scaring the wits out of her. She registered a general feeling of male hardness and warmth before she instinctively flipped her assailant and planted her knee in his throat.

Gray eyes regarded her steadily with more than a hint of annoyance. She'd seen him across the room at the cocktail party and tailed him from a distance, but none of that prepared her for the impact of his gaze up close and personal. It was almost as powerful as his rear view.

"If you would kindly remove your knee from my windpipe, perhaps we could discuss why you're training those binoculars on my house." His voice was as cool and steady as his eyes.

Kat complied and stepped back as Andrew picked himself up, brushing sand off his magnificent backside. She gathered she wasn't making a good first impression.

She glared at him. "Don't grab me again."

He towered over her, glaring in return. "You were sneaking around my beach house in the bushes. I believe I have a right to confront you."

Even barefoot and in sweats—which she was amazed he owned since they couldn't be starched—Andrew Winthrop exuded icy arrogance.

Kat drew herself up to her full height, all five feet four and a half inches, and tilted her chin. "I certainly was not sneaking. And you spilled my coffee and my candy.''

His thin, hard lips compressed even further. "Oh, pardon me. What do you call lurking behind shrubbery?" He stepped closer, watching her carefully as if he thought she might try to flip him again.

She retreated, the soft, white sand sifting into her canvas sneakers. God, she loathed sand in her shoes! "I wasn't lurking."

"Well, pray tell, what were you doing then?"

Checking you out because my biological clock has hit warp speed and I want you to father my baby. Seemed a little early for that. She raised her head, stared into his gray eyes and lied brazenly.

"Bird-watching."

He raised a sardonic dark brow, his short laugh reflecting skepticism rather than amusement. "Bird-watching?"

Probably not the best lie she'd ever come up with, but she actually didn't lie often. She'd have to practice when she got back home.

Andrew gently but firmly took her arm. A shiver of awareness raced along Kat's nerve endings. Andrew Winthrop's touch wasn't nearly as cool as his eyes and his voice.

"I'm very interested in hearing more about your bird-watching." He steered her back toward the cottage. "Especially since you watched for birds at my office yesterday, as well."

Uh-oh. He'd spotted her yesterday. Had he seen her follow him today? She narrowed her eyes. "If you knew I was out here, why'd you parade around without your clothes?"

Amusement thawed the Arctic depths of his gray eyes. "Parade around?" He shook his head in mock consternation. "Showers are usually more efficient without clothes."

"Oh."

Andrew ushered her up the weathered deck. "I'm afraid 'Oh' isn't going to do, Ms..." he said as he threw open the back door to reveal a minuscule kitchen. "Why don't we start with your name?" His smile didn't reach his eyes, but it did reveal perfect teeth. She'd figured as much. "I trust, given your extensive, um, bird-watching, you know who I am."

He stood behind her, waiting for her to enter the cottage.

She crossed the threshold.

He stationed himself next to the open door and awaited her answer. So far lying hadn't worked very well for her. She might as well give him her name.

"Devereaux. Kat Devereaux." She watched him mentally process the name, searching for an association or a link. Coming up with nothing, Andrew folded his arms across his chest and leaned against the counter.

"Okay, Ms. Devereaux, what kind of bird were you looking for exactly?"

"Well, I wasn't exactly looking. I was watching."

He lifted a skeptical black brow. "What were you watching for?"

She shrugged. "Anything, everything, nothing."

"And how did you come to be watching the fascinating habits of *this* particular bird?"

With each passing second he impressed her as the perfect candidate to marry. Arrogant. Stuffy. Irritating. There was absolutely no possibility she'd become emotionally involved. Perfect.

"Fascinating? That's definitely a stretch."

"Let's stick to the subject at hand. How'd you find out about this bird?"

Kat found herself at a loss as to how to broach the subject. Should she start with the part about his sister and her being friends? Should she start with her overwhelming need to be a mother?

Kat sidled toward the doorway, and stood close enough to Andrew to catch the clean tang of sandalwood soap. It was one thing to watch the man from a distance, but being this close to him sent her mind skittering in directions it didn't need to go.

"I need to secure Carlotta and fetch Toto, and then we can talk."

Andrew wrapped his hand around her upper arm, his touch halting her in her tracks. "Hold it. Exactly who are Carlotta and Toto?" He dropped his hand to his side and Kat absently rubbed at the tingling spot. Emotionally he might not appeal to her, but he scored high in the physical reaction department. Either that or she'd hit premature menopause and was hot flashing.

"Carlotta's my car."

"You mean that wreck you followed me in? I believe it's safe unless someone mistakes it for scrap metal."

Kat drew herself up and stared down the length of her nose. Unfortunately, she had to tilt her head way back, because Andrew was considerably taller than five feet four and a half inches, which ruined her attempt at haughtiness.

Carlotta, as she'd christened her '79 Toyota, had been a good friend to her—steadfast and loyal. Kat had a deep and abiding affection for her. "I'll thank you not to refer to Carlotta as a wreck. She runs beautifully."

Except for the clicking noise her motor made, her backfiring muffler and the fact that her air-conditioning hadn't worked for the past five years. But, really, those were trivialities. Just thinking about them made Kat squirm at her own disloyalty.

Andrew ignored her disclaimer with a wave of his hand. "I'm scared to ask, but what or who is Toto?"

As inopportune as it was, she appreciated the elegant line of his hand, the sprinkling of dark hair on the back.

Kat turned at the first step of the deck stairs. "Toto's my dog."

A frown marred the perfection of his face. "A dog? You're bringing a dog in here?"

The prospect of a dog in his house seemed to upset him more than being flipped onto his back by an unknown woman. She skipped down the last three steps. "Toto's more than just a dog. Just wait, you'll love him."

Behind her, Andrew muttered something indistinguishable, although she was fairly certain it wasn't complimentary. Just wait until he met Toto. Everyone loved Toto.

ANDREW WATCHED the petite bundle of energy bounce along the road. He ran his hand over his jawline, contemplating the mystery of Kat Devereaux—who she was and why she was shadowing him. Shadowing wasn't exactly correct. Following him, none too discreetly, was a more apt assessment.

He'd first spotted her yesterday, lurking behind an abstract sculpture in the lobby of his office building, wearing the prerequisite dark shades and tan trench coat. Fortunately for him, she hadn't worn a wig. Her riotous ginger curls had heralded her presence all the while she'd trailed him. She'd darted behind him like some exotic bird for two days now and he'd had enough. Despite himself, she intrigued him.

She was probably just another determined female who'd read the article naming him one of Florida's top five eligible bachelors. Andrew rued the day he'd given in to impulse and agreed to be interviewed. He had a neat, orderly life—he loved his work, played handball three times a week and casually dated. *Impulse* was not in his vocabulary. Perhaps he'd entertained a faint inkling of discord and discontent at the very orderliness of his life. And for once he'd given in to impulse and allowed himself to be identified as a prime male candidate. That had taught him a lesson. He had enough on his plate trying to maneuver himself into a partnership. He didn't need Kat Devereaux hanging out behind the sculptures. And he'd get rid of her—just as soon as he satisfied his curiosity.

He flexed his right shoulder and winced at the stiffness. He'd be sure he got his answers from a distance.

Her car backfired from the driveway as she killed the engine. He flinched when she slammed the door. He hoped she hadn't parked too close to his Mercedes. He wasn't anxious to pick up any dents—and they could be catching from the looks of that thing she drove.

Andrew forgot all about dents as Kat Devereaux waltzed up the deck stairs, for all the world as if she were a dinner guest, a mass of fur running circles around her, yapping incessantly. She stopped when she reached the kitchen doorway. "We're back."

Andrew eyed the small, shaggy dog of indeterminate pedigree. "Toto, I presume."

Hearing his name, the little dog perked his ears and paused before charging over to sniff and yap around Andrew's legs.

"Be careful. Sometimes he...."

The lower leg of Andrew's sweatpant suddenly grew warm and wet. He didn't need to glance down, and he didn't need to hear Kat finish her sentence to know what had just happened. He closed his eyes, rubbing his temples wearily. This was going from bad to worse.

"No, Toto, no! Bad dog! Oh, I'm so sorry."

Toto licked at Andrew's bare toes while Kat grabbed a dish towel and dived for his wet pant leg. He threw up his hands to ward her off before she could come any closer.

"It's a little late for that. If you'll just call off Toto, I'll change into something a bit drier."

"I'm so sorry. Really I am." Dancing blue eyes belied her contrite tone. Or maybe she was sincere in her apology, but she also thought it was damned funny. She scooped up the wriggling canine and sought to reassure Andrew. "He usually only does it once and that's only if he likes you."

"What does he do if he doesn't like you?" Andrew quizzed on his way out the door. "No, never mind. I really don't want to know. Just let me change pants and then, if Toto can contain his enthusiasm, you and I are going to talk, Ms. Devereaux."

In the space of one brief hour she'd flung him on his back in the sand, and her dog had lifted its leg on him in his own home. It wasn't a matter of living to regret having met Kat Devereaux and her little dog, Toto. He already did.

THIS WAS NOT going well at all.

Kat supposed she should scold Toto, but it really wasn't his fault. Excitement and incontinence went hand in hand for poor Toto. Instead, she absently scratched him behind his ears while he burrowed into her shoulder. She'd hand it to Andrew—he'd handled the mishap with surprising grace.

She glanced toward the bedroom door where he'd disappeared to change clothes and heaved a sigh of relief. So far Andrew Winthrop was turning out to be exactly what he seemed, exactly what she needed: a stuffy, albeit attractive, lawyer with a degree from Harvard, a ton of money in the bank and a pressing need for a wife. She could offer him a temporary version of wedded bliss and he could give her the baby she so wanted.

Andrew padded back into the room, having replaced his sweatpants with a pair of worn but creased blue jeans. He still wore the faded Harvard T-shirt.

Kat bent and put Toto on the floor. Andrew eyed the little dog warily. "Once, right? He only does that once?"

Toto ran over to snuffle Andrew's feet. "Usually..."

Kat couldn't resist teasing a bit. "Although he might make an exception in your case."

Sardonic humor glinted in the depths of his eyes. "Only if I'm lucky."

With one last sniff, Toto trotted off to discover parts unknown in the beach house.

Kat offered Andrew a friendly smile, which wasn't a hardship, because she was overall a friendly type. It also seemed like a good lead-in to her proposal.

"Nice place you've got here. Cozy." Actually she'd been here once last summer with Bitsy and her daughter. Bitsy's husband, Eddie, also a lawyer, and Andrew had been out of town at a conference.

"I'm so relieved you like it. Now, why don't we discuss your bird-watching?"

His voice might be pleasant and relaxed, but determination was written on his face with a bold marker. It was there in the hard line of his lips, the thrust of his chin.

Kat felt like a bug pinned to a board by Andrew's piercing eyes. His suggestion hung between them, demanding an explanation. Kat's stomach chose that moment to protest loud and clear. She glanced at him reprimandingly. "I'm hungry. You spilled my lunch earlier."

Andrew stared at her as if he thought she was indeed a bug. "You call M&M's lunch?"

"They had peanuts in them. That's a protein source." Really, all that money for a Harvard degree. You'd think he'd know his food groups.

"Shy little thing, aren't you?"

"You know some people wouldn't believe it, but I really am shy." And nervous as hell. Her entire future hinged on this. Her baby hung in the balance. Her last-ditch effort at motherhood stood sexily before her.

His brows shot up to his elegant hairline. "Count me

in as a nonbeliever in the shy business." He drummed his fingers on the countertop.

Kat stared at his hands. His fingers were long and blunt, his hands broad. She swallowed hard. Now was a bad time to develop a hand fetish. Actually, a fetish in any way, shape or form that concerned this man was not allowed.

She braced her hands on the countertop and hoisted herself up, which put her at eye level with Andrew.

"Could I have a glass of milk?" she requested from her perch.

"You're a strange woman." Andrew pulled out a gallon of milk.

Ha! I'm a strange woman? Kat had seen his sleek, plastic girlfriend and, excepting Bitsy, had a fair idea of the type of women who inhabited his world. After all, she'd lived in a similar world for her first twenty-four years. "Considering the women you probably know, I'll take *strange* as a compliment."

Andrew closed the refrigerator and studied Kat Devereaux. He wasn't trying to insult her, it was simply what had come to mind. He'd never met a woman like her. He was used to sophisticated women who employed every available means to enhance their beauty, be it spa or salon or a discreet visit to a prominent Palm Beach plastic surgeon. Women who cooed and simpered and sought to impress.

God and Madame Mimi's Spa knew that was modus operandi for his mother.

Kat Devereaux sat on his kitchen counter with her face devoid of makeup and her hair standing on end, and she certainly didn't seem to care if she impressed him. Oddly enough, she did. She was pushy, opinionated, physically assertive and sexy as hell. Maybe it was a compliment, all things considered. Strange, intriguing, different, whatever she was, she had managed to divert his attention from the matter at hand. Regardless of how cute her nose was with its sprinkling of freckles or how shapely her legs were swinging from his countertop, he wanted some answers!

He topped off a glass with milk and presented it to her. "Here's your milk. Now tell me why you've been playing Mata Hari with me."

Whatever, or whoever, Kat Devereaux was, she wasn't much of a liar. At least not a good one. Bird-watching! She'd be terrible at poker. Far too transparent. Even right now, he could almost see the wheels turning.

She stalled by drinking her milk. All of it. Without stopping.

Andrew folded his arms and waited expectantly—he had plenty of time. Kat placed the glass on the counter and smiled at him winningly, her blue eyes widening. A milk mustache ruined the effect. Andrew bit back a smile.

"So, you're definitely not buying bird-watching, huh?"

Her sheer temerity arrested him. He gave in to the smile. "No. I don't buy bird-watching."

Kat abandoned her perch to pace the kitchen floor. "Okay—"

The front door slammed, interrupting her explanation.

"Yoo-hoo…Andrew, where are you?" Andrew recognized his sister's singsong tone. He'd never get to the bottom of this. His frustration vented itself in sarcasm. "Come on in. Make yourself at home. We're out here in the kitchen."

Bitsy waltzed through the swinging door, barely spared him a glance and beelined over to Kat. "I spotted Carlotta out front. Have you talked to him yet?"

He glanced from one woman to the other. This was getting stranger by the minute. "Bitsy? Kat? You know each other?"

Bitsy remained next to Kat but turned to face Andrew

and giggled. "Kat works at the school where I volunteer. She's a dear friend."

Red alert! That was not comforting news. His sister meant well, but trouble seemed to follow her like the wake behind a boat. He still marveled that they shared the same gene pool. Why was he not too shocked to find her involved in this wackiness? "Why don't you two explain what the hell is going on?"

"Well, big brother—"

Kat threw up her hand to stop Bitsy. "Wait, Bitsy. We were just about to have this discussion when you arrived. Let me explain."

Andrew was fast running out of patience. If one of them didn't tell him something soon, he'd throttle both of them.

Bitsy glided over to a kitchen chair and plopped down. "Just pretend I'm not even here."

"You *could* leave," he suggested.

"Oh, no. I'll be fine. I promise, you won't even know I'm here."

Kat offered him a sunny but nervous smile. "I'm not quite sure where to begin."

"How about the beginning?"

"Well, there isn't really a beginning. I guess if you wanted a beginning it would be a couple of years ago when I turned thirty—"

Andrew cut her off. He didn't want her life story. "Forget the beginning. Just try spitting it out somewhere around the middle."

Kat narrowed her eyes at him. She obviously didn't appreciate being rushed.

"Bottom line? I need a husband. You need a wife. Let's get married." She crossed her arms across her breasts. "There, was that brief enough for you?"

Andrew prided himself on his ability to maintain a poker face and this was no exception. However, he mentally gaped. Unless he was mistaken, a veritable stranger had just proposed marriage. What a preposterous idea!

Bitsy snickered from the corner of the room.

Andrew ignored her. Being a calm, rational man, he wanted to hear the arguments they'd come up with to convince him. As he stared into the azure blue of Kat Devereaux's eyes, he understood now why sometimes people couldn't look away from a train wreck. "Perhaps we should go back to a few weeks before your birthday and take it from there."

"As I was saying, a few weeks before the big three-o I started evaluating my life, which I think is a fairly common thing, and realized it was close to perfect. I love my job—I teach art to elementary school children. I'm disgustingly healthy, I treat myself to good vacations, and I have a comfortable place to live. There was only one thing missing."

She paused and Andrew smirked to himself. *A man. She wanted a man.*

"A baby. I've always wanted children, or at least a child. It's the one thing missing in my life." She paused and stared at him expectantly. "Any questions so far?"

Andrew ceased smirking. *A baby?* She wanted a baby. He didn't think so. "Several. But why don't you continue and we'll see how many you leave open."

"That just sort of sets the stage. About two weeks ago Bitsy told me your father refused to make you a partner unless you got married."

Andrew glared at Bitsy, who remained unrepentant. "I was in the library when you and Father had your little discussion in the study."

Andrew didn't take her to task for eavesdropping since it would have been a total waste of time. However, he refused to let her matchmaking go unchecked. And was his whole damn family obsessed with his matrimonial state or lack thereof? "That's it, Bitsy. This time you've gone too far. I don't need you discussing my private affairs with strangers.''

"Kat's no stranger to me. And you know her family. Rand Hamilton's her father and Jackson Hamilton's her brother.''

"Nor do I need you soliciting a wife on my behalf.'' Irritation tinged his tone.

Kat watched the interplay between him and his sister with avid interest, seemingly unperturbed at being the object of discussion. He'd never have pegged her as Rand Hamilton's daughter. Rand was as much of a cagey manipulator as his own father. Her friendship with Bitsy made sense.

"Well, for goodness' sake, if I didn't do something you'd end up marrying that horrid Claudia. There are plenty of horrid people in our family already without you adding to the numbers.''

He had, in fact, spent some time assessing Claudia as a marriage partner. "What, dear sister, is wrong with Claudia?''

"She called Juliana a brat!''

Andrew considered the antics of his precocious six-year-old niece. "Juliana *is* a brat.'' An indulgent smile softened the blow. He'd never been able to stay angry with his sister.

"I know she is. You know she is...but, it was the way Claudia said it!''

Kat piped up. "You wouldn't happen to have any ice cream, would you?''

Andrew eyed her flat stomach. "You're not...you know...that way already, are you?''

Kat rolled her eyes upward. "No. If I were, I wouldn't consider marrying you. I'm just hungry.''

Andrew marveled at her matter-of-fact tone regarding the issue. Not that it mattered, because he wasn't buying into their plan. He waved a generous hand, "By all means, help yourself.''

The electronic chirping of a beeper cut off Andrew's sentence. Bitsy read the digital display and grimaced. "Well, kids, I hate to cut out on the fun but this is Juliana's baby-sitter and she's given me the 811 code."

"Don't you mean 9-1-1?" Andrew corrected.

"Nope, 8-1-1 is our code for brat attack. Last week she tried to tie the postman to a stake. Said she was playing Salem witch trials." Bitsy stopped en route to the door to envelop Kat in a hug. "Welcome to the family, darling." She bussed Andrew on the cheek. "Congratulations, big brother. You're making a wise decision."

Without further ado, she sallied out the back door.

Andrew ignored her parting comment. Reasoning with Bitsy was in the same league as turning the tide. But it didn't mean he'd go along with this flaky scheme she'd concocted, even though he did need a wife because he damn well meant to get that partnership, whatever the cost. And his father had already named the price.

Kat threw open the freezer and rummaged about until she surfaced bearing a pint of premium ice cream like a trophy. She grinned at him as she pulled off the top. "Spoon?"

He indicated the silverware drawer.

"I can't believe you buy this stuff. I hadn't figured you for a Chunky Monkey man."

Just what the hell did she mean by that? "Bitsy likes it so I always keep the stuff on hand."

She flashed that saucy grin again. "A woman with excellent taste, your sister."

Andrew watched in horrified fascination as she spooned a bite directly from the carton. She paused, her spoon in midair. "What? Why're you looking at me that way?"

At least she hadn't used her finger. "I don't believe I've ever seen anyone bypass the bowl and go straight for the carton." And she and his sister thought he'd actually consider living with her?

"For goodness' sake, relax. It's only a pint. It'll be gone in no time. Now a half gallon would've been another story. Unless you wanted some." She offered the open carton. "Do you want some?"

She stood before him, a cross between a pixie and Medusa on a bad hair day and, out of nowhere, his libido kicked into overdrive. He reminded himself they were talking about ice cream. He reminded himself she'd concocted a nutty scheme to marry him and bear his child.

"No, thanks." To all of it. The ice cream. Her. Her plan.

"You're sure?" She still held the carton toward him. "Positive."

Kat shrugged and spooned up another mouthful. "So, do you just not like ice cream, or is it Chunky Monkey you object to?"

"I didn't say I objected to it, I simply said I didn't want any."

She nibbled at a walnut. "Let me guess, your favorite flavor is…vanilla. With the little bean specks in it, of course."

Had she trailed him to the grocery store? Slipped in behind him at an ice-cream kiosk? And what if he did like vanilla? She made it sound criminal.

"Vanilla's a good basic." This was ridiculous! Getting defensive over ice cream. "But enough about ice cream. Why me? Don't you know any eligible men?"

She ran her tongue catlike over the spoon and Andrew felt a totally unwelcome and unexpected stab of want.

Kat looked at him as if she were dealing with a child who couldn't grasp a simple concept. "Of course I do. I have quite a few male friends."

"So, what's wrong with them?"

"Nothing's wrong with them. That's the problem. I like them. Why would I want to ruin a perfectly good friendship by marrying someone I like? And they'd want to stick around or at least be involved with the baby afterward. On the other hand, you and I would make a perfect match.''

"You've lost me on that one.''

Once again she waved the carton in front of him.

"Chunky Monkey. Vanilla. Carlotta. Gertrude.'' She said, and went back to eating, as if no further clarification were necessary.

Lost. He was definitely lost. "Gertrude? Who in the hell is Gertrude?''

She brandished her spoon toward the front of the house. "Your car. I named her Gertrude. She looks like a Gertrude.''

She'd named his car now! "Gertrude?''

"Sorry, it just seemed to fit. But you could call her Trudy.''

"I won't be calling it anything. But please explain.''

She spoke slowly as if he might have trouble following her. "You're vanilla. I'm Chunky Monkey. You're Gertrude. I'm Carlotta. You're not my type. I'm not your type. We have nothing to worry about if we get married.''

He had to agree with her on that one. They had nothing to worry about because they wouldn't be getting married.

"Pardon me for being so crass as to bring up such a minor point, but exactly why would I want to marry you?''

"Ah, that's my point exactly. You don't want a wife, do you?''

"No.'' He'd give her points for that one.

"Exactly. And I don't want a husband. Or, I should say, I only want one for a while.''

He was beginning to follow her thought process, which alarmed him in and of itself. His father had been adamant concerning a wife. Good old dad considered it part and parcel of his partnership. "Go ahead," he said, now intrigued.

"Let's take that skinny blonde you've been tooling around town with, Claudine…"

"Claudia."

"There're two?"

"No, one. Her name is Claudia."

"Oh, okay. Anyway, let's marry you off to her, hypothetically. How likely is Claudette—"

"Claudia."

"Okay, okay. Claudia. Will she sign a prenuptial agreement? And what happens two years or five years from now when the marriage hits the rocks?" Kat made a slicing motion in midair. "Half of everything that's yours walks out the door with her."

He'd have to give her credit for her read on Claudia. No way she'd sign a prenup. Especially not with the proverbial ball in Claudia's court—it had never been a secret how important a partnership was to Andrew. Andrew harbored no illusions about marriage and divorce. It formed the basis for his cynical view. Perversely, he found himself a little piqued Kat had so readily written him off as a failure at marriage. "Who says we'd wind up divorced?"

Kat arched a skeptical brow in his direction. "To begin with, the national average isn't running in your favor and don't forget to factor in you're not exactly frothing at the bit to enter the esteemed state of matrimony."

Andrew crossed his arms over his chest. "Sorry, Ms. Devereaux, but you've got to build a stronger case than that."

"Well, aside from the fact that I have no personal interest in you…"

Andrew's brows shot up to his hairline.

"I suppose bearing your child might be considered personal, but you know what I mean. Anyway, I've got one other thing in my favor that Claudia doesn't."

His look both challenged and invited her to continue. "Claudia is beautiful, sophisticated. She attends all the right functions. She has beautiful nails." At his incredulous look, she defended herself. "I noticed…women notice these things. And then you have me. I'm not beautiful or glamorous and there's not a sophisticated bone in my body. I loathe cocktail parties and I'd rather shovel manure for my garden than have a manicure any day."

Andrew assessed her from her riot of red hair to the tips of her canvas sneakers. She'd accurately assessed herself. She wasn't beautiful. She wasn't glamorous. She wasn't sophisticated. The chivalrous thing to do would be to deny it, but he wasn't chivalrous. Instead he inclined his head in understanding.

"You and I both know Claudine is exactly the kind of woman your father wants you to marry. On the other hand, I met your father briefly once before. We both know he'll dislike me intensely." She leaned in closer and dropped her voice. "Wouldn't that be sort of poetic justice, since he's the one making you get married?"

He couldn't suppress a smile at the Machiavellian beauty of her thought. Kat Devereaux was right. The old man would turn inside out if he married her. With her unorthodox, brash manner she was a far cry from what he knew his father had in mind in the way of a daughter-in-law.

Also, she'd hit the nail on the head. He didn't want a wife. But he sure as hell wanted this partnership. That was an understatement. It had been his driving goal since boyhood. Or as his sister Bitsy summed it up—that partnership slot was his spot in the cosmic universe. And he was ready to take his place except for that small matter of a wife. This business with Kat Devereaux might prove a bit messy but perhaps not nearly as sloppy as a nasty divorce settlement.

Frighteningly, she was beginning to make sense.

2

KAT DRUMMED HER FINGERS on the countertop as she awaited a reaction other than Andrew's smile, which hadn't been a smile at all. Although he kept his expression shuttered, she hadn't lived with a lawyer through her formative years without picking up subtle nuances. He was beginning to buy into her plan.

"What about a sperm bank?" he fired at her.

"No way." She had seriously looked into that alternative and long ago dismissed it. She'd exhausted every remote possibility and alternative. Otherwise, she wouldn't be proposing to Andrew.

"Why not?"

"The school board wouldn't be happy with an artificially inseminated unwed mother, whether that's fair or not. Also, I don't trust the screening process. There are too many loose ends medically if some inherited genes proved a problem later on. And from a genetics standpoint you're great material."

A glimmer of humor warmed the chill in his eyes. "I know your father professionally, and I've met your mother once or twice. Except for the fact that you have your father's eyes, I'd say genetics aren't apparent."

Little did he know she also had her father's drive and determination to make things happen once she'd set a goal. And right now her goal was Andrew Martin Winthrop III. Or his genetic contribution, to be exact. "Recessive genes. I'm just like my maternal grandmother. And that would've been my stepmother you met."

"Did she stalk your grandfather?"

"My stepmother?"

"Your grandmother. Did she stalk her potential husband?"

Kat glared at him indignantly. "I haven't stalked you, I was investigating. You can't expect me to marry a virtual stranger."

His black brows etched up a notch as he slipped his hands into his pockets and crossed his ankles. "Exactly my point. Who in their right mind would expect someone to marry a 'virtual stranger'?"

She caught his subtle dig. "That's what this is all about. Getting to know each other. Go ahead, ask me anything you want to know."

"Devereaux, not Hamilton. Divorced or widowed?"

"Sort of divorced. I guess actually divorced."

"You don't seem too sure on that point. I hate to break it to you, but you can't marry me if you're already married to someone else. Our legal system considers it bigamy, and they tend to frown on it."

"Our legal system also takes a dim view of embezzlement, which is why I came home to an empty house one day." He was a Harvard brain, let him figure it out. Six years and counting and the humiliation still stuck with her like stink.

Andrew didn't disappoint her. She watched realization dawn on him. Nick had made national news in absentia.

"You were married to the guy who disappeared several years ago with about twenty-five million of his investment clients' money?"

"One and the same. It was six years ago and twenty-five-and-a-half million. No, I haven't heard from him. No, I don't know where he is. The courts granted me a divorce on grounds of desertion. Next topic. What else do you want to know about me?"

"Adoption?"

"On the waiting list for three years. I came close."

Kat studied the linoleum pattern on the kitchen floor. She could barely stand to think about Daphne, the bright-eyed two-year-old who'd come so close to being her daughter until the teenage birth mother changed her mind yet again and decided to keep the child. Kat couldn't bear the emotional wrenching again. Resolute, she shifted her attention back to Andrew. "I can't go through it again."

A brief nod acknowledged that closed door. "Which are you more interested in, my genetics or my bank account?"

Kat got the impression Andrew was deliberately trying to goad her. In fact, she considered his question more than fair. He and his family were worth a small fortune. Plus there'd been that magazine article a couple of months ago naming him one of Florida's most eligible bachelors. She wanted his genetic contribution, not a financial portfolio.

"Of course, there'll be a prenuptial agreement. I'll waive all rights to any of your money, as well as any future claims our child might make. In return, you'll agree to forgo all parental rights. I want a sperm donor, not a dad." That was important to her. As she'd explained to Bitsy, she refused to have her child bounced back and forth between parental households, subjected to stepparents who barely tolerated his or her presence. Kat had been down that road herself and wouldn't send her child there. For a time, her son or daugher might wonder about the father's apparent disinterest, but Kat planned to make his dedication to his career the culprit. It would also serve as a reason for their divorce. It might hurt for a time, but it would be less painful for the child than years of being the ball in a custodial tennis match.

"You've got this all worked out, don't you?"

Kat knew she didn't imagine the hint of admiration. "Pretty much. We'd have to iron out a couple of details, but we'd both enter this agreement with everything laid out on the table.''

''You won't object to me checking you out?''

''Oh, of course not. I checked you out.'' His bare buns came to mind and ignited a slow heat. ''Although there is one thing I'll have to insist on.''

''Yes?''

''A physical showing a clean bill of health.''

''That's understandable. Of course, I'd expect the same from you. If...and it's a big if...I decide to consider this, when would you want to do it?''

Kat, still thinking about his bare butt, mentally slid between the sheets. ''Not until after we're married. That's the whole point of getting married.''

''I *meant* get married.''

''Oh, of course. The sooner you make a decision the better.'' Kat rummaged through her canvas bag and pulled out the only piece of paper she could find, a bank deposit slip. Where the heck was a pen when you needed one? She settled for an eyeliner pencil and scribbled out her number. ''Think about it and give me a call.''

Andrew stared at the paper lying on the counter between them. Kat shoved it nearer to him and walked to the door where she summoned Toto from the nether regions of the cottage. Something nagged at her. Something she was forgetting. She mentally ticked everything off. She had her purse, her keys and her dog.

When it hit her, she whirled to face him. ''And I'll want a sperm count. There's no point in wasting each other's time.''

''SHE SAID WHAT?'' Edward Sommers threw back his head and laughed until tears rolled down his face. Andrew stopped pacing Edward's book-lined office and sank into one of a pair of matching leather chairs. He eyed his brother-in-law and fellow attorney across the desk and wished Kat Devereaux's parting comment amused him as much as it had Edward.

"It's the first time I've had a woman refer to sleeping with me as 'wasting time.'" And it rankled.

Edward gave way to another bout of laughter. He sighed and mopped a handkerchief at his face. "That's Kat."

"Why haven't you or Bitsy mentioned her before?"

"As in introducing you? Matchmaking?" Edward assumed the virtuous look he usually reserved for juries.

"Bitsy's been throwing women at me since I was in grad school. What about Ms. Devereaux?"

"She tried. Kat was never interested."

Andrew discovered, much to his chagrin, that was not the answer he wanted to hear. "So she didn't want to date me but now she wants to marry me?"

"That seems to sum it up."

Just what the hell had Kat Devereaux considered wrong with him? "Why didn't she want to meet me before?"

"Said you sounded too much like a...I believe the exact term she used was 'stuffed shirt.'"

Andrew experienced a knee-jerk reaction. "I am not a stuffed shirt." Conservative. Perhaps a bit reserved. But a stuffed shirt? He'd stepped out of his conservative mold when he'd agreed to appear as one of the state's most eligible bachelors. And that had proved nothing but trouble since.

Across the desk, Edward smirked at his denial and toyed with a pen. "May I be frank?"

"By all means."

"How long have we known each other, Andrew?"

"It's common knowledge we've known each other for the better part of fifteen years."

"Correct."

Andrew templed his fingers and prodded. "The point, Edward?"

"You just made the point, Andrew—we've known each other fifteen years, ten of which I've worked at the same firm with you and eight of which I've been married to your sister, and you still call me Edward. Not Eddie or Ed or even Sommers, but Edward. No one calls me Edward."

"Well, you've never called me anything but Andrew," he countered.

"That's not true. I called you Andy—once. The look of distaste on your face was so plain, I never made that mistake again."

"Okay, I concede," Andrew said, knowing Edward was right. But he wasn't interested in what he called his brother-in-law, or vice-versa. Kat and her proposal kept flitting through his mind. Along with her incredible legs.

"You're seriously considering this, aren't you?" Edward didn't seem surprised.

"This firm has been a part of my family for almost a century. It's my heritage. I refuse to let my father deny me a partnership just because he believes partners should be married and stable. Marriage was his sole stipulation. What's your opinion?"

"It could work. It could get you what you want without costing you half of everything in the end if you have a prenuptial. The way I see it, you have two immediate choices—Kat or Claudia. Straight up, I'd take Kat any day. I only have one reservation."

"Yes?"

Edward picked up the embossed leather frame on the corner of his desk. The photograph captured all of Julianna's exuberance as she laughed at her parents.

"She's a beast. But she's my beast and I wouldn't trade her for the world. Sure as hell not for a partnership." He settled the frame back on the corner of his massive desk. "I question whether you can walk away from your child when the time comes."

Apparently Kat thought he could. That seemed to be

one of the more salient points in his favor. He'd never considered himself father material. Much like his own father, he spent too many hours at the office and liked it that way. And while he didn't envision himself reading bedtime stories, he also didn't envision tossing his child's legacy aside. He wasn't interested in parental visitation, but he'd damn well retain the right to name his son or daughter as his heir. He and Edward could deal with the legal ramifications later.

He reached for Edward's phone. "Mind if I use your phone?"

"Go ahead."

Andrew punched in his office extension. "Gloria. I need you to make a doctor's appointment for me for tomorrow afternoon. Clear my calendar if you have to. And round up a private investigator ASAP, not one of our regulars though. Thanks."

He checked his watch, a smile tugging at the corners of his mouth. "Now I need a good attorney. If you know one, I'm willing to spring for a working lunch."

Edward grinned and shrugged into his jacket. "It'll cost you a pastrami on rye at Baker's."

"I'll even buy you a beer to go with it." Andrew paused at the office door. "So, *Eddie,* do I qualify as a wild and crazy guy now?"

KAT SLID INTO THE SEAT facing the doorway. "Thanks, Umberto. I'll have a glass of Chianti and a basket of garlic rolls while I wait."

"Anything for you, *cara mia.*" He treated her to a soulful look before moving off toward the kitchen. Kat shook her head slightly and smiled. Umberto always swore undying devotion to her, as he did to every other female patron. It was fun, harmless flirting that made for a lively dinner and usually a generous tip.

Tonight she and Andrew were meeting, with their attorneys in tow, for the first time in the week and a half since she'd propositioned him, although they'd had several short, perfunctory phone conversations in the interim.

"Hi, sis." Her older brother ambled across the restaurant.

Kat stood and hugged him. "Thanks for coming, Jackson." He might be her sibling, but he was also one of the best lawyers she knew, and the only one she trusted to keep this agreement confidential.

"You realize this whole thing is against my better judgment. And Father's going to be furious when he finds out," he said without preamble.

"Jackson, practically everything I do is against your better judgment." Kat winced when she thought about her father's reaction, but she'd made up her mind. "Unfortunately, it won't be the first time Dad's disapproved of me."

Umberto interrupted with a basket of fragrant garlic rolls and Kat's wine. He bowed slightly in Jackson's direction. "A glass of Chianti for you?"

"Thanks." Umberto glided away and Jackson picked up the conversational thread. "I don't understand why you can't just fall in love, get married and have a baby."

He didn't add "like everyone else." He didn't have to. It hung between them unspoken. Kat had lived a lifetime of being different.

"In case it slipped your mind, I tried that with Nick and it landed me a charming case of desertion."

"If I ever get my hands on that…"

"… low-life, slime-sucking son of a bitch, you're gonna kill him." Kat finished the diatribe she'd heard so many times before. "You'd have to take a number."

She patted Jackson's hand. She wasn't bitter, but she'd learned her lesson and learned it well. "It's okay, Jackie. Honest it is."

"Well, I hate to bring it up, but you know sometimes you're a little excessive."

"I have several excellent behavior modification tapes that have really helped."

"Several? Humph. What about that time you bought all that pink paint because you liked the color and it was on sale?"

"*That* was a long time ago!"

"How many pairs of shoes do you own? And how many had you just bought at that sale the last time I met you for lunch?"

"I'm not shopping any more shoe sales and I promise these tapes are great. Try to understand I need to do this my way."

Umberto placed a glass of wine in front of Jackson and slipped away.

"I respect that. I don't agree with it, but I respect it. By the way, I've got an ethics question for you."

Jackson had plied her with ethical dilemmas from the time he'd entered law school. Kat had always marched to a slightly different drummer, and he swore it gave him a fresh perspective.

"Shoot."

Jackson toyed with the stem of his glass. "You have a client who gives you specific instructions. But, as an attorney, you don't feel they serve your client's best interest. Your client's current wishes would, in the long run, pose a serious problem. Do you adhere to his wishes or act in his best interests?"

Kat knew better than to ask for details or specifics. Jackson would never betray client confidentiality. For a fleeting second she thought about her own case. Jackson made no bones about his disapproval. However, she'd given marrying Andrew and having a baby a lot of thought—it wasn't a whim. Besides, Jackson knew she'd kill him if he was playing games with her. She tossed out the idea and went on to consider the question from a general perspective.

Kat recognized clients were often distraught. Usually

by the time they got around to contracting the services of a lawyer, they were an emotional mess. Most of them didn't know the intricacies of the law, which often rendered their requests or instructions ill informed. It was the reason they paid exorbitant fees for legal counsel.

"Earn your money and act in his best interests."

"Good answer." Jackson reached into his suit pocket, pulled out a cigar and clamped it between his teeth.

"Don't even think of lighting up that thing," she warned as she fished a garlic roll out of the basket.

"I'm not, but it couldn't possibly smell any worse than that." He defiantly waved his cigar at the bread.

Kat broke off a small piece and launched into the question she'd avoided asking since Jackson's arrival. "So, is the contract in order? Everything's clear? You spelled out all the stipulations?"

Jackson didn't blink. "Yes, yes and yes. But I still think—"

"Jackie, I know what you think. But if everything's in order, I plan to marry Andrew Martin Winthrop III."

She looked forward to seeing him tonight. She needed a blast of arctic ice from those cold gray eyes. It had been far too easy to forget his aloofness and lose herself in his voice over the phone. His voice brought to mind a good bourbon. Potent. Heady.

As if conjured up by her thoughts, that voice interrupted her reverie. "Good evening, Kat."

She glanced up with a start. Edward Sommers and Andrew were standing beside the table.

Her gaze riveted on Andrew. Good Lord, if he wasn't a total package. Coal black hair cut precisely and brushed back from a face saved from being pretty by a slightly crooked nose and a harsh mouth. And summa cum laude from Harvard. Fabulous genetic material. She buried a sigh. It was a good thing she didn't go for his type. Otherwise she *would* be making a big mistake marrying him.

Kat rose from her seat and Eddie enveloped her in a bear hug. "Welcome to the family." Edward spoke low in her ear.

Kat laughed at his forwardness. "Good to see you again, Eddie."

She shifted to face Andrew. She could hardly hug his lawyer and then shake her fiancé's hand, could she?

Kat stood on tiptoe and twined her arms around Andrew's neck. He stiffened beneath her hands when she bussed his cheek. He was all hard, masculine angles. If she thought he sounded and looked good, he felt and smelled even better.

Kat withdrew from him and sank into her chair, glad of the support it offered, while the men indulged in a flurry of handshaking.

"Andrew, Eddie, this is Jackson Hamilton, my attorney and brother." She sent Jackson a teasing glance, determined to lighten the atmosphere. "Our mother had a fixation with dead presidents when he was born."

Edward interrupted her introductions with a friendly nod. "It's okay, Kat. We've all met in the courtroom before."

"And I take it Katrina Anastasia was your mother's Russian nobility phase?" Andrew drawled.

Clever. Very clever. Kat snickered her appreciation of his parallel witticism, relieved to discover Andrew possessed a sense of humor. Next to her, Jackson nodded his approval.

"Thank God, someone's finally paid you back for that dead president joke."

ANDREW WATCHED Kat Devereaux walk back to the table. She'd excused herself to go to the bathroom when Jackson and Edward had left with minor contract changes. There was nothing provocative about either her walk or her manner but she exuded an unselfconscious sensuality. He also watched their doe-eyed waiter mooning over her.

She slid into the seat next to him and treated him to a warm smile. "Ready to eat?"

"That's fine." Andrew noted their smitten waiter hovering in the background. "I'm sure we'll have the opportunity to order posthaste." No sooner had Andrew spoken than the waiter approached the table. Andrew indulged in a scowl. Regardless of the underlying reasons, Kat was his fiancé. Almost.

"We're ready for our salads now." She bestowed an equally warm smile on their waiter, who hurried off at her bidding.

"We don't order because there's no menu. Mama Leone serves whatever she's in the mood to cook. But I can promise you, it'll be the best Italian food you ever tasted." Kat waved a hand at the humble furnishings. "And I didn't think you'd run into anyone you knew here."

"That's fine." He hadn't come for the gastronomic experience. He reached into his jacket pocket. There was no way he would have given her this with Jackson and Edward watching, but he'd rather get it over with before dinner arrived.

He slapped a sealed envelope on the table and stared past her at a charcoal drawing of a fishing village. It tilted crookedly on the wall.

She ripped into the envelope. "Oh, my. According to this, your sperm count is above average."

He retrieved the single sheet of paper and tucked it back into his pocket. "So they said."

Kat shifted toward him, her indigo eyes alight with avid curiosity. "I've always wanted to know, did you have to…"

Andrew cupped her pointed chin in his hand and leaned in close. "We are not going to have this conversation. Not here and now. Not later. You'll have to find

someone else to quiz for details or continue to wonder.''
It had been damned humiliating. They'd put him in a
room with a little cup and… It was the closest he'd come
to calling the whole charade off.

Kat's full bottom lip puckered into a pout. On any
other woman it would have been a studied ploy of seduction. A move calculated to drive him to acquiesce to
her request. On Kat it was pure and simple sulking. And
tenfold as enticing. ''But I just wanted—''

Andrew slid his thumb to rest against her lips. ''Shh.
Let's talk about something else.'' He sure as hell hoped
she came up with another topic of conversation, because
all he could think about was the lush fullness of those
lips against him. He released her and leaned back in his
chair, only to notice her hand tremble as she tucked her
hair behind her ear.

Romeo arrived bearing salads. He situated Kat's before her with a flourish and a murmured, *''Cara mia.''*

''Thanks, Umberto.''

Umberto, not Romeo. Romeo seemed more appropriate. He placed Andrew's salad before him with much
less pomp.

Kat broke the tension-laden silence. ''I have my own
medical evaluation if you want to see it. And you had
enough time to check me out?''

''It's not necessary for me to see your evaluation. And
yes, I've had plenty of time to check you out. Otherwise
we wouldn't be here.'' Plenty of time to ascertain
through his P.I.'s report that she was an elementary art
teacher, immensely popular with students, parents and
faculty alike. She shared a similar background with him.
She lived fairly modestly except for what appeared to
be a proclivity for the shoe department at Dillard's.

''Right. Have you told Claudette yet?''

''No. And I'm not going to until after the fact. Claudette…I mean, Claudia…would go straight to my father.
She knows he expects me to marry her.'' For some an-

noying but inexplicable reason Andrew felt compelled to justify his relationship with Claudia to Kat. "Claudia doesn't care a whit about me, but she isn't going to take it well when she finds out I married you instead of her. Missed opportunity and such. That's why we should get married quietly in the next week or so and then tell everyone."

"I think we can count on several people 'not taking it well.'"

Andrew stared in fascination as she nibbled a cherry tomato. He swallowed hard and reached into his pocket. "I believe you're right about that."

He grasped the small velvet box. Perhaps she'd put down the damned tomato. He slid the jeweler's case onto the table next to her salad.

Kat's knife clanged against her plate. She eyed the box suspiciously. "What's that?"

"It's a bomb," he answered with a hint of sarcasm.

"What?"

"What does it look like? It's a ring."

"But I don't want a ring. At least not an engagement ring. A *plain* gold band will suffice."

She was far too transparent for her own good. With her emphasis on "plain," she might as well have come out and said she thought he'd give her something ostentatious.

"As my wife, people will expect you to wear something other than a plain gold band." He nudged the box closer to her. "Open it."

Momentary reprieve arrived in the form of Umberto carrying two generous servings of gnocchi. When he left, muttering over the two barely touched salads he'd cleared away, Andrew pressed the box into Kat's hand. "Just take a look at it."

With a decided lack of enthusiasm, she cracked the box open and stared at the ring, speechless, which seemed a novel state for Kat from what he'd observed thus far. Finally she pulled it out. The fiery iridescence of the opal flanked by twin sapphires came to life in the light. "It's beautiful. Simply beautiful."

"I'm glad you approve. You didn't seem like the diamond type."

"I'm not. I'm just surprised..." Her voice trailed off, as if loath to finish the thought.

"What? That I realized it?"

"Well, actually, yes." Wariness gleamed in her eyes. He took the ring from her. "May I?"

"Okay." She presented her hand with reluctance. "But I need to ask you a question."

Andrew slid the ring onto her finger, noting the small callus that marred her palm. He frowned at the hint of desperation tinging her voice. "What's the question?"

"Do you read the *Wall Street Journal?*"

Andrew recalled a long-ago trip to the fair. He'd been about ten and had gone through the fun house. Mirrors and tilting floors had left him slightly off-kilter, disoriented and thoroughly delighted. Much the same as having a conversation with the entrancing Kat. He stared at her for a moment and then did the only thing he could. He threw back his head and laughed.

Bemusement replaced amusement. Where the hell had that question come from, besides left field? "Of course."

She nodded her approval and speared a bite of her gnocchi. "You really should try this. It's outstanding. Early-morning delivery?"

"Actually, I'm on-line." She appeared positively gleeful at that news. "Why? Are you a fan?"

"Nope, I think it's dreadfully boring."

Andrew shook his head slightly to clear it. Obviously he was missing something. "Then what's this all about?"

"Consider it a reality check. One more thing. Would you mind eating at least part of a garlic roll?"

Katrina Anastasia Hamilton Devereaux soon-to-be-Winthrop was a hell of a conversationalist. Talking with her was rather like chasing a roller coaster. "Would you mind explaining?"

"I've had quite a few of them and, they're rather strong." That was an understatement. They were safe even if they found themselves in the midst of a vampire coven. "And I thought it would be a good idea if we kissed before we went home—to test and make sure one of us isn't repulsed by the other when it comes down to it. And with all the garlic rolls I've had I just thought it'd be a good idea if we started out on an equal footing. You know if you haven't eaten one, you could be really put off by…" The tip of her tongue wet the fullness of her lower lip in nervousness, and he felt an instantaneous tightening in his groin.

Andrew plucked a roll from the basket.

He didn't like garlic.

He ate the entire thing.

KAT AND ANDREW LEFT Mama Leone's behind and stepped into the soft glow of a streetlight.

"I'd recommend carrying out our test in the privacy of a car, preferably mine. I believe it offers more room," Andrew suggested.

Kat would have argued in favor of Carlotta if she'd detected even a hint of criticism, but she recognized that Trudy was much roomier. "Where are you parked?"

"This way." Andrew guided her with a light touch to the small of her back. She stepped over the uneven pavement and realized her future hinged on this one kiss.

Her *Wall Street Journal* reality check earlier had served its purpose. Andrew had shown such insight in presenting her with the simple yet exquisite opal-and-sapphire ring instead of the cold elegance of diamonds, it unnerved her. She absolutely did not want emotional attachments or compatibility with this man. Ye gods,

she'd almost crowed with relief at the news he was an
on-line subscriber. She was safe. And one step closer to
getting her baby.

Now she just needed to verify they were physically
compatible.

They stopped next to the gray sedan and Andrew
opened the passenger door for her. Kat slid onto the cool
smoothness of the leather seat. She knew she enjoyed
looking at him—especially the rear view—and his touch
elicited a tingling awareness, but she had to know how
they would both respond to the intimacy of a kiss. Better
to know now than after they'd married.

Andrew slipped into the driver's seat, breaking her
contemplation of their compatibility. He casually tossed
his suit coat into the back seat before he turned a CD
player on and the low, plaintive wail of a saxophone
wove itself around them.

"I figured you for a Beethoven or Mozart kind of
man." Surely it was the intimacy of the music and confines of the car that lent her voice that husky quality,
not anticipation.

Andrew reached across the distance separating them.
"No Beethoven. No Mozart." He traced the line of her
brow, his touch featherlight but sure. She shivered from
his heat against her cool skin. "Does that repulse you?"

"No. Not yet."

"Good."

Kat tucked one leg beneath her and shifted closer,
trailing her fingers over the hard line of his jaw, savoring
the slight rasp of his beard against her. She felt the pulse
beneath her fingertips race. Was it hers or his? Perhaps
both. She wasn't sure. "How's that?"

"Fine, just fine."

He stroked the sensitive softness behind her ears, easing his hands into her hair, drawing her closer. Kat quivered as a slow, languorous heat stole through her. Dark-

ness shadowed his face, but the rapid rise and fall of his chest beneath her hand told its own story.

She loosened his tie and undid the top button of his shirt, her fingers shaking as she came into contact with the heated satin of his chest. Andrew sucked in a harsh breath and she heaved a sigh, finally remembering to breathe. As a prelude to a kiss, this was a doozy.

Impatient, Kat hooked her finger above the knot of his dangling tie and tugged him to within a fraction of her mouth. His ragged breath mingled with her own. "Are you ready for this? What do you think?" she said, her voice raspy.

His hand wandered to caress the nape of her neck. She arched ever so slightly, grazing the tips of her breasts against the hard planes of his shirt-covered chest.

"I think you talk entirely too much," he muttered against her lips before claiming them with his own.

There was nothing tentative about his kiss and Kat responded with equal forthrightness. She lost herself in a whirling kaleidoscope of sensation. The taste of red wine and garlic mingled with passion. The rumpled silk of his hair as she ran her fingers through it. His branding touch that stroked up her calf to her thigh.

Somehow, during the course of the kiss, Kat wound up in Andrew's lap, wedged between the hard wall of his chest and the unyielding steering wheel. Her arms draped around his neck and his hand kneaded her buttock at the edge of her panties. Without removing his mouth from hers, he murmured, "Does it feel like I'm repulsed?"

Snuggled in his lap, she had ample evidence to the contrary. "No. I'd say definitely not repulsed."

Kat was nibbling at his lower lip when a sharp rap on the passenger window startled them both into looking up. She sat in stunned confusion as a flash blinded her. Footsteps pounded away.

Andrew abruptly shifted her back onto her side of the

car and raked a hand through his hair. Without uttering a word, he radiated tension.

"What the heck was that?" Kat asked, although she had a sinking feeling she already knew the answer.

"That, Ms. Devereaux, is an overzealous photographer for the local paper. You and I will make tomorrow morning's news. Leave your phone off the hook and, since both our families read the paper, I suggest we find a nice, discreet justice of the peace tomorrow."

Kat tugged her skirt down as Andrew confirmed her suspicion. That promised to be one provocative photograph. She knew all about the press. She shuddered as she remembered how they'd ravaged her like a pack of vultures when Nick had skipped out with his embezzled millions. But what was newsworthy about Andrew Winthrop and herself? "Why would they want a photo of us?"

"It's that damn eligible bachelor deal." Andrew massaged his temple. "It brought out matchmaking mothers and one hounding photographer."

Oh yeah. She'd sort of forgotten about his prime catch status. One day she wanted to hear more about those matchmaking mamas, but right now she needed to concentrate on the photo disaster. "No self-respecting paper will turn that shot down. Well, maybe the *Wall Street Journal* would."

Andrew grunted a harsh laugh.

Kat gathered her sensually scattered wits. Andrew was right. They'd planned to present their marriage as a fait accompli. Also, if they were married it would take the impact out of the photograph. Kat was very much aware she was marrying a conservative man so he could gain a partnership in his extremely conservative, family law practice. Not to mention the school board and her students' parents were likely to take a dim view of a photograph of her sprawled in Andrew's lap. She didn't think they'd find it much of an example for the students.

She'd never considered that his recent designation as one of Florida's most eligible bachelors had elevated him to local celebrity status. Thanks to Nick, Kat was well versed in damage control. "Meet me at your house tomorrow morning at eleven. You bring a justice of the peace, Eddie and Bitsy. I'll bring Jackson. Surely they can have our contracts ready by then if we call them tonight."

"Tomorrow then. Eleven o'clock."

Kat jumped out of the car and slammed the door. She didn't have time to sit around tingling from a kiss— make that a helluva kiss.

She had a wedding to go to tomorrow.

Her own.

3

ANDREW SWUNG OPEN his front door and found Edward and Bitsy regarding him with sly amusement. Edward held up a folded section of newspaper to Andrew's face and cocked his head, comparing the two. "What do you think, Bitsy? The chin and the nose are the same, but I don't know about that hair standing on end and the unbuttoned shirt...." Edward trailed off.

Bitsy laid a speculative finger against her nose. "I don't know where he could've come up with a body double on such short notice, so I suppose it is my darling, straitlaced brother."

Andrew glared at the smirking couple before him—to think they wondered why their child displayed a penchant for mischief.

Edward regarded the photo in mock wonder. "Eight years I've known you, and this is the first time I've ever seen you even slightly disheveled."

Between the expanse of Kat's shapely legs and his shirt gaping open, disheveled was an understatement.

"Yeah, *Eddie?*" Andrew deliberately used the nickname. "Well, you've never seen me get married, either, so consider it a week of firsts. Now if you two have finished the Laurel and Hardy routine, perhaps you'd like to come in."

Andrew had seen the photo as soon as his paper was delivered. He'd spent the morning trying not to think about the reaction of his well-heeled clients—or the sleek line of his future wife's legs, the feel of her firm buttocks pressed against his lap.

Bitsy and Eddie moved past him, into the den. "So what kind of ring was Kat wearing?" Bitsy quizzed.

Andrew closed the door and answered automatically, "Opal and sapphire." Her question sank in and he spun to face her. "You noticed a ring in that picture?"

"Of course. And you can bet every other woman who looked at it noticed it as well."

"You're kidding, right?"

Bitsy sighed dramatically. "How can you seemingly sophisticated men be so incredibly naive sometimes? No, I'm not kidding."

Andrew sought confirmation from Edward, who shrugged off the unvoiced query. "Don't look at me. The workings of the female mind remain a mystery."

Bitsy ignored his comment. "Dad's furious. Livid. Enraged. Beside himself."

"Now that's a surprise. When did you talk to A.W.?"

"Puh-leeze. Give me a little credit. After you called last night we screened our calls. We let him leave a message on our machine. Don't tell me he didn't call you as well."

"Sure he did. Left a message much the same as yours, I suspect. Who was the girl and what the hell was I doing?"

"That's it in a nutshell. What're you going to do about it?"

"I'll talk to him later today, and then it's what *you're* going to do about it. It'll be quite interesting when the rival paper runs the story tomorrow that the mystery woman in the photograph is actually my wife. Of course, this will be leaked by an anonymous but reliable source." Andrew decided she deserved teasing for her earlier body-double comment. "And I can't think of anyone better suited to leak gossip than you, Bitsy."

Bitsy swatted at him and then rubbed her hands together in glee. "Do you want me to call now?"

"Why don't you wait until after the fact," suggested Edward, "since neither the bride nor the justice of the peace has shown up yet."

"Okay. Speaking of the bride, did you bring in the camera?"

"No, it's in the car."

Andrew held up a hand. "No cameras. No photos."

Bitsy shook her head in disgust and continued toward the door. "Maybe you don't care about any photos, but one day your child will want to see her mother and father's wedding photos. Juliana loves looking at ours."

Andrew didn't offer a rebuttal. He knew he'd make a lousy parent—he didn't have time in his life for anything other than his work—but he'd never deliberately do anything to hurt the child he and Kat would create. Not even something as trivial as denying her, or him, wedding photos.

Quite the contrary, in fact. He waited until the door clicked behind his sister to turn to Edward. "The stipulation's the way I wanted it? Even though I waive parental rights, I retain the right to name this child as my heir?"

Edward nodded an affirmative.

"How'd you get Hamilton to sign off since it's not what Kat wanted?"

"Hamilton's no fool. Even though their family has enough money tied up in trust funds to take care of the kid, he felt it was in both the child's and Kat's best interests not to waive rights to Winthrop money."

"Excellent."

The front door slammed, heralding Bitsy with camera in tow. "I'm going to check on Juliana and make a cup of coffee. Either one of you want anything?"

"No thanks." Unless she could serve him up his partnership and he could forgo this farcical foray into matrimony.

"Nothing for me." Edward lowered his voice even though Bitsy moved onto the kitchen. "Yeah, well it's not going to be so 'excellent' when Kat finds out. She's going to be plenty angry with all of us."

A twinge of doubt surfaced before he dismissed it. She'd left no room to negotiate the point. Andrew stared out the window, unseeing. "I can handle one woman's anger, but I will not sign away a Winthrop's birthright."

"Hell hath no fury like a woman deceived." Eddie misquoted in final warning.

Outside, a car sputtered to a stop, backfired once and died.

Andrew squared his shoulders at the surge of adrenaline rushing through him. He stood one matrimonial step away from getting what he'd worked for all these years—his partnership.

"I believe my blushing bride just arrived."

KAT PARKED BETWEEN the gurgling fountain gracing the circular driveway and the front walkway. She checked her rearview mirror to make sure Jackson pulled in behind her. She'd driven by the house when she'd investigated Andrew, but it was set far back from the quiet residential street and she'd never seen it this close. They'd met at his beach house.

An impeccable lawn gave way to impeccable evergreen shrubs. Everything was unmitigatingly serene, unrepentantly verdant. Kat shuddered at the uniformity.

She snapped a retractable leash onto Toto's collar—she didn't know how understanding her groom would be of Toto's incontinence today—and waited for Jackson to join her at the brick-paved walkway. Toto darted about, intent on introducing himself to every shrub.

"Nice house." Jackson surveyed the whitewashed stucco with the red-tiled roof.

Kat shrugged at the rectangular structure, smiled at her brother and led the way to the front door. "I'm not particularly interested in his house, just his sperm." She needed to remember that was *all* she was interested in. Last night had proved their physical compatibility. She'd just have to keep it in check.

Jackson seemed decidedly unamused by her attempt at humor. "Are you sure you want to do this? You and Andrew haven't signed these documents yet." He lifted his briefcase. "Or made any binding legal commitment. You can still change your mind."

"That binding legal commitment is known as marriage, and no, I don't want to change my mind."

"If you're marrying him because of this—" Jackson indicated the section of newspaper folded against his briefcase "—don't worry about one racy photograph...and it is racy. The fickle public will forget soon enough."

Kat patted his cheek. "Don't worry so, Jackson. You know I'm not marrying him because of that photo. I'm past ready to have a baby. It may have moved the schedule up a little, but the deal was already put to bed." She glanced at the photo and laughed. "Don't take that literally. Although Andrew is one heck of a kisser."

Jackson scowled and straightened his already straight tie. "That definitely falls into the category of more than I wanted to know."

As he reached for the doorbell, Kat stopped him. "Jackie, you and Eddie settled all the details in the contract?"

He tensed beneath her fingertips. Apparently he still didn't approve of her marrying Andrew. "Of course we did."

Bored with marking his territory, Toto plopped onto her foot.

"Okay, I just had to check." Kat squeezed Jackson's

arm and released it. "You know you're my favorite brother."

"I'm your only brother."

She reached around him and pressed the doorbell. "Yeah, well, if I had another one, you'd still be my favorite."

The door opened and Kat found herself poised on the threshold of her new, temporary home, face-to-face with her groom. For the next few months, possibly the next year, she'd see this man across the breakfast table. Despite the fact they qualified as polar opposites, it wasn't a dismaying prospect. A quiver of anticipation arrowed through her. He appeared as immaculately groomed as his lawn, but far more arresting.

A low heat began to simmer inside at the look in his eyes as they swept over her. Kat was glad she'd chosen the sleeveless linen dress. She'd told herself it was because it was elegant, cool and comfortable and it matched the stones in her engagement ring, but she also knew the sapphire blue complemented her eyes. She'd left her legs bare—she didn't wear panty hose, not even for her own wedding—but she had rushed out this morning and bought a pair of strappy sandals, right after she'd purchased Andrew's wedding ring. She'd also conceded to vanity and brushed on a light coral lipstick.

She moistened her lips as the seconds dragged on and they continued to study each other. She absently hoped the baby inherited his nose and cheekbones.

A flash shattered the moment.

"The groom greeting the bride at the door." Bitsy sang out a caption for the photo.

Andrew welcomed Kat and Jackson with a sweep of his hand. "Please, come in."

Kat reeled Toto in when he headed toward Eddie's pant leg, and shared a conspiratorial grin with Andrew. Her mouth gaped open. She faced the largest custom-built aquarium she'd ever seen. A literal wall of fish loomed before her. Toto quickly forsook Eddie's leg to yip at the myriad of colorful fish. Kat felt as if she were snorkeling without getting in the water. It was breathtaking. Exhilarating.

"Wow!" she breathed to no one in particular.

"I like fish," Andrew responded simply.

"It was the one thing the interior decorator couldn't talk him out of," Bitsy volunteered as they moved en masse around the glass wall to the living room.

While Edward and Jackson popped the locks on their briefcases, Kat examined her surroundings with mounting dismay. Despite her earlier flip comment to Jackson, she would live here for several months. Pale peach tile offered the only hint of color in a room of creams and tans.

"The decorator planned the theme of the house around tranquility," Bitsy offered by way of explanation.

"She was obviously addicted to sedatives."

"*He* was quite expensive." Andrew's tone was stiff.

"*He* had to pay for all those sedatives somehow." Kat stood her ground.

"The truck's bringing your things on Monday, isn't it? Feel free to change whatever you want to. I certainly want you to feel comfortable while you're here," Andrew offered.

Kat nodded an acknowledgment. "Thanks." Exactly where would her flea market rocker fit into this urbanely somnolent room?

Jackson cleared his throat. "If you two could just sign the papers, it's probably best to get this out of the way before the J.P. gets here."

Kat released Toto from his leash and moved over to Jackson's side. She picked up a copy of the contract and began to read.

Jackson interrupted her. "Just sign on the back page. It's all there."

The doorbell pealed, reinforcing his directive. Even though Harry Murdoch, the justice of the peace, was known for being closemouthed, they wanted this contract out of sight when he entered.

She hastily scribbled her name, Katrina Anastasia Hamilton Devereaux, for the last time and, with rock-steady hands, passed the pen to Andrew, who followed suit.

Jackson and Edward breathed a collective sigh of relief as they stuffed the papers back into briefcases, closed them and slipped them out of sight. Bitsy backed into the corner to get a better photo angle. Kat simply stood and admired the rear view of the man about to become her temporary husband as he crossed the room to answer the door.

"BY THE POWER INVESTED IN ME by the state of Florida, I now pronounce you man and wife," intoned Harry Murdoch. No organ broke into "Oh, Promise Me." Toto's snoring provided the only background accompaniment.

Despite the unusual circumstances of their nuptials, four pairs of expectant eyes watched Kat and Andrew. He turned her to face him, his hands wrapped around her bare arms. Andrew's expression remained unfathomable, but his intention was clear as he bent his head toward her. Standing on tiptoe, Kat braced her hands against his broad shoulders and met him halfway.

At first pass, it was the briefest brushing of mouths, the merest tempting taste that left her hungry for more. She sought more, reveling in the taste of him, the hard, masculine line of his mouth against the full softness of hers. Andrew tangled his hand in her hair and pulled her closer.

Kat went willingly.

She sighed softly as his tongue teased against the corner of her mouth. She saw stars behind her closed lids.

A cough interrupted the sensual daze enveloping her. She opened her eyes as another star flashed by in the form of Bitsy and her camera.

For the briefest second she recognized the passion darkening Andrew's eyes as equal to her own before it vanished beneath his cool composure. He disentangled his hand from her hair, the loss of his touch leaving her oddly bereft. She absolutely could not, would not, should not crave his touch. *That* was not part of the deal. *That* could lead straight to that excessive business she was determined to avoid.

While Andrew shook hands with Harry and thanked him for performing the ceremony on such short notice, Jackson wrapped her in a congratulatory hug.

He muttered in her ear, "That was some show, sis."

"I told you he was a hell of a kisser," Kat murmured in return. Good grief, if he was half as good at the rest of *it*...

Jackson released her, feigning disgust.

Bitsy embraced her with open arms. "I can't believe it! We started out as friends and now we're sisters-in-law!"

Kat held her close, touched by Bitsy's obvious pleasure in her becoming a family member, however temporary. "Better keep thinking of me as a friend, since we'll remain friends a lot longer than sisters-in-law."

Bitsy quizzed her with a raised brow and a knowing smile. Kat felt herself blush to the roots of her flaming red hair. Even though she and Andrew were physically compatible, Bitsy needed to remember that had nothing to do with a real marriage. And anyway, Kat wasn't looking for a real marriage.

"There's a hormonal attraction. I'll grant you that, but that's all it is."

Bitsy's brow slid up another notch.

Harry Murdoch was occupied with Andrew across the room. Still she lowered her voice. "Don't be goofy,

Bitsy. You know I'm not looking for a real marriage, and neither is your brother. Remember, we've got a plan here, an agreement. Andrew and I are simply taking care of mutual needs in a slightly unorthodox but relatively uncomplicated manner.''

Bitsy, ever playful, looked uncharacteristically serious. ''Perhaps you'll take care of needs the other one doesn't know exists.''

Kat refused to touch that with a ten-foot pole. ''What? Is my new husband a gourmet cook?''

Bitsy's smile acknowledged Kat's attempt to lighten the conversation. ''Andrew screws up making Jell-O.''

Kat flopped onto the beige leather sofa. ''We're doomed. You know what a lousy cook I am.''

''Nah, Mrs. Fitzwillie will save you.''

''Mrs. Fitz-who?''

''Fitzwillie. She comes five days a week and takes care of the house and laundry. Lucky for you two culinary inepts, she also takes care of all the cooking. She even stockpiles food for the weekends when she's off. And then there's Anton. He's a dear old man who works part-time as the gardener.''

Kat brightened considerably. ''Maybe it won't be too bad living in the tranquil palace after all.''

She missed Bitsy's response. Andrew caught and held her attention as he escorted Harry Murdoch to the door. Standing on the other side of the aquarium, he seemed a part of the exotic seascape. With his broad-shouldered good looks, he could have been Neptune commanding the depths.

''Yeah, and I'm Charlie Tuna,'' Kat muttered to herself.

''Huh?''

''It's actually a bit disconcerting.'' She continued her solo conversation.

Bitsy waved a hand in front of Kat's face. ''Earth to Kat. What's disconcerting?''

"Andrew."

As if he knew he was the object of discussion, he watched Kat and Bitsy from across the room even after he joined Edward and Jackson. Kat refused to back down from his inscrutable gaze. After what seemed like minutes but proved only seconds, he shifted his attention to the two men beside him.

"Andrew? How's that?"

"It's those damn fish and his music."

"What've you got against those poor fish? And what music?"

Kat realized she may have made a slight tactical error. She'd taken Andrew Martin Winthrop III at face value. Slotted him into a neat little box. She didn't like finding parts that didn't fit.

She eyed Bitsy accusingly. "The fish are so… so…well…alive. And did you know he likes jazz music?"

"Kat, it's an aquarium. It would be really weird if the fish weren't alive, and yeah, I guess I knew Andrew liked jazz. What's the big deal? Are you feeling okay?"

Kat gulped in a deep breath. Bitsy was absolutely right. She was overreacting. She needed to listen to her behavior tape again!

"Sorry. You're right. It's no big deal. I guess I'm more keyed up about today than I realized."

Andrew, Edward and Jackson joined them. Kat deliberately avoided glancing at Andrew, as if she'd have a clue what was going on behind his shuttered gray eyes.

Edward took Bitsy by the arm. "Well, we'll be going now."

"But what about the champagne?"

Edward tugged her to her feet. "The baby-sitter needs us, dear."

"But I called just before the ceremony and everything was fine."

Edward hustled her toward the door, leaving Andrew,

Kat and Jackson to trail behind. "And I called just a few minutes ago, and she needs us home as soon as possible."

Edward opened the front door, hugged Kat, shook hands with Andrew and Jackson, and urged his wife outside.

Bitsy grabbed a gift-wrapped package off the front seat, which she thrust at Kat and Andrew. "But they need to unwrap their wedding gift...."

"Say goodbye, Bitsy."

Kat elbowed Andrew and Jackson. The trio called out in unison, "Goodbye, Bitsy."

"Funny. Very funny," Bitsy managed before Edward stuffed her into the car. She winked knowingly at Kat from the passenger seat. "I'll talk to you tomorrow."

Jackson cleared his throat. "I need to get going, as well."

Andrew shook his hand, every inch the gracious host. "Thanks for coming on such short notice. We'd love for you to stop by whenever you can. And now if you'll excuse me, I have to make a phone call."

Kat would bet the farm there was no phone call. He was allowing her a private goodbye with her brother.

Jackson stopped short of a hug and squeezed her shoulder instead. "Just let me know if you ever need any help, kid."

Jackson's concern rendered Kat perilously close to tears. "Thanks, I will. And Jackie?"

"Yeah?"

She offered a gentle shove out the door. "Don't call me kid."

He laughed. "Okay. Okay. Don't forget to tell the parents before tomorrow's paper comes out."

"Don't worry. I'll call right now."

"Better you than me."

Kat closed the door and turned around to face her new

husband. She held out the gift. "Bitsy's your sister, so why don't you do the honors?"

"Go ahead."

She shoved the package at him. Since it was from Bitsy, there was no telling what might be inside. "Really. You open it."

"Okay. I'll bite." Andrew tore off the paper and lifted the box top.

How prophetic. From one finger dangled his and her matching edible underwear.

"DO YOU WANT TO GET the phone calls out of the way first, or would you prefer a quick tour of the house?"

"I'd rather get the phone calls over with."

"There's a phone over there, or you can call from the study if you want privacy."

Kat shrugged. "I'll call from here. Everything's been out in the open so far. I don't see the need to start keeping secrets."

Andrew reminded himself that the secret he kept from her was for the good of the child they were planning. Kat curled up in a chair and punched a series of numbers into the portable phone. Andrew attempted to study her with detachment.

He noted again that Kat Dever...make that Kat *Winthrop*...was no beauty. In fact, she bordered on plain with her freckles and the pugnacious set of her jaw. Her legs were good, lovely even, but he'd seen better. God knows she didn't attempt flattery. So what was it about his new wife that had made him forget their audience when he kissed her? Why did he ache now for another taste of her lips?

Kat looked at him strangely and he realized he was staring. "That was a wash."

"Huh?" Now that sounded like a successful attorney.

"Dad and Phoebe weren't in. I left a message with Hayes—he's the butler who came with Phoebe when she married Dad—but I'll be surprised if I hear from him today."

"Will he be upset tomorrow when he finds out we got married without him present?"

"You've got to be kidding! Dad'll be upset because I'm in the news and it might reflect on him. I could convert to Buddhism and move to Tibet, and Dad wouldn't care as long as it was quiet and didn't reflect on the Hamilton name."

An odd note colored her voice; odder still, Andrew felt an alien urge to comfort her. "Maybe you simply misread him."

Kat snorted. "Nope. Dad laid a solid case of blame on me for the bad press when Nick embezzled those millions and then walked out on me."

Andrew glimpsed old hurt in the rigid set of her shoulders. It wasn't difficult to imagine Rand Hamilton blaming his daughter instead of standing by her. Since they were both attorneys, he'd had some dealings with Rand in the past. Andrew had always considered him a bastard, he just hadn't known how much of one.

And how had she wound up married to someone like Nick Devereaux? "Did you love him?"

Surprise widened her azure eyes. The question astonished Andrew. How she felt about her first husband should mean nothing to him.

"It was a long time ago and I was young."

Kat's non-answer told everything. Not that it mattered to him anyway.

Andrew lowered himself to the sofa, automatically creasing his trousers.

Kat thrust the phone toward him. "Your turn."

Andrew declined. "A.W. and Mother are entertaining our esteemed senator this afternoon on their boat. I guess we'll both break the news later in the day."

"I've still got another call. I have a mother you know." She punched in a series of numbers.

"The one with the dead president and Russian nobility fixations."

"One and the same. Hello, Mom?...yes, I know I should've told you I was seeing someone. But, I need to tell you...yes, Mom, he *is* quite a looker, but I need to tell you...."

Apparently even the loquacious Kat was no match for her mother. Kat heaved a sigh and took a deep breath, straining her breasts against the bright blue dress and accelerating his pulse.

"Mom, I'm married," she announced. "What do you mean *who?* Of course the one with his hand on my thigh!"

From his seat on the couch, Andrew heard the warbled tone on the other end of the line escalate in volume. Kat held the phone away from her ear.

"Today...yes, I know you're going out of town for the week." She threw Andrew a panicked look and motioned frantically. "My new phone number? Okay, I'll hold while you get a pen and paper." She covered the mouthpiece and hissed, "Quick, what's your number? I can't not know your number...*our* number...if I just married you."

Andrew scribbled the number on the back of a magazine off the end table.

Kat grabbed it from him as he wrote the final number and relayed it to her mother. She wrote a single word and shoved it at him.

Birthday?

He mouthed the information and she repeated it into the phone. "Okay, call me when you get to California and get settled in."

She clicked the off button and rubbed the back of her neck. The same neck he remembered as warm and silky. "Whew. At least that's over."

"What's the birthday all about?"

Kat launched herself out of the chair. "Numerology.

She and my stepfather leave this afternoon for a New Age convention in California. She wanted to get a fix on your numbers on the way out.''

He'd heard of mismatched couples, but Kat's parents won the prize. "*She* was married to Rand?"

"The numerology came after the divorce, but they're a case in point. Opposites may attract, but it's only for a short period of time."

Andrew reasoned the attraction he felt for his wife was novel. Kat Devereaux Winthrop stood apart from any woman he'd met before. So he was attracted to her quirkiness. Unusual on his part, but not totally irrational. He further reasoned the novelty would wear off quick enough and he'd be back on an even keel.

He hoped it was damn soon.

KAT TRAILED DOWN THE HALL behind Andrew, the plush beige carpet absorbing their steps. Aside from the overwhelming neutrality of the interior, the house was quite lovely. A long rectangle, all interior rooms opened onto a central courtyard with a small garden pond.

The home tour was almost over and Kat vowed not to walk behind Andrew once she knew her way around. It was too darned distracting—which was why she didn't hear what he said. She was too busy appreciating the immediate view.

"Huh?"

Andrew stopped abruptly and Kat plowed into him. She latched onto the first thing she came in contact with to steady herself. Taut, firm buttocks tightened under her touch. She resisted the urge to squeeze, instead dropping her hands to her side immediately.

"Sorry about that. Um, what were you saying?"

Andrew turned to face her and the hallway seemed to shrink considerably. "I said, this is our room."

He threw open the door behind him and ushered her inside. A general impression of more of the same hit her, but the bed captured her attention. Swathed in yards of mosquito netting draped from the ceiling, it dominated one wall. Kind of erotic that netting...visions of her and Andrew playing a private game of Tarzan and Jane beckoned like a jumbo pack of double-stuffed Oreos.

"*Our* as in yours and whose?"

"*Our* as in yours and mine."

Kat quivered at the thought of those tight buns snuggled up next to her every night. "Um, thanks, but that's really not necessary. You've got plenty of space and I'll be happy in any of your guest rooms." She'd bargained for sharing a house when they got married. She'd even bargained for sleeping together—after all, she intended to make a baby—but sharing a bedroom for however long she was here insured an intimacy she hadn't bargained on.

"Absolutely out of the question."

She didn't care for his tone. "Why? Give me one good reason."

"I could give you several, but for starters I refuse to have Mrs. Fitzwillie speculating as to why we don't share a room."

"So, for your pride's sake we have to—"

Andrew cut her off. "No. My pride plays a secondary role, but Mrs. Fitzwillie would be devastated if she found out I'd entered into an *arrangement*." His entire countenance softened. "Her husband died just before she came to work for me. They didn't have any children and she was lonely. In the past nine years, she's been more like a mother to me than my own mother."

Well, Kat wasn't exactly thrilled about disappointing a nice little old lady—especially one who cooked—but there had to be a way around sharing a bed with this man on a nightly basis. She knew herself. Too much of a good thing... "I could get up before she gets here and she'd never know."

"She'd know." Andrew advanced until he stood before her. He clamped his hands on her shoulders and drew her to him. His voice lowered to a provocative level. "For Mrs. Fitzwillie to believe anything less than we're passionately, head-over-heels in love is not acceptable." His hands slid to her upper arms in a caress.

Expensive cologne mingled with his essential maleness, the heady scent intoxicating her. Even as she swayed toward him, she objected, "I'm not sure either one of us is up to pretending to be head-over-heels in love."

His breath brushed the planes of her face as he lowered his mouth to hers. "Then we'll just have to practice."

His lips nuzzled and nipped at hers until she responded to his sensual coaxing. His tongue teased the moist heat of her mouth and her nipples tightened in desire of such ministrations. An aching lethargy unfurled between her thighs.

The giving, generous kiss brought to mind his consideration for Mrs. Fitzwillie. Kat anticipated cool courtesy for his employee, but his tender concern dismayed her. The thought had her wriggling out of his arms and stepping out of reach.

His eyes questioned her. The hand he ran through his midnight-black hair trembled.

"I'll do my best to uphold my end with Mrs. Fitzwillie." Her own hand proved unsteady as she combed her fingers through her hair, but she strove for a flippant tone. "And we'll share this bed, but just for the record, Toto always sleeps in my room."

"Not on the bed."

"No, he has his own bed, but in the room." Kat swallowed a smirk. One night of Toto's snoring and Andrew would beg her to move into a guest room.

"Okay."

Kat backed toward the bedroom door. "I'll go get my suitcase."

"Can I help?" Every vestige of softness and passion had vanished, replaced by his customary cool and correct demeanor.

She heaved a sigh of relief. This was the Andrew she knew and didn't find dangerously endearing.

"No, that's not necessary." She knew she had to clamp down on thoughts of *me Jane, you Tarzan* and strategically draped mosquito netting. "Oh, and unless I'm ovulating, we don't need to bother with sex."

She closed the door behind her on the thick silence.

Sometimes self-preservation was a bitch.

4

Damn his wife with her perky breasts and sleek legs! Andrew stalked into the bathroom and splashed cold water over his face. Twice now in as many weeks, she'd referred to intimacy with him as a waste of time unless it involved procreation. What, did she consider his ego her own personal trampoline to trounce on whenever she felt the urge?

Spending plenty of time at the office in the upcoming months sounded like a plan. He could decidedly do without desperately wanting to bury himself in that quixotic woman while she casually announced making love was a chore they could postpone until she was ovulating.

Cold water trickled under the edge of his collar. The cool marble counter beneath his fingertips soothed his male pride. His partnership hovered within his grasp. It was all that had ever mattered. It was all that mattered now.

He heard his *wife* enter their bedroom. Andrew quickly dried his face.

He opened the bathroom door and found her engaged in a futile wrestling match with a suitcase nearly her size. Her contortions molded her dress across her rounded behind and hiked her hemline to midthigh.

Desperate for a distraction, he offered, "If you let me help you with that, I'll still respect you in the morning."

The faint blush that crept up her cheeks surprised him.

"I guess I could use some help," she conceded.

He hauled the behemoth on top of the bed and felt a

rising tide of annoyance at the thought of her dragging the heavy case all the way from her car rather than accept his earlier offer of help.

However, his irritation vanished as insight blindsided him. Kat hadn't conceded anything to him when she'd agreed not to touch his money in their prenuptial agreement. Oh, she'd used it as a selling point when she'd presented her case, but he'd bet not touching his money was more important to Kat than to him. Beneath her unorthodox manner lay a formidable streak of independence.

"It must've been galling to need a husband," he said casually as he dropped to the bed.

She unzipped her suitcase and faced him clutching a handful of serviceable white underwear. "Which dresser drawers do I get?"

"Those three." Andrew motioned to the trio nearest the bathroom.

She didn't respond until she'd pitched the cotton panties into the drawer and turned to stare him in the eye, her blue gaze unwavering. "Not particularly galling. More along the lines of inconvenient."

He groaned mentally. Now she'd relegated him to an inconvenience. "One thing you couldn't take care of on your own?"

"You don't have to make it sound as if I'm eccentric."

"I'd settle for unusual."

"Nothing unusual, nothing eccentric, nothing hidden. What you see is what you get. This is it." She threw her arms wide and then dropped them to her side. "I just don't want to be played for a fool again. Ever. I freely admit to making a fool of myself occasionally. And I've been known to do things others considered somewhat foolish—marrying you, according to Jackson—but I will never, ever allow anyone to play me for a fool again."

Andrew uttered a single word. "Nick?"

Kat carried another handful of underwear to the drawer and nodded. "While an international audience watched—so, thank you very much, once was enough."

Would she think he'd played her for a fool? That hadn't been his intent in changing the terms of their prenuptial agreement. Rather he'd seen it as simply protecting his own. He knew Kat's interpretation would differ. It was a good thing he wasn't in this for the long haul or committed to a real marriage because he'd shot that chance to hell with those contract changes.

"Devereaux was a fool." A nagging sense of guilt lent his voice harshness.

Her sunny smile seared him. "I appreciate your gallantry, but actually Nick did me a favor. I took a good hard look at my life, reevaluated my priorities, and learned an important lesson."

Kat brushed her hands together, dismissing the subject, and rooted through the jumbled mess in her suitcase. She pulled out a gift-wrapped package and tossed it onto the bed between them. "I bought you a wedding gift this morning." Her voice was demure, but her eyes danced with devilment.

Andrew played her game and prodded the package with one finger. "Should I expect an explosion?"

A sly smile curved her full lips. "That depends on you."

He picked up the package—obviously a book—and ripped at the paper, fully expecting how-to instructions on becoming pregnant with the least amount of bother.

However, one glimpse at the cover and a gut-wrenching laugh rumbled through him. "I'll treasure it always." He grinned at her cheekiness. "It was far too thoughtful."

His own playful attitude sobered him. He reminded himself she was a means to an end. The key to his partnership. Nothing more.

He shoved off the bed. "I'm heading into the office for a couple of hours. I'll be back around five. Make yourself at home."

Andrew placed *101 Uses for A Dead Lawyer* on the nightstand and got the hell out of their bedroom.

KAT HUMMED A NOTHING TUNE as she tamped potting soil around the final clump of fuchsia petunias. She wiped her grimy hands across her thighs and lugged the clay pot around the corner of the house as Andrew turned into the driveway.

He'd told her to make herself at home and she'd taken him at his word. With a quick visit to a nursery and the lovely potting shed out back, she'd added some much needed color to the monochrome landscape.

All the plants she'd bought, she'd potted. Like herself, none were here to stay. She'd take them with her when she left. In the meantime, they offered friendly faces in a strange place. Not to mention she'd worked off a little tension. Even though it was her idea to marry Andrew, she'd been nervous earlier.

Kat arranged the newcomer at just the right angle to complete the grouping of potted plants now sitting by the front door. The mix of gaily colored flowers spilled forth a welcome, their perfumed sweetness hanging in the humid heat. The crunch of Andrew's footsteps and the feel of his gaze on her back sorely tested her concentration.

"I see you found the nursery center and the potting shed."

She turned to face him. He stood as handsome and immaculate as he'd been when he'd left earlier in the day. No wrinkled shirts or mussed hair on her husband. In contrast, Kat felt positively grubby in her sweaty T-shirt and dirt-stained shorts.

She indicated the mass of color with a flick of her wrist. "Hope you don't mind."

"Not at all."

"Do you like it?"

"It's different."

The rioting reds, yellows, purples and hot pinks overflowing the clay pots punctuated the endless green of the landscape. Judging from his tone, Andrew didn't find that pleasing.

"Why does *different* sound like a dirty word when you say it?"

"I don't mean for it to. It just takes some getting used to."

"Well, you told me to make myself at home. Once I unpacked my one suitcase there wasn't really anything for me to do and I noticed the nursery on my way over this morning. And, there's really nothing I'd rather have been doing."

"You made that abundantly clear earlier."

"That's not what I meant. I like working with plants. Digging in the dirt is good therapy." She smiled spontaneously.

"Probably cheaper than stretching out on a therapist's couch." Andrew returned her smile. Not the polite gesture he'd offered before but a heart-stopping, genuine smile.

Kat's breath lodged somewhere in her chest. She swallowed hard.

How had a discussion on plants suddenly turned so intimate? One minute it was purple fountain grass and red salvia, the next she could hardly breathe.

"Uh-huh," she managed to say.

Andrew rubbed his flat belly. "I'm starving. What do you say to Chinese? I know a great place that delivers."

Food. Now they were on safe ground.

"Mmm. How fast can they get it here?"

"Come on in and let's order."

Kat toed off her ratty gardening sneakers and followed him into the house. She stood inside the front door, awed once again by the initial impact of the eight-foot aquarium. Would she get used to this before she left?

Andrew stopped and scrutinized the flowers she'd arranged in the den. The unusual tropicals complemented the exotic fish. Along with the aquarium, they offered a splash of vibrancy amidst the room's neutrals.

"I put flowers in every room. What can I say? You like fish. I like plants."

Andrew resumed his course to the kitchen. "It's a nice touch."

Kat wanted to believe him, but a small frown drew his brows together. He opened a kitchen drawer and pulled out a worn menu, then laid it on top of the island.

He gestured toward the purple iris gracing a crystal vase. "Mrs. Fitzwillie will love these."

For once, an issue took precedence over sustenance. Her new husband's approval was suddenly important. She'd lived with disapproval for a long time. She couldn't remember a time her father hadn't disapproved of her. Jackson clearly doubted the wisdom of her marriage to Andrew. She'd decided after the fiasco with Nick, the only approval that mattered was that of the school board because it affected her career. Otherwise she wouldn't be here now.

Kat left the menu where it lay and scrubbed the potting soil off her hands and forearms. She grabbed a hand towel and assured herself it was only because it was his home that his approval mattered. "What about you? Do you love them?"

Cynicism shaped his mouth into a semblance of a smile as he unbuttoned his shirt cuffs. "They're fine, but cut flowers don't last long. Even if I do like them, they won't be around long, right?"

She traced the gleaming white tile on the island with a ragged nail and shrugged. "Well, then I can just replace them."

He rolled up one sleeve, baring a tanned forearm.

"Do whatever you need to do to feel comfortable for as long as you're here." He dealt with the other sleeve with equal efficiency.

No quip tripped off her tongue. He was right. The flowers would die, and she'd keep replacing them until she left. But once she was gone, there'd be no more flowers. He *shouldn't* plan on getting used to them. She found the thought curiously dismal.

And she refused to need anything from him other than what they'd laid out in their contract. Certainly not his approval.

Her rumbling stomach beckoned her to deal with more mundane matters, such as take-out Chinese. She shrugged off the momentary melancholy and scanned the menu for her favorite. "Yu Shian shredded pork. Extra peppers, please."

A grimace of distaste marred the aristocratic lines of Andrew's face.

She laughed at his expression. "Does that mean we're not sharing our Chinese tonight?"

"You can rest assured."

Predictable. How could she have doubted herself? She had Andrew Martin Winthrop III's number. Her smile smacked of smugness. "Too hot for you?"

He shook his head slowly, his eyes alight with un-customary merriment, as if he was about to deliver the punch line to a joke. "Actually, no. I'm a vegetarian."

Visions of a tofu Thanksgiving danced in her head, dropping her jaw.

How many more surprises was she in for with this man?

ANDREW GRINNED AS HE PLACED the cardboard containers of Chinese on the countertop. He'd thoroughly enjoyed displacing Kat's smugness by announcing his vegetarianism. She'd stood across from him thinking she had him pegged. And those thoughts had been clearly reflected in her sweat-stained, dirt-streaked, impudent face.

Staid. Predictable.

Not that being a vegetarian rendered him a wild man, but it had rendered Kat speechless.

Tantalizing aromas wafted from the closed cartons, reminding him he hadn't eaten all day. He checked his wristwatch.

How much time did one petite woman need to shower? There wasn't that much of her to clean. His stomach growled a warning. Five more minutes and he wouldn't be held accountable.

Andrew pressed the intercom buzzer and was met with dead silence. He dropped his hand in disgust. The thing was still on the blink. He'd have Mrs. Fitzwillie call the repairman. Again.

He started to the bedroom but paused in the den, Kat's flower arrangement catching his eye. In less than a day she'd stamped his house with more of herself than he had in a decade. Standing in his own kitchen with her earlier, he'd felt the outsider, the observer. She'd been dirty and sweaty because she'd put something of herself into the place. He'd felt the odd man out in his button-down shirt and cuffed trousers.

A slight whimper interrupted his reverie. Stretched out on the rug, Toto twitched in his sleep. Doggie dreams, Andrew surmised as he quickly slipped out of the room. He might feel slightly overdressed in his own home, but he wasn't eager for another showering of Toto's affection.

The closed bedroom door brought him up short. Living with someone else—sharing a bedroom with someone—meant adjustments. He rapped the wood panel and called out, "Dinner's here."

Her reply reached him, undecipherable and muffled. She was obviously still in the bathroom. He threw open the door and stepped inside, announcing once again, "Dinner's—"

He stopped in mid-sentence and mid-stride, every semblance of coherent thought fleeing as Kat threw open the bathroom door at the same time and froze, naked, before him.

Hunger of a different kind consumed him. Another woman might have covered herself or gasped her shocked outrage. Kat stood before him proudly.

Looking away wasn't an option.

Feasting his eyes on her, he attempted to appease his appetite by taking in the sight of her glorious nudity. Her hair clung to her head in damp, subdued ringlets. No hint of merriment lightened the depths of her dark blue eyes. She slightly parted her full lips. He recalled their sweetness and ached with need.

His gaze slid from her freckled shoulders to the pale, succulent fullness of her breasts. Her nipples peaked and pouted beneath his devouring gaze.

Desire and need pooled hot and heavy in his sex.

He visually caressed the womanly, slight rounding of her belly. He drank in the tight red curls cradled between her rounded hips and the sleek line of her thighs.

He stood, rigid with the need to partake of the feast before him. He longed to test the texture of her skin against his. To taste her.

Her glittering, sapphire-dark eyes engaged him, radiating a heat that mirrored his own. She slowly reached up to brush her fingertips against a swollen nipple. A soft moan escaped her.

Watching her touch herself, desire roared through him like a fire out of control. It threatened to consume him, destroy him.

He tightened his grip on the doorknob. The need to make love to her nearly dropped him to his knees. It was that *need* that formed and stiffened his resolve to walk away. He'd wanted, and had, a number of women, but he'd never *needed* anyone like he needed Kat now. He fought to regain control.

When he performed his husbandly duties, it'd be just that—a performance, a duty. Not giving in to this alien need.

"Dinner's here." Hot want thickened his voice. Frustration edged it with harshness. His announcement broke the erotic spell that bound the two of them.

"Oh." Kat blinked, her expression dazed, as if she were waking from a dream. She reached behind her for a towel, draping it around herself sarong-wise. As she crossed the bedroom to the closet, she avoided looking at him.

Andrew relinquished the doorknob and moved toward the bathroom. "I need a shower before dinner." He slammed the door on the silence behind him.

Kat's lingering scent in the still-steamy room aggravated his unabashed craving. The thought that he'd just cut off his nose to spite his face—it felt like other body parts—occurred to him.

Andrew turned the cold-water tap on full blast, not bothering with the hot.

He was plenty hot.

He stepped into the shower. A seldom used but very appropriate epithet echoed in the stall.

Thoroughly drenched, Andrew stood beneath the icy deluge fully dressed.

KAT, NOT PRONE TO SELF-DOUBT, wondered if she might have made a mistake with this marriage.

Andrew had turned her on more with a two-minute look than Nick had in four years of touching. He'd also threatened her earlier resolve. Who was she kidding? She'd forgotten all about contracts and agreements and partnerships. She'd wanted him like she'd never wanted any other man.

Dangerous territory to tread on a temporary basis.

And nothing had changed. Theirs was a temporary arrangement and that's all it would ever be. She wanted it that way.

She thunked the cartons of Chinese on the wrought iron patio table and paced back to the kitchen.

The refrigerator door stood open. Andrew hunkered down before it. He slanted her a sideways glance. "Want a beer?"

The day had been unbalanced enough and she still had to get through the night with this man. "Thanks, but no thanks. I'll stick with water."

In one lithe movement he rose, elbowed the door shut and turned to face her. A polo shirt hugged the breadth of his shoulders. Khaki shorts showcased muscular, hairy, thoroughly masculine legs. The slow burn she'd sought to control flared within her. But one look at his shuttered expression doused the flame. Those same eyes that had devoured her earlier now chilled her to the core.

She pushed a wild lock of hair off her forehead. "I thought we could eat outside on the patio."

"That's fine." His clipped tone offered just the perspective she needed. Desperately needed. According to her ovulation prediction kit, she was fertile ground, which probably explained her incredible response to his perusal of her earlier.

In heavy silence he followed her out to the patio, where they settled into opposing seats. Pots of hibiscus, gardenias and jasmine scented the warmth of the evening. A bird trilled in the distance. Still neither spoke.

Kat opened her carton and reached for the dinnerware, determined to outlast his silence.

Andrew's food remained untouched as he watched her across the table. He took a long pull of his cold beer and broached the subject between them. "About what happened…"

Kat remained silent, curious to know Andrew's thoughts on the intimacy they'd shared. She'd been caught up in a magical spell he'd cast merely by looking at her. She'd recognized his hunger. She hadn't been able to move. She hadn't *wanted* to move as his gaze touched her intimately. Had he felt the magic as well?

"I didn't mean to..." He gazed at a point past her shoulder. "It won't happen again."

Relief and frustration warred within her. Frustration stemmed from her need to know how he'd felt. Relief, at not having to examine the escalating awareness between them, won out.

Kat mounded shredded pork on a bed of rice. "We both have to get used to living with someone else. I'll be more careful in the future."

An imperceptible nod attested to his relief at her willingness to drop the matter. She studied him across the table as he reached for his dinner.

He was handsome—no denying the appealing combination of black hair, gray eyes and chiseled features. She'd expected a pleasant physical relationship. She hadn't anticipated this incendiary, smoldering heat between them. She didn't want it. And then there was his obvious affection for the widowed Mrs. Fitzwillie. And the fish. And the music.

She wanted the staid, safe man she thought she'd married.

She'd just concentrate on the things that mattered. Like the *Wall Street Journal.* His perfectly creased trousers and starched shirts. The way *different* rolled off his tongue like an expletive.

This was still a brilliant plan. She'd make it work. From here on out, Andrew Winthrop was simply one giant, walking sperm.

"Would you care to try this?" He offered, ever so civil.

Kat wrinkled her nose in distaste at the tofu concoction on his plate. "No, thanks. I'll stick with what I ordered.'' Take-out Chinese and her groom suddenly became interchangeable.

Amused by her own private joke, she forked a mouthful of her own meal. One bite and fire flamed in her mouth. Eyes watering, she grabbed her water glass and drained it.

Unruffled, Andrew regarded her across the table. ''Are you okay?''

She nodded, convinced she'd breathe fire if she opened her mouth.

''More water?'' he asked as he took her glass and turned toward the kitchen. She nodded mutely.

Kat examined her plate in his absence and realized her oversight. She'd expected one thing and gotten another. The cook had used whole red peppers instead of chopping them up. She'd bitten into an entire Chinese hot pepper.

Andrew placed a glass of water before her and sat back down with a fresh beer for himself. She muttered her thanks.

''Guess it was a little spicier than you anticipated?'' A taunting spark of humor belied his noncommittal tone.

''No. It was exactly what I ordered. I just need to pay closer attention from now on and not get distracted.'' She drank another generous portion of water, determined to put out the fire.

White teeth flashed against his tanned skin. ''I promise not to distract you again with my tofu and mung beans.''

Kat ignored his gibe and took another bite after carefully checking for peppers. ''We need to plan this reception. I'd like to get it over with as soon as possible.'' She and Andrew had discussed the necessity of hosting a reception for family and, more importantly, his business acquaintances, since they'd married so quickly and quietly.

''There's very little for us to do except decide on a

date and show up. Gloria, my secretary, is incredibly efficient and used to dealing with this kind of thing. She'll take care of all the details in no time.''

A swift stab of emotion, perilously close to jealousy, stabbed her at his esteem for Gloria. Doubtless, the paragon Gloria was a blond Amazonian beauty. Or perhaps svelte like Claudia?

What in the world was wrong with her? She was obviously overtired from the excitement of the day. She shook her head to clear it.

Misreading her action, Andrew frowned at her. ''I assure you, you'll be pleased with the whole affair.''

She clamped down on her wayward interpretation of what he said. Simply a poor choice of words on his part. ''Fine. Next weekend may be short notice but let's plan for that anyway.''

''I'll let Gloria know on Monday.'' He angled himself in the chair and fished in his shirt pocket. ''I also picked up a wedding present for you this afternoon.''

A single key clattered noisily across the wrought iron tabletop and pinged against her glass. Now they were back on safe footing with such a romantic gesture.

A house key stretched her definition of a gift. She left it lying next to her water glass.

''Umm, thanks. I realized once you left today that I didn't have a house key. I had to leave it unlocked while I went to the nursery.'' He raised his eyebrows and she hastened to reassure him. ''I left Toto here to guard the house though.''

He laughed outright at Toto's status as a guard dog, the sound playing along her nerve endings like a caress.

''It's not a house key, although I do have a spare I'll give you.'' He leaned forward and picked up the key, pressing it into the soft flesh of her palm. His fingers wrapped around hers a fraction longer than necessary. ''It's a car key.''

How could he shake her up with one lousy touch?

Maybe this ovulation business had her sensitized. "But I already have a car."

"After a fashion."

"It runs."

"After a fashion."

"What are you going to drive if I drive yours?"

"You're not going to drive mine. I bought you a new car."

"What? You did what?" It came out annoyingly close to a squeak.

Andrew didn't blink. "I bought you a car."

She'd bought him a book—paperback at that—and he'd bought her a car! She pushed the key across the table to his side. "I don't want another car." For the briefest second she fantasized about air-conditioning, before loyalty squashed it. "I'm very fond of Carlotta."

"We got married for two reasons, one of which was my partnership." Andrew massaged his temple. "Whether either one of us likes it, my firm and our clients expect certain standards. As my wife, you can't drive around in that road hazard." He pushed the key back to her.

She acknowledged the veracity of his reasoning. She wavered and might have agreed, had he skipped his snide description of poor Carlotta. Kat leaned over the table, dropping the key into his khaki lap. "Easy. I won't drive in front of your friends." She plopped back into her chair.

"Even if that were reasonable, which we both know it isn't, there's still the other reason we got married." He steepled his fingers over the bridge of his nose. "Monday morning the dealership's delivering a station wagon. It's one of the safest cars on the road. If you insist on turning me into a laughingstock before my colleagues, that's your prerogative. Don't drive the damn Volvo."

He leaned forward. Steel threaded his voice and was

evident in his gaze that pinned her to her chair. "But after the first time we make love, when there is even the slightest chance you might be pregnant, you lose the option. You will not endanger our baby by driving around in that death trap you call a car. You'll drive the Volvo if I have to strap you in myself."

Kat swallowed convulsively. He'd said "our baby." Not *the baby* or *your baby,* but "our baby." Not a single argument came to mind. She was dismayed she hadn't considered Carlotta was neither safe nor reliable for a baby. There were times when giving in didn't mean crying "uncle."

"Okay. I'll drive it."

Andrew shoved back his chair and tossed her the key.

"You could've at least let me pick out the color," she groused, compelled to object to his high-handedness.

He gathered the remains of their meal and started toward the kitchen. "Luckily they had a cancellation on a special order." He paused at the door. "It's purple."

Toto trotted out as Andrew disappeared into the kitchen. Insects droned with the coming of dusk and Kat continued to stare at the doorway Andrew had disappeared through. He'd bought an expensive new car to keep them safe. He'd bought her a purple car!

Toto jumped into her lap and lavished her with a doggie-breath kiss. She scratched behind his ears and sighed into the night. "Houston, we've got a problem. Where's my tape? I need to listen to my tape."

"WHICH SIDE DO YOU PREFER?"

Kat shrugged her ambivalence, lifting the hem of her lime-green, oversize T-shirt to just above her knees. "It's your bed. You choose."

Despite having spent the better part of the evening in his study, a stroke of bad luck sent him to bed at the same time as his wife. He wasn't looking forward to sharing a platonic bed with this woman who, in turn, bewitched and frustrated him. Andrew wondered if she always wore the hideous shirt to bed or if, fearing he'd lose his head after seeing her naked earlier, she'd donned it deliberately. "Go ahead and take the side closest to the bathroom."

While Kat settled Toto in a doggie bed situated by the closet, Andrew stripped down to his briefs. Doubtless, she expected pajamas.

By the time she finished with Toto, he'd settled between the cool cotton sheets. Her eyes widened when she turned and noticed his bare chest above the sheet. He recognized the surprise on her face. She didn't know whether he was naked below the sheet or not. He grinned to himself. Let her continue to wonder. Served her right for wearing that atrocity.

"Did you talk to your father tonight?" she queried as she crossed the room. He'd swear his bold, brazen wife had a case of nerves.

"Yes. Did you?"

"Talk to your father?"

"No. Talk to *your* father."

The mattress shifted slightly as it absorbed her weight. "Oh, yeah. I called Dad about half an hour ago."

Out of the corner of his eye, he watched her try to discern whether he had on any clothes as she drew the sheet around her. A flicker of annoyance told him she still didn't know.

"Let me guess. He was thrilled to welcome me into the bosom of the Hamilton family," Andrew said.

She turned to face him, dramatically reducing the space between them. She smelled faintly of mint toothpaste, and in his mind he easily stripped her of the green abomination. He knew what was underneath, and wasn't likely to forget anytime soon. His jockeys seemed to shrink. Certain parts of him remembered all too well.

"I wouldn't call him Dad the next time I see him in

court, if I were you." She grinned, quick and irreverent. "And your father's thrilled I'm a Winthrop?"

"A.W. and Rand probably have a lot in common." Thank goodness, she hadn't inquired about his phone call to Claudia. Graciousness hadn't been in Claudia's vocabulary.

"Did he mention your partnership?"

"No. Let's just say he was surprised that it wasn't Claudia."

Doggie snores filled the silence between them.

Kat shifted underneath the covers. Her soft calf whispered against him for the briefest moment. His mouth dried.

Awareness filled the space between them. She didn't look at him, but it was there in the budding of her nipples against her T-shirt. If he hadn't married her, he'd consider seducing her, because he wanted her in the most basic way and her body seemed to respond in kind. But he'd become a sperm donor when he'd signed on the dotted line.

Kat dusted her hands together. "Well, we seem to have some more business to take care of tonight. I checked my ovulation prediction kit and it seems I'm in season. You know, now's the time. We should probably get the sex thing over with."

5

UH-OH. KAT NOTED the slight narrowing of Andrew's eyes. Perhaps she should have been more select in her terminology. However, she was determined not to go overboard. She'd show moderation. Keep it to a business level. Theirs was a business arrangement after all. No need to lose her head just because they were about to get naked together. If he wasn't already...

Andrew propped on one elbow and leaned closer to her. The sheet slid down, baring his flat stomach. "I've never done the 'sex thing' with procreation in mind. Anything I need to know? Does it matter which of us is on top? Should you be facing east?" The low timbre of his voice caressed her even as he reached over and traced a small circle on the back of her hand in a rhythmic motion.

Damn him. He was toying with her. All she wanted was a wham-bam-thank-you-ma'am. Just the thing most women got with most husbands. But no. She had the rotten luck to stumble onto one intent on seduction. And darn good at it. She felt slightly dizzy and he'd only touched the back of her hand. So far.

It had been a really long six-year dry spell since Nick had hit the door. Six long, abstinence-filled years in which she'd avoided entanglements like the plague—because of that blasted all-or-nothing tendency of hers. She'd heard somewhere that sex was like riding a bike. Except she suspected she'd upgraded from a three-speed to a ten-speed along the way. Suddenly nervous, Kat ran her fingers through her perpetually disheveled hair.

"The only requirements are once a day for the next three days."

"Only once a day? Surely twice a day would double our odds." He slid his bedeviling hand beneath the neckline of her T-shirt and trailed her collarbone. Frissons of delight danced across her skin.

How was she supposed to keep her wits about her with his touch igniting small fires? "Uh, no. It doesn't work that way. It decreases the potency of the sperm if you…" His mouth whispered along the shell of her ear. "If you, uh…oh my, uh, do it, um, too often."

"You're the boss. If you say once a day, then it's once a day." Andrew pushed the sheet into a tangle at the foot of the bed.

"What're you doing?"

"I have a job to do and it's time to get down to business."

Now this was more like it. Now they were getting to the wham-bam part. Business. This was a business arrangement.

Baby for her. Partnership for him. Cut-and-dried. No crazy excesses.

Andrew leaned away from her, his gaze sweeping her from head to toe. She looked her fill of him. Peering at him through binoculars didn't come close to this. Golden skin lightly covered with dark hair. No bulging muscles marred the classic lines of his body. He was all hard planes and angles bisected by a pair of white briefs that evidenced his willingness to get down to business. Want and intent warmed his eyes to a smoky gray.

She closed her eyes and inhaled his male scent.

"You have the most exquisite legs." The low, heated timbre of his voice opened her eyes and increased the ache building inside her.

Not *okay* or *nice*, but *exquisite*.

With a gossamer touch, he stroked from the arch of her foot to her calf. He followed that same path with kisses that sampled and savored. The moist heat of his mouth against the sensitive skin behind her knee mightily weakened her earlier resolve.

Andrew lavished her thighs with kisses. Instinctively she parted her legs in supplication. But her wicked, wicked husband taunted her with a look that only promised, and pushed her T-shirt aside to nibble his way to the slight rise of her belly.

Kat tugged her T-shirt over her head and tossed it to the floor. Her senses begged to indulge in him. She stroked the hard line of his shoulder and felt a faint shudder ripple through him at her touch. She stroked the sleek muscles of his back as he explored her ribs and the underside of her breasts, the faint rasp of the stubble on his face, stoking the fire he tended with his sensual exploration. With deliberateness, he bypassed the aching peaks of her breasts and moved on to the pulse tattooing a rhythm of desire at the base of her throat. Braced on his forearms above her, only his mouth touched and caressed her.

His muscles bunched beneath her fingertips as her hands clutched at him, transmitting the fever building inside. Her breath grew ragged as he pushed aside her hair to sample the sensitivity of her neck and the shell of her ear. Trekking across a desert could not have left her with a greater thirst.

She groaned in frustration and invitation as she pulled his mouth to meet hers. It was the sweetest of tortures. Rather than gaining some satisfaction from the taste and feel of his mouth, it only turned up the heat coursing through her.

When his tongue touched hers, the last tenuous hold on her moderation slipped. She touched him as she'd wanted to the first time she'd seen him at his beach house. She purred her appreciation for the tight ripple of his buttocks when she slid her hands beneath his briefs and stroked and kneaded.

Andrew had teased and incited her earlier, but she'd sensed he did so while fully in control of himself. She'd sensed his measure of restraint in his touch, the cadence of his breath. Now spiraling urgency replaced his control.

He found her breasts and measured their fullness against his palms, intensifying the ache of his earlier neglect. She murmured a request on their behalf and he took one pearled tip in his mouth.

Pleasure rocked her, rippled through her and left her wanting more. Impatient to feel the hard length of him against her skin, she tugged at the waistband of his underwear. "These have to go. Now."

"You're the boss." He took over for her and shucked his briefs.

My, oh, my. Kat lay very still and closed her eyes. The cool cotton of the sheets against her fevered skin *felt* real.

The heady scent of aroused male mingling with her own excitement *smelled* very real.

"Kat, please tell me you're not falling asleep." The sexy thrum of Andrew's voice *sounded* real.

The questing probe of his hand down her belly to the slick wet between her thighs felt, oh, so very real.

She moved against him in an age-old request, opening her eyes.

No doubt about it. She wasn't dreaming. She was in bed with her husband, who happened to qualify as the all-time sexiest man.

"Do you know what redneck foreplay is?" Her voice sounded husky, even to her.

His finger stroked against her silky fold. "Hmm, I hope not."

She nudged his shoulder and delivered the punch line. "You awake? You awake?"

He chuckled as he slid his finger in her.

Kat arched. No more jokes. Coherent thought lessened with each dip and stroke. She wrapped her hand around the length of his shaft. "And no, I'm not asleep."

His fingers found the sensitive nub of her womanhood. "If you are, you're having one hell of a wet dream."

She writhed beneath his ministrations, excited by his touch and his comment. Could this man with his naughty talk possibly be the same stiff shirt she'd married? She rubbed her hand up his hardness. He was stiff all right, but it wasn't his shirt.

Kat lost herself in a kaleidoscope of sensation. Of touching and being touched. Of tasting and being tasted. Want became need—the need to feel him deep inside her.

Then he was. And amidst the maelstrom of pleasure she recognized an emotional connection. She hadn't sought it. She didn't want it. But it was there, almost as tangible as the thrust of him within her. This was not some nameless, faceless sperm donor. This was stuffy, sexy, thoughtful, quirky Andrew.

She gave herself over to a pleasure so intense it bordered on pain. She panted and moaned, close to tears from the tension that mounted with each rhythmic plunge. And then she transcended to a place she'd never been before. She soared even as she shattered and became part of the kaleidoscope.

As if her satisfaction had pushed him over the edge, Andrew found his own release. She had never heard a sweeter sound than his harsh rasp of her name as he spilled into her.

STILL DAZED and somewhat befuddled, Andrew turned off his bedside light with a snap. He'd set out to teach his wife a lesson and fulfill an obligation. Somewhere along the way he'd lost sight of both objectives and given himself over to pleasure. And something else he couldn't name. Or wouldn't.

Kat followed suit with her light, but instead of plunging the room into its customary nighttime darkness, a faint glow illuminated the bedroom.

Andrew propped himself on one elbow, trying to find the source. The glow seemed to originate somewhere to the right of Kat. "What's that?"

Beside him, Kat faced him in a similar fashion. "*That* is a night-light."

The emotional intensity of their lovemaking still disconcerted him. "Why do you need a night-light?"

"If I had my own room, it wouldn't bother you."

"I didn't say it bothered me. Not exactly. But why's it on?"

"Maybe Toto can't sleep without it."

Andrew harumphed his disbelief. "Toto could sleep next to a freight train."

In the shadows, the vulnerable look on her face told its own story. Just because he was annoyed by his own lack of control, he'd tried to bait her. He kicked himself for being an insensitive moron, anticipating her answer before the words left her mouth.

"I'm afraid of the dark." Embarrassment tinged her defiance. "So, now you know. Go ahead and laugh."

The indomitable, unflappable Kat Hamilton Devereaux Winthrop feared the dark. He realized what the admission had cost her. He was an ass for asking.

Without forethought, he reached out and smoothed his hand over her unruly hair, drawing her down to the bed. He settled beside her, rubbing her back with a soothing rhythmic motion. It had been a hell of a day for both of them.

"It's okay. I don't like spiders." He'd never divulged that to anyone.

She relaxed. "The light won't bother you?" Impending sleep slowed her speech.

"No." Beneath his fingertips she tempted him again, a bewitching heady mixture of feminine flesh and muscle, wrapped in the scent of satisfaction. He swelled a bit recalling his role in her satiation.

"You sure?" She sounded one step closer to slumber.

"Positive." This impromptu back rub qualified as torture. He'd given in to an urge to comfort her and look where it had landed him—more than ready to make love to her again, but they were on a once a day ration and she was almost asleep.

Snoring intruded on the quiet.

"Kat?"

"Hmm?"

"Does Toto always snore?"

"Uh-uh." Though she verged on sleep, the smile in her voice wrapped around him.

"A'drew?"

"Hmm?"

"Thanks," she slurred into her pillow.

For the back rub? For marrying her? For his sperm donation? For being the kind of guy she wouldn't fall in love with, one who'd walk away from his own kid?

Kat snuggled her delectably plump rear against him, her even breathing punctuated by a gurgle of contentment. Andrew frowned into the dark of the night as his hand rested against her belly. Maybe even now in the aftermath of mind-boggling lovemaking, his numerous sperm were competing for a chance to form a new life—a red-haired little tyrant with serious gray eyes and a penchant for mischief.

He'd never wanted a child. It wasn't part of his plan. He was too dedicated to his career. Too remote. Too emotionally distant. He might be great at sperm donation, but he wasn't good dad material. Was he? Could he be?

His hand flexed in a protective gesture until sleep claimed him.

KAT ROLLED OVER AND STRETCHED without opening her eyes, her face buried in Andrew's pillow. The warmth of his body and his scent lingered. Still fuzzy with sleep, she breathed in the increasingly familiar combination of expensive aftershave and Andrew's own masculinity.

She turned her head and squinted at the nightstand. Six forty-five loomed at her from the digital readout. Closing her eyes, she snuggled deeper into the pillow, content to drift back to sleep.

"Wake up," a voice rang in her ear.

Good God! The pillow not only smelled of Andrew, now it was sounding like him too! She jackknifed to a sitting position, slamming her head into a solid wall behind her.

"Ugh." A groan sounded in her ear.

She whirled, now on her knees in the bed. The "wall" was Andrew. He stood by the bed, one hand nursing his right eye.

"Are you okay?" She reached forward to examine his face. Even dim-witted with sleep, she appreciated the still-damp crispness of his hair, the clean line of his freshly shaved jaw, the scent of soap and sandalwood. And the rapidly discoloring flesh around his eye.

He stepped back and snapped, "You could've warned me you were lethal first thing in the morning."

"Only when I'm scared out of my wits!"

He felt beneath his eye and winced. "What scared you about a wake-up call?"

"I was asleep and the next thing I know the pillow's talking."

A hint of a smile played at the corner of his mouth. "You thought the pillow talked?"

"Go ahead and laugh, you're the one with a heck of a shiner coming up." She mustered a grin that turned into a big yawn. "Just the thing for a successful attorney about to make partner."

"Thanks, Kat. A new wife and a black eye, all in one weekend."

She wasn't a morning person. Never had been. Never would be. Her brain was mush first thing in the morning—overcooked oatmeal. She flopped back on the bed and pulled the sheet up to her chin, prepared to resume sleep. She spoke with her eyes closed. "Did you wake me up just to harangue me?"

"No, I was hoping for a black eye."

She curled into a fetal position. "I'm going back to sleep."

"Kat?"

The laughter in his voice irritated her.

"What?"

"Today's Monday."

"Thank you. I'll sleep better knowing that."

Within a matter of seconds, the implication penetrated her brain. She threw off the sheet and leaped from the bed, yanking down the hem of her T-shirt. "Monday. It's Monday. Mrs. Fitzwillie!" Kat raked her hands through her hair.

Andrew glanced at the bedside clock. "That's it. Our first audience arrives in about ten minutes."

"Why didn't you tell me?" she accused as she scrambled for the bathroom.

"That just happened to be the pillow talk you heard."

Kat, incapable of a witty rejoinder at 6:50 a.m., contented herself with slamming the door on his smug, albeit swollen-eyed, countenance.

"YOU SHOULD'VE ICED your eye while I was in the shower. It would have helped the swelling."

Andrew had never sported a black eye before. Although it hurt like the devil, he rather liked it. Stuffy guys didn't walk around with black eyes. Not that he'd confess his surprising pride to his wife.

He opened the bedroom door and waited for Kat to

precede him into the hallway. "And deprive my loving wife the opportunity to tend to my wound? I wouldn't dream of it."

She snorted as he fell into step beside her. "Keep it up—there's still that other eye you mentioned."

Eight minutes flat. That's how long she'd taken to pull herself together. Despite the frown tugging between her red brows, he realized his initial assessment of Kat had been wrong. He'd thought her plain. Actually, she enchanted him.

He laughed. "Has anyone ever mentioned you're not a morning person?"

Andrew heard Mrs. Fitzwillie humming in the kitchen.

"Not and lived to tell about it." She tilted her head coquettishly. "If you'd really wanted to play the loving husband, you'd have brought me a cup of coffee to wake up to—not sneaked up on me."

The humming ceased.

He slipped his arm around Kat's waist, pulling her to his side. He'd memorized every curve in the past two nights—intimately and with great satisfaction. Those curves tantalized him now. Soft and full and womanly. What had previously appealed to him in Claudia's race-horse lines?

"Ah, honey, I love it when you say those sweet things to me." His tone deliberately caressed for the benefit of Mrs. Fitzwillie.

Stopping in the kitchen doorway, he nuzzled the top of her head, his black eye turned away from Mrs. Fitzwillie. Kat smelled like bottled sunshine—clean and fresh.

Mrs. Fitzwillie beamed at the two of them from across the room.

Still averting his shiner, Andrew introduced the two women.

Kat disentangled herself and stepped forward to greet

Mrs. Fitzwillie. "I'm delighted to finally meet you. Drew's spoken so highly of you."

Andrew blanched at the nickname, sure she'd used it deliberately. He moved toward the coffeepot. The quicker she got a cup, the better.

Mrs. Fitzwillie focused on Kat. "Oh, I just couldn't believe it when the dear boy called me with the news." Kat speared him a questioning glance over Mrs. Fitzwillie's shoulder and he shrugged.

He'd phoned Mrs. Fitzwillie with the news because she deserved to find out from him, not read it in some newspaper.

"He's been lonely so long. I'd almost given up hope. But now you've captured his heart." She stared deep into Kat's eyes and nodded, apparently satisfied. "I can see why."

Andrew realized with startling clarity that he *had* been lonely—until Kat bombarded his well-ordered existence. Damn if he needed Mrs. Fitzwillie letting Kat in on something he was just finding out himself.

He pressed a steaming mug of coffee into Kat's hand. "We're fresh out of IVs today. This'll have to do."

"Thanks, Muffin."

Drew, he could stomach. *Muffin* went too far. She'd pay for that. He sat down at the butcher-block table.

Mrs. Fitzwillie turned, took one look at him and screamed, clutching her chest. "Dear boy! What in the world happened to you?"

Andrew juggled his cup at her shriek. Occasionally he forgot Mrs. Fitzwillie's affinity for melodrama.

Kat jumped in with a mischievous smile. "I'm afraid it happened this morning in bed."

The little vixen, heaping fuel on Mrs. Fitzwillie's fire.

Sure enough, Mrs. Fitzwillie's imagination kicked in. "Goodness. My Burt and I used to have quite the frolicking time but never a black eye. My goodness."

Mustering what he hoped was an I'm-so-in-love look,

he gazed up at Kat. "You were just about to fetch some ice for it, weren't you, Bunny?" He all but grinned at the grudging admiration that flickered in her eyes.

"I'll hop right to it." Kat filled a sandwich bag with ice, wrapped it in a dish towel and moved to stand behind his chair. With a gentle touch, she held the makeshift ice pack against his swollen eye. The softness of her breast brushed his shoulder and her hip pressed against his arm, giving rise to an ache an ice pack wouldn't assuage.

Abruptly, Mrs. Fitzwillie threw open the kitchen door. "Yoo-hoo. Anton, come meet the new missus," she bellowed at the top of her lungs.

Kat nearly jumped out of her skin, jamming the hard ice against his tender eye. Andrew stifled a yelp of pain. He vowed to avoid Kat around kitchen knives and power tools. The woman was dangerous.

"Sorry," Mrs. Fitzwillie said. "Anton's close to deaf."

The weathered, slight man ambled across the patio and entered the kitchen. Andrew settled into the background. Mrs. Fitzwillie clearly itched to handle the introductions. She dragged the wizened man across the kitchen.

"Anton, the dear boy got himself married this weekend, and this is Kat, his wife," Mrs. Fitzwillie boomed. "Kat, meet Anton Brock, master gardener and groundskeeper."

Age-opaqued eyes studied her. "You are the one in my shed this weekend? You are responsible for this?" He jerked a thumb over his shoulder at the mass of color gracing the patio. Though Andrew had known him for years, Anton's harsh voice still sounded at odds with his kind face.

Kat fidgeted with the ice pack on his eye. Andrew winced and stilled her hands. "Yes. I'm sorry if I—" she began.

A broad grin split the lines of Anton's face. "Finally! For years, I try to talk him into a little color here, a little color there, and always 'No, Anton. Color goes away. Always count on the green.' Now, after all this time, you bring color."

Andrew didn't need his landscaping preference discussed with his wife, especially as if he weren't present. He tried to quell Anton with a scowl. The man ignored him.

"You don't mind if I use the potting shed?" Kat smiled with charm.

"No, no! Everything you bring in a pot." He cast her a sly glance. "Maybe we will put some color in the ground, yes?"

"Yes. No. I don't know." Kat glanced at Andrew. "Let's talk about it later."

Once again, Andrew felt the odd man out in his own home. He hadn't planned on Kat turning things upside down this way.

The old man grinned. "I begin the plans now." He waved a hand at Andrew's frown. "Simple. A bed here. A bed there." He turned and hurried toward the potting shed with a bowlegged gait.

Andrew grimaced. "Something simple? I doubt it. Anton's probably off to plan south Florida's botanical extravaganza."

Mrs. Fitzwillie began unloading the dishwasher. "He may indeed. And he'll have a grand time designing it. Even if a plant never goes in the ground." She sighed. "Oh, Missus Kat. You're just what the dear boy needed. You'll bring this place to life."

Andrew pulled away from the ice pack and Kat's touch, scraping his chair back. "I've got to go or I'll be late."

He'd had all he could take of hearing how much he needed Kat in his life. All he needed from her was a means to his partnership. It would still be integral to his life ages after the dust had settled from Kat leaving. Andrew had long ago learned what you could count on.

He picked up his briefcase and headed for the door.

"Have a good day." Kat sounded subdued.

Before he managed to leave, Mrs. Fitzwillie stopped him. "Now dear boy, I know you want to kiss your bride goodbye before you leave. Don't mind me. Go right ahead." She planted herself against the sink and waited expectantly.

Kat didn't budge from beside the table. Andrew stood at the door.

Mrs. Fitzwillie waved a pudgy hand. "Go ahead, go ahead. I won't mind a bit."

Andrew had the odd feeling, intensified by the glint of suspicion in Mrs. Fitzwillie's eyes, that he and Kat were facing a test. He knew a peck on the cheek wouldn't pacify Mrs. Fitzwillie. He leaned his briefcase against the wall at the same time Kat took a step and they met halfway.

He slid his hands around Kat's waist to rest in the small of her back. His fingers brushed the soft satin of her skin where her shirt gaped from her shorts. He knew the taste of that very spot and his body tensed at the memory.

Standing on tiptoe, Kat linked her arms around his neck and murmured against his mouth. "Relax. It's a kiss. Not an execution."

Easy for her to say. He died a slow death of want every time they touched. Lowering his head, he captured her mouth with his and sampled her full lower lip. She trembled as she leaned into him.

He raised his head to break the kiss. For a fraction of a second, her lips clung to his. Drawing on every vestige of willpower, he pulled away. Kat slid her hands from his neck to frame his face, and pulled him back down to her. Bypassing his mouth, she gently touched her lips to his swollen, discolored eye. "Sorry about that."

"It's fine." Her tender caress threatened his composure.

Kat lightly traced his jawline with her fingers before she dropped her hands to her side.

She'd given a heck of a performance on Mrs. Fitzwillie's behalf. Passion tempered with tender concern. He couldn't get to the office fast enough.

Mrs. Fitzwillie clutched her hands to her breast. "Now that was a kiss!" She sighed, beaming at the two of them. "Isn't love grand?"

KAT SCRAMBLED ACROSS THE SOFA toward the ringing phone, wondering for one heart-racing moment if Andrew might be calling from his office. Not that he should and not that it mattered.

"Hello?" She attributed her breathlessness to her aerobic contortions to reach the phone before the answering machine snatched the call.

"And how is the blushing bride?" Bitsy chortled in her ear.

Kat's heart slowed to a normal pace as she silently called herself all kinds of a fool.

"Hi, Bits, how are ya?" She slumped onto a needlepoint pillow.

"I'm fine. The question is, how are *you* after a day of wedded bliss with my brother? And what'd you think of my wedding gift?"

Kat considered the havoc Andrew's baby making had wrought and opted for flippancy. "Blissed beyond belief. And your gift was unusual. We have them on display with the china."

"Sweetums, that is not where they belong, but this *is* my brother, so please, no details."

"I wouldn't dream of it." Kat grinned up at the whirring ceiling fan. "Especially not the part about—"

"Stop. I don't want to hear this. I'm just glad you're

no longer single-handedly supporting the battery market. No pun intended.''

''Very funny. Just for that I won't mention the black eye or new car.''

''Tell all,'' Bitsy demanded. ''Tell all now.''

Kat recounted an abbreviated version of both stories.

Although Bitsy howled at Andrew's black eye, the new car caught and held her attention. ''So he bought a new car to keep you and the kidlet safe. That's an interesting slant.''

''Humph! That was just his selling point. I'm sure he's much more concerned with making the right impression for his clients.''

''Oh, come on, Kat. A convertible Mercedes would've made the right impression. Give him credit.''

That was just the problem, she silently mused. He was gaining too much credit. Way too much credit. She'd already listened to two moderation tapes today.

Mrs. Fitzwillie's mention of a lonely Andrew had nagged at Kat all morning. Ignoring Bitsy's reprimand, she changed the subject.

''Bitsy, do you think Andrew's lonely?''

A sigh drifted over the line. ''Andrew cut himself off from almost everyone a long time ago. Growing up, he was more of a parent to me than A.W. and Mother. He's six years older than I am and he took care of me. But only a string of nannies took care of Andrew.''

The lock on Kat's heart struggled to hold tight against the picture of a vulnerable little boy, a solitary man.

''Speaking of your parents, I guess I'll meet them soon. We're holding a reception this weekend at Andrew's club. Mark your calendar.''

''Now *that* I wouldn't miss for the world. The Montagues meet the Capulets at cocktail hour. Kids allowed, or do I need a baby-sitter?''

''Forget Romeo and Juliet. It's more like the Hatfields

and McCoys armed with law degrees. And of course you'll bring Juliana.''

"A neighbor of mine runs a catering service, if you don't already have someone in mind," Bitsy offered.

"Andrew's secretary, Gloria, is handling all the details." She paused, and then tacked on casually, "Do you know Gloria?"

"I've met her once or twice when I dropped by the office. Why do you ask?" Bitsy's voice teased and Kat knew she'd guessed why Kat asked.

"Just curious. Andrew described her as a paragon of efficiency."

"I don't know about efficiency, but she's got the body of a Venus and a mind like a steel trap. Brains and beauty." Bitsy sighed melodramatically. "Some women just have it all."

Before Kat could respond, a shriek sounded in the background on the other end of the line.

"Motherhood beckons. Gotta go. Talk to you later."

Kat hung up the phone and huffed off the sofa. Maybe Andrew should have married Miss Venus, aka Gloria.

Pacing the length of the room, she dug deep in a bag of fudge cookies with pecan chunks.

But then again, Miss Venus probably wouldn't have offered what Kat had. How many women would let a man like Andrew go with no strings attached and without putting up a fight?

None she could think of, who might be in her right mind.

THE EARLY EVENING SUN SLANTED over her back as Kat scooted forward on her knees.

"Stick it right there. No, not that hole. The one next to it. Perfect. You might not be too sure of what you're doing now, but with my training you'll be an expert in no time," she promised. The sight of Andrew on his knees with her left her breathless.

"Yes, mistress of dirt," Andrew intoned.

Kat passed him a six-pack of perennial plants. "Quiz time. Put these wherever you think they ought to go." Andrew's interest in the flower bed had surprised her. Accepting her challenge to lay it out and plant it had quite frankly amazed her.

Andrew rocked back on his heels to study the layout of the flower bed she and Anton had spent the day preparing. Rock-hard muscles bunched in his thighs with the motion. Kat flushed with a heat that had nothing to do with the ambient air temperature. Those same muscles had bunched up last night just like that right before he... Kat plucked at her shirt, suddenly feeling warm.

"How about right here?"

"Looks good to me." And the plants were fine there, as well.

Andrew eyed the containers skeptically. "They certainly are small."

"They're like anything else. Take care of them, nurture them and they'll grow. And the best part is they'll come back year after year."

"Guaranteed?"

"Not as sure as death and taxes, but if you take care of them they'll come back for years."

"I don't know if I'll have time to take care of them."

"You'll find the time if it's something you really want."

Andrew covered the last root with soil, leaving a trail of dirt on his thigh. Her fingers itched to brush it away. She did nothing to mask her obvious appreciation of his body.

"Andrew, there's something really sexy about dirt."

A sly, sexy smile played about his mouth. "I bet you say that to all the gardening help. Small wonder Anton's looked so spry lately."

She'd just be damned, her Harvard stuffed shirt dug

her ogling him. "I only say it to the ones with the great buns."

"You know, I never noticed Anton's...uh, posterior attributes. You, on the other hand, I have definitely noticed. And you, my garden fairy, have lovely assets."

"Awfully cheeky for a garden boy toy, aren't you?"

"You haven't seen the half of it yet." In one lithe move he stripped off his T-shirt.

Somewhere along the way, she'd tapped into a playful sensuality that could literally charm her pants off. She licked her suddenly dry lips. "I definitely approve of the first half."

Still kneeling, he stalked her on the garden path like a dark panther scenting his next meal. She felt ripe and lush and ready for the feasting. She met him halfway.

"You're far overdressed for a garden fairy." He slowly tugged her shirt up, his knuckles trailing against her sensitized skin, until he pulled it over her head and tossed it behind her. She reached out to steady herself against the roughly furred planes of his chest and wound up caressing the expanse of it. His fingertips blazed a trail of fire down her shoulders.

The late-afternoon sun warmed her bared back. It was nothing compared to the molten heat building inside her. Kat flicked her tongue against his nipple. The sharp hiss of his indrawn breath spoke volumes in the still of the garden.

"We could go inside." She'd meant to sound sultry and inviting. Instead she croaked.

Andrew slid her bra straps off her shoulders. "It's after hours and no one's here but us. I'm perfectly happy where I am, if you are. You just happen to be overdressed."

He nuzzled down her chest, and used his teeth to pull the cups of her bra down, baring her breasts. His gray eyes darkening to slate, he fondled and squeezed until she couldn't stand it any longer and pulled his mouth to one aching nipple.

Hot, slick heat drenched her panties. Kat thought she'd come unglued with the need to feel Andrew deep inside her. She'd been waiting a lifetime to be here with him now, the grass a soft cushion beneath her, the aroma of the fertile earth mingling with their scent.

Instinctively she arched her throbbing core against the hard line of his arousal. Reaching for the waistband of his shorts she pleaded for release from his sweet torture, "Andrew...please...now."

His eyes never left hers as he removed first his shorts and then hers. "Tell me what you want, Kat."

She leaned back on the soft green carpet of grass and spread her legs in invitation. "I want you to make love to me."

Bracing himself over her, he nudged her slick wetness. Her hips arched against him. With one smooth thrust he plowed into her warmth. Kat moved against him in a rhythm as old as mother earth herself until they completed each other. With a tenderness that did nothing to restore her equilibrium, Andrew brushed his lips against hers.

"I think I may like this gardening business," he remarked as he rolled off her.

Kat tossed her shorts at his head. "Just make sure you don't do any planting without me. And speaking of planting, can you bring that bag of manure over here?"

Wearing nothing but a puzzled frown, Andrew hoisted the fifty-pound bag of cow dung. Good Lord, but he was a fine specimen. And quite talented. "Where?"

Kat shifted so that her hips were in the air. "Here."

"Huh?"

"Yeah, put it underneath me. I read that you should elevate your hips for twenty minutes afterward to optimize chances of fertilization."

Andrew settled the bag underneath her, smoothing out his shirt for her to lie on.

"And what scientific publication was this?" Andrew stepped into his briefs and shorts.

"No need to cover up on my account. And actually it was a magazine. They suggested pillows or a rolled blanket."

He stretched out on the grass beside her. "Ah, so the bag of manure is your own personalized version." His eyes skimmed her sun-kissed body with appreciation. Kat had always felt comfortable with her body, but Andrew's blatant regard made her feel beautiful, sexy, powerful.

"Consider it a fertilization ritual."

Andrew threw back his head and laughed. The warm, carefree sound was almost as satisfying to her as the love they'd just made.

"Maybe the pH balance will determine X or Y chromosome."

Kat giggled at his inanity. "Shut up."

And in that instant, lying naked in the sun with her hips propped up on a bag of cow poop, Kat realized her plan had gone seriously awry. She'd married Andrew because she didn't expect to be attracted to him.

Instead she stood in serious danger of moving far beyond mere attraction.

This situation really stunk.

6

RETURNING FROM WORK the next day, Andrew knelt to greet the ball of fur that barreled toward him. He assured himself it was merely in the best interest of his pant leg that he allowed Toto to slop wet doggie kisses on his hand. He'd never gotten around to quizzing Kat on Toto's incontinence. This seemed the safest way to avoid another episode.

Such enthusiasm on the little dog's part dictated some return of affection, he further reasoned. Andrew scratched behind the scruffy ears, reluctant to admit to himself he looked forward to Toto's welcome. He chuckled as he remembered Kat's assurance that Toto had guarded the house on their wedding day. Had it only been four days? In some ways it felt as if Kat and Toto had been a part of his life much longer.

"So, hound, you kept the castle safe in my absence today? How many warring enemies did you keep at bay?"

Toto rolled over and presented his stomach by way of answer. Andrew chuckled at Toto's forwardness.

"Aye, milord, and it's a relief to have you home," Kat retorted from the kitchen doorway, hands planted on her rounded hips. Sunlight danced behind her, turning her hair into a fiery halo, outlining her shapely thighs through her thin cotton dress.

An increasingly familiar stab of lust besieged him. For a tempting second he fantasized tossing the wench over his shoulder and having his way with her.

Sanity prevailed. Ovulation had come and gone, just in the nick of time. Yesterday at work the memory of their gardening exploits had proved a terrible distraction. And last night's less exotic but equally satisfying love-making actually had him doodling on a brief today. He never doodled and certainly never on a brief. Now the only reason to make love to his wife was desire and that wasn't part of the deal.

He rose to his feet, annoyed by his lasciviousness and at being caught in a conversation with a dog.

"Hi. Let me change clothes before dinner, okay?"

Laughter sparkled in her blue eyes. "Take your time. Dinner'll keep. Just don't let Toto tie you up in anything too philosophical."

Andrew smiled at her wit and then sobered at a jolting thought. "I'm not sure exactly what you two discuss, but you don't need to mention this to Bitsy." He shuddered to think of her merciless teasing.

"What? That you change clothes before dinner?"

"The dog."

A smile quirked at her delectable mouth. "Oh, you mean that you talk to my dog. Don't worry. I wouldn't dream of telephoning Bitsy with it."

"Thanks." He started down the hall to the bedroom.

"Then I wouldn't have anything to talk about at the reception on Saturday."

He stopped and turned slowly to face her, aware of the stiffness in his neck that had plagued him all day. "What color's your dress for the party?"

"Royal blue with jewel tones." She answered without hesitation, then paused, suspicion narrowing her eyes. "Why?" Before he could say anything, she answered for him, her expression clearing. "You want to get a corsage for me?"

He paused for effect. "No. So, I'll know what color muzzle to order."

Kat sputtered behind him as he continued to the bedroom. Andrew unknotted his tie, pleased at having one-upped his impudent wife.

He dropped his briefcase onto the worn rocker resting in a corner of the bedroom. Mark Antony, his decorator, had designated the house's interior scheme minimalist tranquility. Now, with Kat's things tucked into corners and nooks, he realized that translated to stark.

Since Kat's arrival, his house felt like a home. The room across the hall with his exercise equipment could easily be turned into a nursery. His house was fast becoming cozy and warm.

Andrew scowled at the thought and at the little dog that had followed him. Toto hopped up beside him as he sat on the bed and unbuttoned his shirt.

"Dammit, I don't want warm and cozy."

In the distance, Kat banged around in the kitchen, for all the world as if she belonged there. As if she belonged here.

The thought further tightened his already tense neck muscles.

He'd seen it time and time again among his peers and his parents. Warm and cozy didn't last. He doubted if his parents had ever had warm and cozy between them. Perhaps in the beginning? Certainly he'd never seen a vestige of it in their relationship. With painful clarity he remembered a nanny who'd showered him with affection. At eight, he'd soaked it up like a dry sponge. He'd been devastated when she had to leave to take care of an ailing mother. Oh yes, he'd learned early on to maintain a distance.

Adulthood had merely reinforced his stance. How many colleagues had he seen marry with enthusiasm only to end up in divorce court a few years later? Bitsy and Edward seemed the exception. But they were exceptional. And the loneliness was all the more painful when it was over.

Toto cozied up to him and rolled over, offering up his

warm belly for scratching, and without thought Andrew immediately complied.

If he grew fond of Kat's dog so easily, how would he respond to his and Kat's baby?

SIPPING A GINGER ALE—her wine cooler days were over until she knew for sure if she was pregnant—Kat lounged on the patio and tried to finalize her curriculum for her summer art students. Or at least she *intended* to think of curriculum. Despite a valiant effort to concentrate, visions of Andrew danced through her head. Andrew tickling Toto and chatting nonsense. The sparkle in his eyes when he'd threatened her with a muzzle. Andrew's naked, hair-roughened chest and tight buns...

She shook her head. She'd better concentrate on her job. If everything went according to plan, she'd have another person to support in the not-too-distant future. She patted her tummy, torn over the desire to already be carrying their child yet hating the thought that if she was pregnant there'd be no more lovemaking.

She'd already listened to one motivational tape earlier today. She'd better dig out another before bedtime, as well.

Andrew joined her on the patio and eased into his chair. He leaned his head against its back and heaved a sigh into the quiet of the evening.

Kat eyed him sympathetically. "Rough day?"

"Yeah. I went up against Jackson today. He's good and he's tough."

Kat had known the time would come when her husband would go head-to-head with either her brother or father. She loved Jackson dearly, but oddly felt a shifting of allegiance to the man who would father her child. Only because Andrew would contribute genetically, she assured herself.

"Who won?"

"I was better today." Arrogance, pride and a touch

of humor shaped his grin. "But he's a helluva lawyer. Next time, who knows?"

"Congratulations. For today at least."

"Thanks." He winced as he looked toward her.

"What's the matter?"

"I slept wrong last night. My neck's hurt all day." He admitted.

Kat remembered Andrew rubbing her back until she drifted off to sleep on their wedding night. Placing her ginger ale on the table, she moved to stand behind his chair.

Andrew glanced up at her, or at least as far as his impaired neck allowed. "What're you doing?"

"My mother used to get a stiff neck when she'd spent too much time at her easel. I could always make her feel better." She positioned her hands on the corded muscles of his neck.

He stilled her by placing his hands over hers. "Thanks, but that's not necessary. I was out of the office today, but Gloria can help me out tomorrow. She's taken care of this for me before."

Kat's instinctive response rang in her head: It'd be a cold day in hell before she gave the Valkyrie—as she'd come to think of the paragon Gloria—a reason to put her hands on her husband. Even if he was only temporary. And it had nothing to do with jealousy, she reasoned. It simply wasn't circumspect for her husband's secretary to rub his neck. And she'd just discovered a newfound regard for circumspect.

She shook off his hands and slid her palms inside his shirt and over the rigid lines of his shoulders. "There's certainly no need for you to suffer through the night," she admonished, beginning a rhythmic massage. Oh no, she'd be the one to suffer through the night. Ovulation was over and hence the excuse...uh, reason...to make love with her husband. Anything now would just be gratuitous indulgence, leading her close to that precipice of excess for which she was renowned.

Slick, heated satin came to mind as she kneaded and molded his knotted neck and shoulders. The feel of him beneath her fingertips stoked the smoldering fire inside her.

His head lolled forward. "Oh, God. That feels so good."

His voice poured over her like warm whiskey on a cold night. Kat desperately sought a diversion. Anything to distract her from fantasizing about nibbling those edible briefs right off her husband's gorgeous body.

"Andrew?"

"Yes?"

"We're going to pretend to be married in front of a slew of people."

"Kat."

"What?"

"We're not pretending. We are married."

"You know what I mean. The majority of the people at this reception know more about us than we know about each other."

"So, what do you want to know?"

"Why'd you become an attorney?" she questioned. She *was* curious. Not to mention desperate to concentrate on something other than mussing the neat edge of his straight, dark hair.

"Just lucky, I guess." He laughed, a low throaty chuckle. "Some people spend their whole lives trying to decide what they want to be when they grow up. I knew before I graduated from kindergarten."

Even though they dined together every night, their conversation was never this personal. Other than the mind-boggling lovemaking each night and the goodbye kiss each morning for Mrs. Fitzwillie's benefit, they'd carefully avoided physical contact. In fading twilight, she breathed in the scent of him, a mixture of expensive

cologne and pure, unadulterated Andrew. Kat slid her
fingers along his spine, careful not to cross the line from
stress-relieving massage to caress, tempting as it might
be. She was an adult in control. She could do this.

While he relaxed she was in serious danger of turning
to Jell-O.

"Go on," she said. Andrew as a little boy intrigued
her.

"Hmm. I must've been about five and a half when
my mother took me to my father's office. She had an
appointment with her masseuse or something equally
pressing. My latest nanny had just walked off the job,
so she dumped me on A.W.'s secretary. The poor
woman didn't know what to do with me. She stuck me
in the boardroom since it was empty at the time. Portraits
lined the walls. Every Winthrop who'd practiced law for
almost a hundred years."

Kat shuddered, envisioning somber-faced men staring
down at a small boy. "How awful for you." She
kneaded his shoulder with an extra dose of sympathy.

"Are you kidding? It was great. I knew then that one
day my portrait would hang beside theirs."

His words hammered home how much his partnership
meant to him. How steeped in tradition. She rested her
hands against the velvet warmth of his skin. "You'd do
almost anything for this partnership. It's that important
to you, isn't it?"

"It's who I am. It's all I've ever wanted." His cool
voice seemed at odds with the warm flesh-and-blood
man beneath her palms. "And, yes, I believe I've proved
I'd do almost anything for that partnership."

Kat inwardly squirmed at her role in "almost anything." He had power, position, wealth and good looks
to boot. Why then did she suddenly feel as if she'd taken
advantage of him? As if she'd discovered and exploited
his vulnerability? She hastened to reassure herself she'd
saved him from Claudia van Dierling.

Andrew pulled away from her touch. "Thanks." He twisted his head from side to side. "That's much better now."

She sank into her seat on slightly unsteady legs. "Don't mention it."

"What about you? How'd you wind up teaching art?"

Kat didn't care whether his question stemmed from genuine interest or if it was merely a polite shift of conversation. She welcomed the change.

"I suppose I inherited it, much the same as you. My mother's a landscape artist. From the time I can remember, she was always working on a canvas."

"I think I've seen one or two of her paintings. She's very good."

"Yes, she is."

"So, why did you decide to teach instead of paint?"

"I love art—it's exhilarating. The colors. The textures. But I also love kids. Watching them learn about themselves through art is an incredible experience."

Kat peeled the label off her bottle. "I've always wanted children of my own—or at least one child. And I want to be there for them. I don't want to skip dinner because the evening light is just right for painting. Or miss a school play because it coincides with a gallery opening."

Dusk veiled the day, casting private shadows between them.

"I take it your mother had a different slant on things."

"Don't get me wrong. Mom's great. And she's always supported Jackson and me in whatever we undertook. But we knew her painting came first." Kat shrugged. "I happen to think people are more important than careers. If great art comes at the expense of a personal life—which seems to be the consensus among most artists—I'll pass on the great art."

Andrew acknowledged her viewpoint with a slight

nod. He snapped a leaf off the hibiscus beside his chair and toyed with it between his long fingers. It almost qualified as fidgeting.

"If children have always been a part of your plan—and it sounds as if they have—why didn't you and Devereaux start a family?" Curiosity marked his question.

She'd discussed her and Nick's relationship with a number of friends after he'd left. It had never felt as intimate as discussing him with her current husband. She'd once married a man she thought she loved, only to discover he was a stranger. Now she'd married a stranger she thought she couldn't love.... She slammed the brakes on that particular train of thought.

"Before we married, Nick said he wanted a family. But once we were married, he changed his mind." In an instant, all their old arguments crowded in. "He said he wasn't father material, that he'd make a lousy father. It was one of the few times he bothered with the truth."

Andrew remained silent. Except for his continued creasing of the hibiscus leaf, he could have been asleep. Kat knew she'd opened this Pandora's box with her career question, but Andrew had taken it one step further. Now it was her turn. The dark invited confidences.

"Why haven't you ever married?" He *was* married. To her. She needed to remember that. "Before now?"

His fingers stilled. The leaf fluttered to the ground. "Because, much like your first husband, I'm neither husband nor father material."

His cold words shattered the soft warmth of the night that cocooned them. An instantaneous denial sprang from her core at Andrew comparing himself to Nick. Until she reminded herself that bedtime back rubs, nighttime confidences, great procreational sex and a purple Volvo did not a marriage make.

"TOTO, I'VE GOT TO TELL YOU, I'm not looking forward to tonight."

The little dog cocked his head toward Andrew questioningly.

Waiting for Kat to finish dressing, Andrew and Toto watched fish dart about in the aquarium. They hadn't even left for the reception yet and Andrew already wished it was over.

"Well, let's look at the guest list. My father-in-law despises me as a professional rival. Then there are my parents who despise each other. As a rule of thumb, I generally avoid spending time with them, especially when they're together."

Toto whimpered his sympathy.

"Kat's father and my father despise each other. And Gloria, who knows more gossip than flies on the wall do, told me Claudia wangled a date with Trent Braxton."

Toto performed his dead dog routine, rolling onto his back with all four paws sticking up in the air.

"Yeah, that's what I say."

And his delectable wife was driving him mad. More than once this week, thoughts of Kat and their baby had disrupted his concentration. He'd found himself considering the reality of being a real, long-term husband and dad. Nothing had ever interfered with his work before.

And then there were the endless nights with her curled up beside him, when she would slide a silky leg between his in her sleep. But there was no need to share that with Toto.

"Sorry I took so long. I'm ready." The cause of his insanity, or at the least, his insomnia, glided down the hall. Exotic. Elegant. Maddening.

Her dress, patterned in vibrant colors, clung and flowed in the appropriate places. He cleared the knot of desire wedged in his throat.

"This is for you. I hope you like it." He thrust a small bouquet of flowers toward her, feeling—and sounding—

as gauche as a teenager on his first prom date. "They're for your hair."

"What, no muzzle?" Her sapphire eyes sparkled.

"It wouldn't be fair to deprive our guests of your delightful wit. It's half your charm."

Her eyebrows skewed a question. "And the other half?"

Unbidden, a list formed in his head. Her sunny smile, her enthusiasm for her work, her loyalty—that wreck she called a car was parked in the garage because she refused to consign it to a scrap yard—her fierce independence, the feel of her hips beneath his... Andrew shook his head in mock disapproval. "A lady never digs for a compliment."

"And a gentleman never makes her." She dropped her head forward to admire the bouquet, revealing a freckled expanse of neck that tempted him to trail kisses along its satin smoothness. "But thanks for these. How'd you know they're my favorites?"

He shrugged off her thanks and thrust his hands into his pockets. "I've seen them around the house."

Kat arched a brow. "And you knew the name of them?"

Dammit. Why couldn't she just leave well enough alone?

"No. I picked them out at the florist."

"You actually picked out flowers that're just going to die?" A cheeky grin relieved her comment of any sting.

"They're only required on a temporary basis, as long as they last through the evening. I thought tonight might be difficult for you, and knowing how you feel about flowers, I thought you'd enjoy them, that's all."

As Kat smelled the bouquet, Andrew inhaled *her* uniquely sweet scent. She eyed him over the flowers. "Why'd you think tonight would be a problem?"

Did she have to examine everything under a microscope and then discuss it?

"I didn't say 'problem.' I said 'difficult.' You once mentioned boycotting cocktail parties." He wasn't deaf to vicious society gossip, and he knew she'd borne the brunt of many wagging tongues with Nick's desertion. He'd just wanted to make tonight a little easier for her.

"It's true, I'd prefer a quick and tidy flogging." She stepped over to the mirror hanging in the hallway and clipped the flowers in her hair. "But then I wouldn't have gotten these, and they're beautiful."

"No. You're beautiful." *Just where in the hell had that come from?*

"Thanks. We both know I'm not." She tugged a curl into submission. "But thanks anyway." Kat eyed him from his combed hair to the tips of his polished shoes, her blatant approval tightening his groin. "You don't clean up too badly, yourself."

Her flippancy about her appearance annoyed him. Facing the crowd at the reception tonight would be tough for her—hell, his parents alone would be enough to send anyone running. She needed every ounce of available self-confidence.

Besides, he spoke the truth. She was beautiful.

"Stop it, Kat."

She halted in the middle of putting on her earrings, eyeing him as if he'd suggested they dance naked in the street. "What? It's just an earring."

He waved a hand. "I couldn't give a damn about the earring. Don't tell me you're not beautiful."

A hint of vulnerability shadowed her blue eyes before she masked it. "There's no audience here. Save it for the party, Andrew. You don't need the practice." Kat turned away from him. "I'll be in the car."

Andrew watched the play of silk fabric over her hips and rounded behind in bemused fascination. He'd always considered himself fairly adept with women.

Until his wife.

7

"DO YOU KNOW WHAT he had the nerve to say to me tonight?" Kat fumed.

Bitsy backed her further into the empty corner of the club ballroom. "What?"

"He told me I was beautiful." She all but spit out the last word. *And she'd believed it for one brief moment.* Her choices had been indignation or puddling at his feet. She'd opted for the safest and tidiest of the two—indignation. "Can you believe it?"

"String him up. That's the sentence I'd hand down for something so offensive." Bitsy waved a cheese cracker for emphasis. "Imagine. He called you beautiful." Rolling her eyes in mock disgust, she popped the cracker into her mouth.

A uniformed waiter flourished a champagne-laden tray before them. Kat passed a glass to Bitsy.

"Go ahead. Make fun. It just gets worse." She touched her hair bouquet, careful not to damage the fragile flowers. "To top it off, he gave me these."

Kat swigged the effervescent wine.

"That brother of mine! It's barbaric—a compliment and flowers for his wife."

"For goodness' sake, Bitsy. He's not supposed to do these things." She lowered her voice as a guest drifted by. "He only wants his stinking partnership. And I only want my baby." A baby with gray eyes and a thatch of black hair.

"Are you sure about that?"

Kat wasn't sure of anything anymore. She felt as if she was standing on shifting sand. And she loathed sand. "We signed an agreement."

"Well, hey. You've got your agreement, so I don't see what the problem is." Bitsy peered over Kat's shoulder, "Unless you consider that Mother and Father just arrived. Oops. And there's Claudia bringing up the rear with her date." Bitsy grabbed Kat's arm. "Come on. It's party time!"

"YOUR PARENTS ARE HERE." Playing to their guests' expectations, Kat slid her arm about Andrew's waist, and was surprised to find odd comfort in his solid warmth.

"I know." Andrew dropped an arm around her shoulders, and pulled her closer. His breath stirred against her temple, unleashing a rising tide of need. "Let's get this over with." With a subtle movement of his broad shoulders, he nudged her in the direction of the older Winthrops.

The band segued into a classical piece reminiscent of a funeral dirge. Kat considered it an omen on her imminent meeting of the in-laws. Actually, with Andrew by her side, she wasn't nearly as uptight as she'd anticipated.

Nodding and smiling at guests, they skirted the room.

"There's no doubt who you look like." Andrew was a replica of his father, except for A.W.'s gray hair and lined face—and a ruthless air mercifully absent in Andrew. Her husband might possess an aloofness, but she'd seen more than a generous amount of kindness in him, as well. A.W. didn't look as if "kind" existed in his vocabulary.

"Yes, I've always been my father's son."

And none too pleased about it, if his tone was anything to go on. Did he base his own supposed shortcomings as a husband and father on the fact he shared similarities with his father? Kat tucked the thought away to examine later.

"Your mother looks much younger than your father."

"Actually, only a year or so. Mother believes in aging as gracefully as financially possible. It's the up side of keeping one of the finest plastic surgeons on retainer."

As they navigated around a small cluster of people, Andrew's hand bumped against her silk-clad breast. An instinctive and instantaneous response rippled through her, tightening her nipple into a bud of want and anticipation. Had he tensed as well?

"Oh. What's the down side?" She managed to keep her voice steady.

A shadow of a smile softened the hard line of his mouth. "It costs the old man a hell of a lot of money."

The older couple awaited Kat and Andrew—regents receiving peasants. Kat quelled the urge to genuflect before their haughty bearing.

"Good evening, Mother. Father." Andrew's arm tightened around Kat's shoulders until it was as rigid as his tone. "Kat, I'd like you to meet my parents, A.W. and Margaret Winthrop."

No hint of softness cushioned the steel of A.W.'s gray gaze. "You seem to have a penchant for scandal, girl. That's not something we Winthrops embrace."

"Consider yourself lucky, darling." Andrew retorted, earning himself a scowl from his father and a star from Kat.

A waiter paused at the group, proffering a tray of canapés. Kat sighed and loaded up a small napkin. Good Lord, what she wouldn't do for a pint of Chunky Monkey right now. Instead she popped an anchovy into her mouth.

Margaret Winthrop stared down the length of her surgically perfected nose, a chilly smile revealing even, white teeth. She fairly dripped West Palm, understated elegance, from her perfectly coifed blond hair to her designer gown. "Wherever did you find that dress, darling? It's so...well, quaint."

And welcome to the family. Kat had spent the better portion of a paycheck on her dress, determined to uphold her end of the bargain with panache. She'd help Andrew secure his partnership, but she wouldn't be a doormat for these people with more money than manners.

Andrew began to say something, but she silenced him with a slight nudge.

"There's a great thrift store near my old house. Maybe we can go shopping together sometime." Andrew's arm, slung across her shoulder, relaxed considerably, and in that instant she knew everything was okay. Whatever this evening brought, they'd face it together.

Margaret's nose wrinkled as if she'd caught a whiff of something stuck to the bottom of her shoe. "I don't think so. My schedule's terribly busy."

Far too busy to make time for a little boy with a string of nannies.

Andrew dropped Kat a lazy wink of approval before turning to face his parents. "Kat's got a great nose for a bargain. It's one of the things I love about her." He squeezed her close, planting a kiss on the end of her nose. "Isn't it, Bunny?"

She recognized Andrew's act for what it was, nonetheless, his declaration of love set her heart rate to double time. "Oh, Muffin..." She didn't have to try to sound breathless. She was.

"For God's sake..." A.W. grumbled.

Margaret sniffed an admonishment. "Really, Andrew! You seem to have forgotten yourself."

"Kat tends to affect me that way." On the Richter scale, his cavalier grin registered a ten. The husky note in his bourbon voice stroked her like an arousing caress.

She liked him on a good day. When he switched on the devoted husband routine, he turned lethal. She munched another cracker under her in-laws' disapproving stares.

A.W. and Margaret prepared to excuse themselves and Kat prepared a sigh of relief at their impending departure. All the preparation proved for naught. Claudia wafted over on a cloud of perfume and the arm of a bespectacled man.

Kat swallowed her sigh, bracing herself for round two. Claudia exchanged perfunctory kisses with A.W. and Margaret, cooing, "A.W., you're looking as handsome as ever. And, Margaret, you're stunning tonight."

In the momentary lull, Kat heard the opening strains of "The Party's Over." She couldn't check a grin. Even if tonight turned out to be a total wash, the band leader had impeccable timing.

Ignoring Kat, Claudia eyed Andrew as if he were her next meal, her lips puckering into a practiced pout. "And you're certainly looking well."

Kat noted with satisfaction that Andrew didn't show even a hint of interest in his former girlfriend. His eyes reflected only a cool remoteness.

"Marriage agrees with me, Claudia." Reaching past her proffered pout, Andrew shook hands with her date. "Glad you could make it, Trent. I'd like to introduce my wife, Kat."

Andrew turned, his smile tugging at her. "Kat, Trent Braxton and Claudia van Dierling."

Murmuring a greeting, Trent retreated, looking for all the world as if he'd rather be anywhere than in the middle of the unfolding power play. Kat empathized, but she'd be damned if she'd let these people intimidate her.

Claudia struck a model pose, bony hipbones evident beneath her dress, her store-bought breasts jutting at Kat's eye level. "So, you're the little woman."

"That's me. And I've heard so much about you, Claudette."

"Claudia." Claudia and Margaret corrected in unison,

matching frowns marring the perfection of their respective brows.

"Oh, of course. Claudia."

"Exactly how did you and Andrew meet? It seems as if one day he and I were an item and the next the two of you were married."

"We'd all be terribly interested to hear," Margaret chimed in, glancing significantly toward Claudia. "We expected, well, it was certainly a surprise to learn Andrew had married a stranger."

A.W. stood silent, a spectator enjoying the sharks circling.

"Love at first sight," Andrew smiled.

Kat had no idea Andrew could sound so...sappy. "I suppose I just knocked him off his feet."

Kat and Andrew exchanged a smile borne of a shared experience. He obviously remembered his landing in the sand as clearly as she did.

"How clichéd," Claudia drawled.

"It's a good thing you and I were just pals, Claudia, because this woman has left me breathless from the moment I met her." Andrew spoke to Claudia, but he gazed adoringly at Kat.

Despite the audience and the playacting, the heat in his eyes left her shaken.

Claudia's eyes narrowed to catlike slits. "Well, since Andrew and I are *pals*, perhaps you and I can do lunch one day." Claudia tilted her head, pretending to study Kat before she lowered her voice to a stage whisper. "I'd be delighted to introduce you to an excellent plastic surgeon."

A retort trembled on the tip of Kat's tongue, but Andrew jumped into the verbal fray ahead of her. "I can assure you, Claudia, every inch of Kat is perfect." Steel threaded his smooth tone.

Kat laid her hand on the rigid muscles of Andrew's arm, thanking him with a slight squeeze. She'd made her own way for a long time, depending only on herself. It felt good to have Andrew standing beside her. Somehow it felt right.

Claudia shared an arch look with Margaret, clearly implying that Kat's lack of inches could use some help.

Trent Braxton shuffled uncomfortably while A.W. nursed a drink and a smirk.

Mustering a confiding smile, Kat leaned toward Claudia. "It's such a relief you're taking this so well, Claudine, with you and Andrew being pals and everything. I wasn't sure what to expect." She lowered her voice to the same stage whisper Claudia had affected earlier. "Mean-spiritedness can be such an unattractive trait, don't you think?"

"Absolutely, my dear." Claudia's tight smile promised retribution while conceding Kat had backed her in a corner.

One second Kat was watching Claudia's feline snarl and the next she felt a thud against her back as an overenthusiastic dancing couple bounced off her. The two canapés sailed out of her hand as if flung on a planned trajectory. Everything slowed down to slow motion, just like in a bad dream. She watched in horrified fascination as the caviar-covered crackers soared straight toward Claudia.

Plop.

With unerring accuracy one landed between her eyes. The other smacked her chest. Fish roe slid south, disappearing between her two mounds of surgically perfected breasts.

Trent broke the silence. "Good shot!"

Claudia, wearing fish eggs and dripping venom, silenced him with a murderous look before rounding on Kat. "You…you…moron! How dare you attack me like that."

"I'm sorry. It was an accident." Kat tried not to laugh as she apologized.

Someone pounded a choking A.W. on the back.

"A couple bumped into her, Claudia. We'll take care of the cleaning bill," Andrew offered.

Trent pulled out a handkerchief and dabbed at the murky mess on her chest. Claudia slapped his hand away and turned to wreak further verbal havoc on Kat.

Andrew tugged at Kat. "And now, if you'll excuse us...they're playing our song."

Kat laughed with delight at Andrew's escape tactic as he pulled her into his arms, settled her against his hard angles and whisked her away from the mess. "Since when is the orchestral rendition of 'Old Man River' our song?"

A devilish grin echoed her amusement. "As of about one minute ago, when I decided you'd been subjected to enough nastiness."

Held close against his lean body, awareness of every thoroughly male inch of him tingled through her. The play of sinew and muscle against her palm, her hips and thighs, her aching breasts. The sound of his breathing mingled with her own, playing like a sensuous symphony in her head. Kat trembled with the hot heat that flooded her and pooled into a slick wetness at the juncture of her thighs. She ached for this man, and this man alone.

Concern darkened his eyes to storm gray as he sobered. "Are you okay?" His hand tightened on her waist.

No. She wanted to shout at him. *You could break my heart if I let you.* Actually, he was well on his way without her permission.

And she'd better remember where she was and her role for the evening.

"I'm fine. It really was an accident, you know." Kat smiled adoringly at Andrew and picked an imaginary speck of lint off his lapel for the benefit of their guests.

"Admit it. I did you a big, big favor when I saved you from Claudia. She's dreadful."

Andrew pulled her closer still, the rush of charged sensuality sizzling between them echoed in the pounding of his heart beneath her cheek and the hard ridge pressed intimately against her. "Mmm. I suppose I owe you a favor in return."

A wolf had jumped into the clothing of the safe, although sexy, sheep she'd married. Short of dying from desire, which seemed imminent, she pretended not to hear his suggestive comment.

"What in the world did you ever see in her?" Claudia's surgically enhanced bosoms and jutting hipbones came to mind. "Never mind. Don't answer that." Kat peered past his shoulder. "It's your turn to meet the in-laws. Dad and Phoebe just arrived. And let me tell you, Phoebe elevates bitchiness to new heights."

"Glad you could make it."

Rand Hamilton possessed the handshake of a dead fish—limp and slimy—Andrew decided, fighting the urge to wipe his palm down the side of his trousers.

"We would have come to the wedding, too, but we weren't invited." Phoebe Hamilton's tone dripped with saccharine sweetness.

"Sorry to disappoint you, Phoebe. But we wanted to keep it simple."

Andrew admired the way Kat handled Phoebe, Claudia and his mother—graciousness with an edge. An exceptional woman, his temporary wife.

"I must say, you two are quite the odd couple. Katrina's always been somewhat...shall we say, eccentric," Rand drawled down the fine line of his nose.

"Thanks, Dad."

"You know exceptional people often are." Andrew's look dared Rand to dispute him.

"Handsome, rich and clever. However did you manage, darling? Well, never mind. Let's just hope you can keep this one.'' Phoebe smiled, a barracuda swathed in silk as she raised a glass of champagne in a mocking salute.

Rand Hamilton's wife *did* elevate bitchiness to new heights. Made Andrew reconsider that there just might be someone for everyone in the world.

Color washed Kat's face. She might have bargained a name for her baby, but when they divorced she'd face a host of unkind comments if Phoebe proved any barometer.

Moving behind her, Andrew bracketed Kat's shoulders with his hands and eased her against his chest, trying to absorb some of the tension radiating from her. Her untamed hair tickled against his chin, and he breathed in the citrus shampoo she favored.

''Frankly, Mrs. Hamilton, I'm honored a woman of Kat's caliber was ever interested in me.'' Sincerity marked each word, scorching him with the truth. He'd been married to his career for a long time, and he'd lived with his emotional detachment even longer. Kat stirred feelings in him he thought had withered and died long ago.

Beneath his fingertips, some of the tension eased from Kat's shoulders.

''We trust you don't have any plans to embezzle,'' Rand observed with a clever smile.

''Or run off with your secretary,'' Phoebe added.

Andrew felt Kat's flinch.

Phoebe portrayed contrived dismay. ''Oh dear. I guess you didn't tell your Andy about Nick taking his secretary with him when he skipped the country with his millions. I never would have mentioned it had I known.''

''Nick Devereaux is a son of a bitch and deserves to have his ass kicked one day.'' Andrew's tone left no doubt he knew just the man for the job. And he meant every word.

Rand and Phoebe Hamilton gaped.

Kat gasped and muttered, "Take a number."

Andrew continued. "I'd appreciate it if you'd bear in mind that I don't like being compared to Nick. In fact I don't particularly like to hear his name mentioned." He smiled his most charming smile to the speechless couple. "If it's all the same to you, of course."

His gaze locked with Kat's and he felt ten feet tall at the surprise and admiration reflected in her eyes. Nick wasn't just a jerk, he was a stupid jerk.

"Look, honey, here comes Juliana. I guess she's over that highly contagious strep throat if Eddie and Bitsy brought her, huh?" Kat asked with feigned concern.

Juliana was as healthy as a horse, make that a small pony, but he noted the look that passed between Rand and Phoebe.

"Actually, I think she's still a little under the weather, but the baby-sitter backed out at the last minute." He leaned in toward the Hamiltons confidingly. "Good help is so hard to find."

Now there was a topic Phoebe could relate to—woes with the domestic help. Fortunately she was too repulsed by a sick child to embrace that soapbox. "Absolutely. Rand, darling, I believe I see Senator Bertram over there. If you'll excuse us…"

Rand and Phoebe beat a hasty retreat at the threat of impending germs.

"Well done, my dear. Masterful, in fact."

Kat glowed at the compliment.

Juliana concluded her march across the room—a six-year-old with a mission. She stopped before them, curiosity dancing in her brown eyes.

"Hi, there. Everything okay?" he asked. Juliana stared at him as if he were a bug under a microscope.

"I'm not sure yet. Could you pick me up, Uncle Andrew?" Juliana's thin, reedy voice held a note of worry.

For a split second, Andrew looked to Kat for insight. She shook her head, shrugging her puzzlement.

"Sure. I can pick you up." He reassured Juliana as he hoisted her in his arms. "What's the matter?"

Juliana's gaze darted between him and Kat.

"Do I need to leave, sweetie, so you can talk to Uncle Andrew alone?" Kat offered softly.

Juliana weighed the question. "No, it's okay." With a determined thrust of her little chin, she began tugging at Andrew's shirt.

Andrew started in surprise, nearly dropping her.

"I knew Mommy was wrong. Daddy too, 'cause he said she might be right." A snaggletoothed grin split her face. "All your buttons are still on real tight. Mommy told Daddy you weren't buttoned up so tight since you'd married Aunt Kat, but you are too." She gave his shirt another yank to prove her point.

Andrew threw back his head and laughed, uncaring of the curious glances sent his way. At his shoulder, Kat leaned against his arm and chuckled. Juliana giggled for good measure.

Although Bitsy's runaway mouth had caught up with her, he realized it was true. If Kat walked out tomorrow—make that *when* she walked out in the next year—he wasn't so sure he'd ever be the same man he'd been before.

He wasn't so sure that's what he wanted anymore. From the moment he'd spotted her behind the sculpture in the lobby of his office building, his life hadn't been the same. He'd never been one to crave excitement, but since Kat, the world somehow seemed brighter, more vivid. Until Kat, he'd lived life though a filter.

Closing his eyes for a second, the noise of the party faded to nothingness. Andrew felt with crystal clarity the extent of what he had signed away. At that moment in time, it could have been seven years in the future. The child in his arms could be his and Kat's. They could be a family sharing a joke.

He opened his eyes and focused on Juliana's freckled nose, the loss of what he'd never have facing him.

"Uncle Andrew?"

Kat's eyes met his, every vestige of humor replaced by a soft understanding. Andrew felt as if she'd stripped away his covering and gazed at his bared soul. And instead of allowing him to rewrap himself in his blanket of ice, Kat sparked a tiny flame.

Impatient with his lack of response, Juliana pressed her nose against his, cutting Kat out of his vision and making him go cross-eyed. "Why do have that funny look on your face?"

He leaned back until he regained his focus and then smoothed Juliana's hair with an unsteady hand. "It's nothing, girlo."

"Can I get down now? I want to tell Mommy and Daddy you're still all buttoned."

Everything he'd ever wanted—and those things he'd thought he didn't—seemed within his grasp. The prestige and power of a partnership in his family's firm. This maddening, delectable woman as his wife. A child. A family.

In the far recesses of his mind, for a fleeting second, he questioned the pecking order of the things within his grasp.

Juliana wiggled again, breaking his reverie. He released her with a quick wink. "You do that. But tell them it's a new shirt."

As Juliana raced off to set her parents straight, Kat's smile blew across him like a warm breeze off the Atlantic. "I like your new shirt. It fits you very well."

And the spark she'd ignited in his soul grew a little brighter.

8

"THEY SEEMED LIKE a nice couple, but that's it. No more lawyers tonight. I've met my quota."

The last of Andrew's fellow attorneys from the firm wandered off and Kat sagged against Andrew. His low chuckle whispered against the sensitive skin of her neck.

"Speaking of lawyers, where's Jackson?"

"His goddaughter's christening is this weekend in Detroit." For the first time, Kat mourned the fact that her daughter or son would be without a father. Not just any father, but Andrew. Seeing him with Juliana this evening had her longing for a future that was out of the question. Tears threatened at the back of her throat.

She and Andrew had signed an agreement. And even if she disregarded that agreement, Kat still didn't know if she was willing to take a chance on him. Being wrong about Nick had been hard. Being wrong about Andrew...she didn't think she could recover. She also didn't know how she would find the strength to leave when the time came.

"Too bad he couldn't be here tonight, but maybe he can come over for dinner one evening." Andrew threw out the invitation casually.

Surprise momentarily silenced her. He'd just suggested dinner plans as if they were a normal couple.

"That would be nice."

"Good." He glanced around the room with a sharp eye. "I think we've made the rounds with all the guests. Come on, there's someone I want you to meet."

Andrew threaded his fingers through hers. The faint rasp of a callus against her palm awakened an increasing familiar craving inside her, as he tugged her in the direction of the kitchen.

"The caterer?" she hazarded a guess.

"No. Gloria."

"The Valkyrie!" Kat all but stopped in her tracks.

"No. Not Valerie. Gloria." Pulling her along, he spoke slowly and distinctly, as if she were hearing impaired rather than hormonally challenged. "What's the matter?"

"Maybe I've had enough of buxom blondes for one evening."

With an upward quirk of his black brows, he dragged her along. "Then it's a good thing we're going to meet Gloria instead of Valerie, whoever she is."

Kat considered refusing. She'd face Claudia any day rather than Gloria. Andrew might have dated Claudia casually, but he respected Gloria. Claudia had never been anything more than a burr under her saddle. But Gloria—brains, beauty, efficiency *and* respect.

She might have initially selected Andrew for his great genes—and okay, the view wasn't too bad, either—but she'd come to respect him in the past few weeks. Respect counted for a lot. As if embezzling millions hadn't been enough, Nick had taken his secretary along for the ride. His betrayal had shouted his lack of respect for all the world to hear.

How could she have a baby with this man if he didn't respect her?

She stopped in her tracks, yanking Andrew to a halt, as well.

"What the...?"

She lowered her voice while waving across the room at the wife of a retired general she'd met earlier. "Do you respect me?"

"What?"

"I said, do you respect me?"

"What kind of idiotic question is that to ask in the middle of our reception?"

"Are you avoiding an answer?"

"No. Of course, I respect you. I told your parents earlier I'm lucky you'd even consider me."

"Well, we don't have an audience now," Kat glanced around at the otherwise engaged couples.

He trailed a finger down her cheek, setting parts farther south aquiver. "I'm very aware of that. I admire how you decide on something and then make it happen." His grin wreaked havoc with her equilibrium. "Like marrying me."

She wanted to let out a whoosh of relief but opted for casual instead. "Okay. That's good to know." She started to slip away.

Andrew blocked her retreat with his arm. "Now, why don't you tell me what this is all about?"

"Well, I know you have a tremendous amount of respect for Gloria..."

"Of course I do. She's—"

"I know. Blond, beautiful, brainy and efficient."

"Now where did you pick that up? Never mind. Let me guess. Bitsy."

"She mentioned it. After I asked."

Andrew shook his head. "Kat, don't you know you can hold your own against any woman?"

Her knees threatened to buckle at his tender assertion. Her composure suffered more when he twined his fingers through hers, brushing his lips against the back of her hand. "Now, come on, honey. I've got a big surprise for you."

They'd almost reached the door leading to the kitchen when it opened and a short, stout woman with gray hair bustled through.

"I was just coming to find you, Mr. Winthrop." The

singsong voice could have belonged to a much younger woman.

"And we were intent on finding you. Gloria, this is my wife, Kat. Kat, meet Gloria Stuart, my right hand."

Kind brown eyes regarded her from wire-framed glasses. "Pleased to meet you Mrs. Winthrop." Gloria Stuart pumped her hand.

"Please, call me Kat. And it's a pleasure to meet you. You did a lovely job on the party. I can see why Andrew thinks so highly of you."

Relief swamped her, dismayed her. She shouldn't care so much that Gloria Stuart was Aunt Bea with a secretarial degree, instead of a Valkyrie. It shouldn't matter.

But it did.

"KAT, I NEED YOUR HELP."

Anxiety deepened the blue of her eyes. "What's the matter?"

Andrew turned his head carefully, wincing at the white-hot pain the simple movement sent shooting up his neck. "It's my neck. I turned wrong a minute ago and it feels the same as it did the other day, only worse."

Asking for help didn't come easy to Andrew. He'd learned early on to make his own decisions, his own opportunities. But with Kat it felt different. It felt right.

"Sure. Let me see if I can help. Why don't we go over there?" She indicated the alcove with velveteen drapes obscuring the recessed area. Her glance swept the dancing couples, the conversation clusters scattered throughout the room. "Otherwise we're likely to cause a stir if I give you a rubdown here."

Andrew also scanned the crowd, easing his entire body around without turning his neck. "Our fathers are competing to see who can outnetwork the other one, and our guests are flattered at having the heads of the best two law firms in the city vying for their attention. Probably no one would even notice, but let's go over there just to be safe.''

Right! As if sharing a small, darkened space with Kat, her magical fingers touching him, constituted safe.

He slipped into the curtained recess behind Kat, his body tightening as he anticipated her small hands moving over him. The sound of their shallow breathing filled the tiny nook. Her womanly scent wove around him, enveloped him.

Andrew pulled the curtain behind them while Kat unfolded a metal chair leaning against the wall. ''Here. Have a seat.'' The breathless tremor in her voice indicated she shared his awareness of the tension flowing between them.

Andrew plopped into the chair. Probably the only damn thing wrong with his neck was the stress of not giving in to the craving for his wife that grew every day.

Kat moved to stand behind him and tripped, grasping at the lectern crammed next to them to catch herself.

''Are you okay?'' he asked, reaching out to steady her with a hand at her waist.

''I'm fine.'' She wedged between the back of the chair and the wall. His head fit neatly in the valley of her silk-covered breasts. Exquisite torture.

''Do you have enough room?'' He rasped.

''It's sort of tight, but I can still use my hands.'' Her touch burned through his clothing. She began to work on his muscle.

''Mmm, can you move a little to the right?'' Her fingers were truly magic. He groaned his relief. ''Yeah, that's better.''

''I don't know how much I can take care of here.''

''Whatever you can do. Right now it's so stiff it hurts, but it's already feeling better. If you can just relieve it a little now.''

Something niggled at Andrew, hovered on the periph-

ery of his consciousness, but with his senses so befuddled by Kat, he brushed it away.

"Oh, that's it. That feels good."

"It's not too hard? I don't want to go too deep." She
eased off the muscle a little.

"No, you could even go a little harder."

The problem was she was too darned short. Slipping
off her shoes, she sought a foothold on the metal folding
chair.

"If I could just get on top of you a little more."

She grunted slightly as she hoisted herself up. She
could really work those muscles in his neck now.

"That feels better to me. What about you?"

Her fingers pressed deeper into the muscle, her palm
kneaded. "Mmm, that's much better. I don't think you'll
have to touch it when we get home. It's not even stiff
anymore."

"Andrew? Kat?" Bitsy's disembodied voice called
from the other side of the curtain.

Kat's hands stilled.

"Yes."

"I'm not sure, uh, exactly what you two are up to in
there, but I thought you needed to know you're on the
PA system."

"The PA system?" Kat echoed.

Jumping up, Andrew bent over the lectern, a microphone attached to it. A red light glowed on the underside, indicating the PA system was indeed turned on. It
must have happened when Kat stumbled against it. He
felt along the flexible stem of the microphone dangling
over the front of the lectern and pressed the button. The
red light clicked off.

Dead silence reigned. No music. No muted conversation. No clink of silverware and glasses. Nothing.

"Wireless remote microphone."

Snatches of remembered conversation floated between

them...*let me get on top...can I go deeper...it's not stiff anymore.*

"This is bad. This is not good." Kat croaked, still atop her chair, wedged between the wall and the lectern.

Andrew rubbed his brow. "It could've been worse. We could've said something incriminating about our agreement. God knows what we could've said about our parents."

He mentally replayed the last few minutes of conversation.

"Instead, three hundred people think they just heard us..."

"Yes. I know what they think."

Reaching for a handful of velvet drapery, he checked with Kat. "Ready?"

"I STILL SAY YOUR MOTHER falling down in a faint was overkill!" Kat kicked off her high-heeled pumps at the kitchen door and flexed her toes in relief.

"Claudia offered smelling salts and condolences." Andrew shrugged out of his jacket.

"I personally thought that was uncalled-for." Kat rummaged through the freezer until she snagged a virgin carton of Chunky Monkey. "So, on a scale of one to ten, how would you rate this evening?"

Andrew loosened the knot of his silk tie, his long fingers coaxing the folds of the pliant material. Kat quelled a wolf whistle and silently encouraged him to continue disrobing. Her hormones were on a feeding frenzy.

"Definitely a ten for sheer entertainment value. I don't think any of our guests were bored. God knows what they'll expect at the Christmas party."

Christmas. Five months. By that time she should be pregnant and he should be a full partner. "When can you expect your partnership?" She rooted around for a walnut.

"I've got a meeting scheduled next week to discuss it. Your eating habits really are deplorable."

Kat grinned at his insult. A week ago she would have been affronted. Tonight she was merely encouraged. Somewhere beneath his vanilla preference beat the heart of a Chunky Monkey man.

She savored her bite before responding. "Dairy and fruit. Two of the four food groups."

"Kat, there are six food groups."

"Only four are essentials. Dairy—preferably ice cream. Fruit—preferably in ice cream. Protein—peanut M&M's. And chocolate."

Andrew leaned across the tile-topped island, his warm breath belying his cool exterior. "Darling, I hate to break it to you, but chocolate does not qualify as a food group."

Even the faint sarcasm tinging his "darling" couldn't quell her shiver of delight at his endearment. "It's all a matter of perspective."

The click of doggie toenails on the tile floor heralded Toto's arrival. Ignoring Kat, he pranced over to Andrew. Kat cast a baleful eye on the pair. "So, I guess I'm chopped liver now, eh, Toto?" Actually, she couldn't much blame the little traitor. She'd had some powerful urges to fall at Andrew's feet more than once in the past week.

Toto whimpered at the back door. Andrew opened the door for Toto and turned to face her, lines of tension etched across his forehead.

Kat scooped a bite of ice cream. "It's good to be home."

His cool regard searched her face. "Is that how you feel? Like this is home?" Kat thought she detected a hint of longing in his smooth voice.

"Yes." She hadn't realized it until that moment, and the truth surprised her. "It does feel like home here."

She had no idea whether her admission appalled or delighted him. If it delighted, he excelled at hiding it.

"You don't miss your condominium?"

"Not really. It's nice to mess around in the potting shed. And Toto and I both enjoy Anton's and Mrs. Fitz-willie's company."

A flash of loneliness in the depths of his gray eyes transformed him from a successful, confident man to a small boy no one had made time for. Then he thrust his hands into his pockets and turned to contemplate the night through the glass door.

"Good, I'm glad."

Kat didn't stop to consider the ramifications of her actions. Instead she responded to his bleak expression. She tossed the carton of ice cream onto the island. Nothing seemed as essential as her husband at that moment. Closing the distance between them, she wrapped her arms around him, hugging the solid wall of his back, inhaling his scent. She felt the loneliness cloaking him as surely as she felt his tight muscles beneath her cheek, echoing her own soul-deep loneliness. God knows the price of honesty, but she couldn't run any longer from whatever simmered between them.

"And you. Toto and I have grown accustomed to you. We enjoy your company. Late suppers at twilight. Back rubs in the dark."

His heartbeat thundered against her cheek; his harsh breathing, loud in the silence, broken only by the hum of the refrigerator. Slowly he turned to face her, her arms still wrapped around him, bringing them into intimate contact.

Kat tilted back her head to search the gray morass of his eyes, but he'd effectively shuttered whatever he felt. His hand drifted along her jaw to tangle in her hair, leaving her trembling in the wake of his caress. He lowered his head until the hard line of his mouth hovered above hers.

"And what happens when you leave, Kat? Because you will. We both know it." The warm intoxication of his breath tickled against her skin as the harsh stubble of his beard scraped, mirroring the dichotomy within her. She felt like shouting for joy and crying from melancholy, all at the same time. Dammit to hell, she'd made the deal to leave, but she wasn't so sure of that path now.

"I don't know anymore," she whispered against his lips. *"Carpe diem, quam minimum credula postero."* She pushed past his cool, crisp shirt, not content until she contacted the warm flesh that was Andrew.

"Seize the day, trust the least possible to the future," he translated as his hand tightened in her curls and the other explored the frantic pulse at the base of her throat. "I don't think either one of us can do that, since the future is why we're here." His eyes glittered with a hunger that defied further suppression. "But I fully intend to seize the moment, because if I don't kiss you right now, I think I might die."

The rough want texturing cool, calculating Andrew's voice excited her. She flicked at the corner of his mouth with her tongue, savoring the taste of his skin. "That won't do at all—" she no longer knew where her breath ended and his began "—since you've yet to make partner."

"Contrary to your book, a good lawyer's a terrible thing to waste," he murmured before his lips spanned the millimeter separating them, effectively ending further coherent thought.

ANDREW DRAGGED HIS MOUTH away from the luscious fullness of Kat's as they cleared the bedroom door. "I have one request."

Kat ripped away the few remaining buttons she hadn't conquered as they'd kissed their way from kitchen to bedroom. Pushing aside the starched fabric, her small hands feathered his bare skin, further intoxicating him. He felt drunk from the taste and feel of her.

"Yes?" Her husky purr brought to mind any number of additional requests. Her fingernail scraped against the hardened nub of his male nipple, the sensation arrowing straight to his groin.

"The green T-shirt. Put on that green T-shirt."

Her hand stilled its exploration. "The lime-green one?"

"The one you've worn every night for the past week."

Despite her evident uncertainty, she walked to the bathroom. "The green?"

He enjoyed the alien surge of reckless abandon invading him, compelling him to make love to his wife for no good reason except driving, mind-stupefying want. "The green."

She closed the door between them and he quelled his impatience. He knew he should seek out and don his customary detachment. Like a man tossing back one too many drinks, he knew he'd regret his glib indulgence in the morning.

Kat emerged draped in the enormous, hideous T-shirt.

What the hell. He was destined for a Kat Winthrop hangover.

He rounded the bed in answer to the question in her eyes, advancing until her erect nipples brushed against his bare chest. Taking her hand in his, he moved slowly until her palm rested full measure against his straining erection. "I want you to know the effect your green T-shirt has on me."

Her eyes widened once again as she cupped his obviously undiminished arousal. Her curves arched into him in full appreciation. "Oh, my."

He slid his hands under the cotton shirt, impatient for the silk of her thighs and the rounded curve of her fanny that had kept him up so many nights—literally. He'd had any number of beautiful women and none had ever threatened his control like his wife.

His entire life had been one ongoing exercise in emotional restraint. Intellectually, he knew Kat was a means to an end. Emotionally, he felt she might be the meaning to all ends. And physically, he planned to immerse himself in her silken warmth until he satisfied her beyond reason.

KAT WRAPPED HER LEG around Andrew's well-formed thigh and sighed from the pure bliss of sexual satisfaction. She reached into the drawer of the bedside table and pulled out a package of chocolate-covered raisins.

"Exquisite. Extraordinary," she breathed, sinking back against the pillows, mired in a delicious languor.

Andrew arched a lazy, relaxed brow as she tugged open the cellophane candy wrapper. "Good chocolate?"

She curled her foot against the back of his knee, popping a raisin into her mouth. "The chocolate's okay. The...that...us...just now." She stumbled around her explanation. What they'd just experienced went beyond great sex. Andrew, with his tenderness and enthusiasm, had restored her feminine self-confidence that Nick had eroded throughout their marriage and finally stripped with his defection. And this time there'd been an emotional honesty between them. Unlike their previous lovemaking, there'd been no hiding behind ovulation and sperm counts.

A queer jolt flip-flopped inside her at Andrew's smug grin. "Don't you know it's considered bad form to comment on performance?"

His relaxed teasing was heady stuff. She nibbled at the chocolate shell coating on the candy until it cracked. The sweet richness melted against her tongue. She and Andrew had been honest with each other from the beginning. Their truthfulness was one of the exhilarating components of their lovemaking.

"I'd say it's bad form to let such a spectacular performance pass without proper accolade." The last word slipped out on a breathless note as Andrew traced a circle on the slight mound of her belly.

"It was an honor to rise to the occasion." A slight shifting of the sheet indicated a second occasion in the making. His hand traveled up to trek maddeningly against the soft underside of her breast. "Of course, I did have sublime inspiration."

The dusky tips of her breasts tightened in response to the swift, slick heat brought on by his words and his touch. Kat arched against his hand. "Sublime?"

His tongue teased the corner of her mouth. "Absolutely sublime."

She tossed the empty candy wrapper over the side of the bed and laid claim to his mouth hovering above hers. If she'd just defined sublime, she was ready to redefine it.

He withdrew his mouth and faced her with awe. "You ate all the candy, didn't you?"

"Mmm-hmm." She ever so gently commandeered him onto his back. With all his beautiful, male splendor stretched out before her, she kneeled over him, reveling in his visual caress. She tasted the sweat-slicked skin of his stomach as her hand explored his well-muscled thigh. Her voice thickened to a husky murmur as her hand drifted upward and her mouth moved to meet it. "I'm a woman given to indulging in excess."

Andrew's deep groan expressed his appreciation of that tendency.

9

"THINK OF IT AS AN organ donation of sorts," Andrew argued. He found it downright frightening that he was beginning to not only understand but anticipate Kat's logic. He knew convincing her to get rid of her junk heap and drive the Volvo was going to take some smooth talking.

"I just can't bear to think of strangers disassembling Carlotta. We've been through a lot together." Kat's genuine distress brought him to the couch. He leaned over the back and rubbed the spot on her shoulder he'd discovered in the past week.

"Carlotta's old and tired, honey. And think how many cars can be kept on the road because of her."

Kat glanced up at him suspiciously. "Are you laughing at me?"

"Absolutely not. I'm just trying to find a solution that works for everyone." He refrained from adding that it'd be over his dead body that she ever placed herself in that wreck again.

He felt her shoulders relax as he rubbed lower. "I could arrange for you to ride with the tow-truck driver if you want." He'd initially thought her attitude toward her old bomb plain nutty. Now Kat's loyalty and capacity for caring overwhelmed him. She would make their kid a terrific mom. And he'd begun to believe he might make a pretty okay dad.

She sniffled. "Thanks, but I think a clean break might

be for the best. I've been driving Charlemagne, and Carlotta looks so sad every time I pass by her."

He didn't ask. He knew. She'd christened the purple station wagon Charlemagne.

"I think that's a good idea."

Fessing up about that clause in the contract would be an even better idea. In hindsight, Andrew realized he should have negotiated the point up front. He should have worked out a compromise so that he had rights to the baby, also. His deception was going to cost him in her emotional trust and the longer he delayed the higher the stakes.

"Kat, there's something else we need to talk about—"

The doorbell chime cut him off in mid-sentence. Someone had lousy timing.

"It's two o'clock on a Sunday afternoon. Who could this be?" he muttered as he stamped to the door.

"Jehovah's Witnesses?" Kat offered.

Andrew checked the peephole. A couple caught in a sixties' time warp stared back from the other side. "I don't think so."

He opened the massive door, and the woman launched herself at him. "Son!"

Behind him, Kat jumped to her feet. "Mother!"

"IT'S THE NINETIES, not the sixties. New Age, not hippies," Kat explained while squirting cheese from a tube on a cracker. Raising her voice, she called out, "We'll be just a minute, Mom, Vince."

"Take your time, baby. We're just absorbing the karma."

Andrew smirked at the karma comment. "What about these matching love beads for a wedding present?" He fingered the necklace dangling about his neck.

"Crystals. They're crystals, not love beads." Kat

licked a glob of gooey cheese off her finger. "And I think it was a lovely gift."

"I agree. It gives a whole new meaning to wedding crystal." Andrew arranged the bottled seltzer on a tray. "Crystals—the gift that keeps on guiding."

Kat snickered. "Bring your crystal and that seltzer and let's get back out there."

Kat's mother and stepfather were in the den, busy soaking up karma like a pair of New Age sponges. The pair beamed beatifically while Kat and Andrew settled the trays.

"So, dear, we not only wanted to bring you your wedding gift, but we wanted to let you know how your numbers came in."

"What numbers?"

"Why, yours, and Andy's." Marcia laid out a chart, glowing at them like an oracle of good fortune. Vince maintained his meditative pose on the floor.

Kat tugged a still-puzzled Andrew onto the love seat beside her. "Remember, Mom's into numerology."

"Right. My birthday."

"I ran yours and Kat's." Marcia looked up from her charts to shoot them a coy look. "You've got some *very* good numbers together."

"How long have you been involved in the study of numerology, Mrs. Stevens?"

Kat recognized the attorney tone. Andrew was going somewhere with this, she just wasn't sure where.

"Right after Rand and I got a divorce. Too bad it wasn't before we got married. But then I wouldn't have my two wonderful children, so I guess I don't mean that. But I've studied numbers for about twenty-five years. And the numbers don't lie. Mom. Call me Mom. According to the numbers, we're going to be family for a long time, son."

Kat indulged her mother because she loved her, but she figured Marcia would be just as well off interpreting tea leaves. Vince continued to stare off into space. Even for Vince, he was acting weird. "Uh, Mom, is Vince okay?"

Marcia waved an airy hand. "Sure. He took a workshop on trance channeling in California. He's been trying for days."

"Did you run the numbers on Nick?" There was nothing subtle about Andrew's question. Good thing she was already sitting down, because his question floored her.

"Does ginseng have a root? Of course I did. That Nick, he was a bad number. A very bad number. Made me wish the numbers were wrong, but of course they never are."

Kat was shocked. "Mom, you never mentioned it. Are you serious? Nick's numbers came up bad?"

"Some of the worst I've ever seen. I'll tell you, it took some heavy-duty meditation to work through that."

"Why didn't you warn her?" Andrew's question held a hard edge.

Kat wished he'd remember this was a conversation, not a hearing. But it was rather sweet that he seemed so indignant on her behalf.

"Our children don't always make the choices we'd like, and the only true recourse is to accept them graciously and be prepared to stand by them when the bottom drops out. If I'd told Kat she'd picked a bad number in Nick, do you really think it would have swayed her decision to marry him?"

Two pair of eyes pinned her for an answer. Kat remembered her desperate resolve at twenty-one to live up to everyone's expectations. She'd also fancied herself in love. Her answer came swift and sure. "Absolutely not."

Something flickered in Andrew's eyes at her response before he resumed his cool demeanor.

"That's what I thought. My headstrong little girl

would've told me to find some tea leaves to read and gone about her merry business.''

A guilty flush climbed up Kat's neck.

Marcia winked at her knowingly before turning her attention to Andrew. ''One day when you're a parent you'll know what I mean. You'll go through the same thing with your kids.''

Kat mentally noted the reference to kids. Emphasis on the *s*. Plural. As in more than one.

''Kids?'' Andrew's stunned voice echoed her reaction.

Marcia beamed. ''Kids. I don't want to take the surprise out of it, but it was in the numbers. And it doesn't matter a whit to me that big families are out of vogue these days.''

Kat couldn't stop the thrill her mother's words brought. She'd always wanted her own little brood. That's why having this one was so important. She couldn't imagine her life without a child. Somewhere along the way she'd tripped herself up and now she couldn't imagine herself without *Andrew's* child.

His eyes met hers. Behind his dubiousness lay a spark of tender excitement.

''YOU'RE SURE YOU don't mind if they stay the night,'' Kat asked as she helped Andrew scout out blankets and pillows.

''I don't mind them staying over. It's just not clear to me why they can't avail themselves of a guest room.'' Kat's mother and stepfather were entertaining and charming but pushing the weird side. And how the hell could he talk to her about his clause in their contract if he had in-laws bunking down with them? Not that he was looking for an excuse to put off an explosive topic.

''I know. But when Mother decides the karma's good in a room, there's no changing her mind.'' She opened the laundry room door. ''How about in here?''

Andrew quirked a wry smile. "I guess good karma's hard to find these days."

Kat laughed, an undercurrent of sexuality sparkling in her eyes. Andrew tucked away a mental note card—his wife found humor arousing. Maybe they'd spend next weekend in bed watching the comedy channel.

They both squeezed into the confines of the laundry area. Kat's hip brushed against his thigh, throwing his body and imagination into overdrive. He came up with a new use for the ironing board mounted on the wall. What the hell was wrong with him? He didn't even have an imagination. And if he did have one, it'd never encompassed ironing boards.

Kat explored a row of narrow shelves. "Bingo!"

Laughing over her shoulder at him, Kat bent forward to select a pillowcase from the bottom shelf. Andrew's erection swelled further. He framed her delectable derriere with his hands and pulled her backward, until her soft curves met his jutting angles. She wriggled against him. Not in protest, but enticingly. Still pressing against her from behind, in blunt, straightforward terms he outlined his plans for her, him and the ironing board.

Kat's breath came in ragged, short gasps as she arched her back, much like a cat soliciting attention. He slipped a finger past the leg of her shorts and the elastic of her panties to find her soft woman's folds. Moist heat slicked his finger and he slid in another one.

With his fingers, he fondled and rubbed against her core. She mewled softly and thrust herself against him. Andrew thought he might explode from her unrestrained response. At that point, bringing her pleasure seemed the most important and natural thing.

Bending his head, he traced the shell of her ear while his fingers plumbed her. He shared with her in a low growl how much he enjoyed touching her. His hardness nestled against her soft bottom told its own story.

He felt the magic tension coiling tighter and tighter

within her as he stroked against her core until she exploded, drenching his fingers with her nectar.

When her shudders subsided he turned her around to face him, bracing her between his thighs. She slumped against him as he pressed kisses into her rioting curls. He ached to sink himself into her honey-drenched warmth.

"What planet is this?" she murmured huskily. "No wonder Claudine was so uptight when you married me."

Exuberant at her obvious pleasure, he tilted her head back to meet her dazed expression. "Claudia." He sobered. "And it's never been this way with anyone else. Only you." And he knew it never would with anyone else.

A lazy, dreamy smile lit her generous mouth at his assertion, but it was quickly followed by a stricken look. She reached between them to touch his unrelieved tension. "Oh, no. What about you?"

Andrew gritted his teeth and removed her well-intended hand. "Just get your mother and Vince settled as quickly as possible. Tell them I got an important phone call."

"Andrew, the phone hasn't rung." The little minx shot him a cheeky grin as she seemed to regain her equilibrium. "I'll tell them you had an important call to make."

Leaving him where he was, she scooped up the linens and made for the door. She leaned forward and brushed her full mouth against his, her tongue foraging swiftly. "Meet me in our room in ten minutes. And where's that underwear Bitsy gave us?"

And then she was gone.

Ten minutes to more ecstasy.

"THAT GIRL IS MAKING a goddamned spectacle of all of us. Get rid of her." A.W.'s order filled Andrew with a cold fury. Nonetheless, he leaned back in the leather club chair with an air of nonchalance. His Monday morning meeting regarding his partnership was off to a less-than-stellar start.

"That's my wife you're talking about. Not a piece of furniture you object to." He stared his father down across the massive desk.

"Not much of a difference really. Think of wives as accessories, like a membership in a good golf club. They enhance who you are—show the world what you're made of. Why the hell do you think I spend so much money on keeping your mother looking good?"

His father's philosophy was nothing new to him, but suddenly he found himself sickened by the attitude.

"I love her." What should have been an act came out as the gut-wrenching truth. Inwardly he reeled at the impact of the revelation.

A.W. smiled condescendingly. "Andrew, my boy, you're thinking with that head between your legs, and it never makes good business decisions. You're like me, son. You were born to practice law. You love it just like you love the power and prestige that goes with it."

His father's words struck a chord. He did love his work and everything that came with it. Since he'd been a small child, it had defined him. His adolescent fantasy had been his name on that brass plate downstairs. With desperation, he held on to his feelings for Kat. "Don't talk about my wife that way. I love her."

A.W. dismissed his assertion with a wave of his hand, as if it were a pesky gnat. "Infatuation. It'll pass. But this firm's been here for ninety years. It's your heritage—it's in your blood."

"I don't want to talk about Kat anymore. I want to talk about my partnership."

"Ah, but the two are intertwined."

"You wanted me married. I am. Now announce my partnership."

A.W. stood and paced behind his desk, his hands

clasped in back of him. "I'd like to. I really would. There's just one problem." He stopped pacing and faced Andrew. "You made a bad choice."

"What are you talking about?"

"You joined the wrong country club, son. You bought a suit off the rack when you should've had one custom-made." His eyes were flat and cold despite his jovial tone.

Andrew quelled his instinct to knock the supercilious look off his father's face. "You've gone too far. You've always been manipulative, but I never expected you to be a cheat."

"Drexall and Altman want you off their account. Let's see, Ben Altman's exact words were, 'After that showing on Saturday evening, I don't trust his judgment.'" A.W. resumed his seat.

Andrew enunciated in brief, very impolite terms what Ben Altman could do.

"Ben would probably like that, but I'm afraid it's physically impossible. What *you* need to do is very quietly, very quickly, get a divorce. You made a mistake, recognized it and took care of it. We'll announce your partnership when the divorce papers are signed."

Andrew paced to stand before the bookcase lining one wall. He stared at the leather-bound tomes with blind eyes. He didn't care for A.W.'s power plays, but all things considered, wasn't his father merely bumping up the time-line he and Kat had privately set? "And if I don't divorce her?"

"Well, I fear I'd have to say I don't think you have the sound judgment to be a partner in this firm."

Andrew turned to face him. "You manipulative bastard."

"You're upset now, but you'll thank me one day. This is for your own good. Trust me, son, I know you better than you know yourself. You *think* you love her, but I *know* you love this firm. You've got a week to decide which one is more important. I know you'll make the right decision.''

Andrew wanted to tell him to go to hell then and there, but he couldn't. God help him but he didn't trust his feelings for Kat enough. He couldn't throw away the partnership he'd courted for so long. Instead he walked silently out of the polished mahogany door.

The intercom on the secretary's desk buzzed. A.W.'s disembodied voice filled the room. ''Sheila, put Andrew on my schedule for next Monday at the same time. And go ahead and begin the renovation on the office next to mine.''

KAT JUMPED TO HER FEET when she sighted her brother heading toward her table at Mama Leone's and toed the shopping bag further under the table. Jackie definitely didn't need to know about the stock of edible underwear she'd purchased earlier. Andrew, it seemed, was very fond of cherries.

They exchanged a brief hug.

''I'm glad you could make lunch today. How was the christening?'' she asked.

''It was fine. The little guy's cute. How was the soiree? What'd I miss?'' quizzed Jackson.

Kat relayed an abbreviated version but still included the fish eggs sliding between Claudia's cleavage. She and Jackson shared a conspiratorial smile. ''You're hell at a party, aren't you, sis?''

Pulling apart a garlic roll, Kat shrugged as she popped a piece into her mouth. ''I'm a weird magnet. I think it's something to do with my natural force field.''

''Careful, Kat girl, you're starting to sound like Mom.''

''Speaking of the weekend, she and Vince stopped by last night.''

''And?''

''Just the usual. His 'n' her crystal pendants as a wedding gift. Our numbers update. They spent the night on the sofa because they were so enchanted with the karma there.''

''I'm sure Andrew thinks he's surrounded by loonies.''

''Undoubtedly.'' She grinned foolishly. She felt like singing. ''I think he likes it.''

Jackson sliced her with his best interrogating-attorney look.

Kat continued. ''I made a big mistake with Andrew. No, not that kind of mistake. He's just not what I thought he'd be. Beneath that cool, starched shirt, he's warm and caring and considerate. What am I going to do?''

''Exactly what are you saying?''

''This just sucks, but I think I'm in love. I've been listening to my behavior tapes several times a day now and it's just not helping.''

''Have you mentioned this to Andrew? Maybe he feels the same way.''

''No. I know he cares about me, but that's not the same thing as love. And I don't want him to feel obligated to keep a wife and child he doesn't want.''

''Kat girl, maybe I'm not the sharpest knife in the drawer, but he did marry you, and it was specifically so you could make a baby.''

''Exactly. Making a baby and keeping a baby—there's just a tad of a difference between the two. Remember the contract you helped draft? Both Andrew and I were so up-front about everything up until now. I feel I'm not holding up my end of the bargain. I feel deceitful.''

''Are you pregnant?''

''Too soon to tell.''

Jackson passed a weary hand over his eyes. ''Perhaps he's not as eager to give up this child as you think.''

"What makes you say that?" It wasn't as if Andrew and Jackson were confidants.

"Just talk to Andrew about it." Guilt washed his face.

Suspicion unfurled and spread through her. "No, I think you and I will talk right now."

"What the hell. I knew this day would come, I just thought it'd be a lot later than sooner."

Kat had the same queasiness in the pit of her stomach coupled with calm dread that she'd experienced when the FBI had raided her home looking for Nick.

"Spit it out, Jackson."

"There's a clause in your contract that gives Andrew the right to name the baby as his heir. You know how Andrew feels about family heritage. I thought it was in your and the baby's best interest."

Betrayal slapped her in the face.

"Are men genetically incapable of trustworthiness? Or have I just managed to surround myself with jerks? Since you obviously have all the answers, maybe you can tell me."

"Kat—"

"It doesn't matter." She yanked money out of her purse and threw it on the table. "I've lost my appetite."

She jumped up, cutting him off. If she could just reach the sanctuary of her car before the threatening tears flooded.

"Kat, let's talk about this—" Jackson trailed her out of the restaurant.

"I don't want to talk to you, Jackson. Not for a long time." She threw off his restraining hand. "But I can't wait to get my hands on that low-down, conniving, back-stabbing husband of mine."

She slammed the door and threw the car into reverse. Jackson jumped out of the way.

Andrew, the vegetarian, would be dead meat when she got through with him.

ANDREW TURNED INTO his driveway. After his meeting with A.W., he'd instructed Gloria to clear his calendar for the rest of the day. A drive out to the beach house and miles of walking the shoreline of the gray Atlantic hadn't come close to clearing his head.

Logically, there should be no choice. He either went with a lifelong goal—his heritage—or a woman he'd known for the span of less than a month.

He parked Gertrude in the garage—hell, he was even calling his car by that ridiculous name these days—and noticed Kat's station wagon packed with boxes. Probably that summer art program she'd been planning.

He let himself into the house. Something felt different. His in-laws had left. Perhaps that accounted for the odd atmosphere he sensed.

He started down the tiled hallway, loosening his tie, and called out, "Kat?"

A noise in the den caught his attention. Sheer instinct guided him to duck to the right as something flew past his head. Glass crashed against the wall behind him. "What the...?"

Another Waterford tumbler sailed past his head. Thank God she had terrible aim.

"Kat? What's wrong?"

She looked like absolute hell. Her eyes were red and swollen, and she could have doubled for Rudolph in a Christmas play. She'd either indulged in a crying jag or developed a severe allergy.

"You double-crossing, belly-crawling snake." His allergy theory flew past with another piece of crystal.

"Can you stop throwing glass long enough to talk?" Surely today would go down in his personal history as the worst day of his life.

"Talk? You want to talk?" Kat stalked around him like a prizefighter biding time on a punch. "That would be an exercise in futility, considering I can't believe a word that comes out of your mouth."

Andrew slumped onto the sofa, tasting bitter regret. His day of reckoning had arrived. How she'd found out didn't matter. "The contract. I'm sorry, Kat. I wanted to talk to you about it. I'd planned to last night."

Stubborn hurt etched her face as she sneered, "How convenient my mother and stepfather dropped in. But what about before? I trusted you. I thought if there was one thing this ridiculous marriage had going for it, it was that we'd been totally honest with each other. I can't believe that, once again, I've allowed myself to be played for a fool."

"It was never my intent to play you for a fool. I'm sorry. And I don't think our marriage is ridiculous. We can work through this."

"There's nothing to work through. And don't worry, I know you're still waiting on your partnership. I'll uphold my end of the bargain until it comes through. We should know within a week whether I'm pregnant. If I am, I'll fight you on that contract. If not, well…that's the end of that."

"Where are you going?"

"I'm not sure yet. And it's really none of your business."

Desperation swelled at the thought of not knowing where she was or how to get in touch with her. She was already so angry with him, he'd go one step further if it meant keeping her nearby. "Go to the beach house." As her mouth opened in sure protest, he continued, "It's hardly ever used. At least I can tell everyone you wanted to spend the week at the beach instead of that you left me. Don't forget your end of the bargain on my partnership." *And you may very well be carrying our child.* Her lips tightened, but she didn't throw anything else, thank God.

"Okay. But I don't want to see you."

"I won't bother you there."

"That doesn't mean squat. I just found out today how much your word can be trusted."

Andrew didn't try to defend himself. He could try to build a case for his deception, but there was no way around it. Motive aside, he had deceived her. He took the beach-house key off his key ring and placed it on the coffee table.

"The freezer's fairly well stocked, but you'll need to pick up some fresh things." He squared his shoulders against the onslaught of loneliness that her leaving would precipitate. Hadn't this been inevitable from the start? When had he begun to hope that it might be different? "Do you need any help with loading anything in your car?"

"No. I'll send for the big stuff in a few weeks. I'll clean up the glass and then I'm gone."

"Don't worry about it. I'll clean it up." He felt so goddamned guilty about her red swollen eyes he'd walk barefoot through the pieces if it would atone for his deception.

"Okay." She scooped Toto up from his perch on the love seat and swept past Andrew.

"Kat."

She slowly faced him, bitter hurt behind the anger sparking her eyes.

"Take care of yourself."

Without a word she turned and walked out of the room. Moments later, he heard the door slam.

Had she just walked out of his life as well?

10

STUPID. STUPID. STUPID.

Kat loaded a mass of peanut butter onto a slice of whole wheat bread and slapped it on another piece laden with jelly. She bit into the sandwich and stared out the window at the waves beating against the shore. Life was at a low ebb when a PBJ brought no joy.

Who was she kidding? All the flipping misery and public humiliation meted out by Nick's embezzlement and defection had been child's play compared to finding out she couldn't trust Andrew.

And then to turn around and agree to spend a week at the beach house—of all the idiotic things to do. Everywhere she looked, memories assaulted her. She'd proposed to Andrew in this very room. She'd been hiding behind that oleander when he'd sneaked up on her and she'd flipped him. She'd had such high hopes then.

The doorbell interrupted her morose reverie. Dropping her sandwich onto the counter, she marched to the front door. All she'd asked for was a little time. Couldn't he even respect that wish?

"Go away," she shouted without opening the front door.

"Please let me in, Kat." Even though the door muffled Bitsy's voice, her distress came through clearly.

Kat sagged against the door in relief. She hadn't realized just how much she really needed someone to talk to until she heard Bitsy. But Bitsy was no longer just a friend. She was still a sister-in-law. Had she known about the clause in the contract?

Turning the lock, she slowly opened the door. Bitsy wasted no time bulldozing in and wrapping her in a huge hug.

"Oh, sweetie, I'm so sorry."

Kat pulled back and posed the question that begged asking. "Did you know?"

Bitsy's lips formed a straight line. "Not until about an hour ago."

Kat shut the door. Of unspoken accord they moved into the den.

"Andrew called you?"

"I don't think he would've except—" Bitsy pulled a wrapped object out of her purse "—he was adamant you needed this tonight."

Curiosity overcame pride. Kat unfolded the toilet paper to reveal her night-light. "I forgot it when I left." Tears spilled over. Why'd he have to be so damned nice and thoughtful? Why couldn't he just leave her to wallow in her anger over his lie?

Bitsy gaped at the pink plastic. "He came clean with me and then forced me over here for a night-light?"

"I don't like the dark." Kat dashed away her tears and blew her nose on the crumpled toilet paper.

Bitsy fell to the couch as if it was too much for her to stand up. "What am I going to do with the two of you?"

"Bitsy, you can't imagine how it felt to once again find out that my husband had a little secret he'd been keeping from me. And, once again, I was the last to know."

"You're right. I don't understand what it feels like to be deceived by my husband. But what I *do* understand is this thing with Andrew is not the same thing as Nick."

Kat wrapped her arms around her middle and leaned her head against the window frame. "It feels the same.

And he knew, Bits. He knew it was the one point I was adamant about.''

"I'm not saying I agree with the way he did it, but I can't say that I disagree with the underlying principle. Andrew will make a terrific dad. I've always known that, but I'd about given up on it ever happening.''

Kat silently agreed he had some pretty powerful father potential as she turned to face Bitsy. "Maybe. But I wasn't looking for a stick-around dad or husband. You know—The Plan.''

Bitsy's eyes narrowed. "Maybe your plan needed a little tweaking.''

"Oh, the plan was fine. I just picked the wrong man.''

Bitsy humphed inelegantly. "And I say you did a fine job picking.

"You would. He's your brother.''

"Nothing to do with it. He's yin to your yang or whichever way it goes. You two need each other and it doesn't have anything to do with partnerships or babies." Bitsy pushed back a strand of blond hair and queried with an arch look, "Or are babies already an issue?''

Kat remembered their weekend activities and felt the slow heat crawl up her face. "It's a possibility." She couldn't stop her hand reflexively rubbing over her stomach.

Bitsy resembled the proverbial cat munching a canary. "Mmm-hmm.''

"We did have an agreement, you know.''

"Oh, okay. So it was all cool and detached. A business agreement fulfilled.''

She didn't have to close her eyes to picture Andrew's sweat-slicked body merging with hers in the garden. They'd been fulfilled all right, but there'd been nothing cool or detached about it. A wet warmth pervaded her just thinking about it. "Bitsy, I absolutely am not discussing my sex life with you.''

"Did I ask you to? Sweetie, I can't tell you how thrilled I am to know you have one finally. What are you gonna do if there's a little bun in the oven?"

The beginnings of a headache nudged her, and she massaged her temples. "I don't know. I could drag Andrew to court to fight the clause in the contract, but neither one of us wants or needs the publicity."

"And that's the only reason?" Bitsy certainly knew how to press an issue.

"And I...care about him. I'll stay until he gets his partnership. I know it means everything to him."

"It used to. I'm not so sure anymore." Bitsy scooted off the couch and stood. "I've got to pick up Juliana. Call me if you want to talk. And take care of yourself. You may have my niece or nephew in your Easy Bake oven there."

Despite herself, Kat smiled at Bitsy's nonsense as she followed her to the door. Kat hugged her. She'd needed a sounding board. Although she still felt terrible, at least she had vented.

"Thanks for listening. I'll call you later in the week."

"Anytime."

Halfway to her car, Bitsy turned around. "Oh, I forgot to tell you. When I went by to pick up the night-light, Andrew was watering your plants."

Hell's bells. He was nurturing those plants. He really knew how to kick a girl when she was down.

KAT AWOKE from a not-so-sound sleep to a pounding on the door. The numbers on the clock read 11:30 p.m.

"Come on, Kat. Let me in. Ya gotta talk to me." Her mystery guest was no longer a mystery.

She padded to the door without turning on any lights. "Go away, Andrew. It's late."

"I hafn't talked to you in five days and three'n half hours. C'mon, honey."

Kat's astonishment that he'd been counting the

days—and hours, apparently—was quickly followed by the realization that Andrew's usual precise diction registered less than precise. Downright slurred, in fact.

"Have you been drinking?" She'd never even seen him tipsy. Not in any of the two and a half weeks she'd been married to him.

"Jus' a few beers with Eddie. He tol' me to talk to you."

"Go home and go to bed. I'll talk to you tomorrow." And *tomorrow* Eddie just might face castration.

"Uh-uh. It's misable there without you. I need you."

Kat pulled her humiliation at his betrayal around her like a suit of armor.

"You need me for your partnership. Go home."

She nearly jumped out of her skin when he began belting out "You Are the Sunshine of My Life" in an off-key tenor.

Oh my God. Her straitlaced, *Wall Street Journal* reading husband stood drunk, and butchering good Stevie Wonder lyrics at the top of his voice.

Kat jerked open the door. "Shut up—"

Flashing blue lights racing down the road stopped her mid-sentence. Unfazed, unaware, uncaring—she wasn't sure which one, perhaps all three— Andrew didn't miss a beat.

Horrified, Kat watched the police cruiser pull into the driveway behind a waiting taxi. A burly officer jumped out and rushed toward them, his weapon readied. Andrew finally seemed to figure out he wasn't at a Kmart special and turned to investigate the flashing blue lights.

"Wha' the…?"

"Freeze, mister. Ma'am, are you okay?" The cop barked.

"Fine. I'm fine. Why are you here?" The revolver trained on Andrew froze Kat in her tracks.

Unfortunately, it didn't have the same effect on her

inebriated husband. He took a step toward the man in blue. "Yeah, wha's the problem, Officer?"

"You seem to be, buddy. One of your neighbors called about a possible burglary in process." The cop waved his gun toward the patrol car. "Spread 'em over there."

Andrew shambled toward the car, a grin splitting his face. "If it's a strip search, could I request *her,* Officer? She's ma wife, ya know. And I haven't seen her in five day and three and something hours." The glare of the headlights illuminated his skewed grin. "And she's wearing my favorite nightie."

Kat tugged self-consciously at the hem of the lime-green T-shirt.

"Buddy, in case you ain't noticed, I'm not Dear Abby, and your ass is about to be arrested if you don't spread-eagle against that car pronto."

Toto chose that moment to dash from the house and run gleeful circles around Andrew. Kat lunged after him. "No, Toto, no. Bad dog."

Andrew, unsteady on his feet, lurched against the officer and landed on top of him. In a moment of joyous reunion, Toto celebrated in his favorite manner, lifting his leg on both Andrew and the outraged officer.

Quick as a flash the policeman slapped a pair of handcuffs on Andrew and yanked him to his feet.

Andrew seemed much more interested in Toto than his new steel bracelets. "At least you've missed me, hafn't ya, little guy?"

Someone had to look out for Andrew, because he was doing a very poor job of it right now. Kat grabbed at the officer's arm. "Wait a minute."

"This is none of your concern now, ma'am." The burly cop shrugged her off, opened his back door and bundled Andrew inside. "Buddy, you're under arrest for obstruction of justice. You have the right to remain silent...."

ANDREW SAT ON A HARD BENCH in a holding cell and tried to block out the surrounding chaos. How the devil long could it possibly take for Eddie to raise bail and get him out of here? Nothing quite like being arrested to sober up a man. Fast. He and his arresting officer wouldn't be getting together for a game of racquetball anytime soon.

"Okay, buddy, let's go."

Andrew glanced up in inquiry.

A skinny young man in uniform smirked at him. "Yeah, you. Your fairy godfather just arrived. Better hurry before he leaves without you."

Andrew rose to his feet, ignoring the wiseass comment. He'd leave with a whole new perspective of the men in blue.

Eddie waited for him in the processing area, trying to swallow a grin.

"Don't say a word until we're out of here," snapped Andrew.

"Okay. And you're welcome that I got out of bed and came down here at three o'clock in the morning to haul you out of the tank."

"Thank you. Now shut up."

"Why don't you take it outside, fellows—unless you just happen to like it here?" Sergeant Smartmouth suggested.

Andrew withheld comment until he and Eddie were out of the station and in Eddie's car.

In the close confines of his sedan, Eddie wrinkled his nose. "Jeez, you stink. Did you sit too close to a drunk or what?"

"No, *buddy*." That was a new name he'd learned to loathe this evening. "You're smelling genuine dog urine. After Toto helped me body-tackle the policeman, he relieved himself on both of us."

From the driver's seat, Eddie made a choking sound. Andrew showed remarkable restraint in not finishing the job for him. He hated to render his only sister a widow and his niece fatherless.

Suddenly, bone weary, he laid his head on the back of the seat. "Edward, my life is out of control. My life has never been out of control. In the past three weeks I've been photographed publicly groping a woman, gotten married, had my eye blackened, had a room of three hundred think they heard me having sex with my wife, had my wife toss crystal at me like I was target practice before she left me, been double-crossed by my father, peed on by a dog twice and now arrested." He didn't throw in *and fallen in love.* It was too illogical for him to accept. "And do you know what I've done every night since Kat left?"

Eddie held up a hand to stop him. "I'd rather not know if you've been seeing Mary Thumb and her four sisters."

Andrew shook his head. He'd resorted to several cold showers but not that. Not yet anyway. *That* couldn't begin to compare to his memories of the taste, feel and smell of his wife that were driving him mad. "Oh, no. I go home after work every night and water her damn flowers."

"Congratulations!" Eddie blew the car horn for good measure.

"What?"

"Congratulations on joining the real world."

"Pull over."

"Why?"

"You must be tipsy, and I'm not riding with anyone who's been drinking."

"Um, I think that'd be you. When I told you earlier tonight—or I guess last night now—to talk to Kat, I didn't mean right then. But think about it. You've lived more since you met Kat than you have in your entire lifetime. And you just wait until the baby comes."

Andrew recognized the truth when he heard it. But

that didn't mean that he had to like it or accept it. He countered, as much out of habit as conviction, "The law has always been my first love."

Eddie pulled up in front of Andrew's house. "That's a load of bull! Sometimes I can't believe you managed to graduate summa cum dummy from Harvard. The law is the law, whether you're practicing at Winthrop, Fullford, and Winthrop or Lawyers 'R' Us. But you know what? There's only one Kat Winthrop, and I believe they broke the mold with her." Eddie reached across Andrew and opened his door. "Now get the hell out of my car, and try not to get arrested in the next twelve hours. I need my beauty sleep."

11

KAT BURIED HER HEAD underneath her pillow and willed the pounding to go away. Another minute and she realized it wasn't her head. Reluctantly, she pulled herself out of bed. Pushing her hair out of her eyes, she shrieked at the face pressed against the bedroom window. Her mother appeared unrepentant as she motioned for Kat to let her in the front door.

Kat made the increasingly familiar trek from bedroom to front door. She'd come to the beach house seeking solitude. This was more like Grand Central Station. At Thanksgiving. Maybe even Christmas. She opened the door.

"I knocked and knocked, and when you didn't answer, I thought maybe you were dead or something, so that's why I was looking in through the windows." Her mother sailed past her, backed up and gave her a quick hug. "I'm glad you're not."

Kat hadn't gotten back to sleep until Eddie had phoned her on his cell phone, assuring her that Andrew was home and the charge would be dropped. Sleep-and caffeine-deprivation scrambled her mother's rambles. "Huh?"

"Dead. I'm glad you're not dead, dear."

Kat headed for the kitchen, or more specifically, the coffeemaker and hit the red On button. "Thanks. I consider that a bonus this morning."

She opened a package of Fig Newtons and offered one to her mother. With practiced ease, Kat managed to fill two coffee mugs and replace the glass carafe under the streaming liquid with barely a spill.

Her mother gestured to a behavior modification tape. "What's that?"

Desperate, she now listened to several a day. "My new best friend." Was that a problem when you became excessive with your moderation tape? She was too tired to think about it.

Joining her mother at the table, Kat sipped the hot, strong brew. "Aah, nectar of the gods. Would you like to tell me why you're here, Mother?"

"Jackson spilled your beans, dear."

"I'm already not speaking to him for the rest of this life. He just screwed up the next one as well." Kat paced to the deck door and back. "Can you request a particular reincarnation? I'd like to be a bulldog with rabies just so I can bite Jackson in the ass." And she was only partially teasing. The idea held great appeal.

"That's blasphemous. I think." Without blinking an eye, her mother picked up Kat's coffee cup and emptied it down the sink. "Anyway, he did what he thought was right."

Kat's mouth gaped open at her empty cup. "Why'd you do that?"

"You've got to lay off the high-test if you're pregnant." Her mother opened the refrigerator, filled Kat's coffee cup to the brim with milk and placed it on the table. "Now that's just what our little zygote needs."

Kat shrugged in resignation. Sometimes Mother did know best. *Would her little zygote think the same one day?*

"Kat, since you were a teenager I've tried not to meddle in your life. And maybe that's been a mistake on my part. For years, I've felt guilty that I didn't try to do anything about Nick. I knew he was wrong for you. And sure enough he wound up hurting you."

"Mom, you couldn't have changed anything."

"Maybe not, but we'll never know. But this time I'm not going to stand by and say nothing while you make another mistake."

Kat dunked a fig cookie into her milk. "Mom, I know Andrew's a mistake. That's why I'm here."

"Andrew's not a mistake. That's why *I'm* here."

"If Jackson spilled all my beans, then you know he, Andrew and Eddie deliberately deceived me. I need a straight answer, Mom. Are men genetically incapable of the truth? Or is there a sign on my back that says Fool— Play Me?" Tears threatened to spill over. Kat yanked herself up by her Fig Newtons. She'd never been the weepy sort. She'd made it through her Nick fiasco without shedding a tear.

Her mother gentled a strand of hair behind her ear, much like she'd done when Kat was a small child. "It felt like the thing with Nick, didn't it?"

Kat nodded, managing a single word. "Worse." Anything more and her waterworks would start up. No need to ruin a perfectly good breakfast of milk and cookies with salty tears.

"I think Andrew's taking the heat for Nick, too."

Kat opened her mouth to protest and shoved a cookie in instead.

"You came home one day and Nick was simply gone. You were left with a public and private mess you had to deal with on your own. You never even had the chance to confront him."

How many times had she fantasized about throwing the contents of the china cabinet at Nick's lying face? How much of the Waterford pitched at Andrew had also been intended for Husband Number One?

"Maybe."

"Andrew's not like Nick. Nick used and abused for his financial gain. And, honey, that bad karma's gonna crawl all over him one day."

"I don't care." The words emerged without rancor

and she meant them. She felt the tremendous weight of her anger at Nick slip away, freeing her. Kat jumped up and danced a jig around the table. Nick had been a pimple on the ass of her progress—and he'd been a very big one—but she'd finally let it go.

Her mother's smile echoed her own joy. "I do believe you mean it. Andrew just wants to protect his child. And I don't care about all the contracts in the world, you and that young man love each other. It was plain as day to me and Vince. You and Andrew just need to figure it out."

Her elation over Nick vanished in light of her situation with Andrew. Deflated, she plopped back into her chair. "I have, but I think it's too late. He reads the *Wall Street Journal* and even his blue jeans have creases. But last night I wouldn't open the door and then he started to sing and I didn't know what to do when the police took him away—"

"The police?" Her mother interrupted her babbling with a screech.

Kat gave her mother a rundown of the predawn debacle. "So, now my Harvard-graduated-soon-to-be-prestigious-law-partner husband has a police record. I've made a shamble of things." The last syllable ended in a wail.

"Katrina Anastasia Hamilton Devereaux Winthrop, pull your hormones together. I've always admired your grit. If you wanted something, then, by golly, you went after it. If you want this marriage to work, give it your best shot."

Kat reached for the last fig cookie. "You know I've never mastered that moderation thing." The empty cookie container lent its own silent testimony. The tapes on the table stared at her in silent accusation. "And yes, I want him. To excess. Because that's the way I do things. It's either all or nothing and I can't settle for nothing from him." Despite her bravado, her heart thundered in trepidation. She wouldn't allow herself to even consider the nothing alternative. She'd taken that route this week and it stank.

Her mother tossed the empty cookie wrapper in the garbage with a smile. "That's my girl. I checked before I came over this morning and tomorrow's numbers showed something special."

Kat walked her mother to the door, her brain racing like a runaway locomotive. "I think I'll give my husband today to recover from his jail time and hangover. But tomorrow morning, he won't know what hit him."

Her mother threw out one last piece of advice. "Honey, invest in one of those home pregnancy tests. I believe I'm gonna be a grandma."

ANDREW LEANED AGAINST the stucco wall and aimed the shower of water at the profusion of pots flanking the front door. His reconciliation attempt with Kat last night had wound up an exercise in humiliation. Eddie's words echoed in his brain like a litany. The life he'd had and the future he'd envisioned before Kat no longer meant anything. She'd turned his house into a home. She'd brought him into the land of the living. With gusto. The best sex in his life was mere icing on the cake—although he'd developed quite an affinity for icing.

And if Kat turned out to be pregnant, he'd make the best damn dad any kid could want. Juliana and Toto liked him well enough, and weren't kids and animals supposed to be the best judges of character?

That was all just damn great except for the niggling detail that she wouldn't even talk to him.

He squinted against the afternoon sun as a car turned into his driveway. Claudia. And he'd thought the past twenty-four hours couldn't get any worse. Even if he turned the water hose on himself he wouldn't drown before she got to him. Too bad.

He ignored her as she climbed out of her car and swayed down the walk. "You look like hell."

Aside from trading his dog-marked pants for a pair of shorts, he still had on the previous night's clothes. He hadn't shaved in two days. Nor had he combed his hair today and he knew his eyes were bloodshot. "I look better than I feel. I don't know what you're doing here, but go away, Claudia," he growled in no uncertain terms.

Claudia's practiced pout came into play. "There's no need to be nasty, darling. A.W. told me he thought your, um, circumstances were about to change. Then Mamie Prewitt told me she'd seen *her* out at the beach house all this week. I just wanted to let you know I forgive you for marrying that dreadful woman. I'm ready to stand by you."

Andrew fought to keep his expression neutral. Kat had more going for her in her little finger than Claudia did in her entire phony package. "Just satisfy my curiosity. How much is A.W. paying you?"

"Now darling, don't be that way. He's just concerned about you," she purred. Stepping closer, she trapped his arm in the valley between her silicone mountains. Her eyes narrowed to slitted seduction as her tongue licked suggestively along her lower lip. The perfected moves of a courtesan. "I believe I could satisfy much, much more than your curiosity." She trailed a red nail down his chest to the waistband of his shorts.

The thought of touching or being touched by any woman other than Kat repulsed him. He took a slight step back, eyeing Claudia cagily. She, in turn, took a larger step forward, wrapping her fingers around his arm, a seductive smile stretching her mouth into a red slash.

It cheered him immensely to realize that Kat was the only woman for him. He offered Claudia a genuine smile, deciding her jets needed cooling.

Turning his entire body to face her, the stream from

the water hose caught her square between her jutting hipbones. Her shriek could have woken the dead.

He strove to appear contrite as he redirected the water hose. "Sorry. You just shook me up there, Claudia." That much was true. She didn't have to know she'd revolted him.

He watched with amusement as she strove to contain her anger. A.W. must have really sweetened the kitty. "I suppose I'm flattered I have that effect on you, darling."

If you only knew.

"Perhaps I could come inside and dry off."

Over my dead body. But it wouldn't come to that. Andrew made a slight move with the water. She jumped back like a scalded cat. "Let's not rush anything. I've got a meeting with A.W. in the morning. Why don't you join us. Nine-thirty. His office," he instructed. He planned to get his proverbial house in order before he began his courtship of his wife in earnest.

Premature satisfaction swept away Claudia's annoyance. "I'll be delighted."

If you only knew.

KAT TUCKED THE HOME PREGNANCY stick into her purse and vowed not to look at it again until she reached Andrew's office where they could check it together. The box specified first thing in the morning. Something about concentration of hormones. Exhaustion had claimed her the night before and she'd overslept this morning so concentration shouldn't be a problem.

Odds were that she and Andrew weren't on their merry way to parenthood. She'd always thought she'd magically, mystically feel different when she conceived.

Nothing.

Nada.

Zippolo.

Oddly enough, she felt fine at the prospect of not being pregnant. She still wanted a baby—her and Andrew's child. But it was no longer a mission. Winning Andrew came first.

She tossed a suitcase into Charlemagne. As she opened her door, Toto settled into the passenger seat. Nine o'clock. Half an hour to the esteemed offices of Winthrop, Fullford, and Winthrop. Half an hour until she laid siege to her husband.

"Come on, Toto, we're going home."

ANDREW HUNG UP THE PHONE, satisfied with his conversation with Eddie. A new sense of purpose and determination had claimed him following his arrest. He pressed the intercom connecting him with his secretary.

"Gloria, I'll be leaving for my nine-thirty with A.W. You and I need to meet afterward. See if you can set up a lunch meeting with Joey Chalmers. I'll be out of the office this afternoon. Oh, yeah—and see if you can't find some boxes." He straightened his tie.

One last stab at the intercom.

"Also, have a dozen Waterford crystal tumblers delivered to my beach house before noon." He briefly indulged in a smile before he regrouped. He wouldn't allow himself to think of Kat now. He had to get this meeting over with.

Andrew left his office through the side entrance leading to the partners' hallway. His heritage flanked him. Ornately framed generations of somber, sober Winthrops watched as he made the trek down the long hall. Nodding at his father's secretary, he let himself into A.W.'s office.

His father sat planted behind his desk. Claudia draped herself on the leather sofa lining one wall, an inordinate amount of leg showing.

Andrew stepped forward.

Closed the door behind him.

And embraced his destiny.

"Father. Claudia. I've reached a decision. As you know, the law's always been my first love...."

KAT EYED THE LOBBY of Winthrop, Fullford, and Winthrop with affection. Why, she'd used that very sculpture to stake out Andrew! Toto strained in that direction. Tugging on his leash, she redirected his attention. "Come on, Toto. Let's go see Daddy." She tried out the name for practice. It had a nice ring.

A uniformed guard stepped into her path. "Excuse me, ma'am. The dog's not allowed."

"Dog? What dog?"

The guard's pointed look zeroed in on the leash clasped in her hand.

Kat scooped up Toto in the best interests of the man's pant leg. Covering his canine ears with her hand, she bluffed. "Oh. *This* dog. We don't use that word. He doesn't think he's a *d-o-g*, and it upsets him to no end."

The man eyed her as if she were a nut case. "Oookay. He still can't come in."

Kat didn't want to waste her time arguing with this man. She had a mission. In for a penny, in for a pound. "His grandfather's going to be very disappointed. Perhaps you know him, A.W. Winthrop."

Mr. Lingley—that was the name on the badge—snapped to attention. "Certainly. Mr. Winthrop. He...that is..." The poor man stumbled around the concept of A.W.'s attachment to a dog.

"He just adores him." *If he knew Toto, he would,* Kat justified to herself. She offered Mr. Lingley her most engaging smile.

Moving aside, he pressed the Up button on the elevator. "Sorry to bother you, ma'am. Have a nice day."

She ensconced herself and Toto in the elevator, whisking past the floors of shagging-to-get-their-butts-noticed associates fresh out of law school, to the senior floor. She could care less whether Andrew was a partner, but she knew it meant everything to him. She'd jump through hoops if that's what it took to help him get what he wanted.

She stopped outside the door bearing his name. Not so very different from her father's offices. Was there a code for lawyers specifying two inches of gray carpet and no less than three inches of mahogany millwork? Oops, you're out of business—not enough crown molding? Sucking in a fortifying breath, she forged ahead.

Gloria greeted her from a desk positioned next to a single office door. "What a nice surprise, Mrs. Winthrop! Are you fully recovered from the party?"

Had that only been a little over a week ago? "Yes, thank you. You did a beautiful job organizing everything. Sorry about the spectacle."

Gloria dismissed it with a wave of her hand. "Happens to the best of us." She reached down to scratch behind one of Toto's ears. "You're a cutie."

Kat beamed with something akin to maternal pride. "Is Andrew in?"

"Sorry, dear. He just went into a meeting with Mr. Winthrop. Want to wait here?" She indicated a plump armchair. "I believe he'll be through in half an hour."

It had to be The Meeting concerning his partnership. She could feel it in the pit of her stomach. Or was that the breakfast sandwich she'd scarfed on the way over?

"I'll just wait outside A.W's office."

As if on cue, Bitsy and Eddie waltzed in.

"Hi, Kat. We weren't expecting to find you here."

"I came by to see Andrew."

The couple exchanged smug looks.

"It must be wives' day at the office." Bitsy said, fishing for information.

Kat babbled to cover up her lack of an explanation for being there. "He's in a meeting with your father, so I thought I'd wait in A.W.'s office."

"Come on. We'll take you down there."

As they escorted her down the hall, Eddie questioned, "Was Andrew, um, expecting you this morning?"

What had seemed like a good plan last night and early this morning suddenly lost its appeal. "No. I haven't talked to him since he was...since Saturday night."

Kat couldn't interpret the look passing between Eddie and Bitsy.

"Is something going on that I should know about?" Kat demanded, her suspicions on red alert from all the covert looks.

Bitsy practically shoved her into an elegant waiting room. "Well, here we are."

The secretary seated outside the door peered over half glasses at her in unspoken inquiry.

From behind the closed double doors, a shriek of fury rent the air, followed by a shrill cry. "Andrew, you can't do this to me."

The hair rose on the nape of Kat's neck. She recognized that shriek and that shrill. What the hell was Claudine doing in A.W.'s office with her husband?

She lit out for the door, intent on gaining entry.

The secretary jumped to her feet. "Mr. Winthrop's in a meeting, madam. And he's not to be disturbed."

Kat paused with her hand on the door handle. "Watch me."

She wrenched open the door just as Andrew's words rang loud and clear.

"I have no intention of divorcing my wife to gain a partnership."

ANDREW TURNED, annoyed at the interruption. He watched in amazement as Kat and Toto barged forward, shrugging off his father's secretary, with Bitsy and Eddie in tow.

All hell broke loose as everyone spoke at once.

"Kat, you're here. And Toto, too. I've missed you." God, but she was beautiful.

"What the hell are all of you doing here? Why is there a dog in my office?" A.W. appeared apoplectic.

"I tried to stop her, sir." The secretary wailed.

"Hi, Dad." Bitsy smiled cheekily.

"We found her in your office," Eddie offered to Andrew.

"I wish I could say it was nice to see you again, Claudette."

"Claudia." The entire room chorused the correction.

Mayhem threatened to escalate. Andrew executed an ear-splitting whistle, effectively silencing the roar.

"Kat, I wanted to clear this up before I talked to you, but I'm glad you're here now."

"What do you mean you're not divorcing me for the partnership? You were supposed to marry me for the partnership!"

"This is a damn fool decision, Andrew. The door won't be open when you come crawling back," A.W. threatened with a heavy scowl.

"And I won't wait forever," Claudia chimed in.

"Count your blessings," Kat muttered in A.W. and Claudia's general direction.

"You go, girl," Bitsy cheered Kat from the doorway.

Kat turned her piercing azure eyes to him. The hurt he'd read in her gaze the last time he'd faced her had been replaced with tenderness and something he dared not name. The rest of the room faded to nothingness.

"What's going on, Andrew?"

She befuddled his senses. He couldn't think clearly. He ran the fingers of one hand over her shoulder. "You wore my favorite shirt."

Kat plucked at the lime green T-shirt. "Just for you."

"My God, that thing is hideous," Claudia opined.

Kat and Andrew turned to her with amused smiles. "We know," they acknowledged in sync.

"A.W. gave me a choice—you or the partnership."

"But…"

"You're a mistake, girl. I wanted to help him figure it out sooner than later." A.W. sneered.

"Let me remind you, you're speaking to my wife." Andrew's jaw ached with the effort to remain civil.

"You conniving old poop," Kat sputtered at A.W.

Lucky for "the old poop" there was no glassware handy. Kat looked mad enough to exercise her pitching arm. Andrew shifted slightly, putting himself between his outraged wife and the brandy decanter.

Ignoring Kat, A.W. looked at his son and scoffed, "Might I remind you, you're unemployed?"

"Correction. Self-employed. As of my resignation, I'm in partnership with Eddie. We're having lunch with a realtor to finalize an office location."

In the periphery of his mind he registered Bitsy, Eddie and A.W., all talking at once. Although he answered A.W.'s assertion, his gaze never shifted from Kat. He watched the delight chase incredulity across her face.

"You gave up your partnership for me?"

He hadn't exactly planned on an audience, but what the heck. He felt like shouting it from the rooftop. Cupping her face in his hands, his thumbs caressed the freckles gracing her cheekbones. "I love you, Kat. Nothing else in my life compares to what I feel for you."

His heart thundered in slow motion as he awaited her response.

A smile lit her face like a bright sun peering through a dark cloud. "You know I'm a woman of excess," she warned. "I either eat the entire pan of brownies or I don't touch them." Her gaze devoured him.

"I'm counting on it."

"I love you. To distraction."

"I think I'm going to be sick," Claudia snapped.

Bitsy, Eddie and the secretary played the part of the Greek chorus. "Shut up, Claudia."

"Speaking of sick…" Kat began.

Once upon a time, following her train of thought had been scary. Now he just enjoyed the ride.

"Have you been? Are you?" Was he on his way to being a dad, as well as a husband?

"I took a test this morning. But I wanted to wait until I was with you to check the result." She shifted Toto to one side and turned her purse toward him. "It's in there. Looks sort of like a thermometer."

Andrew rummaged through what amounted to a small suitcase with an unsteady hand. "That's it."

He slowly pulled out the cylindrical stick and took the cap off. His hand shook like a leaf in a storm as he showed the window to Kat. "What does that mean?" He could barely speak as the blood thundered through his head.

"I don't remember. Pull out the instruction box."

He snatched the box and matched the stick to the back. A roaring filled his ears. "We're going to have a baby! I'm going to be a daaaad...."

Stunned, Kat stared at her stuffy attorney husband stretched out in a dead faint.

Claudia sprang from the couch. "I know CPR."

"Touch him and you die," Kat challenged.

Toto took advantage of her lax hold to leap from Kat's arms. Barking like a maniacal bundle of fur, he charged at Claudia.

Kat dropped to her knees and put her ear next to Andrew's mouth to check for breathing—just in time to catch a faceful of ice water tossed by the efficient secretary.

Revived by the cold water, Andrew jackknifed up, catching Kat in the eye with his head. Kat clutched at her eye. "I think you just paid me back for that black eye," she moaned, half laughing, as she clutched at the injury.

With her one good eye, Kat watched Claudia jump up

onto the sofa to escape the marauding Toto. "Get this mutt away from me!"

With exquisite timing, Toto performed his well-rehearsed trick. Outrage distorted Claudia's perfect features as she climbed down from the couch. "I hope I never lay eyes on any of you again." Claudia stamped out with damp indignity.

A.W. growled from his leather chair. "She's going to make your life a three-ring circus."

Kat basked in Andrew's boyish grin. "I'm counting on it. For a lifetime."

She pulled a moderation tape out of her purse, tossing it over her shoulder. "Andrew in excess." She'd never known such complete joy. "Now that has a nice ring to it."

Epilogue

"Breathe. Breathe. Breathe. Okay, baby, relax. Catch your breath." Andrew coached Kat as she labored in the birthing room.

A jumble of emotions assaulted him. Excitement. Tension. Delight. Awe. Nausea.

They were about to become parents! Kat knew the sex. He'd opted for the surprise element.

He stroked Kat's hand, desperately trying to remember the pointers from their birthing class. Encouragement. Yeah, that was it. "You're doing great, baby. Just great. And you look beautiful right now." Huge. Extremely huge, but beautiful.

"Did I tell you yet today just how much I love you?" Kat wiped the sweat off her face with her free hand.

"Yes, love, when they were wheeling you into the hospital earlier."

"I lieeed," she wailed as another contraction hit. She threatened every bone in his hand with a death grip. "This hurts," she panted through clenched teeth.

Damn right it did. His hand would never be the same.

"Is she coming?"

Dear God! He didn't know anything about babies. Birthing class flew out of his head as panic crowded in. "The baby? I don't know. It's a girl? How can I tell?"

"Not the baby. The doctor."

The door opened and Liv Bertwick breezed in, followed by a nurse. The sound of rubber gloves snapping into place echoed in the room. "So, I understand you're ready to have a baby."

Andrew breathed a sigh of relief. Everything would be okay now that Dr. Bertwick had arrived.

Kat's grip relaxed marginally. "I think it's time."

Dr. Bertwick examined his wife. "I believe it's time, indeed. Take a deep breath and really push for me when the next one hits."

Andrew and the doctor coached while Kat pushed and what seemed like hours but was really only minutes later, their efforts were rewarded by a squalling, bloody, beautiful black-haired boy.

In a moment of exquisite joy unrivaled by any other in his life, Andrew cried and laughed as he hugged his wife and his son. They'd done it. Kat had done it. They had a son!

"Okay, Kat. You did great. That wasn't so bad, now was it? You ready for round two?" Dr. Bertwick's words penetrated his euphoria.

"Round two? Two? As in more than one? As in another?"

Andrew didn't realize he'd spoken aloud until he caught the look that passed between doctor and patient.

Kat smiled at him over their son's head. "You said you wanted to be surprised. Surprise, darling! We're having twins."

"Twins? Twins!" He dropped into a chair. Light-headed. He definitely felt light-headed.

The nurse shoved his head between his knees. "Now, none of that, Dad."

After a few breaths, he straightened in the chair and caught up Kat's hand in his.

Her sapphire eyes sparkled with mischief. "Did you

expect anything else? You know I've got that excess thing going on. But don't worry, it'll be okay."

"Okay? No. This is great." He felt a stupid grin cover his face.

With that, the pushing resumed until the other twin made her appearance. And the volume of noise made by the tiny redhead could only be described as excessive.

If you enjoyed what you just read,
then we've got an offer you can't resist!

Take 2 bestselling
love stories FREE!

Plus get a FREE surprise gift!

Clip this page and mail it to Harlequin Reader Service®

IN U.S.A.	IN CANADA
3010 Walden Ave.	P.O. Box 609
P.O. Box 1867	Fort Erie, Ontario
Buffalo, N.Y. 14240-1867	L2A 5X3

YES! Please send me 2 free Harlequin Duets™ novels and my free surprise gift. Then send me 2 brand-new novels every month, which I will receive months before they're available in stores. In the U.S.A., bill me at the bargain price of $5.14 plus 50¢ delivery per book and applicable sales tax, if any*. In Canada, bill me at the bargain price of $6.14 plus 50¢ delivery per book and applicable taxes**. That's the complete price—what a great deal! I understand that accepting the 2 free books and gift places me under no obligation ever to buy any books. I can always return a shipment and cancel at any time. Even if I never buy another book from Harlequin, the 2 free books and gift are mine to keep forever.

So why not take us up on our invitation. You'll be glad you did!

111 HEN C24W
311 HEN C24X

Name	(PLEASE PRINT)	
Address	Apt.#	
City	State/Prov.	Zip/Postal Code

* Terms and prices subject to change without notice. Sales tax applicable in N.Y.
** Canadian residents will be charged applicable provincial taxes and GST.
  All orders subject to approval. Offer limited to one per household.
  ® and ™ are registered trademarks of Harlequin Enterprises Limited.

DUETS00